PRAISE FOR *THE HUMMINGBIRD*

'If you're a fan of Swedish crime queen Camilla Läckberg, you'll love Hiekkapelto' *Kaleva*

'An exceptionally promising debut' *Seura*

'Hiekkapelto knows how to get into people's skin' MTV3

'Extremely promising Northern noir' *Helsingin Sanomat*

'Here is an author who, with her first detective novel, trounces the Swedes. Läckberg & Co. feel clunky once you've had a chance to devour the realistic, engrossing and vitally topical story about Yugoslav Hungarian Anna Fekete, a criminal investigator from a northern Finnish coastal town' *Viva*

'*The Hummingbird* is a confident, thrilling crime novel, which credibly depicts the everyday life of the Finnish police' *Me Naiset*

'When you're reading *The Hummingbird*, it's hard to believe that the book you're holding in your hands is a debut. Absolutely everything comes together: the police work is described realistically, as are the problems faced by immigrants; the plot is skilfully constructed; the characters are lifelike and engaging' Literary Blog, Kirsin Kirjanurkka

ABOUT THE AUTHOR

KATI HIEKKAPELTO is a special needs teacher by training. She lives on an old farm on the island of Hailuoto in Northern Finland with her children and sizeable menagerie. Hiekkapelto has taught immigrants and lived in the Hungarian region of Serbia. This is her first novel. The sequel, *The Defenceless*, will be published in 2015 by Arcadia Books.

ABOUT THE TRANSLATOR

DAVID HACKSTON is a British translator of Finnish and Swedish literature and drama. He graduated from University College London in 1999 with a degree in Scandinavian Studies and now lives in Helsinki where he works as a freelance translator. In 2007 he was awarded the Finnish State Prize for Translation.

The Hummingbird

KATI HIEKKAPELTO

Translated from the Finnish by
David Hackston

ARCADIA BOOKS

Arcadia Books Ltd
139 Highlever Road
London W10 6PH

www.arcadiabooks.co.uk

First published in the United Kingdom by Arcadia Books 2014
Originally published as *Kolibri* by Otava, 2013
Copyright © Kati Hiekkapelto 2013
English language translation copyright © David Hackston 2014

A catalogue record for this book is available from the British Library.

ISBN 978-1-909807-56-3

Arcadia Books is grateful for the financial support of FILI,
who provided a translation grant for this project.

Typeset in Garamond by MacGuru Ltd
Printed and bound by CPI Group (UK) Ltd, Croydon CRO 4YY

Arcadia Books supports English PEN *www.englishpen.org* and
The Book Trade Charity *www.btbs.org*

Arcadia Books distributors are as follows:

in the UK and elsewhere in Europe:
Macmillan Distribution Ltd
Brunel Road
Houndmills
Basingstoke
Hants RG21 6XS

in the USA and Canada:
Dufour Editions
PO Box 7
Chester Springs
PA 19425

in Australia/New Zealand:
NewSouth Books
University of New South Wales
Sydney NSW 2052

That night the Sandman arrived like a Gestapo henchman. When he went on his rounds, hush now, hush, he stuffed the blue clothes in the laundry and pulled on a long leather jacket and a pair of shiny boots, threw me in the car and took me away. His belt had a buckle that he could open quickly. Three guesses why. And I didn't dare fall asleep, though the drive seemed to take forever.

I've seen mutilated bodies as a kid, women stoned to death, honest, and I suppose I should be traumatised, but I'm not. But I know what my own body looks like dead and I've heard about girls that have fallen from balconies, the Angels of Rinkeby and Clichy-sous-Bois, angels that didn't know how to fly. And I know another girl that just vanished, wallahi. Everyone knew she'd been sent back home to be married off to some pervert with a pot belly, a golden tooth and fingers like sausages. In that way the family's honour was restored, phew, the whole fucking family could sigh with relief and smile those everything's-just-fine smiles for the rest of their lives. All except for the girl, that is. And the pervert bagged himself a nice little plaything, something to stick his dirty fingers into.

The Sandman drove me to my aunt and uncle's place in another city, in another suburb, dumped me on the living-room sofa, and I lay there, numb, listening to every sound, wondering when they were going to come in and kill me. I heard my aunt turning on the tap in the kitchen, whispering into the phone, chatting with my uncle, rustling something. I don't know how they were related to me, at least not in Finnish terms. As far as I know Mum's cousins still live in Sweden and my dad's only brother died ages ago. These were an aunt and uncle in our terms: age-old friends of my parents, some distant relation to Dad. They never slept and they probably never ate anything either, but they left me bits of bread on the living-room table. It's like they were constantly at the ready. What were they waiting for? Waiting for someone to say, shove her off the balcony, go on, whoops, it was all a tragic accident. Or was it: your plane's leaving in two hours; we've got you your ticket!

The sofa stank of Kurdistan. I don't understand how they manage to carry the smell with them and preserve it in everything they own: sofas, rugs, curtains, clothes and textiles, kitchen cupboards, beds, sheets, wallpaper, the television, bars of soap, hair, skin. What do they store it in? A jar? And how does it survive for hundreds of years, across thousands of kilometres? Or is it really like they say in that old song, that Kurdistan is the air that we breathe?

This aunt and uncle watched every move I made; they wouldn't even let me lock the bathroom door when I went for a pee. As if I could have disappeared down the drain or through the air vent. There was no way I could run away. I counted the steps to see how long it would take me to sneak into the hallway, rattle open the locks and dash into the stairwell screaming for help and make a run for freedom. But this aunt and uncle were keeping watch in the kitchen, which was situated along that route that felt like an eternity, the open kitchen door like a gaping mouth in the hallway, right next to the front door. They would have stopped me before I'd have been able to get out. And I knew they'd double-bolted the door and that my uncle had the key. They'd explained this to me loud and clear as they'd locked all the bolts and security chains and closed the living-room door, as though they were locking me into a cell. And in Finland I was supposed to be safe. But right now I was more frightened than I'd ever been as a little kid; although there were sometimes pools of blood in the street back home, at least it was a time when Mum and Dad still used to laugh.

I couldn't just lie there and wait for the KGB Sandman to creep in the door and say NOW and let them start doing something really bad to me. I had to act. I pulled my mobile out of my handbag. That was the first miracle: they'd forgotten to confiscate it. That was a really stupid mistake. They must have been nervous too.

I dialled the number they'd taught us on the first day at school – safety first, yeah, that's Finland for you. I remember as a kid I'd been petrified at the thought of actually having to call that number, if I had to report a fire or something or if Mum had a heart attack and I was unable to explain what was wrong, if they couldn't understand what I was saying.

That number did nothing to increase my sense of safety; on the contrary, it loosened it, making it sway and crack and rattle. I had nightmares about all kinds of emergencies. I always thought I'd run to the neighbours' house, the way we would have done back home, but even that didn't feel right when after a few weeks I realised I didn't know any of the people living next door. All I knew was that there was a woman on the ground floor who spat at us.

Now I know the right words. I know a whole new language and I can speak it better than my old one; I could call anyone, the National Forestry Commission, and they wouldn't hear the faintest hint of Kurdistan in my voice. All they would hear would be the hum of the great northern pine forests.

And I know that here you can trust the police, at least in theory, unless you're a Dublin Case, that is, or faulty goods that dictators at the Immigration Bureau decide must be sent back to where they came from. I'm not one of them. I've got citizenship. OMG, it makes me laugh to say it, but I've just got to: I'm a bona fide Finnish citizen, officially. It's like winning the lottery, though I wasn't born here. Okay, not quite seven right numbers. More like six plus the bonus. I had no other option but to believe in miracles. I called 112.

1

THE THICKET FOREST around the running track was silent. The shadows of the branches disappeared into the deepening dusk. A pair of light-coloured trainers struck the sawdust of the running path with dull, regular thumps. Her legs pounded the earth, their strong, pumped muscles working efficiently, her pulse beating at the optimum rate. She didn't need a heart-rate monitor to feel it; she would never buy one. She knew her body well and knew what it required at any given time. After the first kilometre the initial stiffness began to recede, her legs felt lighter and her breathing steadied, and her running achieved that relaxed rhythm which could carry her to the ends of the earth.

It was easy to breathe in the damp, oxygenated air, fresh from the rain. Her lungs drew it in and pushed it out again like a set of bellows that today, at least, wouldn't be tired. Sweat had covered the full length of her body. If I stopped now and stripped off, she thought, I'd glisten like the damp forest. Her toes felt warm. She had long since taken off her gloves and stuffed them in her pockets, though her hands had felt the chill when she'd set out. The sweat-band round her head absorbed the droplets trickling down into her face, and her thick dark head of hair was soaked at the root. Her feet hit the ground in steady paces; the world shrank around their monotonous rhythm, and her thoughts seemed to empty themselves for a moment. There was just one step after another, step, step, step, nothing more in this malignant world.

She felt a twinge in her knee. Her breathing turned shallower, faster; she was becoming tired after all. She slowed down a notch, just to have the strength to walk up to the front door. Not far now. She could make out the figure of the fallen tree that marked the start of the final straight. As it had fallen, its thick, foreboding trunk had taken a couple of slender birches with it. Now its roots jutted into the air like a troll. She'd often thought how easy it would be for someone to lurk behind them.

On another running track the stillness was broken only by the rhythmic hiss of a solitary jogger's tracksuit. The forest was silent, not even the rush of the sea could be heard. Surely the birds haven't left already. Perhaps they've already gone to sleep, the jogger thought just as a crow squawked right next to her ear. The noise took her by surprise, her heart jumped with fright, and immediately afterwards came the sound of rustling, as though the branches had been pulled away and flipped back into place. Someone was moving through the woods. No, not someone, something – a bird, a hedgehog, an insect. For crying out loud, what kind of insect would make a sound like that? A fox, perhaps, or a badger, forests are always full of different creatures; there's no need to be frightened, she nervously repeated to herself, trying to calm herself but not really succeeding. She sped up and started running too fast. All the crises in her life were whirling in her head in a single cacophonous clamour, and she ran to try and empty them from her mind; all summer until this very evening she'd been running like one possessed. If only term would start again soon, she thought, I can get away from here, away from the past. This she had repeated to herself since the day the letter of acceptance to the university had arrived. Still, she felt as though she might never make it.

She was already on the second floor by the time the downstairs door clicked shut. This was her final spurt: up the stairs to the fifth floor at full speed, and though it felt as though her calf muscles were ablaze, she knew she'd make it. Tonight's run was one of the gentler ones in her weekly regime, less than an hour's light jogging at a comfortable pace, unadulterated pleasure and enjoyment. She pulled off her sweaty clothes and threw them in a pile on the hallway floor, stepped into the shower, turned on the tap and let the warm water sprinkle down across her ruddy, pulsing skin, washing the beads of sweat and foaming soap down into the network of drains beneath the city, now the concern of the workers at the water purification plant. The idea amused her. As she stepped out of the shower, she wrapped herself in a thick white dressing gown, twisted her black hair into a towel, cracked open a can of beer and went out on to the balcony for a cigarette. Nothing but bleak concrete and floor upon floor of dark windows. Suburbia. What the hell had made her want to move back here? She laughed out loud at a suburb that, true to form, was trying to trick her. Now it was pretending to be asleep, but she knew it for what it was. She had seen everything that lay hidden behind those concrete walls. Thankfully after a good run it didn't bother her, and strangely enough neither did the challenges of tomorrow. Endorphins were racing through her body, turning her nerves into an amusement park, and the feeling of exhilaration remained with her until she went to bed. *Jó éjszakát*, she whispered to herself and drifted to sleep.

Gasping for breath, the runner jogged through the now silent, darkening woods. Raindrops glistened on the dark-green foliage, water that hadn't made it to the ground. Behind her came a loud crackle. It must be a moose, she thought, or a fox, but still didn't quite believe it herself.

She scanned the area around her. It's too quiet, she thought, unnaturally muted. She cursed to herself that she'd run so fast, couldn't run another step, and though she was genuinely afraid and wanted to get out of the woods quickly, she had to slow to walking pace. This is no way to burn fat, she thought. It'll only turn to lactic acid, and tomorrow I won't have the energy to do anything. But I have to get my body into shape. I must. Everything had to change, she kept reprimanding herself, trying to take her thoughts away from the threatening woods around her, whose shadows seemed to be watching her. This is crazy, she muttered under her breath. I'm going crazy – and it serves me right. I just need to forget everything, put an end to all this sin and lick my wounds. What bloody stupid clichés, at least try to come up with something original. Her voice was drowned out by the sound of rustling from the trees.

Breathing heavily she walked the final half kilometre back to the car, feeling as though she didn't have the energy, that the journey would never end. Just as she made out the shape of the yellow car behind the bushes and was smirking at her overactive imagination, she saw a dark figure in front of her. Someone was crouching down on the running track. The figure stood up and started walking briskly towards her.

2

THE HEAVY RAINCLOUDS that had hidden the sky from view for four days in a row were once again lashing the city with water. The air was grey and chilly. Pedestrians with umbrellas dodged the spray whipped up by cars in the morning rush hour. The smartest people were wearing rubber boots. It seemed that summer had finally come to an end, though the skin yearned to cling to the warmth and the touch of seawater for just a moment longer. The school term had started, the summer holidays had ended, people had returned to work and society was gradually regaining its momentum: work, home, work, home, no more lazing around by the water blowing out dandelion clocks.

At a quarter to eight, Anna opened the main door of the imposing, towering office block in the centre of the city that had once been her home, and stepped into the foyer of the building that never sleeps. She glanced at her watch and noted that her new boss was late. She dug a jar of powder from her handbag, tugged her fringe into a better position, added a little lip gloss. She tried to take deep breaths. She had butterflies in her stomach. She needed the toilet.

Neon lights flickered behind a set of venetian blinds. Anna had slept badly after all. She'd woken in the early hours and started fretting. Despite this she wasn't especially tired. Adrenalin sharpened the morning stiffness of her senses.

A week earlier the past had once again become the present as Anna had rented a van, and with the help of a few colleagues packed up what little she had in the way of furniture and belongings and moved them many hundreds of kilometres from the city where she had studied and where she had lived, working a string of temporary positions, ever since graduating. The majority of her belongings were the same ones she'd had when she began studying ten years earlier.

Anna had rented an apartment in Koivuharju, the same suburb where she had spent her youth and where Ákos still lived. The area's reputation was anything but attractive, but the rent was reasonable. The appearance of Anna's surname on the letter box in uneven block lettering hadn't aroused the slightest interest among the other residents. Even her relatively high level of education was nothing out of the ordinary, as Koivuharju was home to a surprising number of teachers, doctors, engineers and physicists from immigrant backgrounds. The only statistical difference was that Anna was actually in work, gainfully employed in a position worthy of her education. The physicists of Koivuharju would have been pleased to get a job as a part-time cleaner.

Koivuharju wouldn't be considered a place where people *wanted* to live; they simply ended up there. Those who lived in and around the downtown area certainly knew its name and reputation, but they didn't know what it looked like. The spectrum of surnames, each more difficult to pronounce than the next, might have intimidated them.

Anna hadn't even looked at the high-end, high-ceilinged downtown apartments. She had always felt more at home on the flipside of these façades – in the shadows and alleyways.

Perhaps this is why she'd become a police officer.

Chief Superintendent Pertti Virkkunen arrived almost ten minutes late. The short, moustachioed man in his fifties seemed in excellent condition. He greeted her with an enthusiastic smile and shook her hand so that her joints cracked.

'We're very pleased to have you here,' said Virkkunen. 'It's great to get an officer from an immigrant background on our team. They've been banging on about it in national strategy directives for years, but until now we haven't seen a single one of you, not even a junior constable – immigrants, you know. Though, of course, we've met plenty of you in other circumstances. I mean…'

Virkkunen was embarrassed. Anna felt like saying something snappy, making him squirm with shame, but because nothing sprang to mind she let it pass.

'You can take it easy for a few days, get to know people and find your bearings. There's nothing particularly pressing going on at the moment, so you can get organised in peace and quiet,' he said as he accompanied Anna from one department to another.

'After all, this is your first job and your first position in the Crime Unit, so we'll give you plenty of time to settle and learn how things work around here. We meet each morning at eight o'clock, assess ongoing cases and delegate work. The analysis team meets once a week. The secretary will be able to give you your rota and more specific timetables.'

Anna nodded and followed Virkkunen, trying to commit the location of various departments and corridors to memory, to construct some kind of mental floor map. The summer after finishing high school she'd done a stint as a seasonal worker in the documentation department on the ground floor of the daunting police station; she had helped in the processing of hundreds of urgent passport applications as people realised, just before going on holiday, that their passport had expired; she had stamped and filed documents, organised shelves and made coffee, and towards the end of her contract she'd even become acquainted with how passports were manufactured. The rest of the building was a mystery to her. It felt labyrinthine, the way large buildings always seem at first.

Virkkunen led Anna up to the Crime Unit and her new office on the fourth floor. The room was spacious and well lit and was situated halfway down the corridor opposite the staffroom. Folders and paperwork were neatly filed on shelves that covered the walls and the computer on the desk was switched off. Three flower baskets hung in the window and a yucca plant the size of a tree stood in the corner. On the wall was a picture of a blonde woman and three blonde children. They were smiling against the backdrop of an exotic sandy beach, sea and sunshine, the way any happy family would on holiday.

Coffee mugs and a Thermos flask were stacked in the room on a steel trolley. A batch of the mandatory office buns lay beneath a cloth. Anna wondered whether she dared decline. The room was so large that there was room for another table for meetings. Sitting around the table were three people, all plain-clothed police officers.

'Morning all,' said Virkkunen. 'Allow me to introduce our new senior detective constable, Anna Fekete.'

Two of the officers stood up immediately and came over to greet her.

'Good morning and a very warm welcome to our team. It's so nice to get another woman on board – the guys here can really get on your nerves sometimes. I'm Sari, Sari Jokikokko-Pennanen – I know, what a mouthful.'

The tall, fair-haired woman, around Anna's age, reached out a slender hand and took Anna's in a firm, warm grip. It seemed as though her entire body was smiling.

'Hello, everyone. I'm very excited to come and work here, though it's all a bit nerve-wracking.'

'No need for that. A little bird tells me you're a damn good officer – we're really pleased to have you. You speak really good Finnish; I can't hear any accent,' said Sari.

'Thanks. I've lived here a long time.'

'Oh, how long?'

'Twenty years.'

'You must have been just a child when you came here?'

'I was nine, because we arrived in the spring. I turned ten that summer.'

'You'll have to tell me all about it sometime. This is Rauno Forsman.'

Also in his thirties, the funny-looking man extended his hand and greeted Anna with a look of curiosity in his blue eyes.

'Morning. Welcome to the team.'

'Good morning. Nice to meet you,' said Anna as the thousands of butterflies in her stomach stopped beating their wings and the tension in her neck gradually began to relent. She liked these people, Sari in particular.

The third person at the table had remained seated. Virkkunen was just about to turn to him, a note of irritation in his eyes, when the man opened his mouth.

'Hello,' the man mumbled in Anna's direction, then turned to Virkkunen. 'Emergency Services took a call last night. Some refugee or whatever we're supposed to call them these days, rang up and said someone was going to kill her. So, should we get to work?'

Virkkunen cleared his throat.

'Esko Niemi,' he said to Anna. 'Your partner.'

A stifled snort came from behind Esko's sagging cheeks, peppered with rosacea. Either that, or the man had a cold, thought Anna and greeted her new partner. He stood up and held out his hand. It was large and rough, the kind of hand that you could imagine hurling criminals into jail with a steely swipe of the wrist, but his grip felt unpleasantly limp. Anna hated handshakes like this; they gave a strangely suspicious impression of people. And still the man wouldn't look her in the eye. Virkkunen invited everyone to have some coffee and the officers filed towards the trolley from which an enticing aroma was now wafting. The slightly strained atmosphere in the room seemed to relax, and Anna was enveloped in a buzz of friendly conversation. Still warm, the fresh buns tasted good.

Once everyone had drunk their coffee and eaten their buns, Virkkunen asked Esko to brief the team on the events of the previous night.

'The girl gave her home address, somewhere in Rajapuro. A couple of officers went round there, but the girl wasn't at home after all. There was the father, mother and two younger siblings, but not the girl who made the call. Kurdish family, kicked up a right hullabaloo, woke the whole house, I'm sure.'

'A girl? The person who received the death threat was a girl?'

'That's what I just said,' Esko replied without looking at Anna, then continued. 'The girl's father said she was visiting relatives in

Vantaa. The father did all the talking, by the way. The fourteen-year-old son ... I'll be damned if I can remember their names,' he muttered and fidgeted with a bunch of papers looking for the boy's name. 'Mehvan. Fourteen-year-old Mehvan interpreted.'

'Nobody called an official interpreter?' asked Anna. 'You can't use a child as an interpreter, especially in such a serious matter.'

'Of course we asked for one, but the interpreter on duty was at the hospital on another call. There wasn't time to get another interpreter with all the fuss going on – it would have been a waste of public money, paying overtime and what have you for two interpreters. The officers on site were told to sort things out as best they could, there and then. And that's what they did. You can't shilly-shally around with important matters. Our boys were simply following orders.'

'Like in Bosnia, I suppose?' Anna muttered.

'What?' Esko retorted.

Finally he turned and looked at Anna with his swollen, reddened eyes. Anna tried to stare back without blinking. The man already disgusted her, though she'd only known him a matter of minutes.

'Nothing. I didn't say a word.'

Anna eventually lowered her glare.

Esko poured himself more coffee, a satisfied smirk on his face.

'Well, everything in the apartment seemed to be as it should,' Rauno continued in an attempt to calm things down. 'Nobody in the house knew anything of what the girl had done or why. A couple of officers in Vantaa checked the girl's supposed whereabouts. The girl – her name was ... just a minute – Bihar was found to be in good health and was precisely where her parents said she was. She told the Vantaa police that perhaps someone had made a prank call and given her name. Either that or she'd had a nightmare and must have made the call herself while half asleep. Apparently she sometimes walks – and talks – in her sleep and can't remember anything about it the next morning.'

'Sounds suspicious,' said Anna.

'Very,' said Sari.

'What's suspicious about that? The girl admitted she made the call by mistake,' said Esko.

'Who calls the emergency services by mistake?' asked Sari.

'Christ, people call 112 when they lock themselves out of the house or when their pet poodle gets something stuck in its eye,' said Esko.

'That's different. This call was placed by mistake,' said Sari.

'How old is Bihar?' asked Anna.

'Seventeen,' Rauno replied.

'A seventeen-year-old girl calls 112 and says someone's threatening to kill her. Sounds like a real-life nightmare to me,' said Anna.

'And why was she was allowed to travel all the way to Vantaa by herself?' asked Sari.

Esko said nothing.

'I want to hear that call,' said Virkkunen. 'Esko, let's hear it.'

A few seconds of background noise. The operator's matter-of-fact voice. Then, very hushed, the girl's whispers: 'They're gonna kill me. Help me. My dad's gonna kill me.'

The operator asks her to repeat.

The girl says nothing.

The operator asks where the girl is. The girl gives her address and hangs up.

'She was petrified,' said Anna.

'I agree,' said Sari. 'Scared to death that someone might hear.'

'Why didn't she say where she was?' asked Rauno.

'Maybe she didn't know,' Sari suggested.

'Or maybe she wanted to bring the police straight into the hornets' nest,' said Rauno.

'She probably didn't know the exact address, and her home address was the only one she could remember. And she was in a hurry; this was a matter of life and death,' said Anna.

'Maybe she just wanted to give Daddy a few grey hairs,' scoffed Esko.

'Did anyone speak to the mother?' asked Anna.

'They tried. The report says in bold that the husband did all the talking. Through Mehvan,' said Rauno.

'But of course.'

'So what are we going to do about this?'

'Let's get this investigation underway. Finnish law doesn't recognise honour violence as a crime, but we might be able to bring a charge of unlawful threat or even false imprisonment. It's Monday morning and the girl is in Vantaa. Shouldn't a girl that age be in school?' asked Virkkunen.

Esko yawned noisily in his chair and started playing with his mobile, a look of boredom on his face.

'I believe compulsory education ends at seventeen,' he commented.

'Esko, I want you to call these people in for an interview by the end of the day,' Virkkunen ordered.

Esko gave a snort and wiped the crumbs from the edge of his mouth with an air of indifference.

'Yes. Bihar, father, mother, brother and little sister. I want them all here as quickly as possible. And book an interpreter – two if necessary. Rauno and Sari, find out about the relatives in Vantaa, ask the local unit for assistance. Anna, establish what has happened in previous cases.'

'Okay,' Anna responded.

'I've got a bad feeling about this,' said Sari. 'It's as though a premonition has come knocking.'

At that very moment, there came a knock at the door. A woman poked her head around and nodded by way of a greeting.

'They've found a body. On the running track near Selkämaa in Saloinen,' she informed the group.

Everyone fell silent and froze on the spot. Sari and Rauno looked at one another in confusion and disbelief. Esko's coffee cup stopped in mid-air on its journey to his lips. Virkkunen's voice broke the silence.

'So much for a quiet start, Anna,' he sighed.

3

ANNA FEKETE sniffed at the air. The rain had strengthened the natural scents of the forest. The detritus decomposing beneath the boughs of trees was mixed with the smell of sawdust. Mould had begun its annual autumnal feast, but still the air was fresh. Wind rustled in the branches of dwarf birches and in the tangle of thicket, the remaining green leaves flittering in the rain.

The twenty-kilometre journey to Saloinen had taken them south through heavy traffic heading out of the city. Before reaching the rapidly expanding village, Anna turned on to a dirt track leading towards the shore. For about three kilometres the track wound its way through the woods and ploughed fields and came to an end at a rectangular, overgrown parking area. A slimy cluster of slippery Jack mushrooms had popped up along the edge of the car park. Parked in front of the mushrooms were a blue-and-white police Saab, a yellow Fiat Uno and the civilian vehicle used by Esko Niemi. Beside the cars stood a row of uniformed patrol officers.

I've got interval training tonight, Anna found herself thinking as she saw the running track that started behind the yellow police tape. It disappeared into the woods, just like the strands of yellow tape cordoning off the area. The body lay only two hundred metres away, said the policemen, but she couldn't see that far through the woods.

The body had been discovered just before nine o'clock that morning by local resident Aune Toivola, an 86-year-old widow out on her morning walk. She was in the habit of getting up at seven o'clock every morning, making a pot of coffee and drinking half before and half after her daily walk. And as usual, her walk had taken her to the running track winding its way along the shoreline. Aune always kept her mobile phone, given to her by concerned relatives, in her pocket, and this she had used to raise the alarm.

Esko had driven by himself, in his own car. This had irritated Anna, though she had no inclination to spend time alone with the man. Still…

Anna got out of the car, greeted the police officers and approached the patrol car. Aune Toivola was sitting there with Esko. The patrol officers were chatting amongst themselves, waiting for permission to leave the scene. Anna noted the gaze of the younger, more handsome of the two officers; he had stared her as she'd arrived and now scanned down towards her bottom as she leant over to talk to the elderly lady.

Aune's wrinkled face was tinged with a look of frustration. Anna didn't even have a chance to introduce herself.

'I've already told these nice young men everything,' she said pointedly. 'I want to go home now. My coffee will be getting cold, and I can feel a headache coming on. My home help will be arriving soon – she'll start to worry if I'm not there.'

The lady was clearly tired and distressed at the disruption to her morning routine.

Esko smiled in the front seat. 'Aune and I have already gone through everything. It's all in here,' he said, tapping the blue-covered jotter in his hand.

You can't have, thought Anna; you were here at most ten minutes before me.

'Nonetheless, there are still a few questions I'd like to ask,' said Anna, addressing her question to Aune directly. 'Then you can go home. It won't take long.'

The old lady scoffed, but didn't say anything. Esko stopped smiling.

'Do you live nearby?'

'About a kilometre away. 55 Selkämaantie, the same dirt track that runs from the main road out here,' Aune replied crisply and waved her hand in the direction of the path leading away from the car park.

'Have you seen any traffic around here? People coming and going along the running track?'

'I haven't seen a thing. My house isn't quite on the path. Besides, I don't sit around spying on people, never have done,' said the old woman.

'And did you hear anything?'

'Pardon?' she replied, raising her voice so that it thinned almost to a whinny.

'Did you hear anything out of the ordinary this morning? Yesterday evening? Or during the night? The sound of a car, perhaps, or a shot?'

Anna noticed the woman's bony fingers fidgeting with her right ear, behind which she saw the bulge of a hearing aid.

'I didn't hear anything. I was watching television last night – the volume was up quite loud.'

'And have you ever seen the woman you found this morning around here before?'

'There's never anybody around here in the mornings. There might be the odd person in the evenings, but I wouldn't know about that – I don't come out here in the evening. Can I go now, please? The carer will be worried and she'll call my son.'

'Just a few more questions. Does anybody else live in the vicinity?'

'There's old Yki Raappana, but this man here has already asked all about him.'

'What about that car over there? Have you seen it before?'

'I'm not sure. Cars do drive up here from time to time. There must be other people here apart from me, what with the road being lit and all that,' said Aune.

'Thank you. You can go home now, but we'll come and visit you in the next few days and have another chat. If you feel worried about any of this and need to talk to someone, there are people at the church who are trained to help. Here's their telephone number.'

'As long as I can get home to my coffee, I'll be fine,' she muttered. 'This was nothing compared to what I saw in Karelia during the war. That was genuine pain and suffering, men coming in on trucks, howling and wailing, some with legs missing, some with shrapnel in their heads.'

'Maybe you could talk about that with them too. It might do you good,' said Anna politely and asked the patrol officers to take the old lady home.

'Let the vicar know too, okay?' she added and winked at the younger and more handsome of the officers. He was visibly taken aback.

Should I have stayed in patrol after all, thought Anna as she watched Esko Niemi getting out of the car.

The figure was of a man well past the cusp of middle age. The greasy hair on his brow was thinning and lank. His wrinkled shirt was stuffed inside a pair of un-ironed trousers. The buttons of his shirt had stretched into a grimace around his belly, revealing a strip of hairy stomach. Presumably he was unable to button up his thread-bare jacket. Esko Niemi hadn't grown old with dignity, as men are purported to. Women were past their prime by the age of forty, but men simply turned more handsome until the end of their lives. So Anna had often heard; she couldn't believe the rubbish that people – women – held to be true.

After stepping out of the car, Esko straightened his stiff back and was overcome by a rasping coughing fit. Having composed himself again, he lit a cigarette.

How can anyone communicate with a man like that, Anna thought and felt herself gripped by a wave of uncertainty.

With one hand Esko shielded his cigarette from the rain, then loudly cleared his throat and spat a lump of green phlegm on the ground in front of his feet.

Bassza meg, what a pig.

'I'm going to examine the scene and take a look at the body,' Esko informed her.

'Yes, let's go,' said Anna.

'No, you wait in the car. Show Forensics where to go when they turn up. Can you manage that in Finnish?'

'Esko, I'm certainly not going to…'

'Are we on first-name terms? That was an order, by the way. Meanwhile, find out who that car belongs to, and careful you don't contaminate any evidence.'

With that said Esko threw her a set of car keys, dropped his cigarette butt into the globule of phlegm and crushed it beneath his shoe. Anna felt sick.

'The boys from patrol checked the body for any paperwork – that's ID to you and me. They didn't find any, but they did find this set of car keys. Make sure you don't mess the place up,' he repeated as though he was talking to a child. Then he lifted the yellow ribbon, puffed as he crouched beneath it and slowly walked off down the dirt track. Anna stood on the spot. She looked at Esko as he disappeared into the thicket, and she knew that she hated him. She clasped her hand into a tight fist and resisted the urge to scream. The sharp edge of the car keys dug a red mark into the palm of her hand.

Anna turned her attention to the lonely Fiat. Just calm down and do your job thoroughly, she commanded herself. The cold, abandoned car was like a premonition of the horrors that awaited them at the end of the track. Anna pulled on a pair of latex gloves and gently tried the Fiat's door. The metal lent her a sense of self-assurance. This was familiar; she could do this. Back in patrol she had had plenty of opportunities to carry out forensic examinations of cars written off at the side of the road, their engines still warm, to look for fleeing drink-drivers and junkies, to confiscate stolen goods stashed in the boot. A car was the most mundane of crime scenes.

But this time Anna wasn't going to carry out a forensic investigation. The forensics team would go over the car with a fine-tooth comb. If there was anything to find, they would find it. Anna was looking for something else.

The door was locked. Anna pressed a raised button on the key ring with the smudged picture of a padlock. The Fiat gave a click.

She opened the passenger door. The first impression of the car was its cleanliness. The dark-grey seat covers were spotless and there was no rubbish or grit on the floor beneath the seat. There have been no children in this car – or drunks, for that matter. Anna resisted the temptation to sit in the car, to listen to what it wanted to tell her. Instead she carefully opened the glove compartment and took out the registration form.

The car was registered to one Juhani Rautio of 17 Vaahterapolku, Saloinen.

The address was nearby. Very near indeed. Anna felt a rush of excitement in her chest.

Reluctantly she returned to her own car and sat down. She wanted to see what had happened on the running track.

Her daydream was broken by a tap at the window. Esko had returned. Again he was puffing on a cigarette and gestured Anna out of the car. Anna felt a chill. Damp from the rain, her clothes now intensified the bite of the wind.

'Forensics are going to be a while. I called the pathologist too. You can go and look now.'

'What?'

'Go and have a look at what's there – and no funny business, mind.'

For a moment Anna felt like refusing, like obstinately saying she had no desire to examine the scene, and behaving like the child Esko considered her to be. But what would it matter to him if she refused? She would only shoot herself in the foot with that sort of behaviour. She had to see the victim with her own eyes so that she could fully take part in the investigation. Anna felt livid, but managed to control herself as she saw a satisfied smirk creep across Esko's face. This is one game we're not going to play by your rules, she decided.

The yellow police ribbons fluttered in the wind, as though they were marking the route for a marathon.

Anna began walking down the path. Her hands were tacky with

sweat and her heart was beating hard. The first hundred metres gently curved deeper into the woods, and as the path straightened out Anna saw something resembling the shape of a human being lying on the ground. You didn't make it to the finish line, thought Anna, and felt the power momentarily drain from her limbs. She felt faint. The rain and wind chilled her.

Anna pulled on another pair of gloves and carefully began to inspect the body. White female, around 165 centimetres tall, weight approximately 70 kilos. Shot with a rifle at close range. Dead instantly. Her head had been quite literally blasted off, and much of her neck too. She'd been here for some time. The body was cold and damp after a night outdoors, and was now stiff and hard with rigor mortis. It looked almost like a gritty, realistic installation, lying motionless on the dirt track, otherwise intact except for the head, which was now an unidentifiable tangle of flesh. It made Anna feel ill to look at the bloody mess that only yesterday had been a face.

The lime-green tracksuit bottoms had darkened from the rain, the legs inside them were still intact but had twisted grotesquely as death had knocked her to the ground. The hands were like those of any young woman out for a run, clean and well looked after. Her fingernails, painted in a plum varnish, were bitten.

Above the waist was where things looked different. The boundary wasn't clear. Dark spots and red strips were splattered across the tracksuit; by now their edges had soaked into the wet fabric. Around the chest and shoulders the tracksuit was no longer green but decorated in various shades of rust and red. Here too, thankfully, the rain had softened the most shocking contrasts. Finally there was the head. In reality it barely existed any more, nothing but spatter that extended some way along the path. On closer inspection the spatter contained grey strands of brain matter. Mush. The unpleasant word reminded her of porridge or baby food, but it was an effective simile. The brain had literally turned to mush as it had come gushing out of the skull.

The woman was young; there was no doubt about that. Thirty

at most. Probably much younger. Anna could tell from the childish smoothness of the skin on the back of her hands, the innocent fragility of her chubby fingers, and an inexplicable gut feeling that she couldn't quite put into words. The body exuded youth and vitality, something not even death had been able to snuff out. Anna examined the jagged edges of the victim's nails. Were you worried about something, she asked herself. Or were you still so young that you hadn't yet put such bad habits behind you? How old are you?

Her tracksuit was trendy and smart, but clearly supermarket quality. Perhaps you'd only just got into running, Anna thought. The trainers revealed that the girl had been out running when she was killed. They weren't the most expensive ones available, but they were a quality brand with shock absorbers specially designed for running. Someone out for a light Sunday jog wouldn't buy these. The soles of the shoes were dirty and slightly worn. You weren't an absolute beginner, then? Some level of addiction had probably already set in. That, if anything, was something Anna knew all about.

But what did any of this matter now? Running or walking, beginner or marathon runner? There you lie now, and you'll never take another step again, Anna whispered and struggled against the anxiety welling up inside her.

Anna gently touched the dead woman's skin at the point where a patch of flesh was revealed between her pulled-up trouser leg and her reinforced tennis sock. The skin was tanned, smooth and cold, in perfect condition. Not even the first signs of stubble scraped against Anna's hand as she cautiously stroked the woman's leg. Did you shave your legs just before going running? Why? I always do it in the shower afterwards. Anna wrote down the observation in her notebook.

She knew that the patrol officers would have gone through the victim's tracksuit pocket, and presumably Esko would have done so too. Forensics would do the same. But Anna wanted to see what the dead woman was carrying with her. She carefully opened the zips. Front-door keys, wet handkerchiefs. Tied at the end of a thin leather strap was a brooch of some sort, a bead that looked like a stone and featuring a strange figure decorated with feathers. A mobile phone with a couple of bars of battery power left.

Anna glanced behind her to make sure nobody was coming, and quickly flicked through the messages and calls. The last outgoing call was made on 21 August at 11.15 a.m. to Mum. The last incoming call was on the same day at 6.27 p.m., an unknown number. Anna felt a chill in her heart. Message inbox: empty. Sent messages: empty. Who called you last night? And why have all your messages been deleted?

Anna examined the ground around the body. The blood spatter had extended over a wide area. On the ground close to the body the detail of the spatter was clearly visible, while further off it merged with the brown of the sawdust and undergrowth and gradually dissolved into the rain. Forensics would have their work cut out. Amid all this mess, would they be able to identify anything from the killer? A hair? A drop of saliva? A fibre? With the naked eye it was impossible to make out any individual footprints in the sawdust. Anna lifted her head and gazed at the sky. She licked a few raindrops from her lips. Go ahead, rinse all our evidence away, she whispered to the rain. Erase all the prints. She let her eyes scan the woods extending out around the scene, unperturbed. Silent landscape. You witnessed everything and now you're holding your tongue.

'What kind of madman kills someone with a rifle?' Anna commented to Esko once she returned to the car park. She'd decided to try her best. To talk, communicate. To carry on as if nothing had happened.

Esko's cheeks dimpled as he drew smoke through his cigarette, and he stared past Anna into the forest.

'It would have made an almighty bang,' she continued, trying to sound amiable.

'What day is it today?' asked Esko.

Anna was almost startled. He's talking to me.

'The twenty-second,' she replied.

'What month?'

'What, have you got Alzheimer's all of a sudden?'

'Just tell me what month it is and don't take the piss.'

'It's August, of course.'

'Right.'

'Right. And…?'

'For Christ's sake,' said Esko, exasperated, and flicked his cigarette butt to the ground. Anna noticed at least five butts by his feet.

'The shooting season started on the twentieth, the day before yesterday. And do you know what people use to shoot ducks, lass?'

Anna was silent for a moment, then responded: 'Yes, I do.'

'Now think where this godforsaken track is exactly.'

'True,' said Anna and turned to look west. The faint breeze didn't carry the sound through the trees, but you could sense the proximity of the sea in the salty odour of the damp air, in the low-lying juniper bushes growing here and there and in the impenetrable green wall of dense thicket.

'So yeah, if I wanted to bump someone off near the shore, at night and at the height of the duck-shooting season, I'd consider using a rifle. Nobody living round here would pay the slightest attention, no matter how many shots they heard,' said Esko, and as if to confirm the veracity of his words a series of three shots echoed from the direction of the shore.

'Missed. If you don't get it with the first or second shot, you won't hit it at all. Pointless contraptions if you ask me, these semi-automatics.'

'Do you hunt?' asked Anna. 'It's considered quite an elitist sport back home – I mean, where I come from.'

Esko said nothing, just stared at the yellow car in the car park, a mosaic of yellowing leaves glued to its windscreen.

'Last night it was raining harder than it is now,' he eventually stated.

'It was raining quite hard all day yesterday. And in the evening a fair wind whipped up.'

'What kind of idiot goes out jogging in weather like that?' asked Esko and lit another cigarette.

'Not you, that's for sure,' Anna whispered so quietly that Esko couldn't have heard.

4

THE LATE SUMMER LANDSCAPE, betraying the onset of autumn, seemed a blur through the car windows as they drove back towards the city, Esko in front, Anna following behind. As the forensics team arrived at the scene, the rainclouds had suddenly dispersed, proving that the blue sky was still there after all. The cloud had split into long threads and drifted into the distance, much to the satisfaction of the team whose job it was to examine the scene and photograph the body. The sun shone down in all its splendour and the forest began to dry out. Although the leaves hadn't yet yellowed, they already carried a hint of their approaching demise. Only a few weeks now, and summer would finally cede to autumn. Anna had long since given up hope of an Indian summer. At this latitude, even thinking of such a thing was futile. Soon the woods and the patches of garden around the isolated houses would curl up in the long embrace of the winter darkness. The city would try to fight against it with neon lights and fluorescent strips. Everyone would be eagerly awaiting the return of light from the first snow. But nowadays the snow fell late in the year. The boundary between autumn and winter was imperceptible amid the surrounding grey slush.

Don't think about that now, Anna irritably chided herself and jerkily pulled the car straight after noticing it had drifted out towards the right. An approaching lorry sounded its horn at her.

The sun is shining; it's still summer – for now. Concentrate on driving and don't fret about the future.

The coroner gave the approximate time of death as around ten o'clock the previous evening. She too was puzzled by the relatively late hour

of the victim's jog and in such poor weather. Anna didn't say anything, though for her it seemed utterly unremarkable. She always
jogged in the evenings. And the weather was never a reason to miss
a run. The forensics officers had promised to submit their reports as
quickly as possible, and the coroner invited Esko and Anna to the
autopsy, which was to take place the following day. Anna flinched.
This was new. She worried about maintaining her professional poise,
though the mere thought of the morgue made her feel sick. No, not
the morgue itself, but the thought that the girl lying on the running
track would be chopped up there tomorrow like an animal in an
abattoir. As if there were no end to her denigration, the authorities
would continue to mutilate her where the killer had stopped.

One after the other Anna and Esko parked their cars outside the
police station, slammed the doors shut, walked inside and made
their way up to the fourth floor, Anna by the stairs, Esko in the
lift. Each withdrew to their own office, as though the other didn't
exist, as though the tragic scene they had just witnessed was but an
illusion.

This is ridiculous, Anna sighed. We need to talk about this,
analyse the situation, plan what steps to take next, find Juhani
Rautio, examine the girl's phone records and her final movements
before going on that run. Where had she been yesterday, and in
whose company? Who was she? What had Aune Toivola told Esko
and the patrol officers? And what about the Kurdish girl? Who was
looking into that? What should they do next? I should at least try to
get to know Esko, have lunch with him or something. This is no way
to work. And for a sinking moment, the thought occurred to Anna
that she had already failed.

Anna spent her lunch break alone in the station cafeteria, where she
ate a depressing meal of overcooked spaghetti with bland mincemeat
sauce and a salad of mandarin slices and grated red cabbage. This
was winter food, though the harvest season was at its peak. Bitter
home-brewed beer and stale bread buns. The cafeteria food had gone

downhill since her high-school internship; here, too, the object was simply to save money. In future she would go into town for lunch, she decided.

Just as she was taking her tray and dirty dishes to the kitchen trolley, a group of people appeared in animated conversation. Esko, Sari, Rauno and Chief Inspector Virkkunen. Blood rushed to Anna's cheeks.

'Anna, there you are! Have you already eaten?' exclaimed Sari in disappointment.

'We have to talk about the case,' said Anna, pointedly delivering her words to Esko.

'We just did, shame you couldn't join us. Everything's in order. You just take care of your own duties, okay,' he replied, noisily placing cutlery on his tray.

'How should I know what my duties are if nobody tells me?' Anna replied, struggling to control the tone of her voice.

'Anna, we were expecting you at the meeting just now,' Virkkunen explained.

'I don't have telepathic skills, and I don't remember ever claiming such a thing on my CV either.'

Virkkunen gave Esko a puzzled look.

'Esko said he'd told you that there would be a meeting in my office as soon as you got back to the station,' he said.

'He said nothing of the kind.'

'I told you when we got back from Saloinen,' said Esko.

'We didn't exchange a single word. And I do have a phone – why didn't anyone call me?'

The group was silent. Virkkunen seemed at a loss. Rauno and Sari took a few polite steps to one side. Esko was scrutinising the lunch menu on the board with a look of nonchalant satisfaction. He looks like a drunk, thought Anna.

'I'm sure this is just an unfortunate misunderstanding,' said Virkkunen. 'I'm very sorry things seem to have got off to a bad start.'

'So am I,' was Anna's clipped response.

She wasn't far from tears.

'I'll have the spaghetti – it's the only grub with meat today,' said Esko.

That afternoon was almost as warm as summer. The thermometer outside Anna's office window said 22°C. Moisture shimmered from the streets and slate roofs. The weather had taken a U-turn, its brakes wailing; suddenly it was summer again. Such rapid, dramatic shifts had increased in recent years.

Anna opened the window. A faint breeze carried in the stench of exhaust fumes. Anna let the sunshine warm her face. She closed her eyes for a moment and listened to the noise of the traffic from below.

The police station was located next to the train and bus stations, nestled between restaurants, department stores, office blocks and housing complexes in one of the busiest areas of the city. It was an ugly, high-rise building erected in the late sixties.

Anna tried to pluck something familiar from amid the cacophony, a sound that might have awoken a forgotten memory or reminded her of an event from her childhood or her teenage years, of her former life in this city. But the sounds could have been from any city, and the events of the past remained hidden.

My first day on the job isn't even over yet and I'm dealing with a case of suspected honour violence, a brutal homicide and a real arsehole of a partner, thought Anna, opening her eyes. It doesn't look good. Nothing here will be easy. But is that really what I was expecting? Her thoughts drifted to the subject of Ákos.

Before long she would have to confront him. She pressed herself tight against the bay windows and squinted into the bright sunshine. She was nervous. She felt a powerful urge to go out for a cigarette.

So much evil took place last night, she pondered. My job is to find out who committed it and why, to find the guilty parties and the evidence to convict them. That's what I'm paid for. It doesn't matter whether it's my first or my 500th day at work; my job is still my job. I'm good at this job. Well, back in the Guides I was. I don't know about this one yet, but surely it can't be all that different. And I've never yet let bullies get the better of me.

Reluctantly she let her craving for nicotine waft out of the window and into the exhaust fumes in the alley below. There was no point getting into a bad habit like that; one a day was all she permitted herself, and never while she was on duty. She sighed and closed the window. The city bustle was muted behind the panes of glass. In the quiet of the room she could hear the dull ticking of a wall clock.

She turned away from the window.

A tall, ominous figure was standing behind her.

'*Úr Isten!*' Anna screamed. The shock coursed through her veins like poison.

'We've tracked down Juhani Rautio. Pack your tampons and lipstick, we're heading back to the same village we visited this morning,' said Esko.

'What the hell are you thinking? Don't ever creep up on me again…'

But Esko had already disappeared into the corridor.

'Get a move on!' he shouted from the lift.

5

JUHANI RAUTIO was just finishing an extended lunch break, during which he had brokered a lucrative deal, when his telephone rang. Juhani cursed his own absent-mindedness. Ten years ago, answering your telephone anywhere and everywhere had been the hallmark of a successful businessman, but nowadays it was considered downright uncouth. Juhani wasn't uncouth, at least he didn't think he was. In dealing with clients, he took pains to focus only on them, to make them feel that he was there for them and them alone. Children didn't like it either, if Mum and Dad were on the phone or reading the newspaper while they were trying to explain something important. You had to be there for them.

Juhani was about to press the reject button and present an embarrassed apology to his client when something made him answer after all. With hindsight, he saw this as a portentous sign of a father's instinct.

The phone call was from the police. He was asked to return home as soon as possible. His wife Irmeli had also been summoned.

This time Esko took Anna in his car; Virkkunen must have been watching them from the window. Still, they didn't exchange a word throughout the journey. Maybe I can get used to working like this, thought Anna bitterly: we sulk, don't talk to one another, and if we do talk, it's only to take the piss.

The first impression of her new workplace had already begun to crack like an old oil painting. Have I just made the biggest mistake of my life, she pondered.

The red-brick house belonging to Juhani and Irmeli Rautio was located in the centre of Saloinen in an area of old detached houses with spacious yards and gardens, each better pruned than the next. The tall trees, fulgent hedgerows and abundant flower beds made this a pleasant area. Almost every garden featured bushes of berries and vegetable patches, heavy with the late-summer harvest. Anna thought of the panorama opening up from her own balcony. She tried to remember whether she could see even a single balcony with hanging baskets. Her mother had always filled the balcony with troughs of flowers. She recalled the buzz of activity on the balcony each spring, her mother's hands caked with mud, fragile plant cuttings standing in long, slender boxes, the cool of the balcony's concrete floor, the bamboo mats rolled up waiting for shoots to be replanted. Above all, she remembered the pride with which her mother looked at her balcony on her way back from town. It really was beautiful, particularly in late summer when a sea of flowers spilled over the railings. After moving away from home, Anna had never planted a single flower. She found herself wondering why.

Juhani arrived home at the same time as Anna and Esko. They shook hands in the driveway, introduced themselves and stepped inside. The house was calm and tidy. The family's affluence wasn't obvious, but was perceptible in the tastefully designed interior. Either the couple had employed a professional interior designer or Mrs Rautio was exceptionally gifted, thought Anna as Juhani gestured them through to the stylish living room where every detail seemed to be just right.

'You are the owner of a yellow Fiat Punto, is that correct?' Esko didn't beat around the bush.

'That's right,' Juhani replied, a note of concern in his voice.

'With the registration number AKR-643?'

'Yes, yes.'

'Do you know where your car is right now?'

'What's going on? Has it been stolen?'

'Just answer the question, please, and we'll see whether this is a matter for your concern,' said Esko calmly.

'Has Riikka been in a crash? Is she okay? Tell me this minute she's okay,' Juhani shouted.

Anna and Esko glanced at one another. Just then there came a click as the front door opened and Mrs Rautio stepped inside, her face red and sweaty as she took off her cycling helmet.

'Juhani, what's going on? Why do we have to come home?' Her voice was taut with worry.

'Please take a seat, both of you,' said Esko gently but firmly.

So he does know how to behave appropriately, thought Anna.

'We found this car parked by a running track some distance from here. There are a few questions we'd like to ask.'

'Our daughter Riikka uses that car, has done for about a year now, ever since she turned eighteen. We originally got it as a second car for my wife, but we realised we didn't really need it.'

'I prefer to cycle,' said Irmeli. 'Means I don't need to work out separately. Where is Riikka? Let me call her right now,' she continued and made to stand up.

'Please, just sit down,' Esko ordered. Irmeli remained seated.

'Where should your daughter be right now?' asked Anna.

'In town, I should think,' said Irmeli, glanced questioningly at her husband.

'Is that where she lives?'

'Well, she lives here actually. Officially, this is her address, but she spends most of her time at her boyfriend's place downtown.'

'She's nineteen years old, is that right?'

'Yes,' replied Juhani.

'Did she come home yesterday?'

'No. We haven't seen her for a few days. When was it she was here, Irmeli?'

'She popped round to do some washing – was it Wednesday? Jere – her boyfriend, that is – doesn't have a washing machine. There's a laundry in the basement, but Riikka doesn't like using it,' Irmeli gave a forced giggle.

'When did you last speak on the telephone?'

'Riikka called us yesterday. Nothing in particular, just asked if she could take an antique chest of drawers with her to Jyväskylä. She was moving there to study. Psychology. The move's pretty soon.'

'Does your daughter jog a lot?' asked Anna and felt a slight tensing of her shoulders.

Irmeli and Juhani sat for a moment in silence. What had so far remained unsaid flickered through the couple's consciousness.

'Yes,' replied Irmeli. 'She got into it in June. I bought her a decent pair of running shoes to get her started. They're quite expensive, proper running shoes, especially on a student budget. She … she seems to think she's overweight. But it's nothing obsessive; it's not as if she's anorexic or anything like that, just a young woman's normal concern for her own body. She wanted to look good.'

Irmeli's restless fingers began plaiting the tassels of a woollen shawl on the sofa. She peered up alternately at Anna and Esko, her eyes now alert with fear, a deep furrow of concern pressed into her brow.

'What make of shoes were they?' asked Anna.

When Irmeli gave the name of the brand, Esko turned towards the window and clenched his fist so that his knuckles gleamed white. Anna tried to swallow the dried saliva in her throat.

'What about her tracksuit? What kind of running clothes did she wear?'

'I think she had several. At least one dark-blue Adidas tracksuit and a bright green one – that one was brand new. Why are you asking these things? Just tell us what's happened!' Irmeli begged, now unable to conceal her anguish.

Anna looked at Esko. We should have talked about this before-hand, she thought. Who should say what? Is it now up to me to tell these people the worst possible news? What should I do?

Esko cleared his throat.

'We've found the body of a young woman on the running track near where your car was parked,' he said in his gravelly voice.

6

RAUNO FORSMAN was driving to Saloinen through the landscape of a reborn summer. He had always been charmed by how quickly the city gave way to the countryside, by how thin and imperceptible the boundary between these two worlds really was. In his parents' childhood the boundary had been clearly defined, and crossing that boundary was an event people planned with great care. Back then city dwellers were still considered better than everyone else. Country folk were curiously envious of them. That being said, they were also considered slightly stupid, because they knew nothing of hard graft and didn't know how to get about in the woods. In Rauno's childhood, this cultural clash had diminished to an extent, though its remnants could still be observed. Nowadays everyone was an equal part of the online community and living in the countryside was viewed as a trendy form of downshifting. The boundary between town and countryside had been erased by years of daily commutes in and out of the city. Traditional fields were replaced with identical, soulless blocks of flats. A romantic soul might have been lucky enough to find a rustic idyll in the form of an old log house.

Rauno drove past the isolated houses in the vicinity of the crime scene. There were four in total. Two houses stood on Selkämaantie. The first was home to Aune Toivola, who would be left in peace and quiet for the rest of the day, and the second to elderly widower Yki Raappana. The other two houses were newly built detached units in Irjalanperä, a remote area to the south-east of the running track where, in the hope of increased tax revenue, the local council had planned plots of land to house those relocating from the city. These houses were inaccessible from the same path that led to the running

track and to Aune and Yki's properties. Instead you had to drive
back to the main road, drive south for about half a kilometre and
turn right at the roundabout by the shopping centre. Still, an old
forest track a few kilometres long led from the houses to the illuminated running track. The shooter could well have used that.

Rauno decided to start with Yki. The house was small, old and
dilapidated, but beneath the flaking layers of paint and the torn felt
roof someone with a penchant for DIY might well have been able
to make out the potential for a quaint old cottage. The surrounding gardens featured large currant bushes, their branches heavy with
berries. The woods opened out on the other side of the yard, behind
the sauna and the fence. Rauno knocked at a slightly skewed door; its
white paintwork had long since started to peel in slender strips. An
old dwarf of a man in a checked shirt and brown trousers and braces
opened the door surprisingly swiftly. The old man's eyes blinked
sharply. The stench of a potato cellar wafted out to the doorstep.

'Hello there,' said Yki and shook Rauno's hand, his palm as rough
as sandpaper. 'It's a fair surprise to have a real police officer round
here. I get so few visitors these days. I'll put the kettle on.'

Rauno didn't care to decline, though the kitchen looked like a
sure-fire way of picking up food poisoning. The ceramic hob was
covered with layers of burnt food and the coffee pot was stained with
age-old brown spillages. The draining board was piled with rubbish
and dirty dishes. Yki rinsed two cups in cold water. Rauno sat down
at a small kitchen table and decided to man up and deal with it.

Though Yki continuously lost his train of thought and delayed
Rauno's departure with endless stories, the visit wasn't entirely futile.
Despite his age, the old man had a sharp mind and an acute sense
of hearing. He hadn't seen anything out of the ordinary. Like Aune,
his house was out of sight of the track. However, he had heard something. At a quarter past ten he had gone outside to close the flues in
the sauna and he'd heard a car driving towards the village. That certainly can't have been the murdered jogger, thought Rauno. The old
man had heard shots too, both before and after the sound of the car's

engine, but hadn't paid them the slightest attention. At this time of year you heard shots all day long, and had he been a bit younger he too would have been down by the shore taking a pop at the geese late in the evening. But he no longer had a rifle. He had given it to his brother's granddaughter when she'd turned fifteen and acquired her hunting licence. That was a few years ago now.

The visit to Yki's house had taken over an hour, and the aftertaste of three bitter cups of coffee still burned Rauno's throat. He sniffed at the stale air that had soaked into his shirt as he drove to his next visit, which yielded nothing but a sense of burgeoning anxiety. Irjalanperä was home to two families with young children who had moved from the city and who were like clones of one another. Both houses were unfinished, their front gardens nothing but a glorified sandpit, a chaotic mess of toys and two-by-four planks. A flock of pre-school-age children was running around, while their parents looked dead with exhaustion; they were people deep in debt, people who collapsed into bed each night as soon as they'd put the kids to sleep.

Just like me, thought Rauno. Just like us.

Neither of the families had heard or seen anything, for which both couples seemed politely and genuinely apologetic. It was entirely plausible that someone could have walked or driven past, gone to the end of the path leading to the running track and made their way from there to the track or the shore without the couple noticing a thing. Putting the children to bed was such an operation that neither family had paid the slightest attention to the world outside their windows.

However, they might have noticed a car's headlights or the sound of the motor, simply because there was so rarely anyone else around. Perhaps they might have paid it some attention. But if someone had been moving around out there after they had gone to bed, they most certainly wouldn't have woken again. Anything was possible, hard to say, maybe, maybe not, Mummy will come and look in just a minute, you wait now, Daddy's talking to this man. They promised to mull it over and to get in touch if anything came to mind, though they seemed quite certain that wouldn't happen. Rauno left his card at both houses and watched as both sets of children immediately seized it for their own games.

He might as well have visited only one of the houses, thought Rauno as he headed back to the city. Now I've just exhausted myself. The noise, the small children, the parents running around after them – it was all too close to home, as if he'd been interviewing himself. Rauno wondered whether he looked as fatigued as they did. It occurred to him that he could use the stress of the new case to escape the same hullabaloo when he got home. He'd have a pint somewhere, go home once the kids were sure to be asleep. And his wife.

The thought was tempting.

Sari Jokikokko-Pennanen had remained at the station. After the discovery of the jogger, Virkkunen had assigned her to all operations related to the missing Kurdish girl. Looks like I'll be on overtime again, she cursed under her breath and reluctantly called the babysitter who had even more reluctantly agreed to stay for another hour but not a minute longer. Sari's husband was away on business and her mother was on a senior citizens' spa holiday in Estonia. She'd have to get home in time. Sari's two small children prevented her from becoming consumed with work, and for that she was truly grateful.

With a sense of routine Sari filled out the forms used to summon people for interview, printed and signed them, put them in envelopes and left them at reception to be posted. Bihar's family would receive the forms tomorrow. Sari glanced at her watch; half an hour had passed already. She called the station in Vantaa and left a message requesting they call back. She wanted to talk to the officers that had visited Bihar's uncle and aunt, who had seen the situation for themselves. Indeed, it would probably also be worth talking to the officers who had been alerted to Bihar's house. Esko had apparently already done this, but she wanted to form her own perspective on the matter. Sari had always found it hard to get an overall sense of a case simply by reading other people's reports, and this had had a somewhat detrimental effect on her work as a police officer. It was a weakness, she thought. My very own little weakness. Nobody's perfect. Again she looked at her watch. She'd have to go soon. Although she was worth her weight in gold, the babysitter would be annoyed, and this she wanted to avoid at all costs. A good babysitter was hard to find, and she didn't want to let this one slip through her fingers.

She decided to continue working at home once she'd got the children to sleep. Perhaps she would still have the energy to scour the internet for information on honour violence, something that she knew only as a distant concept, something that occasionally cropped up in headlines from Sweden. She switched off her computer and quickly arranged the papers on her desk into two piles: those to be filed away and those that still required her attention. Both could wait until morning.

Poor Anna, she thought as she closed the door of the station behind her and walked towards her car. What a nasty way to start a career as a detective. Then she called home.

'I'll be another ten minutes. I'll take an extra hour and a half off on Friday, okay?'

7

WHAT MUST IT FEEL LIKE to have to identify your own daughter's body?

The question struck Anna as she pulled on her tracksuit in her apartment hallway. It was late. Her body felt tired and stiff. Her thoughts spun around restlessly like small children after a long car journey. The situation was ripe. Her imagination attacked at moments of weakness, drove its rusty nails deep inside her and yanked out painful memories that she had hoped were already forgotten, gone for ever, but that festered at the back of her mind and clung around her shoulders, from morning to night, from one move to the next, from year to year. They never let go.

Anna rubbed her eyes to block the path of the welling tears. Amid the red blotches on her retina, she saw the image of a child raped and mauled by a two-headed eagle. It could have been her. It could have been anyone.

Such attacks had become rarer over the years. It's just a panic attack, the school nurse had told her when she was in high school and suggested she go to the doctor and get herself some medication. Anna couldn't stand the idea of pills that would affect her state of mind. Instead, she'd started training for the marathon. She couldn't even remember the last time she'd had an attack. Perhaps it had been after she'd ended her year-long relationship, the only long-term, serious relationship she'd had. The guy had been another policeman, nice and sensible, all in all a very decent man, but with one fatal flaw: he'd wanted to get married and have children. And though Anna had been the one to end the relationship, the break-up had taken its toll on her. For a while she was quite beside herself. But that, too, was years ago.

Anna lay on the floor in the hallway and stared at the lamp hanging from the ceiling in the hope that it would blind her and dispel the eagle. She remained there for at least ten minutes and forced herself to calm down. It's no use, she repeated to herself. No use, no use, no use. There was someone out there prepared to kill his own child, someone just like Payedar Chelkin. Wasn't there something far more terrible about this than mere death, something impossibly bleaker, blacker? For a moment Anna tried to think what could have happened to the Kurdish girl. Then she sat up awkwardly, and though she felt drained she pulled on her trainers, ran outside and jogged to the start of the running track. Just as she had done yesterday, just as Riikka had done too. One–nil to me, she thought.

After the forensics officers had completed their work, Riikka's body was taken to the coroner's office. Juhani and Irmeli Rautio were already there, and Anna had waited with them. The couple identified their daughter immediately, without a moment's hesitation. They buckled with emotion; now they too would be for ever broken. Juhani Rautio's sobs were so heart-wrenching that Anna could no longer contain her tears. Irmeli sunk into apathetic silence. With expressionless eyes she looked at her daughter as she lay, headless, on a plastic stretcher in the cold room, caressed the skin along her arms, no words, no tears. Anna wrapped her arm around Irmeli's shoulder; she wanted to say something comforting but found herself incapable of words. There Riikka's mother stood, stiff and cold as a statue in her arms, and it all seemed so familiar that Anna began to feel sick.

Anna set off on her usual route, which took her through the yards in front of numerous blocks of flats and headed towards the woods on the outskirts of the suburb. That was her running track, the lonely place where she had taken up running all those years ago while, cans of beer in tow, her peers had trundled from one problem to the next, escaping old ones and running headlong into fresh ones. Her mother had been terribly proud that, despite the ravages of puberty and her own social problems, Anna hadn't become caught up with drugs and was serious and committed when it came to her sport. Still, all those years ago she'd known that she was no different from anyone else.

People can escape the past in so many ways.

Anna dived into the dark embrace of the trees. It was dusky in the forest, but her eyes soon became accustomed. The white of the running track winding its way ahead glowed dimly.

Suddenly she felt frightened. Her mind was darkened by the thought that someone was watching her through the dusk of the trees, following her run in the crosshairs of a sniper's hunting rifle. Something snapped in one of the bushes. The forest seemed to be tensing around her, ready to explode at any moment. Then, the sound of approaching steps behind her. Anna slowed a little, tensed her body in preparation for the attack and quickly glanced over her shoulder. The dark figure was already right next to her. A short, stocky woman in a black tracksuit. She greeted Anna with a smile and a nod of the head before speeding away along the track.

Bolond! Anna reproached herself. Stupid and superstitious. Now's not the time to let my imagination run away with me. You've been out here running in the November darkness too, as a teenager, with no knowledge of self-defence and you've never been afraid of anything, she muttered to herself, sped up almost to the limit of her ability, ran for five minutes at full speed, then slowed down for fifteen minutes. She continued like this for an hour, forcing herself to get through the tough set of intervals, using the torturous regime to shed her fear.

She wondered whether Riikka had tried to do the same. Had she been afraid, sensed something in the moments before her death?

After her shower, she listened to AGF's song 'Lonely Warriors'. A strange and fascinating soundscape of machines and human voices washed over the sofa where she lay wrapped in a towel, her wet hair a tangled mess on the cushions, like a solitary soldier in her barrack at night after all her comrades had died around her. She was alone on the front line, she thought, alone in the universe.

She thought back to her time in the army. It had been a time of awakening, of finding direction. Of opening a door, and of closing one, because it was then that she'd finally realised she would stay in Finland. It hadn't been a conscious decision but something that was inevitable.

She vaguely recalled what Áron had looked like in his khaki uniform as he had left home for the last time.

A lonely warrior.

Best to forget about it altogether.

She switched off the CD player and tried to go through the day's events – without success. There was too much to focus on. She wouldn't wish a first day at work like this on her worst enemy.

And just then something flashed inside her.

Fuck you. That's what she should have said to him, perfectly amiably and without any hesitation, collegially, bloke to bloke. And then: Chief Inspector Virkkunen seems to have been reading too many swivel-eyed nationalist blogs before bed. Then she should have given a faint, nonchalant chuckle, just enough to give the impression that she might be joking, having a laugh, saying something apparently frivolous and insignificant. Though, of course, this was not the case.

That's how she should have dealt with the day's events.

But what with all her nervousness that morning it hadn't occurred to her. Of course it hadn't. And besides, would she have had the guts? To say such a thing to her boss? On her first day at work? Doubtful.

Anna couldn't decide which was more infuriating: the fact that an appropriately snide comment always popped into your head too late or that she probably wouldn't have said it anyway. After agonising over this for a while she fell into a restless sleep on the sofa, her hair still wet.

8

SUMMER HAD DECIDED TO LINGER on after all. The chill of the previous few days had disappeared when Anna awoke on the sofa, naked, as the sunshine pushed its way between the slats of the blinds and crept across her eyelids. It was half past five. The towel, which had served as a blanket, had fallen to the floor, but, thanks to the morning sunshine, Anna hadn't felt cold. She stretched her stiff limbs. A beam of light bisecting the room revealed specks of dust dancing in the air. Anna wanted to feel enthusiasm for the day ahead, the way she always did with new challenges; she wanted to jump up from the sofa and get straight to work. But instead she was worried.

There was something disturbing about the cases of both Riikka and Bihar. They had torn open wounds over which she had grown a thick, supposedly impenetrable layer of scar tissue. She was afraid that being a detective might yet prove too challenging for her. Practice was different from theory, and investigating cases was different from rounding up drunks on the street. What had she been thinking? That the way to move forward in life was to move back to this city, this damned suburb? In the morning light it seemed all the more clearly a regressive step, and the thought of Esko did nothing to ease her sense of malaise.

What's more, she still hadn't tried to contact Ákos.

With a sigh, she went to the bathroom and tried to comb the tangles out of her hair. Her thick, full head of hair, so coveted by Finnish women, was a curse when it dried on a cushion, uncombed. But this, too, she would simply have to survive.

*

Esko didn't even bother greeting Anna over coffee, though the others happily wished her good morning; he simply sat po-faced drinking his black coffee and muttered something to Rauno that elicited an awkward chuckle. Again he looked dishevelled, and Anna thought she could smell the stench of old liquor on his breath when he was gripped by another coughing fit.

You're nothing but a pathetic drunk, thought Anna, and a small glimmer of hope flickered within her. Bitter old alcoholics were nothing to be afraid of, and they were no match for Anna. The thought cheered her up.

Together they went through the previous day's events, considered who the shooter might be. Rauno suggested it could be a hunter with mental-health problems. This sounded far-fetched, though they all agreed it was entirely plausible. Virkkunen told Anna to observe the autopsy by herself. Esko tried to object, claiming that this was technically his job. Virkkunen explained his decision in a tone of voice that left no one in any doubt as to who was the boss. He wanted to give Anna a variety of opportunities to acquaint herself with the day-to-day work of a criminal investigator, otherwise there was no way she could develop professionally. Esko could get on with other things. Anna almost felt the urge to decline, to say she would be happy for Esko to go, that she would have plenty of opportunities to observe an autopsy later on, that there were already so many new and fascinating things for her to learn, but she was unable to open her mouth. Virkkunen had that effect on people. Esko did nothing to hide his annoyance, but at least he managed to keep his mouth shut.

'The victim had engaged in sexual intercourse on the day of her death,' declared Linnea Markkula, the forty-something coroner who gave off an aura of musk, Anna's favourite perfume.

Anna had hurried straight from their morning meeting to the coroner's office, situated in the basement of the university hospital a few kilometres from the city centre. Linnea had already set to work in the tiled autopsy room, bathed in blue light and filled with the smell of death, where the body of Riikka Rautio lay on a steel examination table.

Anna had packed her camera. She was wearing white protective scrubs with a paper mask over her mouth. Breathing through the mask felt difficult.

'That would explain her legs,' said Anna. She felt like pulling the mask away from her lips and taking a deep breath.

'The what?' asked Linnea.

'Her legs. I noticed that her legs were very smooth, recently shaved. It stuck in my mind, because I always shave my legs in the shower *after* my run. And by the following afternoon the new stubble is already showing – on my legs, at least. Of course, Finnish women's leg hair is different. It's tamer.'

Linnea gave a smile and gently stroked Riikka's shin.

'I still can't feel anything here. It's a common misconception that hair continues to grow after death; it only seems that way because the skin retracts, so you would expect there to be some amount of stubble here by now. I imagine they were pulled out by the roots on the day of her death, with wax strips perhaps.'

'She had a date with someone before her run,' said Anna. Or maybe during her run, she thought.

'Well, that sperm got inside her one way or another – and I doubt she'd just visited a fertility clinic. We should check that though, just to be sure,' Linnea joked.

'She could have been raped.'

'There's no evidence of that. You saw for yourself that none of her clothes had been removed by force. Her jogging bottoms and everything else were positioned perfectly normally on the body.'

'Could the killer have pulled her trousers back on afterwards?'

'In theory, yes, but I would have noticed. Re-dressing a body lying on the ground isn't the same as pulling trousers on yourself. The underpants are always awkwardly crumpled up, for instance. And there are no signs of violence around the vagina either.'

'What about elsewhere?'

'Nothing except the blown-off head.'

'Well, it's not entirely blown off,' Anna pointed out.

'Right.'

For a moment the women looked in silence at the body of the young woman on the autopsy table. Anna photographed the full body. Bluish livor mortis had begun to develop around the chest and stomach.

'What are those?' asked Anna pointing to some faintly visible blotchy patches on the lower left shank, just above the hip.

'Old bruises. They're healing now, but they must have been pretty big. A few weeks old, I'd say. The position seems to indicate that she fell. When people fall on their side – if they slip on ice or fall off a bike – the resulting injuries typically affect the area around the hip.'

'Shouldn't there be something on her palms too, then? Don't your hands hit the ground first when you fall over?'

'Usually, yes. But she could have been wearing gloves. Or she might not have had time to put her hands out; that happens, too. But in that case there should be some marks on her left shoulder as well, and there's nothing here.'

Anna tried to think back a couple of weeks. All she could remember was the relentless sunshine and record temperatures. Two weeks ago nobody was wearing gloves, not even at night. She zoomed in on the marks at close range, snapped three shots, examined the images, then photographed the hands.

'Are you ready?' asked Linnea. 'Let's take a look inside.'

Linnea opened up the body with a sense of confidence and routine. It looked so clean and easy, as though this wasn't a real human being at all, someone who had been alive only a moment ago. As Riikka's stomach and internal organs came into view, Linnea explained that people were always shocked to hear what she does for a living, and that in bars she generally said she was a doctor – or preferably a nurse. Telling someone you're a pathologist or a coroner was likely to scare off even the most self-assured flirts, while calling yourself a doctor meant that half the bar expected you to be holding open

surgery over your pint glass. Being a nurse was a safe option. For lots
of people it sounded just stupid and subversive enough to be attractive. The only problem was that Linnea wasn't the least interested in
the kind of men that would be interested in that kind of woman.

'Five years as a single parent is starting to get me down. I need a
man,' Linnea chortled as she weighed the liver. 'Even a quick bit of
fun would do.'

That shouldn't be too difficult, thought Anna as she watched the
good-looking blonde at work. She was beautiful and well educated,
and probably fairly affluent too. Not from Koivuharju, that's for sure.

'Nothing out of the ordinary here,' Linnea concluded. 'A healthy
young woman, no pregnancies. She'd eaten a small portion of something a few hours before her death. Judging by the colour she'd
washed it down with a glass of orange juice. I'll take a closer look
at the stomach contents later on. Internal organs all fine, intestines
fine, no signs of drug or alcohol abuse. We'll send of blood samples
for testing, but I'm pretty sure nothing will show up. Lungs are clean
– this girl didn't even smoke. Well behaved, I'd imagine. Except for
the sperm. I'll extract the DNA, see if we can identify Mr X.'

Linnea continued somewhat more quietly.

'The shower of bullets destroyed the head entirely. She died in-
stantaneously. The shot came from right in front of her, and the
shooter was so close that the barrel of the gun could almost have
been touching her. Terrifyingly brazen, don't you think?'

'It certainly is. What about time of death?' asked Anna.

'The victim was discovered at nine in the morning. I arrived at the
scene around midday. My initial estimate put time of death around
ten o'clock the previous evening, and that still stands. Ten p.m., give
or take an hour or so, because last night was so cold and wet. Funny
time to go out jogging, isn't it?'

'I suppose,' Anna sighed. It was late.

'Join me for a drink on Saturday?' asked Linnea as they pulled off
their scrubs and masks in the coroner's changing room.

Anna was almost taken aback. She drew a deep breath.

'I can't. My brother's coming round,' she lied and could feel herself blushing.

'My kids are with their dad this weekend, and I'm not planning on lounging around the house. Bring your brother along, too. Is he as good-looking as you? Single? How old is he?'

The redness of Anna's cheeks deepened.

'Thirty-nine. And yes, he is single, I think. He can't speak Finnish though.'

'Doesn't matter, I've got a first in body language,' said Linnea with almost a cackle.

Anna tried to laugh with her, though all she wanted to do was run out of the room and make her way up into the daylight. Ákos and the doctor of pathology. The mere thought was a catastrophe waiting to happen.

Anna had lunch in a good Thai restaurant in the city centre and swore she'd never again poison herself with food from the station canteen. With the harmony of coconut milk and lemongrass still lingering on her tongue, she retreated into her office, uploaded the autopsy photographs to her computer and wrote up her notes. After this, it was time to prepare for the interview with Riikka's parents. Virkkunen had told her to oversee the interview with Esko, but Anna had no intention of reminding him. She noted down a few key questions that she mustn't forget, and otherwise decided to let the interview progress at its own pace. At the outset it was hard to put down anything too concrete. Most important was to get a broad overview of Riikka's life and her circle of friends. That should take the investigation a long way. At the very least it would sprawl out around her like a battlefield around a lonely soldier. We're going to need reinforcements, Anna guessed. This is going to be big.

Anna didn't need to remind him or go to Saloinen by herself; Esko appeared at the door of her office at two o'clock sharp and informed her in typically abrupt fashion that it was time to go.

Again, the drive was as quiet as the open-sea ice in the heart of winter.

After a night of agony, Riikka's parents sat in their living room, lost and anxious. Esko placed a Thermos flask and packet of biscuits on the coffee table in front of the couple, a look of empathy in his reddened eyes.

'I thought I'd bring you some coffee,' he said and the Rautios nodded, touched.

He knows what he's doing, thought Anna. Have I been too quick to judge him?

'Tell us about the boyfriend with whom Riikka had been staying. How long had they been dating?' Anna began the interview and immediately cursed her elementary mistake: only ask one question at a time.

'His name is Jere Koski. He studies mathematics at the university. They'd been seeing each other for almost three years,' Juhani answered. The man's voice was hushed. Speech seemed difficult, as though forming each word caused him great pain.

'Where did they first meet?'

'There was a get-together for high-school students a few years ago. I think that's where it started. But they've always known one another. Jere is a few years older than Riikka, but he's from the same village.'

'What did you think of their relationship?' asked Anna.

Juhani seemed at a loss for words. Irmeli stared at her feet as though wondering what on earth they were doing there.

'Well ... what do parents normally think of their only daughter's boyfriends? At first we weren't exactly thrilled, especially given his...' Riikka's father cleared his throat. 'His background. But...'

'But what of it?' Irmeli interrupted her husband with a scowl. Anna was somewhat startled by the chill in her voice. 'You can't – and shouldn't – try and get in the way of young love.'

'Jere's a good boy, he studies at the university and everything. Riikka seemed content, so we accepted the situation and were happy for her,' said Juhani.

'What was wrong with the boy's background?' asked Esko.

'Well, there's nothing *wrong* with it as such,' Juhani Rautio seemed a little embarrassed. 'Jere's father, Veikko Koski, is long-term unemployed and he likes a pint. He's off work on disability leave, for his back apparently, but everybody knows it's because of the booze. His wife's a cleaner at the local school. She's nice.'

Was that the problem, Anna wondered. Better folk didn't think a boy from a poor family was right for their daughter?

'Did Riikka have any boyfriends before Jere?' asked Esko.

'They'd been together for so long,' said Irmeli. 'She was too young to have any others.'

'What kind of man is this Jere? Describe him for me,' asked Esko.

'Just an average young man, not a drunk like his father, not yet anyway. He's an outdoor kind of person, always off camping or fishing,' said Juhani.

'Does he go hunting, too?' asked Esko.

The room fell silent. An expression of restlessness crept across Juhani's face. The corner of Irmeli's mouth twitched nervously. She looked at her husband in horror.

'You don't think…?'

'Of course not. You said that Jere is the outdoor type. Does he go hunting or not?' Esko continued unflinchingly.

'Yes, he does.'

'Can you expand on that?'

Juhani considered this for a moment before continuing.

'He hunts a lot – ducks, hares, grouse. He travelled to Lapland to shoot ptarmigans; Riikka often went with him. He was a member of an elk-hunting club too.'

'So he had access to firearms,' Esko stated.

'Yes, well, I imagine so, without them you wouldn't really…'

'We're going to need Jere's contact details. You do have his telephone number?'

'Yes, of course. We tried to call him last night when … when Riikka … But he didn't pick up.'

Anna and Esko glanced at one another. Esko nodded. He tapped
Jere's address and telephone number into his mobile.

'You carry on,' he instructed Anna. 'I'll bring him in straight
away.'

That went smoothly, thought Anna, bewildered. Almost as
though we were working together.

It was hard to continue once Esko had gone. A sense of suspicion
had descended on the room, and even thinking about it was uncomfortable. Juhani and Irmeli looked anxious and concerned.

'We just can't believe…' Irmeli stuttered.

'You appreciate that we have to check everything,' Anna interjected. 'We have to turn every stone, rule out all possibilities until
there's only one left. But tell me more about Riikka and Jere, their
relationship.'

That was at least three questions, Anna again berated herself.
What a lousy interviewer.

It was clear that Juhani and Irmeli were reluctant to go on. Irmeli's whole body was trembling gently, and Juhani was holding back
tears. They were exhausted and beside themselves. Anna poured
them more coffee and waited. Juhani eventually pulled himself together and began speaking, his voice taut with agony.

'Like I said, Jere is a good boy, he studies hard and enjoys being
outdoors. Riikka had taken up hunting and rambling with him,
and fishing. She was even thinking of applying for her own hunting
licence, so she could take part in the annual hunt. We were a bit
surprised; we've never done anything like that ourselves, though we
enjoy eating game like anyone else.'

'Even berries we'd rather get at the market,' said Irmeli with a
forced laugh.

'Riikka took her high-school exams this spring. All As and Bs,'
said Juhani.

'Smart girl,' Anna commented. Juhani wiped his eyes.

'Did she have lots of friends?'

'Oh yes. The same group of girls had been friends since nursery school. Her closest friend was Virve Sarlin; they'd been in the same class from primary school right through to the end of high school. Two of a kind, they were.'

Anna noted down the name.

'And how long had she been living with Jere?' she asked.

'She moved in with him straight after the school exams.'

'What did you think of the move?'

'Well, it didn't make any sense, especially as she'd applied to university in Jyväskylä and got a place there. We told her moving twice in a year would be too much, but she moved anyway. She didn't have to ask our permission, she was eighteen, after all.'

'Did they ever argue?'

'I don't imagine so,' said Irmeli and gave her husband a questioning look. Juhani shook his head. 'We thought they were quite settled.'

'And what about recently? Have you noticed anything out of the ordinary?'

'About Riikka or the relationship?'

'Both. What about Jere?'

Again the couple looked at one another, as though searching for an answer in the other's eyes. They seemed uncertain.

'We don't really know,' Irmeli began. 'Riikka only visited a few times this past summer, only to do her laundry, really. Perhaps she was a little quieter than usual, now that I think of it.'

Juhani nodded his head.

'But was that out of the ordinary?' Irmeli continued. 'It's hard to say. Even as a child she was a quiet one. Come to think of it, I don't think the two of them visited us at all this summer, did they, Juhani?'

For a moment Juhani was silent.

'They visited at Midsummer. And they turned up together at Riikka's great-grandmother's birthday. That was on the fifteenth of June.'

'Wasn't that odd?'

'What?'

'That they didn't visit you together.'

'Not at all. I've only thought of it now. Jere never visited us anyway. I'd always felt that he would find any excuse not to come whenever possible. Perhaps he was shy. It was disappointing, of course. Juhani had always wanted a golfing partner, but Jere wasn't interested in things like that. So it's hard to say whether it was out of the ordinary or not. I doubt it. Surely we would have noticed if something had really been off kilter. Wouldn't we, Juhani?'

'I would say so. They were doing just fine. Now we'll never know what would have happened when Riikka moved to Jyväskylä. I'd assumed the relationship would have gradually fizzled out.'

Juhani's voice broke.

Irmeli stood up and went into the bedroom. When she returned she handed Anna a photograph, her hands trembling. Smiling back at her in the photograph was a chubby-cheeked girl, a high-school graduation hat upon her shoulder-length, chestnut hair, a bunch of roses in her hands. She was looking straight at the camera. Her eyes were greyish blue, lightly made up, and there was a sense of determination in her somewhat introverted expression. Her lips were full and beautiful. This was the face that had been destroyed. Like all young girls' faces, it was pretty and attractive. Anna could feel her throat tightening.

'She was going to move next week. We'd booked the van and everything,' said Irmeli quietly, her voice frozen and impassive.

When the dam finally breaks, there will be no shoring it up again, thought Anna. Suddenly she felt how much she missed her own mother.

When she arrived back in town, Sari asked Anna to join her at the gym in the police station. Because she only had two hours of her shift left, Anna was happy to go. One of the advantages of being a police officer was the opportunity to dedicate exactly that amount of working time to sports activities every week. Today was a day off from her running schedule, so a good weight-training session would do her a world of good. She wanted to get to know Sari, a woman who seemed the complete opposite of Esko: funny, relaxed, sporty and tolerant.

In the changing rooms Anna stole a few glances at her colleague's athletic body. She was tall and muscular without being too sculpted. In a word, she was handsome. It was hard to believe that two children had stretched her stomach and dangled from her breasts. Women generally started to sag. Sari had the fair complexion and toned body of a Viking goddess.

'How old are your children?' asked Anna.

It was always safe to start talking about someone's children. People loved talking about their own children, as long as they were smart and well behaved and lived up to their parents' expectations without making a fuss.

Sari's eyes lit up. 'Two, and three and a half.'

'Still so young. Did you adopt them? You don't look like you were pregnant only a couple of years ago.'

Sari laughed, clearly flattered.

'I didn't put on weight with either or them, though I ate like a horse all the time. I must have a phenomenal metabolism or something. And I've always done a lot of sport, and Pilates three times a week while I was pregnant.'

'Wow. Are they girls or boys?'

'One of each. Siiri and Tobias.'

'How do you do it? Such young kids and a job like this to boot?'

'I get along just fine, actually. It's a bit embarrassing to admit, but we have a nanny at home – it's an absolute must. Though the kids are still young enough that sometimes I don't sleep all that much. Still, I don't really spend time wondering whether I'll manage or not. I sleep whenever I get the opportunity. I can fall asleep anywhere and everywhere.'

'Now I'm envious! If only I could do that. What does your husband do?'

'Teemu is an engineer; he's always away on business. Thank God I don't do nights, and I'm almost always free on weekends; Virkkunen and I have come to an agreement about that.'

'You didn't want to stay at home for a while?'

'I was on maternity leave for almost a year with the youngest one. But you know what it's like – when you've got an enormous mortgage you've just got to keep working. We built our house a few years ago. To be honest with you, I'd simply had enough of being at home. It can be lonely and fairly boring; I'm not really cut out to be a nursery teacher. For me this job's a way of letting off steam, it means the kids don't get on my nerves as much. You're not supposed to say things like that out loud, are you?'

'Nowadays we can, thankfully. Where did you build your house?'

'In Savela, on a plot of land that used to belong to my parents-in-law. You should come and visit some time. Where do you live?'

'Koivuharju.'

'Oh God.'

Anna laughed. There was something very attractive about Sari's directness.

They walked through to the weights room. The bare concrete walls were bleak and the place stank of testosterone. There weren't many weight machines, mostly dumbbells and free weights. It's a male world, thought Anna as she picked twenty kilos from the rack, slid them on the ends of a bar and lay down on the bench. Sari started off on the exercise bike.

Three sets of twelve repetitions. Her chest muscles were in agony. Anna was out of breath; her arms were trembling under the strain. A pair of hands helped her with the final push; a familiar-looking man in a tight sleeveless T-shirt, his arms solid as a rock.

'Hi, I'm Sami,' the man greeted her. 'We saw each other yesterday at the car park.'

'Ah, yes,' said Anna as she got up from the bench. She walked towards the rack of free weights. The man followed her.

'Do you fancy meeting up some evening? Friday maybe? We

could grab a bite to eat somewhere,' he said without beating around the bush. He came up so close to her that they were almost touching. Anna felt awkward. She didn't need a date at the moment. Particularly not with another police officer.

'I don't know,' she stumbled. 'I've just moved and everything's a bit up in the air. I'm not sure I'll have the time.'

'I got the impression you might have been interested,' said Sami.

Menj a picsába, thought Anna. One wink, and men imagine all kinds of things.

'Well, that was, you know ... I didn't mean anything by it,' she awkwardly tried to explain.

'What about your friend, then? Good-looking lass. Better looking than you.' Sami seemed hurt and fixed his gaze on Sari.

'We're both spoken for,' Sari shouted from the exercise bike.

'I doubt it,' quipped Sami, his expression impassive.

'Why don't you go and have a wank in the changing room,' said Sari. At the other side of the gym, two officers chuckled.

Anna too gave a smirk. Sari was great. How did she have the balls? Sami slung his heavy free weights back on the rack with an indignant clatter and left the room.

'What a jerk,' Sari puffed. 'This is the downside of working in a male-dominated profession: hormonal dickheads everywhere you look. Hey, now it's your turn to spill the beans. Have you got family here? Where are you from? I want to hear everything. I think it's just great that we've got a foreigner on the team, though you don't seem much like an immigrant.'

Anna had no desire to talk about herself, though she knew there were some questions she'd have to answer sooner or later, over and over again. *Why did you come to Finland* was the most common, and it irritated her no end. Though people generally asked out of sheer, benevolent curiosity, Anna always felt there was another dimension to the question: did you have a good reason for coming, one that we real Finns can find acceptable, or did you simply come here in search of a better life?

The question always aroused a sense of guilt, making her feel like an unwanted guest whose secret had been revealed. Anna saw nothing wrong with looking for a better quality of living. Surely it was natural for everyone to search for such a thing? Why should it be restricted to people who already had everything they needed?

'Here you are,' Esko interrupted just as Anna drew a deep breath and was about to begin her story. He had appeared at the gym door. Though Sari had been assigned the Bihar case, Esko seemed to direct his words at her rather than Anna. Anna tried not to show her irritation. It was pointless letting arseholes make your blood boil.

'Jere's disappeared,' he informed them.

'What?' Anna and Sari cried in unison.

'Disappeared into thin air. Phone switched off. Parents, friends, landlord – nobody knows where he is.'

'Great,' sighed Sari.

'Quite. Seems like an open-and-shut case to me.'

'It does, doesn't it,' admitted Anna.

'The boy shot Riikka, probably in a fit of jealousy – wouldn't be the first time such a thing has happened in this country. Then took fright once he realised what he'd done and went into hiding.'

'We'll have to put out a warrant for him,' said Sari.

'Already done. And I've got a search warrant for his apartment too. I'll have to get out there now – with her,' Esko continued speaking to Sari and nodded towards Anna.

'Right now?' asked Anna. Annoying. The shift would go into overtime.

'Be in the car park in fifteen minutes.'

'Okay,' said Anna and hurried towards the showers.

'Anna, wait. Bihar and her family are coming in for an interview on Friday. Can we go through the details of the case tomorrow? I want to talk about it before they come in,' said Sari.

'How about lunch and a meeting at twelve?'

'It's a deal. See you.'

9

JERE'S APARTMENT WAS SITUATED near the city centre in a stale-smelling, 1970s block of flats on Torikatu. On this spot there had once been a beautiful old wooden house with good ventilation and free of mould. Anna had seen photographs of the city taken at the turn of the century; it had changed a great deal since then. In the name of progress, quaint wooden areas of the city had been torn down to make way for concrete boxes, and cobbled streets were covered with tarmac. The remaining art nouveau buildings in the downtown area still exuded a bygone, bourgeois elegance, but only a very few wooden houses had been spared the cull. There were still a few former working-class areas complete with small wooden cottages in and around the city centre. These properties were highly desirable for the rich and famous, who spent hundreds of thousands repairing and extending them.

The door to Jere's apartment block stood anonymously between a local pub and a second-hand store. The caretaker was waiting for them with a set of keys. The lift creaked and rattled as they went up to the second floor. He opened the door and would have followed them into the apartment had Esko not raised a hand in front of him.

'Hey, this is our territory now,' he said and the caretaker retreated into the corridor, disappointed.

On the doormat were a pile of flyers, a bill and a couple of free newspapers; the lowest in the pile was dated 21 August. Anna's letter box bore the words NO FLYERS. She couldn't stand it that in a matter of days the hallway was filled with rubbish. In an investigation, however, rubbish often provided crucial evidence.

The spacious one-bedroom apartment was dim. All the curtains had been pulled shut. The rooms were large, the ceilings high, and the scarcity of any furniture made the place seem almost deserted. A bachelor pad, par excellence, thought Anna.

They looked round the apartment, sizing it up. At first glance, everything seemed perfectly normal. Shoes were arranged in a tidy row on the hallway mat and coats hung on a rack. A T-shirt and a pair of socks lay on the floor next to the bed, but the bed itself had been made up neatly. There were no dust bunnies cowering beneath the sofa. On the coffee table was a pile of magazines and a coffee cup with a dried, brown oval at the bottom. Even the bathroom was clean. There was a tangle of hair in the plughole in the shower cabinet, but there were no layers of limescale around the toilet bowl or dried toothpaste stains in the sink. The kitchen looked as though it had recently been cleaned. The rubbish had been taken out and the dishes washed, and there were no crumbs on the worktop. The metallic draining board gleamed when Anna switched on the lights. There was nothing fresh in the fridge. It seemed that Jere hadn't wanted to leave anything behind that might start smelling or grow mouldy.

It's a pain coming home when the first thing you have to do is start tidying up, Anna heard the voice of her mother. Was that why she always left a mess behind whenever she went on a trip? Was Jere planning on coming back? Hadn't he run away after all? Anna had almost been hoping to encounter something sick and perverted, something that would have struck them the minute they walked in the door and revealed Jere's guilt in an instant, but if there was such a thing, it was well hidden.

'He certainly didn't leave in a hurry,' said Anna.

'Hmph,' Esko snorted.

'He's taken out the rubbish and everything,' she continued.

'And maybe there was something in the rubbish that needed to be disposed of,' said Esko, his enunciation deliberately exaggerated. 'You sure you understand everything I'm saying?'

Anna tried not to rise to it.

'Yes, I do. What about Riikka? Wasn't she supposed to be living here? There are no signs of another occupant here – and certainly not a woman.'

'Maybe that's all been disposed of, too – Riikka included.'

Esko spoke each word slowly and carefully and looked at Anna with mischief in his eyes.

'Well, no point standing around, is there?' said Anna, trying to control her irritation as she pulled a pair of gloves from her pocket. 'If there's something here to find, we'll find it.'

Esko scoffed again.

They started in the living room. It was an oblong-shaped room with a window looking down on to the street. The few pieces of furniture were second hand but in good condition. Beneath the window was a white melamine desk that looked like it had been taken from his childhood home; one of its drawers featured a Turtles sticker. The old brown leather sofa was worn but looked comfortable. A shallow bookshelf featured a television and DVD player and a few books, but no ornaments. Mathematics, physics, Chandler, Nesser and Åsa Larsson. The boy certainly had good taste in crime fiction. *The Hunter's Cookbook, The Deer Hunter's ABC, A Guide to Hiking* and *Fly Fishing: Baits and Lures*. The outdoor type, no doubt about it. There was a shelf of CDs and DVDs, cheap American entertainment for the masses. The belongings of a pretty average young man. On the desk there was a relatively new laptop and a fancy calculator. There were box files full of marked essays and sheets of squared paper covered in complicated formulae. No diaries, no letters, nothing particularly personal except a passport.

'He hasn't gone abroad, at any rate,' said Anna. 'Here's his passport.'

'Just think for a minute, eh? You don't need a passport to get to Sweden.'

True. Or Norway, thought Anna but didn't say anything.

'We'll have to ask Virkkunen for a warrant to confiscate the laptop, see what the IT boys can find on it,' said Esko. 'Kids' private lives are on computers these days, private information posted on Facebook for all and sundry to read. You must have hundreds of dago friends online,' Esko chuckled as though he'd told a particularly witty joke.

Anna counted to five before responding.

'I'm not on Facebook.'

'Well! So we do have something in common. Who'd have thought?'

Esko stared at Anna for a moment, a seedy smirk on his ruddy face. Anna looked away.

'If Jere had posted online where he was going, one of his friends must surely know where he is,' she continued.

'Fancy that. So you can think, after all.'

'I don't get the impression that Jere fled on the spur of the moment. By the looks of it, he planned his departure very carefully,' Anna carried on regardless of Esko's tone.

'This Jere is one cold-blooded character. See, that's why men make better police officers. You women are too vulnerable to fluctuations in your emotions, you southern types probably more so than Finnish women.'

Menj a picsába, Anna cursed to herself and decided not to exchange another word with him.

If this had been a treasure hunt, the door into the bedroom would have been signposted *Getting Warmer*. The room itself was large. Anna opened the dark-blue curtains. A sudden light glinted against the white walls. From the window she saw the wall of the house opposite and looked down into the concrete courtyard, featuring a handful of parking spaces and a wooden seesaw with a small shrub sprouting beside it.

In the middle of the room was a double bed. Even the bedspread was blue. Anna turned up the hem. It was hand made. Riikka? His mother? And why do I automatically assume it was made by a woman, she thought angrily. The boy could just as easily have made it himself.

Esko gave a whistle. He had opened the double doors of a walk-in closet. There was nothing inside that might have suggested that Riikka lived there. Instead, there was a gun cabinet, locked according to official regulations. Anna felt her pulse quickening.

'Well, well, let's see what skeletons this model student has in his cupboard. Try and keep schtum for a minute, eh, so I can concentrate,' said Esko rudely and knelt down in front of the cabinet. He slowly turned the dials of the combination lock, his ear close to the cabinet. In under a minute the door gave a quiet click and swung open. Wow, thought Anna. This is just like in the cinema. Naturally, she didn't say this out loud.

The cabinet contained a Marlin .45-calibre rifle, an old single-barrelled shotgun, a 16/70 Baikal and several drawers full of rounds and bullets.

'There's one rifle missing,' said Esko.

Anna was forced to open her mouth.

'How do you know that?'

'I'm getting vibrations; it's as if the cupboard's trying to tell me something,' he said and stuck his head inside the cabinet, closed his eyes and listened.

Anna waited.

'There should be a .12-calibre Remington pump-action shotgun in here,' Esko surmised as he crawled out of the cupboard. 'Which, as you can see, is missing.'

Anna stared at him in disbelief.

'I checked out his licences before we left – just a few clicks on the computer, that's how easy it is these days. Besides, if Little Miss Senior Detective Constable would like to take a closer look, she'll find two packets of 12/70 steel shots. You wouldn't put them in that monster, and certainly not in that rifle over there.'

Anna felt ashamed. And furious at herself. Why hadn't she thought of this? Checking a suspect's licences is an elementary step.

'Something for you to shove up your arse then, now you've come out the closet.'

'Oh, sweetheart, gagging for it today, eh?' he replied and gave her a dirty wink. Now there wasn't even a flicker of a smile on his face.

'Fuck you.'

'Call the station, tell them he's armed,' Esko ordered her. 'I'm going out for a cigarette and a snoop round the yard. My sense of smell isn't what it used to be. Blame the fags.'

Anna remained in the apartment, waves of disappointment pressing sweat into her armpits and on to her brow. I've completely cocked this up, she thought. Now that drunken git's got one up, he'll be able to laugh at the dago bitch who hasn't got the first clue about police work. She called Virkkunen and told him what they'd discovered – or rather, what they hadn't found. She didn't mention who had checked Jere's licences and who had not. Virkkunen thanked them for their good work and added the words ARMED and POSSIBLY DANGEROUS to the arrest warrant.

Anna went round the rooms one more time, listening carefully to see whether the silence might tell her something as to the whereabouts of Jere and his rifle. If only these walls would reveal their secrets, the stupidity of moments ago would be erased. What's the use of walls having ears if they don't have a mouth too, she thought.

That evening Anna finally called Ákos. She had been avoiding her mobile phone on the kitchen table, trying to think of something else to do, and even picked up the phone several times only to put it back down again. She'd gone out to the balcony a couple of times for a cigarette. What would she say? How would she start the conversation? Eventually she plucked up the courage and made the call.

Her brother answered immediately. In the background she heard voices, laughter and the thump of music. Ákos was in a bar somewhere.

'Anna, *hogy vagy? Baj van?*' There was a crackle, a clatter, then everything fell silent. Ákos had moved somewhere else, outside perhaps, maybe into the gents.

Anna took a deep breath and counted to three.

'*Jól vagyok, köszönöm. És te?*' she said eventually.

'*Hát én is jól vagyok.*'

A second's silence. Anna tried to bolster her courage. Then she told him.

'I moved back a week ago. We're almost neighbours now.'

'*A kurva életbe,* Anna. Why didn't you say anything?' her brother hollered down the telephone.

'Haven't had a chance. I started work yesterday. I've been rushed off my feet finding a flat and everything. I wondered if you'd like to come round on Sunday?'

'Sunday? Why not? The Depraved are playing at Mara's pub on Saturday night, I can't miss that, but Sunday's free. What time?'

'*Valamikor délután.*'

'Okay.'

'Have you heard from Mum?'

'Not a peep.'

'I spoke to her last week. She wants to talk to you. You could chat on Skype.'

'We'll see.'

'She misses you.'

'*A faszom*, Anna, you could have told me you'd moved back,' Ákos tried to change the subject.

'How have you been?'

'You haven't been in touch much.'

Anna said nothing, but felt a sting of guilt beneath her skin. It was true. For the last ten years she hadn't had much to do with her brother. They'd called each other occasionally, and seen each other even less. Anna hadn't wanted to. She hadn't had the energy. Neither have you, she felt like snapping.

'Hey, I've gotta go. Zoran and Akim are waiting. Shall I say hello? Zoran will be happy, that's for sure.'

'Okay. *Szia.*'

'*Szia.*'

Anna ended the call.

Zoran. Damn it, so he was still around.

Anna recalled the last time she'd seen her brother. It had been a few years ago, at the end of a bitterly cold February. Ákos had called her on the verge of death and begged Anna for help. Throwing aside all her principles she had gone to him. Anna cleaned the bedsit, which was swimming in vomit and empty beer cans, and fetched her trembling brother food and sedatives. On the way home she'd hated herself. Thank God I don't live any closer, she'd thought.

And now she was here again. Less than a kilometre away.

10

ORIGINALLY, WHAT HAD FASCINATED ANNA about police work was its dynamism and variety, and in those respects she had not been disappointed in her choice of profession. Still, she was always surprised at how much paperwork was involved, how much sitting at a desk it entailed. Back in patrol, she'd always rounded off her shifts with paperwork, but here it seemed there was even more of it. Her third morning as a senior detective constable began by switching on her computer, and she would sit working at her desk for most of the day. A surprisingly large amount of her investigative work took place indoors, sitting by her computer, because the police force's intranet provided access to all manner of information and registers. The world of television drama series, with detectives running along the streets with a gun in their hand, was a far cry from the calm atmosphere in the station's offices.

She wondered how long it would take before they started to get some results. She hoped they'd find Jere quickly.

At twelve on the dot Sari knocked at the door and fetched Anna for lunch. They decided to go to a wine bar that had just opened up in town and that served lunch during the day. It was a pleasant place with dark wooden fittings and velvet finishings; the ambience was intimate and dusky, even in the middle of the day.

'We should come here some evening, too,' said Sari. 'The wine list looks excellent. Should we have a glass now, wave goodbye to a sober afternoon,' she giggled.

'I'll have one too. The Australian Chardonnay sounds nice and fresh,' said Anna.

'Oh. I wasn't being serious.'

'What?'

'I mean, I wasn't serious about ordering a glass. Not while we're on duty, surely? It was a joke.'

'Oh. Yes, right. Sorry,' said Anna. 'I don't think I'll ever get my head round the strange alcohol etiquette in Finland. I suppose I'm just too foreign. I've never understood what could possibly be wrong with a glass or two, on duty, morning, evening, whenever.'

'You don't go out on the piss, then?'

'Sometimes, if I feel like it – there's a little bit of the Finn in me, after all. But that's exactly what I mean: if you have one glass, it's automatically synonymous with going out on the piss. The way people talk about alcohol here is so strange and hypocritical. Back home only being clearly drunk is frowned upon.'

'Funny you should say *back home*, though you've lived here since you were ten.'

'I go back a couple of times a year, and I spend all my holidays there. Maybe that's why. Though generally I feel like I'm somewhere in between, neither here nor there.'

Anna could feel the blood rushing to her cheeks. She'd had to go and put her foot in it.

'Have you got a man?' Sari asked with a cheeky grin. She didn't appear to notice that Anna thought this a very intimate revelation.

'No.'

'Haven't found the right one?'

'I don't know. Suppose not.'

'What about in your other homeland?'

'No, not there either.'

Anna felt embarrassed. Her mind was flooded with thoughts of the sweltering heat two summers ago, the shadows on the banks of the Tisza, the 30-degree water in the river that had seemed almost cool. She'd been back home for over a month in a single stretch and had enjoyed her time there more than ever before. This summer she hadn't managed more than a week there. It had passed in a flash as she'd gallivanted from village to village and obligatory meetings with relatives. Only one evening had she been able to sit down at a *járas* with her childhood friend Réka, a couple of cans of beer in a cool box, and sit in peace watching the glowing red sun sink into the open, comfortless embrace of the hills. It suddenly occurred to her that she didn't know when she'd next have a holiday.

'You really do seem to be somewhere in between.' Sari's voice was gentle, but her gaze bored deep into Anna's dark eyes. 'You know what, we're going to order that wine. Jesus, I couldn't agree more. Finns' relationship with alcohol is crazy.'

They ordered two glasses of Chardonnay to accompany their lunch of mushroom soup and salmon. There was a buffet with four different side salads. Excellent, Anna enthused, no more lunch in the staff canteen, and definitely no more quickly gobbled trans-fat meals from petrol stations and hotdog stands. She had finally reached a stage in life when she had the time to eat healthily.

'I haven't found anything on the Chelkin family. Nothing important anyway. There's no record of any of them, except with Immigration. Their residence status checks out. Even GP records revealed nothing worse than flu. So if Bihar has been abused, she certainly hasn't been treated at the health centre,' said Sari.

'What about school?'

'She goes to a high school in the city centre, full of yuppie kids. The younger siblings are still in elementary school, in Rajapuro.'

'The high school is a good sign. In very orthodox families, girls are often forced to learn about childcare or something similar, if they're allowed to go to school at all.'

'The head of year said Bihar is a top student, one of the best in the school. She hasn't noticed anything out of the ordinary, except that Bihar can be quite reserved, not at all outgoing or overly sociable. She just put it down to cultural differences.'

'That may be the case. In many cultures girls are brought up to be quiet and meek, closed off. What about friends?'

'According to the teacher she has a few friends at school.'

'A boyfriend?'

'Don't know. But she's been absent quite a lot recently. Spent some time in Turkey last year.'

'Was it a long trip?'

'A couple of weeks.'

'Hard to say anything based on that. They have the right to visit relatives.'

'But what if she felt she had to run away?'

'Still…'

'And what if she was there for some sort of arranged marriage?'

'That's something we'll have to ask them, though they won't tell us. How long has the family lived in Finland?'

'Ten years. Bihar was in first grade when they arrived. They are Turkish Kurds and came here as asylum seekers. Now they all have Finnish citizenship.'

'What about the parents?'

'The father, Payedar Chelkin, is a 44-year-old electrician but hasn't worked a day in ten years.'

'Of course not,' Anna sniffed.

'The mother is Zera. She's only 34. Imagine – she must only have been 17 when Bihar was born. She doesn't have a profession. The youngest child, Adan, was born soon after the family came to Finland. And the son Mehvan is in eighth grade.'

'Have you asked around the Rajapuro school?'

'No. Should I?'

'Try and look up one of Bihar's former teachers. Middle-school teachers know a surprising amount about their students' family backgrounds.'

The mobile phone in Anna's handbag beeped. It was an SMS from Rauno. 'Esko says to tell you Riikka's friend Virve Sarlin is coming for interview tomorrow.'

'What the hell's the matter with that guy?' Anna wondered.

'He can be a bit grouchy sometimes.'

'A bit? I think he's grouchy quite a lot. All the time.'

'Don't worry about it.'

'Can't he send me a message directly?'

'Pff. Seriously, don't waste your energy on it,' said Sari.

'Does this mean that if I want to send him a message, I should send it via Rauno? We can't make Rauno our go-between.'

'Yes, you can. At least for the moment. Esko will calm down soon enough.'

'He hates me.'

'No he doesn't. He's just downright old-fashioned and stuck in his ways. It's going to take him a while to get used to the fact that his new partner is a young foreign woman. He's never travelled further than Sweden. Believe me, he's an okay bloke when you get to know him.'

'It certainly seems so.'

'I mean it. And though Virkkunen pampers him a bit, he also keeps him in order. Have a word with Virkkunen if something happens.'

'What do you mean, *pamper*? Why?'

'I don't know, it's an old story. We've all had our little run-ins with Esko. That's just the way he is – there's no point taking it personally.'

Anna shrugged her shoulders and finished off her wine.

'So, Virve Sarlin tomorrow. The parents told us she was Riikka's closest friend,' she said.

'Well, you could learn all kinds of things.'

'Let's hope so. At least we'll be able to shed a little light on the mystery of Riikka Rautio.'

'Then on Friday we've got the Chelkin family.'

'We've got our work cut out.'

'Your career as a detective has got off with a bang. I spent the first three years investigating stolen bikes.'

'Sounds like an attractive option,' said Anna.

I still remember the day we arrived in Finland. Dad, Mum, Mehvan and me. Adan was already in Mum's belly but you couldn't see it yet and nobody had told me about it. I could sense how nervous Mum and Dad were. Mum was squeezing my hand so tight that it hurt when they told the immigration staff at the airport that we were asylum seekers. I had no idea what it meant, but Mum and Dad knew words like that. Kurds have such a long history of moving and relocating that they just know. A lot of people who turn up here don't know. They think someone will come along and drag you out of baggage reclaim and straight into a job. They're in for a nice little surprise.

I felt embarrassed. I wanted to be like everyone else, gently dragging my suitcase behind me, shopping for Moomin mugs and potholders with poppies on them and bars of chocolate, checking every now and then with the nonchalance of experience to see when it was time to go to the gate. I wanted to be on holiday. I tried to imagine what it must be like to be on holiday.

We were taken into some kind of office and told to wait. We waited so long that I almost wet myself. Eventually two blonde women in police uniforms and a dark-haired man in normal clothes came into the room. Mum and Dad tensed when they saw them. I'd been taught from a young age to be afraid of the police, but these women didn't look all that scary, though they were pretty big. They smiled and looked us in the eye. You could tell we were no longer at home.

The man spoke our language. I thought it was weird that we'd travelled for so long, we were so far away from home, it was so cold outside, and what do you know: there's one of our own waiting to meet us. Of course, I've known since the day I was born that those who have the chance always want to get away.

The man told the police what Dad was saying and told Dad what the police were saying. Dad told him the story of our infernal trek to safety across the mountains. He spoke in that same lilting voice that he sometimes used to tell me and Mehvan ancient stories when we still lived back home. Translated in Finnish, Dad's words sounded strange, as though the man wasn't telling our story any more but some other story altogether. And it was weird too that, though only a short time had passed since all this happened, I'd already started to forget about it. Suddenly the whole thing started to sound like a foreign fairy tale that the man was telling those police officers: once upon a time, then they all lived happily ever after; small smudged pictures on brittle sheets of paper.

Eventually I had to ask to go to the toilet. The worst of it was we first had to tell the interpreter, and he translated for the cops. It was like I had to repeat it a hundred times: I need to go to the bathroom, the toilet, I need a wee, a piss, I need to urinate, to micturate, to empty my bladder, powder my nose, and still they might have misunderstood and thought yuck, maybe she needs a poo – whatever, there's some pressure down below that we're never supposed to talk about. Mum gave me a murderous look.

One of the officers took me to the bathroom. She tried to give me an encouraging smile, and she was really pretty with thick blonde hair in a plait. I didn't dare smile back at her, though I was over the moon. There was a lot of pee; it came pouring into the bowl like Niagara Falls. I was embarrassed because the woman was waiting right outside the door and must have heard everything. I was so nervous I forgot to wash my hands on the way out, and I wondered what she was waving at, what she was trying to say, then I realised she was pointing at the sinks, the taps, the liquid-soap dispensers and the paper towels, and I went bright red and walked back to wash my hands. She must have thought we don't bother washing where we come from, probably thinks we eat off our shitty hands, stuff our faces with cassava from a shared bowl.

Then the officers made a phone call. The interpreter told us we would have to wait a while longer – huh, we'd only been waiting for like ten hours already – then we'd be taken to a centre where we'd be given our own room and abbou *everyone would have their own bed. And eventually they took us there in one of the border agency's dark-green minibuses. It felt amazing, sitting in the bus looking out at the strange new city flashing past the window. It was evening already and it had started to rain, and all the street lights were reflected strangely in the raindrops on the window.*

I pretended we were in a taxi on our way to a luxurious hotel somewhere.

Except that Mum was sitting next to me weeping and Dad was angry with her for it.

11

VIRVE SARLIN was a short girl with a very fair complexion and long, light-blonde hair. She gave off the sweet smell of incense and was dressed in a pair of baggy, red velvet trousers and a dark-green tunic. A collection of chains and wooden beads hung round her neck, and around her wrist jangled a bracelet of small bells. When she wasn't twiddling a strand of hair round her forefinger, she was chewing her nails or fiddling with her abundant jewellery. Dark shadows loomed beneath her grey, make-up-free eyes and the area round her nose was reddened. She looked exhausted.

'Hi, Virve. I'm Detective Constable Fekete Anna.'

Virve gave Anna an agitated glance.

'So you're Riikka's best friend, is that right?'

Virve's chin and nostrils began to tremble and she let out a gravelly squeal as she tried to hold back the tears.

'She's been my best friend since first grade.' Virve's voice was brittle, like a child's.

Anna handed the girl a tissue. She felt like a therapist, the kind of person to whose office her own headmaster and head of year had sent her throughout middle school. There had always been a box of tissues on hand there too. Anna had never needed one. She had never told the therapist anything and had never burst into tears. After her third visit, she had informed the headmaster that she wouldn't be attending any longer, that running was far more therapeutic. The headmaster said he was very concerned about her. She had laughed in his face.

'Let it out,' said Anna. 'This has all been a big shock.'

'It's terrible. I can't sleep properly – I've been wide awake from the moment Riikka's mum called and told me what had happened. I keep seeing her going out on that run, pulling on that hideous tracksuit, again and again. It's like a film stuck in my head, playing over and over.'

Anna's heart skipped a beat. Had Virve been there when Riikka had set off on her final run? She bided her time and pulled the contact information for a crisis helpline from her desk drawer. She handed Virve the leaflet. The girl scrutinised it for a moment, thanked her and stuffed it into her tasselled jute bag.

'You should make use of this service, especially since the state provides it free of charge. But I'm afraid I'll have to ask you all sorts of questions. Are you up to it?'

Virve blew her nose on the tissue Anna had given her and nodded.

'Right, let's get started. Were you with Riikka on the day she died?'

'Yes, yes. I mean, not all day, but almost. She lives … I mean, she used to live at my place.'

'Excuse me?'

'She lived at my place, has done since she split up with Jere.'

'So Riikka and Jere were no longer together?'

'That's right. Split up at Midsummer. Riikka moved in with me straight afterwards.'

'It seems Riikka's parents didn't know anything about this.'

'You bet they didn't. Riikka had decided to tell them once she'd moved to Jyväskylä. She was worried they'd try and force her to move back home, especially because they'd fretted so much about her moving in with Jere in the first place. She didn't want to tell them anything about it, at least not for the moment.'

'Why did they split up?'

'Riikka felt like she needed to move on. She needed a bit of freedom, you know? She was still pretty young when they started dating. Relationships like that rarely last for ever.'

'Did they argue a lot?'

'Towards the end, yes. In the spring, they argued pretty badly.'

'Do you know what they argued about?'

'Riikka thought Jere was too possessive. It annoyed her.'

'So it was Riikka who ended the relationship?'

'Yes.'

'How did Jere take it?'

'He wanted to carry on dating, I think. You don't think he had anything to do with this, do you?'

'Our job is to find out, not just to think things.'

'He couldn't have done something like that, I'll swear to it.'

'Was he violent? Towards Riikka or in general?'

'No. Not like his dad. If you ask me, I think Riikka was exaggerating things a bit. As if she was never at fault. It takes two to tango, you know.'

Anna nodded, as if to indicate that she couldn't agree more. Her mind was going over the books she'd read on interview technique: use gesture, expression and tone of voice to show that you are with the interviewee, that you're listening. Empathise with the interviewee's opinions when appropriate to gain trust.

'Was Jere's father violent?'

'He was a drunk. Round the village rumour has it he used to beat their mother when he'd had a few. I remember Liisa would often turn up for work with a black eye. She's a cleaner at the primary school we all went to.'

'Think carefully back to the day Riikka died. Last Sunday. Starting right from the morning, tell me as much as you can remember,' Anna asked.

Virve again blew her nose and took a sip of water, then began twirling another strand of hair round her finger. Her eyes wandered restlessly across the walls, and every now and then she would sneak a glance at Anna. It appeared that her eyes found it hard to focus on one thing, even for a second. This girl's in a pretty bad way, thought Anna.

Virve closed her eyes, took a few agitated breaths in and out.

'So, we woke up around ten. Riikka was sleeping in the living room. We had breakfast and just hung out. We couldn't be bothered going out because the weather was so awful. I was in my room for the most part, I rent a one-bedroom flat downtown: bedroom, living room and a small kitchen. Then some time in the afternoon she took a shower, started getting herself all dressed up and said she was going into town. She came back around five o'clock, then at around seven she suddenly had another shower and said she was going out for a jog all the way to Selkämaa, and from there to her parents' place for the night.'

'Didn't you wonder what she was up to?'

'What? Going out for a run?'

'That too. And what she was doing in the afternoon.'

'Not really. I wondered why on earth she wanted to go out in the pouring rain. I wouldn't have bothered. I prefer yoga. I suppose I didn't think anything of it because she's been like that all summer. Of course, I knew she had a new bloke on the go, and it pissed me off that she wouldn't tell me anything about him.'

'So Riikka had a new boyfriend?'

'She never said as much, but you could tell.'

'How?'

'She was so excited, secretive even. She'd disappear all of a sudden, dressed up to the nines. That's when she got into all that bloody running – she was trying to lose weight. Often she'd be out all night.'

'When did this start?'

'I can't remember exactly. Maybe around Midsummer or at the very beginning of July. Anyway, it was almost as soon as she'd finished with Jere. If you ask me, I think they started seeing each other before the break-up.'

'Did you ask her about it?'

'I never stopped! But she kept saying there was no one new. She didn't breathe a word of it to me. It was weird. I've always … I mean, we always used to share things like that.'

'Have you any idea why she wouldn't let on?'

Virve was silent for a moment, concentrated on sucking a strand of hair she'd rolled into a ball.

'I kept thinking, what if it's not a man?'

Anna thought she saw something flash through Virve's mind, but the girl continued her account almost immediately. It was as though she couldn't pin down the thought and it escaped.

'Though, I mean, I can't think why she'd be worried about something like that, especially with me. She knows I don't care about gender – it's love that counts. On the other hand, Riikka's about as straight as they come. We're actually quite different. I mean, we were. Talking in the past tense feels just awful.'

Virve began to cry. She pressed her face into her hands and sobbed gently. Anna handed her another tissue and waited for the girl to calm down before she continued.

'Let's go back to what happened before Riikka went out for her run. So, she came home from town at around five o'clock. Try to tell me as carefully as you can what she said, what she did and how she appeared.'

'Now that I think of it, she didn't eat anything. I'd just roasted some aubergines, they were really good, and when I asked if she wanted to join me she said she'd eaten in town.'

'Did you ask where she'd eaten?'

'No. I gave up talking to her because she just lay down on the sofa and said she was tired.'

Anna noted this down on her computer. In addition she had a notepad that she used to make unofficial observations. She took a pen and wrote: *Where did Riikka eat 21.8?*

'What happened next?'

'Then I ate by myself, washed up and went to my room to watch TV. You asked how she appeared. She seemed really down – just lay there on the sofa. Then I heard her going into the shower, and when I came out of my room she was pulling on that green tracksuit and … Fucking hell, I should have tried to stop her going out.'

Virve's final words were lost amid a volley of whimpers.

'What did you do after she'd left?'

Virve glanced up at Anna, a look of fright in her teary eyes.

'I stayed home. I was at home all evening.'

'Can anyone corroborate that?'

'Why should they? I don't suppose they can. I was by myself,' Virve was beginning to panic.

'There's no need to be nervous. It's a routine question. Did Riikka receive any telephone calls that day? Any text messages? Did she make any calls?'

'I didn't hear anything. I spent most of the day in my room. Damn it, I should have pressed her more, forced her to tell me what was going on. Maybe none of this would ever have happened,' Virve spluttered through her tears.

'Let's have a short break. I can bring you something if you'd like. Coffee?'

'Tea, thanks. Who could have done it? And why?'

'That's what we're trying to establish.'

'It wasn't Jere, that's for sure.'

'Why not?'

'He's not a killer.'

'Do you know where he is now?'

'No.' Virve seemed startled.

'Jere has disappeared into thin air.'

Virve said nothing and sat fidgeting with her bracelet.

Anna fetched a cup of tea for Virve and coffee for herself. They drank in silence. There was something odd about Virve. It wasn't so much her studied, new-age hippy look, which was actually a fairly everyday sight around the city. She was clearly nervous, but that too was perfectly normal. Almost everyone is nervous when they have to deal with the police, even if they've got nothing on their conscience. But Anna had a niggling feeling that the girl was hiding something. Then again, aren't we all, she thought.

Esko was right about one thing: in this line of work it was best to put your emotions aside. They could easily lead you astray. The 'intuition' of which we heard so much was generally nothing but luck or the skills gleaned from years of experience.

Anna drank the remains of the coffee, which had stood in the pot for goodness knows how long, and felt a wave of heartburn spread across her chest. That's all I need, she thought as she replaced her cup on the desk.

'Tell me about Jere,' Anna asked once they resumed. 'What kind of man is he?'

The cup of tea had clearly calmed Virve down and helped her focus. The irritating jangle of jewellery had ceased and her eyes were no longer darting here and there. She stared fixedly at her cup, which she held nestling in both hands and blew on to the steaming tea. She seemed to be thinking carefully about what to say. When she finally answered, it was as though she was speaking to the teacup.

'He was okay, I suppose. He's from the same village as me and Riikka, but he's two years older. Everybody fancied him, right through middle school and high school. Everyone except me. He was good-looking and sporty and that, but I always thought he was a bit full of himself. At least, he was when we were younger. He's not like that any longer. Nowadays he spends loads of time in the woods. And he's smart too – he got into the uni to do maths. I suppose I always thought the sporty look was a way of trying to hide his family background. I mean, if he'd stuck a safety pin through his cheek, he'd have looked more authentic, you know? But the girls all liked him, that's for sure. For Riikka he must have been like some pre-teen fantasy come true. She liked athletic guys, even though she's ... she was a bit chubby. She was always a bit superficial – appearance meant a lot to her. Still she was a hundred thousand times more down to earth than her parents. Christ, what yuppies. Have you met them?'

'Are you and Jere close?'

'What do you mean? No, we're not,' Virve responded almost angrily. 'I mean, of course we've seen quite a bit of each other through Riikka,' she continued, striving to catch a friendlier note. 'But nothing more than that.'

'Are you sure you don't know where Jere is now?'

'For God's sake, how would I know? I don't know him that well.'

'Are you on Facebook?'

'Yes.'

'What about Riikka and Jere?'

'Yes, they are. Jere never logs in though.'

'Can we use your account to see whether either of them has written or posted something that could help us?'

'Sure, but I don't think you'll find anything. Jere hasn't posted anything in ages and Riikka…' Virve's voice broke once again and she fell silent.

Anna brought up the Facebook login page and Virve signed in. In her profile picture she was standing bathed in glaring sunshine, in the shadow of an enormous palm tree.

'Nice picture. Where was it taken?'

'Mexico,' Virve answered. 'I was travelling around there last spring, just after our final exams.'

'Wow,' said Anna and began scrolling through old posts.

What's on your mind, Facebook asked. You tell me, thought Anna as she skimmed through the short sections of text that Virve's 286 friends used to keep each other up to date about what was on their minds. Anna clicked on Riikka's name from the list of friends, and her profile appeared on the screen. The diagonal angle and grainy quality of the photograph showed that the profile picture had been taken using a webcam or a mobile phone. The same round cheeks as in her graduation photograph, the same greyish blue eyes that should have seen many decades yet stared back at Anna from the screen. This is sick, thought Anna. Life continues here, in a virtual, online world, though Riikka's comments ended on the twenty-first of the month. After that the page had filled up with her friend's shocked R.I.P. messages. I'll have to remind Irmeli and Juhani to have these profiles removed, she thought.

Riikka had posted intermittently all summer. Perhaps once a week she had decided to share the goings-on in her life with her circle of friends in short status updates dealing with everything from ice cream to a swimming trip. Only once did she mention going for a run. That was in mid-July. Anna quickly scrolled through her list of friends, all 103 of them. Riikka clearly had better things to do than sit staring at the computer, thought Anna. She clicked open Jere's profile: 754 friends, but no signs of life on his wall. Virve hadn't been exaggerating; Jere didn't brag online about the details of his life and didn't take part in others' discussions. Anna wondered why he'd bothered to gather such a vast number of friends, and asked Virve.

'I don't know,' she answered. 'Some people are like that. Like, as if it's really cool the more friends you've got on Facebook.'

Anna logged out and thanked Virve. The search hadn't revealed anything of interest, but she'd still have to go through Riikka's private messages and emails.

'Okay, let's just go through everything once again, so we can get your statement in order. Are you up to it?'

Virve put down her teacup and sat upright.

'Sure, I'm up to it.'

They went through events again and there were no changes to Virve's statement. Virve read through the statement carefully, confirmed that it was correct and signed it, her wrist jangling as she wrote. Finally Anna reminded her that there might be more interviews in the near future. Virve's suspicions regarding Riikka's possible new relationship and her observations on the day of the murder were so significant that they would require further investigation. Virve glibly said she would be happy to help with their enquiries. I think that's your first blatant lie, thought Anna.

After Virve left, Anna should have gone straight to Esko Niemi's office to tell him about the important new information: Riikka and Jere's break-up and Riikka's clandestine new relationship. She stood outside the door to his office, raised her hand to knock but suddenly changed her mind. She couldn't do it, after all, didn't have the guts.

Anna could sense Esko's hostility oozing through the door. It would burn wounds into her knuckles if she so much as touched it. She didn't know how best to survive working with Esko, how to approach him. And if she couldn't survive Esko, how was she ever to survive working in this unit, at this station, in this city?

She lowered her hand, walked away and went to Sari's office instead. Rauno was there too. They discussed at length the information she had gathered from Virve and considered its significance for the course of the investigation. She'd have to find out the identity of Riikka's new boyfriend – or girlfriend. The search for Jere had been stepped up. There was still no sign of the boy or his rifle.

Towards the end of their chat, Anna mentioned her concerns about Esko, about how she'd been offended by the text message sent via Rauno, that she was worried such friction would slow the investigation or make it more difficult – or at worst prevent it from moving forwards altogether. Rauno repeated what Sari had said earlier. Esko will change, just give him time. You have to be patient.

Anna was incensed. She left the room, went outside, smoked a cigarette and decided to call it a day. On the way home she bought a frozen pizza at the local supermarket. The girl at the checkout greeted her brightly and bid her goodbye with a friendly *See you* as Anna left the store. This put Anna in a slightly better mood.

The beep of the microwave echoed round the kitchen. An empty kitchen is somehow depressing, thought Anna, so terribly lonely. Better buy something to put in those cupboards or some kind of wall hanging to dampen the echo. A pair of curtains might help too. She gobbled the steaming pizza and felt so drained that she didn't have the energy to go for her run. That evening she was supposed to do a longer run. She had planned to run for at least an hour and a half, all the way from Koivuharju via Savela to Koskela, and from there to head back north on the cycle path along the shoreline. She would go tomorrow. Instead of a run, she switched on the TV and cracked open one of the beers she'd picked up at the supermarket. Lazily she surfed from one channel to the next looking for something to watch, but there was nothing interesting on. She wondered how this was possible, given that there were dozens of channels in total. She switched off the box and went out to the balcony for a cigarette. Should I get rid of the TV altogether, she pondered as she blew smoke rings towards the windows of the building opposite. A faint breeze blew then apart. I could give it to Ákos. Anna couldn't understand why she'd bought the television in the first place. There never seemed to be anything interesting on. Mindless entertainment made her feel as ill as the pizza she'd just eaten. And she'd been planning on sticking to a healthier diet. She stubbed out her cigarette in the ceramic ashtray that was beginning to fill up. Enough is enough! No more fast food, no cigarettes, no beer and no mind-numbing television!

Anna switched on her computer and googled the term *honour violence*. Thousands of articles, cases all across Europe. Research. Information. Projects. Despite all this, the subject still remained vague; Anna couldn't make sense of it. There seemed to be no recorded cases in Finland. The entire concept was clothed in darkness. The law was chugging forwards like a steam engine, while reality sped ahead like a high-speed train.

Anna sat reading for so long that her eyelids started drooping shut of their own accord. She switched off the computer and crawled into bed, letting the fatigue get the better of her. Yet once she had switched off the lights, she found it impossible to get to sleep.

Sari gently rinsed between her legs. A small scratch had appeared on her labia and it stung each time the water touched it. Water and sperm trickled into the lavatory. There they go; thank God for the hormonal coil, she thought glowing with warmth and happiness. Her husband had returned from a week-long business trip just as the kids were going to bed. After he'd read them their bedtime story, he'd grabbed Sari and carried her into the bedroom and locked the door, and any remaining signs of jetlag were long gone. The fringe benefits of all those work trips. After all these years, their sex life was still exciting. This was the reward for weeks of loneliness, of running the family's everyday life single-handedly. Not a bad reward at all, Sari thought as she towelled herself off and climbed back into her husband's warm embrace. She could have carried on straight away, but knew it would be best to wait a while.

'How was your week?' he asked as he gently caressed Sari's back.

'A nightmare. Two big new cases came in at once: a murder and a case of honour violence. The honour case might be a false alarm, but the murder is going to be a big one. And Esko's being a complete wanker, for a change. I think he drinks every night. He's been pretty rude to our new detective who only started on Monday. Anna Fekete, she's called.'

'What's she like?'

'Really nice. Good at her job. A bit quiet.'

'They hardly need another chatterbox down at the station.'

'You shut up!' Sari quipped and threw a pillow at her husband. 'We went to the gym together yesterday. Her Finnish is perfect, and I mean really flawless; you'd never know she's not originally from Finland. There was no need to worry about her, after all. I've invited her round some evening.'

'That's nice. Where's she from?'

'Was it Serbia? I didn't want to pry. Somebody said she's Serbian. I'll ask her next week. We agreed to go to the gym once a week.'

'Sounds great.'

His hand was now stroking her stomach, his rough fingertips gently scratching her skin.

'How was the trip?' she asked. 'Mmm, that feels good.'

'China is a polluted, strange, chaotic place. Beijing is, at least. But we struck a good deal. Your skin's so soft.'

'Will you have to go back again?'

'Not until after Christmas. Thankfully.'

'What if the kids and I joined you next time? I could take some time off. I'd be fascinated to see the culture over there.'

'Not a bad idea. But I won't be able to spend much time with you while we're there.'

'That doesn't matter. Do you think it'll work?'

'We'll make it work.'

Sari's mobile beeped as a text message arrived, but she didn't care to read it.

'I love you. I've really missed you.'

'Me too,' Sari mumbled into her husband's mouth, and the kids didn't wake up once that night even though the couple made no attempt to hold themselves back.

12

A NERVOUS BIHAR CHELKIN was waiting outside Anna's office. Anna watched her through the venetian blinds in the staffroom. The girl was chewing gum and repeatedly glancing up at the large wall clock whose second hand glided evenly across the white surface of the clock face. Her head was covered in a tightly wrapped hijab and her body was cloaked in a long trench coat. What's she wearing beneath that, Anna wondered. Just a swimming costume? She'll be sweltering.

The warm sunshine had continued since Monday afternoon. Today it was almost 25°C.

The rest of the family had arrived at the station too, and the entire team had been briefed for their interviews. Rauno and Esko were to take care of Payedar and Mehvan Chelkin, while Sari would talk to Zera and Adan. In Vantaa, Bihar's aunt and uncle were currently being interviewed by the local authorities. To her surprise, Anna found a certain satisfaction in the idea of Esko and Mr Chelkin sitting across the table in Interview Room Two. She knew Esko wouldn't assume the role of the sympathetic policeman and conduct the interview like an informal chat. She was convinced that Payedar Chelkin would go home shitting bricks, mentally crushed. Or rather, he wouldn't be going home at all; he'd be taken straight into police custody in handcuffs to await sentencing. Anna recognised her emotion as that of revenge – and it felt damn good.

The Chelkin family had been granted asylum after waiting in a reception centre for over two years. The application process was long but not at all exceptional. That was what to expect if you had the audacity to try and come here: years of waiting.

The shoreline. The screeching seagulls in Munkkisaari.

Table tennis with Ákos.

The worry carved into their mother's face.

Memories began to flicker in the back of her mind, oozing out of their hiding places like a toxin.

Anna had to go outside for a cigarette. Just to keep the level of toxins in my body stable, she chuckled to herself.

Anna smoked her cigarette so quickly that she felt faint. That's that rule broken too, smoking at work, she thought, disgusted at herself. Let this be the first and last time, and yesterday doesn't count because I'd already clocked off. She crushed the butt against the rim of the stinking communal ashtray and dropped it down the brown flue. This is one habit I mustn't start, she decided.

We were given leave to remain relatively quickly, she thought as she walked back up the stairs back to the Violent Crimes Unit. After her cigarette, the climb felt tougher than normal.

At least they hadn't been forced into a cycle of agonised worry, wondering where they could escape to next. But back then there had been a state of emergency law; they were privileged. In any case, they were already – how could she put it? – European, Ákos with his Mohican and a cassette full of Finnish punk music. A boy on civil service at the reception centre had formed a band with him almost immediately. Back then Ákos's assimilation had seemed so certain. Their mother had hated his new friends.

A young Kurdish woman had been invited to the station to serve as an interpreter.

Bihar had informed them that she didn't need an interpreter. Anyone who came to Finland as a first-grader would know Finnish better than their own mother tongue, which was destined gradually to dwindle and lose its fluency. Anna knew all about that, but didn't want to think of it now. Bihar's parents, on the other hand, didn't know a word of Finnish. The interpreter was there primarily for them. Anna had checked a total of three references to ensure that the woman wasn't a relative of the Chelkin family. Getting to the truth would be hard enough, and an interpreter unable to remain objective could put a stop to the investigation altogether.

With a sense of great satisfaction, Anna had asked the interpreter to arrive a full hour before the interviews were due to commence. She remembered only too well Esko's comments about wasting public money, and she also knew that this woman's few hours of interpreting represented the only source of income for her entire family.

Anna popped a menthol pastille into her mouth, went into her office and asked Bihar to step inside.

'We'll be recording this interview,' Anna informed her as she switched on the video camera. 'Interviews with minors are always recorded. And I'd like to remind you that as the plaintiff in this case, you are required to tell the truth. Do you understand?'

Bihar nodded to the camera.

'You placed a call to the emergency services in the early hours of last Monday morning. Is that right?' Anna began.

'I suppose,' the girl replied, a note of defiance in her voice, and turned her eyes from the camera to Anna.

'Why did you place that call?'

The self-confident defiance of a moment ago was shaken. For a fleeting moment Anna thought she could see, behind the girl's dark eyes, an animal cowering in a corner. Bihar closed her eyes quickly, took a deep breath, then opened them again, her fear concealed once more.

'Um … well … I think I was dreaming. I was having a nightmare and I must have been half asleep when I called, didn't really know what I was doing. I woke up when the cops turned up at my aunt's place asking what was going on, what I'd gone and done.'

'What were you dreaming about?'

Bihar shuddered almost imperceptibly. She hadn't expected that question. Perhaps she'd assumed the businesslike Finnish police wouldn't start asking about her dreams; surely they'd stick with the facts, with the real world.

'I can't remember,' she answered instinctively. 'Couldn't remember when I woke up either.'

'And when did you wake up?'

'When the police arrived.'

'And that was?'

'I dunno, four or five in the morning. I couldn't get back to sleep after that – it was almost morning.'

'Was your dad in your dream?'

'Can't remember.'

'Did your dad threaten to kill you?'

'In my dream or for real?'

'It doesn't matter. Did he?'

'Not when I've been awake, he hasn't. I can't remember anything about that dream. He might have threatened me, if that's what I said on the phone.'

'Why were you in Vantaa?'

'Spending the weekend with relatives. Is that against the law?'

'What relatives?'

'My aunt and uncle.'

'How do you travel to school?'

'Huh? What's that got to do with anything?'

'Just answer the question, please.'

'I walk to the bus stop and get the bus.'

'Do you walk with anyone?'

'No, I go by myself.'

'What about Mehvan?'

'He's in a different school. I'm in high school, he's still in middle school.'

'Were you forced to walk with your brother in the past? When you were in middle school?'

Bihar's dark eyes looked away from the camera and stared up and down the walls, avoiding Anna's gaze.

'No,' she replied.

'My colleague says otherwise. She had a chat with your former teacher yesterday, one Riitta Kolehmainen. She says otherwise too. She told us your brother followed you like a hawk right through middle school, never let you out of his sight. She also said you were frequently absent.'

'I always had my parents' permission,' she snapped.

'Yes. This isn't about truanting.'

'Of course, me and Mehvan walked to school together when we were in the same school. Nothing weird about that.'

'Didn't it bother you?'

'Nope.'

'Didn't feel like it was restricting your freedom?'

'No.'

'You went to Turkey last year.'

'Yes.'

'Why?'

'Nothing special.'

'Were you there celebrating your engagement?'

'Of course not,' she scoffed with a forced laugh.

'Really? What do you do after school?'

'Watch TV, do my homework, visit friends. Normal stuff.'

'Who are your friends? Are they Kurds? Finns?'

'Finns at school – there aren't any other refugees in our class, or in the whole school. At home they're mostly Kurds, then there are a few Somali girls that live across the street.'

'Have you got a boyfriend?'

'No,' Bihar answered.

'Have you had one in the past?'

Bihar stared at the surface of the table; her long, black eyelashes fluttered, casting a shadow on her cheeks. She took a sip of water.

'No,' she said eventually and tried to give Anna a convincing look in the eyes.

You're lying, thought Anna.

'Bihar, I'm your friend,' Anna decided to change tactics. 'There's no need to be afraid. Just tell me the truth and I will make sure you get to safety. Right now. You won't have to go home or be frightened of anyone ever again.'

Bihar shuddered again, hesitant.

'I don't think it'll help,' she said eventually.

'What do you mean?'

''Cause there's nothing wrong.' She assumed the bored expression of earlier and blew a chewing-gum bubble that burst across her lips.

'You called 112. Your life was in danger. I've heard the tape. You don't sound remotely sleepy; you sound downright petrified. I can see you're afraid now, too. I can see you're lying to me because you're frightened. Wake up, girl! Do you want to live with that kind of fear for the rest of your life, let them control you like that?'

Bihar started shifting uncomfortably in her chair.

'What am I supposed to be afraid of?' she said.

'Your father, for one. Or your uncle, your brother, your mother. Maybe somebody else. They've threatened to kill you? And what have you done? Gone to a party with some schoolfriends and had a sip of cider? Fallen for a Finnish boy? Come on, Bihar. Think about it.'

Bihar bit her lip and stared at the door. Light and pink blotches appeared on her olive cheeks. She wiped the corner of her eyes on her jacket sleeve, holding back a deluge of tears.

That did the trick, thought Anna. *Telitalálat!*

The girl sat silent for a moment, occasionally glancing up at Anna and the camera.

'They won't kill me,' she said almost under her breath.

'Of course they won't, if you mope around at home long enough to get married to the nice man that your father has decided is suitable for you. Do you even know who he is yet? Are you engaged? Are you happy? Do you love that man?'

Bihar didn't say a word. A single tear escaped and trickled down her left cheek.

'Who are you protecting, Bihar? It's your life at stake here. You shouldn't have to worry what your mother or father think about things or if you're not the good little girl they want you to be. They don't seem to care much for your feelings, or do they? You know very well what motivates them – shame. And they lie to you and tell you it's about honour. *Namus*, Bihar, *namus*. The honour of the family and the clan. The honour of the men in the family.'

Anna could feel herself getting worked up. Her voice had toughened. The subject was getting too close for comfort. Everything got too close eventually. I'm too hot-blooded for this job. Better calm down, so as not to startle her. Anna got up and said she would fetch more water.

'Right,' said Anna as she returned with a jug of water. 'Tell me everything. Don't be frightened. You've lived in Finland long enough to know that we're on your side. You know that, don't you?'

'Yeah, yeah.'

'What have your relatives done to you?'

'Nothing.'

'Do they watch over you? Hit you, threaten you? Threaten to kill you?'

'No, no, no!' Bihar started to shout. 'Stop it, all right? They don't do anything. I'm fine, okay?'

'When are you going to turn eighteen?'

'In three months.'

'You realise that they can't tell you what to do once you're eighteen. You can decide for yourself where you want to live, who you hang around with and what you do. You're only answerable to the law, not your parents.'

Bihar sniffed and looked at Anna, her large eyes full of contempt. 'Course I know that. Why wouldn't I?'

'Do you think they'll let you move away?'

'Just stop it, all right? It was a false alarm. This whole thing is one big misunderstanding. I was dreaming. I wasn't myself. I used to walk and talk in my sleep all the time as a kid.'

'Are you absolutely sure you want to put this in your statement?' asked Anna.

'I'm sure. My parents would never do anything to hurt me.'

'Why don't I believe you?'

'Probably 'cause you're a detective. You've been trained to see something criminal everywhere you look.'

'Bihar, false imprisonment is a crime. Threatening to kill someone is a crime.'

'But none of that has happened to me.'

'Then why did you call 112?'

'I've already told you.'

'You're not telling the truth.'

'Fine, I'll admit it. It was revenge.'

'Tell me more.'

'I was angry 'cause they wouldn't let me go to the school party. I wanted to get back at them.'

'Is that the truth?'

'Yes.'

'Why didn't you tell me straight away?'

'I didn't dare. I thought it might be against the law, you know, making a prank 112 call.'

'You could be punished for it.'

'It was stupid. I wasn't thinking. I was just really angry. Sorry.'

'Why weren't you allowed to go to the party?'

'My parents said people would be drinking there. And they were right.'

'In three months' time you can go to parties. And drink, if you want to.'

'That's what my dad said.'

'I'm sure,' Anna muttered. 'For the last time – is someone threatening to hurt you?'

'No. Not at all. Believe me, okay?'

Anna sighed and terminated the interview. Bihar tucked a few stray strands of hair beneath her veil and tightened the fabric. She took a sip of water and glanced at the camera. Anna stood up and began organising her papers on the desk. Bihar remained seated and

dug around in her coat pocket as if looking for something. Suddenly
she stood up, staring at the camera all the while. She held out her
hand and shook Anna's. With her other hand still in her pocket, she
pulled back the hem of her coat to reveal a garish, printed T-shirt
that looked like it could have belonged to one of Ákos's bands.

'Thanks. See ya,' said Bihar, gazing into Anna's eyes like a puppy
begging for a treat. Then she dashed to the door and ran out.

13

'WE CAME UP WITH SWEET FA, couldn't get anything out of them. They just kept saying it was all a misunderstanding and they've never hurt anyone,' Rauno told Anna as he brought two pints of lager to their table at a bar in the park.

The atmosphere inside the police station had begun to feel tense and claustrophobic. The interviews had drawn on late into the evening; it was a Friday evening and summer was coming to an end. The temperature had risen above 20°C, and after hearing the weather forecast on the radio Anna had felt a sense of urgency.

'This is our last chance,' she had said to Rauno almost dramatically as he walked into the staffroom. The station had already quietened down for the evening; everyone was rushing home to enjoy a weekend of glorious late summer weather.

Anna noticed that, once again, Rauno was in no hurry to get home.

'What? Don't worry, I'll always give you another chance, my darling. No worries.'

Anna was amused.

'I mean it's our last chance to sit outside in our T-shirts, have a drink in the sunshine, get a tan, just hang out. Let's go.'

'You're in an apocalyptic mood. Are you going to string yourself up this winter or what? I'm certainly planning on sitting outside with a pint many times yet. In fact, I'm not planning on stopping,' said Rauno.

They had walked into town together.

Rauno drank half of his pint in a long, single gulp and wiped the froth on his lips with his shirtsleeve. Anna sipped her own pint more slowly, enjoying the sunshine and the cool touch of the beer on her tongue and palate.

'The girl eventually decided she'd done it out of revenge, because Daddy didn't let her go to a party.'

'That's what the parents said too.'

'They'd obviously agreed what to say in advance, and it's a pack of lies. First she'd said she was dreaming and that she made the call in her sleep.'

'And that's precisely what the parents said initially too. Apparently she'd always been a restless sleeper, regularly talked and walked in her sleep. Then they started on about how they have the right to prevent their children going to places where alcohol is available, that the law is on their side.'

'And in that, they're right.'

'You should have seen Esko's face. This was nectar from heaven for the racist old git; if only Finnish fathers would take a leaf out of his book, he said later on, we wouldn't have brats hanging around the station all day.'

'Is Esko really a racist?'

'Don't cling to one word. He's nothing in particular – he just wants people to think he's a grumpy old man.'

'He's horrible to me.'

'He's horrible to everyone – except Mr Payedar Chelkin, oddly.'

'Looks like the case is going to fold.'

'I think so. Let's talk about something else. I don't want to think about work. This sunshine is so warm,' said Rauno as he stood up to get another drink.

He hasn't asked whether I want one, thought Anna.

Of course he hasn't, because my glass is still almost full. Nobody ever asked in Finland. And it was a good thing.

'I bought one of those natural light lamps a while ago,' said Anna once Rauno had returned.

'Crazy. Why on earth?'

'The thought that it's soon going to be dark all day really gets me down.'

'Those lamps are useless – the whole idea of winter depression was invented by urbanites. Take a look: it's August, the sun is shining, there's a fly buzzing around over there. Now is now, there's no point wasting your time worrying about things that haven't happened yet.'

'I suppose not, but I bought one all the same. Are you from the countryside then?'

'Yes, from down the road in Mäntykoski.'

'Family?' Anna asked, though she knew the answer. Sari had already told her at the gym.

'Yeah. Wife and two kids.'

'How old are your children?'

'Four and five, both girls.'

'Sweet,' said Anna with a smile.

'Suppose so.'

Rauno had almost finished his second pint; Anna had barely touched her first and it was getting warm. She watched the people walking through the park in summer clothes; a pigeon wobbling along, picking at crumbs; a dog taking its owner for a walk. The approaching winter was biding its time somewhere north of the Arctic Circle. Her eyes were drawn to a man making his way through the park in gentle strokes, the gravel scraping beneath the tyres of his wheelchair. The man's legs were strapped to the chair with a wide belt. In his trendy jeans his legs looked limp and shrunken; without the straps his feet would have dragged along the ground and possibly toppled the wheelchair. The man rolled himself to the bar, ordered a pint, dexterously swung the chair round in front of the nearest empty table and sipped his beer. Handsome, thought Anna. Look at those muscular, tanned arms, his amazing shoulders.

'So basically my sleeping pattern went out the window because of that bloody lamp. Anna! Are you there? Wakey, wakey!'

'What…? Ah, yes. Well, I thought I'd give it a try. The shop assistant said I should use it for about half an hour in the mornings from the beginning of September until New Year. Apparently you shouldn't use it in the evenings, otherwise you won't be able to get to sleep.'

Anna glanced over at the man in the wheelchair and saw that he was looking back. She smiled; her skin started to tingle.

'You can try, but I don't believe in these lamps,' Rauno continued. 'I reckon this winter depression is simply down to the fact that we're supposed to work just as hard all year round. We should be able to take it easier during the winter months, to wind down and sleep more, do less work.'

'You might be right. But when do you think we'll ever get a chance to live according to the rhythm of nature?'

'Never. Well, maybe if you moved up north and took up a new career as a gold prospector or something.'

'Is that what you're planning?' Anna's interest plucked up.

'Where could I go? Wife and kids here,' said Rauno and downed the remains of his pint. 'Except home, that is,' he continued, a note of disappointment in his voice. 'I promised to put the girls to bed tonight. My wife Nina is going out with her friends. I'd better go.'

'Oh. Shame. Though it's nice that your wife gets the chance to let her hair down. You've had a long week too.'

'Hmph. I suppose. Are you staying?' Rauno glanced at the man in the wheelchair. *Bassza meg* – he's noticed. Anna nodded towards her half-full pint glass.

'I'm so slow.'

'Well, I'm off. See you on Monday.'

'See you.'

Anna slowly sipped her pint and peered from behind her fringe at the man in the wheelchair. He had noticed her gaze and was returning her glances, staring almost. Without a second thought for the situation or the potential repercussions, Anna stood up and walked over to the man's table. Sitting around the same table we are equal, she thought as she sat down opposite the man.

'Hi. I'm Anna,' she said and held out her hand.

The man gripped Anna's hand firmly. 'Hello, Anna. You look stunning. I noticed you the moment I arrived. I'm Petri. Petri Ketola.'

I noticed you too, she thought.

'Fekete Anna,' she said, her hand lingering in the man's powerful grip.

'Ah, you're Hungarian? Cool. She doesn't look at all Finnish, I said to myself. I've always wanted to visit Budapest.'

'Yes, I'm Hungarian. But I don't like Budapest: too big, too dirty. And the people are so uptight.'

'Were you born here? Your Finnish is so good. You haven't even got an accent.'

'Thanks. I wasn't born here. But I'm not from Hungary either – well, at least not from modern Hungary. I'm from the Hungarian minority in the former Yugoslavia. My home town is in the north of Serbia, very near the Hungarian border.'

'Fascinating. I didn't know there were Hungarians there.'

'Well, nobody really knows,' she laughed. 'It's not all that interesting.'

'Yes, it is. It's really interesting. When did you come to Finland?'

'1992. I was almost ten.'

'Was it because of the war, the break-up of Yugoslavia?'

'Yes.'

'How bad was it? Is it okay to talk about this, or…?'

'There was no fighting where we lived – or in the Serb area, for that matter. In the north things were relatively calm, in a way. But we Hungarians were sent to the front. Those that happened to live in Serb territory were sent out with the other Serb troops, first to Croatia, then Bosnia and finally Kosovo, and those that lived on the Croatian side were conscripted to the Croatian army. So, at least in theory, it was entirely possible that two Hungarians could have been fighting against one another. And I have an older brother. Well, two actually. Both of them were a prime age for the army back then.'

'I see,' said Petri.

'It was a crazy time. The Hungarians couldn't care less about all that Serbian nationalist chest-beating. And Belgrade isn't our capital city, and the names Kosovo Polje or Republika Srpska don't bring me out in patriotic goosebumps. But what can you do if you just happen to live there? If someone simply drew the border in the wrong place?'

'I remember watching it on the news. Srebrenica and Kosovo. Still, I was only a kid back then. There were a couple of documentaries on TV about it. It must be twenty years since the war broke out.'

'Yes. I didn't really understand it much back then. But I remember what it felt like, like the world was coming to an end. It seemed as though nobody had any future.'

Petri gave Anna an inquisitive glance.

'You have amazing eyes,' he said, a twinkle in his own eyes.

The man's flirting and flattery felt better than the glow of the sunshine; Anna wasn't the least fazed by it. She sipped her beer, which by now was like lukewarm tea. She felt relaxed and self-assured.

'Can I pry a little?' she asked.

'You may.'

'What put you in that chair?'

'My dad was drunk and crashed the car when I was five. I was in the car.'

'Shit. I'm sorry.'

'It's okay. I'm glad you asked. Normally people are too embarrassed.'

'Maybe I don't have normal inhibitions.'

'I noticed that already, saw it in those dark eyes,' said Petri, staring at her intensely. 'What are your plans for the evening?'

Anna smiled. 'Well, first I thought I'd have another beer and chat with you for a while, then I'll go home.'

Anna was quiet for a moment and looked teasingly at Petri. He could barely hide his disappointment.

'And then I thought I could get to know an interesting man in my apartment a bit more closely. Quite a lot more closely, actually. If that man wanted to join me, that is.'

Petri swallowed and nodded, then laughed out loud. Anna fetched them another couple of pints.

After finishing them off, they headed off along the gravel path, away from the park and towards the taxi rank at the end of Aleksanterinkatu, Petri's head at the level of Anna's chest.

'You smell of beer again. For God's sake, can't you come home without having a drink first?'

Nina Forsman was standing in the hallway blow-drying her chestnut hair. She was a short, slender woman. In the past, Rauno had always felt a desire to protect her. Recently he had been tempted to hit her on more than one occasion, to slap that chiselled face, that small nose and full lips, to shut the infernal mouth that spouted words that crushed him and made him feel worthless, words that he was unable to answer in the same way, in any way.

'I went for one drink with the new detective. We need to show we're there for her. It must be terrible turning up for a new job and getting Esko as your partner. Sari and I agreed to be supportive friends to her.'

Why the fuck do I have to explain myself, Rauno cursed under his breath. Why can't I say to her face that I'll drink as much as I damn well please?

'I doubt that's much of an imposition. She's a good-looking young woman, apparently, an exotic foreigner. Sari told me. I'm sure you're drooling after her already. Where did you go? Why did it take you so long? Have you shagged her yet?'

'Come on.'

'You never go anywhere with me.'

'You always want to go out with the girls and let your hair down. I'm not one of the girls.'

'Hah, you could've fooled me these last few weeks.'

'Give it a bloody rest,' Rauno raised his voice.

Two small children pattered into the hallway shouting for Daddy. Rauno picked the girls up, one after the other, trying to disguise and swallow his anger. He pressed his nose into their clean heads of fine hair, the grip of their chubby arms all but strangling him. At least someone in this household is happy. Perhaps I'm a happy man after all, he thought. Somebody loves me.

Nina dabbed foundation on her face, her brow almost touching the mirror, pencilled on some eyeliner, puffed her eyelashes with black mascara and powdered her cheeks with blusher. She's pretty, no doubt about it, thought Rauno as he felt a twitch at his left trouser leg.

'What are you staring at? Go and play with the girls; they've been waiting for you all day. I'm calling the taxi now. I'll try not to be late, but you know Jenni and Mervi. A night out with them always drags on. See you. There's liver casserole in the fridge.'

Rauno stood there sniffing the air that Nina had left behind her, and he didn't feel the slightest sense of longing or sorrow. He felt indifferent, almost relieved that she was gone. He went to the living-room window, carefully pulled back the curtains and secretly watched her as she nattered into her mobile, relaxed and carefree. A taxi pulled up in front of the house and his wife disappeared inside it. The taxi drove away leaving the driveway empty once again. Does Nina feel more at ease when I'm not here, Rauno wondered. He put the casserole in the microwave and went into the children's bedroom to build Lego towers.

14

BY MONDAY MORNING clouds had drifted back across the city, just as the weather forecast had promised. They seemed to be waving a grey calendar in people's faces, one that foreshadowed heavy rain, forcing people to look around and to accept that August was over. Autumn was now on its way.

Anna had spent Sunday on the balcony with Ákos. She had been nervous at the prospect of her brother's visit. She had anxiously paced back and forth through her apartment, finally trying to unpack the remaining boxes of clutter and put everything in its place. She had thought carefully about where to display the old family photograph: on the bookshelf or on the bedside table. What would Ákos say when he saw it? Did he have a single photograph of any of them, she wondered. Eventually she had slipped the photograph back into its box, and was just wiping her sweaty palms on her trouser legs when the doorbell rang.

But Ákos had been in a good mood; straight away he'd seemed close and familiar again. The gig the previous night had been amazing, the pub filled with youngsters. It had made him believe in the future once again. Punk hadn't died, after all, and the sun was shining – it warmed the shaded balcony to almost tropical temperatures. They had rolled *csevap* sausages from mincemeat, cooked them under the grill in the oven and eaten out on the balcony. The heat had made the atmosphere languid; they felt relaxed and lazy. At one point they had felt like going for a swim but couldn't find the energy. Their bellies were full of raw onion, *csevap* and cold beer. And Ákos hadn't overdone it on the drink. Perhaps her brother had finally settled down a bit, finally grown up.

They had reminisced about the baking summer days of their

childhood, days when the entire family, the entire town had escaped
the sun and sat in the shade of the poplars and weeping willows
along the banks of the River Tisza. Their tall boughs provided more
shade than the whitewashed clay walls of the houses and the tightly
fastened shutters across the windows. They had cooked fish soup and
gulyás on an open fire; Anna could still recall the smell of smoke and
paprika. They hadn't gone home until well into the evening, as the
crickets and frogs began their nocturnal concert once darkness had
fallen. Even at night, the humidity never let up.

The Tisza was a magnificent river in shades of grey-green and
brown, sometimes almost black, flowing all the way from Romania
through Hungary and northern Serbia, past Anna and Ákos's former
hometown and merging with the Danube just outside Belgrade.
There was a mystical beauty about that river. Its silence and calmness
were treacherous, as the current was strong. The river was the first
thing that came to mind whenever they thought of home. Uncover-
ing this shared memory had felt somehow significant. The Tisza, a
river flowing thousands of kilometres away, brought them together
here, far away in the north where they had ended up as the result of a
string of coincidences. It felt as though the river were flowing within
them, in their veins. It was in the Tisza that they had learned to
swim, and on those riverbanks that they had spent their childhood
and Ákos his teenage years. The river had been important to their
father, and their mother still swam there all summer long.

They had planned a trip home together as soon as Anna could
get some time off work. She assumed she would have to pay for the
flights, but it didn't matter because Ákos had only visited once since
they had left all those years ago. Anna was prepared to pay whatever
it took to get her brother back home to see their mother.

Ákos hadn't agreed to a Skype call. Maybe next week, he'd said,
and Anna hadn't wanted to push the matter. Not now, not when
they'd just had such a nice time together and even the sunshine
seemed to warm their frosty relationship.

*

It was spitting with rain. The temperature had dropped and Anna shivered as she cycled into the city centre. She had decided to cycle after missing her planned runs over the weekend. It was a mistake. Her hair was damp and her ears felt chilled, and she was afraid she might catch a cold. The people walking past her bore an expression of disappointment. Where had the sun disappeared to? Where on earth had those nasty clouds come from to taunt us, and why?

Her working week started with a long meeting in the auditorium on the fourth floor. The entire Violent Crimes Unit had assembled along with representatives from the analysis team. Domestic violence, accidents in the workplace, assaults, and the cases of Riikka and Bihar were all on the agenda. They certainly had plenty to be getting on with, Virkkunen commented from beside the projector. Its bright light was reflected in his glasses so powerfully that Anna couldn't make out his eyes at all.

'We'll have our work cut out until the human race dies of extinction,' Anna whispered to Sari, who was sitting next to her on the sofa. Sari nodded and yawned absent-mindedly, then gave Anna a wry smile and whispered back that her husband had been home for the weekend.

Anna glanced around the room. There was no sign of Esko.

The analysis team gave a rundown on the most important events of the previous week, and when it was time to discuss the case of the murdered jogger the door at the back of the auditorium opened and Esko crept inside. His eyes seemed even more swollen than before – if such a thing was possible; his face was ashen and pink, and his hair tangled. Virkkunen looked furious.

'I think he's in for a talking-to,' Sari whispered to Anna. 'He's clearly hung-over.'

Virkkunen gave a short summation of the facts surrounding the discovery of Riikka Rautio and the cause of death. He then placed a topographical map of the area around Selkämaa on the projector so that those present could get a grasp of events as a whole. Then he asked Senior Detective Kirsti Sarkkinen from Forensics to say a few words. Kirsti stood up from her seat in the front row, twiddling a memory stick in her fingers.

'We didn't really find anything at the scene,' she began. Anna could sense a sigh of disappointment sweep across the room, or perhaps she only imagined it. Perhaps it was only in her head.

Kirsti inserted the memory stick into the laptop on the table, pushed the projector's mirror to one side and clicked on a photograph from the scene of the murder. Once again the blood and spatter hit Anna's eyes and she began to feel sick. She turned away and looked towards the front left-hand corner of the room. Thankfully Kirsti quickly changed the image on the screen. Now the screen showed a close-up of the surface of the track; only in the corner of the picture could you make out a bit of blood.

'It's impossible to discern any individual shoeprints in all that sawdust; the material is too soft and pliable,' she explained. 'Besides, even if we had been able to identify something, it would be impossible to enter it into evidence as the track has obviously been used by plenty of people other than the killer. Still, it was interesting to examine. In a thousand years scientists will be able to use our material as an archaeological investigation into the development of Gore-tex. Decade upon decade of rubber and exercise fabric is layered among the sawdust. It's fascinating.'

Sari gave Anna a look of amusement. 'We've always said that Kirsti is a good archaeologist going to waste,' she whispered.

'Good job for the police,' Anna whispered back.

'In the car park, however, it would have been possible to distinguish tyre tracks and even shoeprints had the heavy rain that night not washed everything away. So that's that. And we can't be sure that the killer arrived by car, though the old man living in the vicinity said he heard the sound of a car at around the time of the shooting.'

'There are three primary ways of reaching the location,' Rauno interjected. 'Along the track through the woods leading from the new detached houses or through the scrubland from the shoreline.

But, of course, the easiest way to get there would be along the path coming from the main road. I think we can assume the killer arrived at the site by car. The running track is so out of the way that someone walking or cycling there would likely attract more attention.'

'Does the missing boyfriend own a car?' asked Sari.

'Yes,' Anna replied. 'Former boyfriend, actually. He has a blue Renault Laguna from 2004. It's currently parked in the yard behind his apartment. The keys weren't inside the flat.'

The image on the screen changed. Riikka Rautio lay on the sawdust, her head blown off. Anna gulped back a wave of nausea and forced herself to look at it. *A fene egye meg*, I'd better get used to this if I'm going to survive this job, she berated herself.

'The autopsy report has been available for everyone to read since last week, so I won't go into that any further. In the victim's sock we found a very long, blonde hair, which cannot belong to the victim because her hair was dark.'

'It must belong to Virve Sarlin,' said Anna. 'Riikka's best friend. Virve told us that Riikka had been living with her all summer.'

'That would explain things.'

'Virve seemed agitated during our interview – and she doesn't have an alibi for the evening of the murder.'

'Let's keep that it mind,' said Virkkunen.

'That brings us to the ballistics report,' Kirsti continued.

The officers in the auditorium appeared to sit up straighter, as though this was the bit they had been waiting for. If they could isolate and identify the murder weapon, at least they'd have something concrete to go on, something to find, to use as evidence when the time came.

'At the scene we found a total of 181 3.5-milligram steel pellets with a combined weight of 32 grams. In plain English that means we're looking for a .12-calibre smoothbore rifle with room in the barrel for at least 70 rounds. This is one of the most common rifles among game hunters in Finland. There are hundreds of thousands of them in circulation. In theory, the round that killed Riikka Rautio could have been fired by any one of them. The only way to identify the individual firearm would be if there was some damage to the barrel that might leave striations on the pellets. In this case, needless to say, there were no marks. The firearm could also be a 12/76 – a magnum, that is – or a 12/89, a super magnum, making the range of possible murder weapons even larger. Judging by the plug found among the brain matter, we can identify the round as one produced by a company called Armusa – a widely used manufacturer. So there's nothing to get your hopes up. With such paltry information, we won't get anyone – I mean, anyone – up on charges for this.'

'Jere owns a 12/70 Remington,' Esko piped up. His voice rattled with the sound of the booze and cigarettes he'd got through that weekend. 'And it's missing from his gun cabinet, just as clearly as the boy is missing from the flat.'

'Well, obviously that's quite a coincidence,' Kirsti admitted as she removed the memory stick from the computer. 'But with only general ballistics evidence to go on, you won't be able to prove Jere's guilt. You'll need something more concrete.'

'Isn't it proof enough that the boy and his rifle mysteriously disappear the very day his girlfriend is shot dead with an identical rifle? If you ask me, it is. I'm sure the prosecutor would agree, too,' Esko puffed. 'Now we just have to find the bastard.'

'Do we even think Jere is still alive?' Sari asked the group. 'Perhaps he's taken another life, and now he's lying somewhere with a round of pellets in his head.'

'I reckon he's more likely cowering somewhere licking his mental wounds. He regrets what he's done and now he's shit scared,' said Esko. 'Still, dead or alive, we'll soon find out. If he's dead, someone will find him before long. If he's alive, he'll turn himself in sooner or later; his nerves will cave in. Mark my words.'

Kirsti Sarkkinen picked up her folder and stepped back from the lectern.

'Do we have any information about the girl's movements on the day of the murder?' asked Virkkunen.

'Apparently she ate somewhere in town,' said Anna. 'And she showered twice that day; the second time just before going out on that final jog. It seems quite odd.'

'She had some other kind of sport in mind,' Esko scoffed.

'Her debit card wasn't used at all that day, so if she ate in town she must have paid in cash.'

'Either that or someone treated her to lunch.'

'According to her friend Virve, she'd spent quite a time getting herself ready before going out. Perhaps she had a date with her new boyfriend.'

'And another date immediately afterwards? So why go home in between? Didn't Virve say that Riikka had come home and slumped on the sofa without saying a thing? As if she was upset or something.'

'Something happened.'

'Maybe she had two blokes on the go.'

'Virve said she suspected it might have been a woman,' Anna commented. 'Though I don't think the gender of her partner is relevant here – I mean, as regards the murder. Virve simply suggested that that might have been the reason why Riikka wanted to keep the new relationship quiet.'

'We haven't found anything in Riikka's Facebook messages or email account,' said Virkkunen. 'And the number that called her is unlisted, so we can't trace it.'

'The pendant in Riikka's pocket seems strange to me,' said Anna. 'First of all because nobody would keep a necklace in their tracksuit pocket, and just strange in general. Should we look into this?'

'What's strange about that?' asked Esko. 'She was out running, the necklace was slapping against her neck and irritating her, she took it off and put it in her pocket. Strange, huh? I think we should focus our attention on locating Jere.'

'Right,' Virkkunen confirmed. 'The most obvious solution is often the right one.'

'What about the mobile phone?' asked Rauno. 'Riikka received a call from an unlisted number.'

'We examined the necklace, and there were no traces of sweat or anything else on it. It must have been brand new. But what's most interesting is that there was nothing on the phone, no grease stains, no fingerprints – not even Riikka's own,' said Kirsti. 'And that's almost impossible unless the device had been deliberately wiped clean.'

'The killer must have deleted the messages and wiped the phone,' said Sari.

'Pretty cold-blooded, if you ask me. First blow the girl's head off at close range with a shotgun, then stick around to wipe down the phone.'

'And what did I say about Jere?' Esko smirked. 'As soon as we find him, this will all be cleared up.'

'I agree,' said Virkkunen. 'In the light of what we've just heard, finding and apprehending Jere Koski is now our priority as far as this investigation is concerned. Let's break for five minutes, then move on to the Chelkin case.'

'There's nothing we can do about that Chelkin family,' Esko began. His break had taken ten minutes. Anna had expected some kind of reaction from Virkkunen, chastising him or at least warning him – after all, it was the second time Esko had been late for the same meeting. But nobody said a thing; nobody even seemed to notice he'd turned up late. Can that man get away with absolutely anything, she wondered.

'The girl retracted her statement,' he continued. 'The 112 call was just a bit of theatre, a way of getting back at Daddy for not letting his underage daughter drink herself silly at the weekend. The relatives in Vantaa confirmed this. The father seemed surprisingly smart for a wog…' Esko swallowed the end of his sentence as Virkkunen's gaze fixed on him from behind his spectacles. 'I mean, many a Finnish father could take a leaf out of his book; it would make our lives much easier.'

'So we might as well discontinue the investigation,' Virkkunen stated.

'Well, there's making a prank call to the emergency services, and at least, in theory, there's making a false accusation and resisting an officer. So the girl would face all the charges herself, if we decided not to play so nicely. But I don't think there's any point making a fuss about this. She'll have learned her lesson, if she's got any sense,' said Rauno.

'Quite. After all, she's still a minor with an otherwise clean slate. You'd think having the whole family dragged in for questioning would be a sufficient lesson about the consequences of making false accusations,' said Virkkunen.

Anna was suspicious. Something was bothering her.

'Sari, you talked to the former teachers,' she said.

'That's right. Two, in fact: Riitta Kolehmainen and Heli Virtanen, both teachers at Rajapuro elementary school. Both said the same thing. There were times when Bihar had a suspicious number of absences from school. Not often, and they were always accounted for. The little brother had always walked his sister to school. Bihar is good at school, so there was no need for Social Services to get involved. Riitta Kolehmainen mentioned that sometimes she had the feeling that something wasn't quite right in that family, but that it had only been a passing hunch. She couldn't explain what had caused it, couldn't remember. Bihar's high-school teacher mentioned that last year the girl spent several weeks in Turkey.'

'These absences could be linked to honour violence,' said Anna.

'Either that or the flu,' Esko muttered.

'It's also common for the males in the family – even younger brothers – to become their sisters' keepers,' she continued.

'It could be the other way round. Maybe Bihar was told to look after her little brother on the way to school. Rajapuro is a rough neighbourhood; nobody in their right mind would want to walk around there by themselves.'

'I think Bihar is lying,' said Anna.

'We must assume that plaintiffs are telling the truth in interviews and we have to act accordingly,' said Virkkunen.

'I know. Still.'

'If there's no evidence, and the girl herself has taken back the accusations – and, what's more, if she can give a perfectly logical explanation for her actions – there's nothing for us to do but drop the matter,' he continued.

'Did anyone ask why Bihar spent Sunday night in Vantaa, though she was supposed to be at school on Monday morning?' Anna asked agitatedly.

'Our colleagues in Vantaa asked, and her uncle said that Bihar was supposed to leave on Sunday evening but that she missed the train,' Sari explained.

'Yes, I remember that, too,' said Esko. 'Bihar's father said the same as the uncle: she missed the train. She left in the morning. Maybe you should have asked, too, then we'd have three confirmations. Does one of us need to explain to you how these things work?'

'You're my partner, so why don't you explain it to me?' Anna quipped. 'They had agreed what to say in advance. We should have taken them into custody straight away instead of waiting around.'

'Let's not forget, the girl retracted her story on the night of the call. What's more, the officers who visited the scene didn't see anything to indicate that any violence had taken place,' Virkkunen interrupted. 'The police can't do anything without evidence. This matter is closed, Anna. I'm sorry.'

'Let's not sweep this under the carpet, at least not yet?' she pleaded. 'Let's keep an eye on them, whenever we have a minute, maybe on alternate days or just a few times a week, especially when Bihar is on her way to and from school, so that they realise we're still watching them. Or in the evenings we could park outside their house for a moment. Just to be sure, to make certain nothing more serious happens.'

'Is there any point?' asked Rauno. 'For a start, when do we ever have a spare minute?'

'Damn right, there's no point,' Esko raised his voice, drowning out Rauno. 'I'm not going to start spying on people unless I'm legally bound to do so.'

'I don't believe she's safe there,' Anna gave it one more try.

'I'm sorry, Anna. I've got to say, I agree with them,' said Sari, a little embarrassed. 'We'd be overstepping the mark. Though I have to say, I agree there's something going on in that family.'

'Surely it can't be illegal to take pre-emptive action to stop a crime from taking place.' Anna felt frustrated and was almost shouting. 'It's our fundamental responsibility.'

'We have no reason to suspect that a crime is about to take place. With that logic, we'd have to look out for almost everyone, just to make sure people stayed on the straight and narrow. It's simply not possible,' said Virkkunen.

'Bihar is in danger,' Anna repeated quietly.

'I'm sorry, Anna, but that's the end of the matter,' said Virkkunen and switched off the projector. Now his eyes expressed nothing but determination. 'We should think ourselves lucky. Now we can concentrate our efforts on the murdered jogger. Right, everybody, let's get to work.'

15

IN A RAGE ANNA RAN straight down to the smoking area in the courtyard and dug a packet of cigarettes out of her handbag. Why the hell do I carry these things around with me if I shouldn't smoke them during the day, she wondered as she lit a cigarette and felt a rush of satisfaction as she drew the smoke into her lungs. Nicotine flowed into her blood, almost dizzying her, and made her mouth tingle.

'I knew you were a smoker.'

Anna gave a start and almost dropped her cigarette.

'You must really have a fetish for creeping up behind people and startling them,' she snapped at Esko who had once again taken her by surprise.

'Have you got any fetishes?' he asked, his voice slimy and lascivious.

Harassment too, she thought. *Útálotos.* She didn't respond, but took another drag on her cigarette. Esko lit one of his own. For a moment they stood smoking in silence.

'Bihar Chelkin is lying. I'm convinced this is a matter of honour violence,' Anna said eventually. She felt compelled to repeat herself one last time, especially to that arsehole.

'Finnish law doesn't recognise such a crime,' he replied impassively.

'Still.'

'Just drop it, yeah? I know you feel great sympathy towards these girls, being one of your own and all that.'

'I can tell when someone is lying,' she said, trying to remain calm.

'Bloody Muslims are always lying. It's a twisted religion – terrorists and liars the whole lot of them. What faith are you?'

'For Christ's sake, Esko. What's the matter with you? What has any of them, any of us, ever done to you?' Now Anna raised her voice.

'You're telling me you don't know?' he said, inhaling deeply on his cigarette and staring at Anna with a maniacal gleam in his eyes. 'You darkies all expect to come here and live the life of Riley on the dole – that's taxpayers' money, you know!' he shouted and flicked his burning cigarette to the ground, lit another one immediately and glared at her, as if challenging her to argue back. 'Either that or you turn up and take our jobs. Just like you.'

'Whose job have I taken?'

'I doubt you were the only applicant.'

For a moment Anna said nothing. She knew it would be pointless explaining how she'd subsisted from one temporary job to the next ever since graduating, how she'd applied for countless permanent positions – all for nothing. She also knew from experience that it was futile talking to Esko and people like him about despair, fear, war, torture, oppression, discrimination, poverty and hunger, about how the world was full of people whose lives were a daily struggle against all of those terrible things.

When she was younger she had often let herself rise to this, aggressively gone on the defensive, tried to beat facts and common sense into the heads of her opponents, shouting, raging and upsetting herself, but it was always pointless. The Eskos of this world were every bit as fanatical as extreme religious zealots, as obstinate and stubborn as donkeys. There was nothing you could say to these people.

Nothing except: 'Sorry,' she said and walked away.

She sprinted up the stairs to her office, taking out her frustration in the stairwell, to punish herself for the cigarette to which she had just succumbed. Once she reached the third floor, her mobile beeped in her handbag. She shut herself in her office, sat down at her desk, out of breath, and took out her phone. One new message. She opened the message, read it and sat in shock, a sense of anxiety clenching her stomach. The message had come from a number she didn't recognise.

Hey there, cutie. You're quite a catch. I wanna taste.

She sent the number to directory enquiries. The blunt response arrived a second later: an unlisted number or sent from a prepaid phone. Who could have sent it, she wondered. Petri? I didn't given him my number, even though he asked for it. Had he managed to fiddle with my phone at some point in the evening? Or had he found it on one of my cards? There was a pile of cards with the name Sgt Anna Fekete in a drawer in the hallway bureau.

If this was from him, it was a nasty trick.

And what if it wasn't from him?

Anna felt a shiver run through her body. She rummaged in her wallet for the number Petri had given her as he'd left her apartment, shyly, almost embarrassed, and asked her to give him a call. Anna looked at the number. The text message had been sent from a different number. Call him and ask, she commanded herself. That way you'll find out. But something within her resisted. She didn't want to contact him and give the impression that she was somehow interested. He was a kind, wonderful man, a very pleasant acquaintance in every way, but for Anna one night was enough. She didn't want to get his hopes up, because there was no hope of anything further. So why am I holding on to this piece of paper, she wondered as she replaced the phone number in her wallet and deleted the unpleasant message.

There was a new message in her email too. This one was from Linnea Markkula. Judging by the degree of digestion, the meal in Riikka's stomach had been ingested at around 4 p.m. on the afternoon of the murder. Salmon, rice and pine nuts. Apparently Linnea had got lucky on Saturday night, for the first time in ages.

Anna chuckled. So did I, more's the pity.

She decided to go into town for lunch. That would give her a chance to examine the lunch menus of the downtown restaurants and to show Riikka's photographs to some of the waiters. If only they could establish where Riikka had eaten and who she was with. She also wanted to visit the florist; she wanted to cheer up her balcony with pots of heather and other plants that would survive the winter.

Why am I always sent to visit the old folk, Rauno wondered. He looked at Aune Toivola as she sat at the kitchen table, her wrinkled hands resting on the waxed tablecloth. The coffee that she poured him was weak and tasted of nothing. Rauno handed her photographs of Riikka and Jere.

'Do you know these people?'

Aune put on another pair of glasses – she had a selection of spectacles beside a pile of newspapers – and began examining the photographs. Rauno strummed his fingers on the table and glanced intermittently at the ticking second hand of the clock on the wall. Damn it, this is going to take all evening, he thought impatiently, though he couldn't understand why he was so restless. He was in no hurry to get home. He had barely exchanged a word with his wife since Friday evening, except for a few compulsory conversations about the girls. Nina hadn't come home until the following morning; she hadn't told him where she'd been and he hadn't asked.

But the thought was gnawing away at him.

'This girl here I've never seen before, but I know the boy,' said Aune, awakening Rauno from his thoughts. He sat up and sipped his tepid coffee.

'This is the Koski boy, isn't it?'

'That's right. Jere Koski.'

'Oh, I know the Koski family. Veikko and Liisa. Veikko was the son of Ilmari, who was a year older than me at school. He married a girl called Lotta Siitonen, and they had Veikko. There were no other children. They've both been dead for years now.'

'What can you tell me about Jere?' Rauno pressed her.

'I don't know the youngsters all that well, of course. Ilmari was a drunk and that's what they said about Veikko, too.'

'And Jere?'

'Isn't he at the university? Maybe he'll be able to stay on the straight and narrow.'

'The murdered girl is Riikka Rautio. She was originally from Saloinen, too. Does that name mean anything to you?'

'Rautio … it doesn't sound familiar.' Aune adjusted her glasses, took a sip of coffee and scrutinised Riikka's photograph once again. Rauno felt like snatching the picture from her hand and leaving. But where would he go? For a pint? On a Monday evening?

Why not?

'Just a minute … The daughter of Kalevi and Sanna Paakkari – Irmeli, her name was – I think she married someone called Rautio.'

'Riikka's mother's name is Irmeli.'

'Yes, I have a vague recollection of Irmeli. This is a terrible shock – your own child murdered in broad daylight, and so close-by too. I've kept the doors locked ever since. I'm worried someone will turn up here with a gun.'

The coffee cup in Aune's hand had started to tremble, spilling coffee on to the shiny tablecloth.

'I don't think you're in any danger,' said Rauno, trying to sound convincing. But how the hell can I be sure of that, he cursed to himself.

'The girl's time of death has been placed at around ten o'clock in the evening. Do you remember anything about that evening?'

'Excuse me?' said Aune, touching her hearing aid.

'I said, do you remember anything about the evening before you found the girl? Anything out of the ordinary?'

Aune thought for a moment.

'No, nothing in particular,' she replied eventually. 'In the evenings I watch television and go to bed early. Every night.'

'How do you get by, here all by yourself?'

'I do well enough. I can still move around and there's nothing wrong with my head, nothing much anyhow,' she laughed. 'It's just my hearing. But now I'm worried. Mind you, it's a good thing the care assistant visits every morning. At least it won't take them long to find me, if something should happen.'

'Is there anyone you could ask to stay for a few days? A relative?' Rauno suggested as he stood up.

'My son is so far away. He's too busy at work.'

Aune wiped the crumbs from the table and gathered them in her quivering hand. She remained sitting at the table, lost in thought, and didn't get up to see Rauno to the door.

The woods on either side of the running track were shadowed and quiet. So what, thought Anna. It's the same track, the same stretch of forest, the world is exactly the same as it is in daylight, she tried to convince herself the way her mother had done when she was a child and afraid of the dark. I'm not going to start imagining things now. But why on earth do all tracks like this have to run through the woods? They could just as well run through the city like soft streams, through the suburbs, from one yard to another, one car park to another, from the shopping centre to the church hall. People could run surrounded by lights and people; we wouldn't always have to be by ourselves in the dark.

Her legs felt horribly stiff. Anna jogged as slowly as possible and still found it hard going. She had smoked far too much in the last few days.

She'd actually stopped smoking years ago. That's what she tried to tell herself as she lit up every evening. The last time she'd smoked during the day was before joining the army, and even then she hadn't smoked very much. One pack easily lasted her a week.

A fene egye meg with the cigarettes, she cursed to herself. It was because of the nicotine that coffee had started to give her heartburn. Her mobile beeped. Happy at having an excuse to stop for a moment, she pulled the phone from her pocket. One new message. It was from the same number as the message earlier that day. Unknown. Prepaid. *A faszom*, she said out loud.

Did you get my msg this afternoon? I'm really interested in you. And hey, be careful out there.

There was a rustling in the trees nearby. The darkness behind the branches was almost impenetrable. Anyone could be hiding there and Anna wouldn't notice a thing. The branches gave a crackle. Anna glanced around and put the phone back in her pocket. She was determined to find out who was sending these messages and why. It was probably the invalid; he'd clearly decided to start harassing her. Some people just can't accept that I don't want to see them a second time. But he could at least play fair; the unlisted number made the messages seem horrid, pathetic and frightening. Was that really his intention?

Just then she heard the sound of someone running towards her. She felt the instinct to scarper into the woods and hide among the trees.

A francba, there are other people running out here and they're perfectly entitled to do so, Anna cursed as a jogger in a dark tracksuit ran past her with a wave. A regular, just like Anna. When she was younger, Anna had known all the local joggers. They had always greeted one another whenever they passed or overtook one another. Of course, she didn't really know them, didn't know their names, where they lived, their backgrounds, professions or their other hobbies. They only recognised one another on the running track, in their tracksuits, sweat on their brows. Anna knew that if she went for a run on a Monday at six, the middle-aged woman in the red tracksuit would also be out. On Thursdays there was the cute guy, who much to Anna's disappointment had never paid her any attention except to greet her in passing. In all likelihood they wouldn't have recognised one another in a different place or wearing different clothes. Despite this, the sense of camaraderie was powerful. They were like bikers or people in caravans who waved to one another anywhere in the world. Sometimes Anna had thought of those nameless, faceless runners as closer to her than her own mother.

Humans are the perfect pack animal, she thought, and increased her speed until she began to feel the lactic acid in her muscles drain the energy from her body. She tried to forget about the text messages and her childish fears. Gritting her teeth, she forced herself to complete one more lap of the track and didn't pay any attention to the strange rustling that sounded as though someone were following her through the trees. She wanted to prove to herself that her fears were unfounded. Then she ran home and took a shower, more fatigued than she had been in a long time. This time she was forced to use the lift, and she was determined not to smoke before going to bed.

When she came out of the shower, Anna glanced at the time. It was half past nine. Quite late, but she'd made up her mind. She fiddled with the settings on her phone so that the recipient wouldn't see her number and called the number that had sent the messages. The officious-sounding female voice answered her: *The number you have called …* But of course, she thought, took out Petri's number, tapped it into her phone and listened as a phone rang somewhere. She counted eight rings and was about to hang up when a sleepy voice answered. 'Petri.'

'Hi, it's Anna,' she said and drew a deep breath.

'Hey there, how are you doing?' Any signs of tiredness were gone; Petri sounded positively elated. 'I almost thought you'd decided not to call me. Great!'

Shit, she thought. That's exactly what I didn't want.

'Have you sent me any text messages today?'

Straight to the point; it was for the best.

'No. You wouldn't give me your number.'

'Are you sure?'

'I'm sure.'

'If they did come from you, I'll find out. I'll have you charged. Come on, admit it. Stop harassing me and I'll forget about it.'

'That's a bit harsh. Is that how you talk to all criminals? They'd be wetting themselves.'

Anna wasn't sure whether he was teasing her or not.

'Do you admit it?'

'Anna, really, I don't even have your number. But I will admit I really hoped you'd call. This wasn't quite what I had I mind, though.'

'I bet.'

'Can we meet up? I've been thinking about the whole Hungarian minority thing. And you.'

It sounded as though he was begging and it irritated her.

'Sorry, I'm afraid I'm too busy at work – I haven't got time at the moment. But let's see,' she said, instantly regretting it.

Let's see. What on earth was she raving on about?

'I honestly haven't sent you any messages.'

'Okay, bye then.'

'Anna, don't—'

Anna hung up.

And went out for a cigarette.

She believed him. He had sounded so genuinely surprised and excited to hear from her. At first. Imagine the disappointment she must have caused him.

Anna anxiously clambered in beneath her sheets and tried to relax her exhausted limbs, and just as she was about to slip into a sleep as quiet and cool as a hole in the winter ice, her phone beeped again. *Bassza meg*, do I need to change my number, she snapped as she fumbled for the light switch. The phone continued to beep. It wasn't a message; someone was calling.

It was Esko.

It was almost midnight.

Jere had turned up at the station.

16

'I'VE ALREADY TOLD YOU a hundred times, I was in Kaldoaivi,' Jere yelled with such force that a droplet of spittle flew on to his stubbly chin. Jere wiped it on the sleeve of his camouflage jacket.

'What is that? Speak Finnish, please,' Anna replied calmly, though she felt the urge to raise her voice. She was annoyed that the boy seemed so cocky after everything that had happened, and she could see that Esko felt the same.

Anna had dragged herself out of bed, forced herself awake, pulled on some clothes and driven to the police station through the night-time drizzle. On the way she nervously smoked another cigarette inside the car. As soon as she tossed the butt out of the window, she felt a deep sense of disgust at herself. The air inside the car was thick with poisonous smoke and the smell of tobacco wafted from her hair as she walked across the station car park. Esko's Opel was parked there too, lonely and expectant like a faithful old dog tethered outside a pub. Has he been home at all, she wondered.

'I don't know what language I should speak to you, but I get the feeling it isn't Finnish. I was in Kaldoaivi. End of story. I left last Sunday and got back a few hours ago. My mum called me the minute I turned my phone on – that was this morning – and told me the police were looking for me, that Riikka's dead, shot. What's been going on here? And why are you looking for me? You don't think I shot her, do you?'

'What is Kaldoaivi?' Anna asked again.

'It's an area of Lapland, in the moorland between Sevettijärvi and Pulmankijärvi,' Esko replied on Jere's behalf.

'What were you doing there?'

'Hiking and fishing, of course.'

'Who were you with?'

'I was by myself.'

'Why?'

'What d'you mean, why? Why was I by myself? Surely a man can go off to Lapland by himself if he damn well pleases. What else could a man possibly want?'

'You didn't tell anyone where you were going and you turned your phone off.'

'That's right.'

'Why?'

'Oh, for fuck's sake. Because I felt like it.'

'I'd drop the arrogance, if I were you. You're currently at the top of our list of suspects. Murder suspects. How does that sound?' Anna asked.

'Fucking hell.'

'Where is your rifle? The Remington,' asked Esko.

'At Riikka's parents' cottage. That's where I normally go duck shooting.'

'Riikka's parents don't seem to know about it.'

'How would they, they hardly ever go there. But that's where it is. You can check if you like.'

'We will,' said Anna. 'What time did you leave on Sunday?'

'In the morning. The train to Rovaniemi leaves at nine.'

'And from there?'

'I got the bus to Ivalo, then another one to Sevettijärvi.'

'Can anyone corroborate that?'

'I've still got the tickets. I'm sure the drivers would remember me. And I booked the train ticket online – I can prove that.'

'The fact that you booked a train ticket doesn't prove anything. But don't worry, we'll be able to chart your journey to the minute.'

'Good. Then I've got nothing to worry about.'

'Riikka was killed at around 10 p.m. on Sunday evening. Where were you then?'

'In a tent in Sevettijärvi.'

'And who can prove that?'

'I spent that evening in the local bar.'

Esko immediately went outside to make a phone call. After a few minutes he returned and gestured for Anna to join him in the corridor.

'It's true. The publican Armas Feodoroff confirmed that last Sunday a young man matching Jere's description came into the bar just after the Ivalo bus arrived, around 8 p.m., and drank seven bottles of beer. They chatted about everything from ptarmigan-shooting to fishing – the boy drank himself into quite a state. There was one other customer too, Antti Bogdanoff, one of the local drunks, so he can confirm Jere's story – apparently he wasn't in too bad a state that night. The lad said he studied mathematics and that he wanted to go hiking before term started again. The same person was sighted in the shop operating next door to the pub. He bought some chocolate and a couple of beers.'

'From Sevettijärvi there's no way he could have got back that same evening,' said Anna.

'Absolutely no way.'

'So it can't be Jere,' said Anna, unable to hide the disappointment in her voice.

'It certainly looks that way.'

'We should send them a photo of Jere, just in case.'

'Sure. I've taken down an email address.'

'I suppose we'll have to start going through the members of the hunting association. Perhaps one of them just lost it.'

'Maybe.'

'Thanks for calling me.'

'Thank Virkkunen,' said Esko.

*I only have vague memories of the reception centre. My life was punctu-
ated with trips to primary school, like all the kids who lived there. Or
nursery school, if they were still young like Mehvan.*

*The adults stayed at the centre all day and slept. It was probably the
adults' sleepiness and vacant behaviour that made my memories of the
centre so messed up. Everything was dusky and obscured behind wisps of
mist; it was like being woozy with fever. That's when the split started, on
the first day at school. It's a split that appears between all kids and their
parents, crack, crack, crack. At first it's just a small hairline fracture,
but it gradually grows and deepens. Eventually it tears apart with a
great rip. The kids are pulled into the outside world. They learn things
quickly, jalla jalla, they learn the language and local customs. They have
a function, morning assemblies at nursery, going to school, studying, a
reason to exist.*

*But what about the adults? They stay behind and sleep. They might
take a language course, if they're lucky. They wait, twiddling their
thumbs, for their kids to come back from school, for their new, wonderful
lives to begin, the life that they had planned so fervently back home and
that aunts and uncles and cousins and neighbours and friends of friends
who had previously left have lied about to them. Ask anyone who's ever
left for the West and they'll tell you how fucking well they're doing. After
time, the parents give up waiting – what's the point? The kids aren't
coming home and life isn't suddenly going to turn into heaven on earth.
After a few years they weep and rage when their kids speak Finnish to
them but are still falling behind at school; they just hang out round the
city listening to shitty American music and don't do anything sensible
now that they've finally got the chance – and at what cost? – though it's
cost the adults everything, EVERYTHING. The adults would even be
prepared to swallow the fact that they no longer have any function here,
but that their kids are throwing everything away too…*

I've thought about this a lot, and I've spent weeks locked in my room so hey, I've had plenty of time to wonder whether it's possible to stop that split from happening. The only thing I can think of is that adults need to be shoved out of the door straight away, just like the kids. Put them straight into work, then you either sink or swim. Less of the Social Services, less of the nonsense about integration, just get these people into work. Working life in Finland isn't so weird and wonderful that an immigrant can't survive. But of course this would mean less funding for integration projects, fewer jobs and meetings for all those experts. So that's that then.

Every single day it felt completely stupid having to go back to the reception centre after school. In the morning the doors pushed me out into a place with a surface, with sounds and tastes and smells, a place that I could be a part of too, then in the afternoons those same doors sucked me back into a bad dream that went on and on without you ever really waking up. Mum told me to call that place home. Four beds in a small room, a table, a bookshelf, depressing blue-grey curtains at the windows, a grotesque excuse for a sky. Cold floors and echoing corridors with endless rows of identical rooms, temporary homes for other people waiting for their real lives to start. Lamps shaped like tubes. A communal kitchen. The kids called it the loony bin. Apparently the building had once been a mental asylum. I secretly worried that Mum would go crazy, that all the madness those windows had seen and sucked up would somehow be transferred into her. That's what it seemed like. For the most part Mum just cried and stroked her ever-growing stomach and stared at the walls. Dad sat outside smoking with the other men living in the house. There were others from our country, the country that didn't really exist. Damn it, I've heard so much about it that my head hurts; I've had a lifelong overdose of it. Dad was happy that he could sit out there and plan a free Kurdistan. Mum had no one to keep her company. I called the place home whenever Mum was listening so that she wouldn't go mad. Whenever Dad said that at least here we didn't need to fear for our lives and that the children would have a future, Mum started crying all the more. Then Dad would go out for another smoke.

In a way, my experience was the opposite of the Sámi. I've read somewhere that back in the olden days the Sámi people weren't allowed to speak their language at school and they were forced to live in hostels, and they weren't allowed to speak Sámi there either, and so their memory of school became blurred. The things they remember most about child-hood were the holidays, because being able to use their own language helped strengthen the memories better. One person said the only thing they remembered about school was when their mother came to visit. Then they could speak. Then they were alive.

For me, my own language never served like an anchor, and though in a way school was fucking awful – there was bullying, and especially to begin with things were really difficult – I actually remember school and the school bus and everything about life outside the reception centre much more clearly than anything that went on inside the centre. Perhaps I was rejecting the life inside those walls, though I don't for one second believe in psychoanalysis or any of that crap. I created a shell around myself, wrapped myself in a protective film. I couldn't talk to Mum; she was a wreck. And with Dad I talked even less. I had the constant feeling that they didn't notice me or Mehvan. It was as though we'd become transparent inside that cling film. And once Adan was born, Mum with-drew even more. She turned into a robot that did nothing but change nappies and breastfeed.

She was depressed. Now I realise what it was, but at the time nobody told me what was going on.

17

ANNA WAS SITTING in a blue-and-white patrol car parked outside Bihar Chelkin's house. It was the early hours of the morning and the sun was somewhere behind the rainclouds. She wanted to make sure that all the local residents – and the Chelkin family in particular – noticed her presence, and for that reason she didn't switch off the motor or the lights. The street lights were refracted in small, glittering spectrums of colour in the raindrops on the windscreen. The car's digital thermometer showed an outdoor temperature of 5°C.

Why do I have to live so far north, she found herself wondering as she glanced up once again at the lights in the apartment on the third floor.

Back home the evening would still be lazy and warm, the last vestiges of summer; the harvest would be at its peak, the maize ripe, and the farmers would still cut the hay at least another three times. The cold and wet weather wouldn't come until some time in December. What on earth is keeping me here? And why do I still think of somewhere I haven't lived for twenty years as 'home', a place where people lost their minds twenty years ago?

Just then, one of the lights in the Chelkins' apartment was switched off and Anna woke from her daydreams. The lights in the stairwell flickered to life, and a moment later Bihar and Mehvan stepped out through the front door of the tall apartment block. Anna flicked on the car's blue lights and slowly drove up next to them.

'How's things?' Anna called to Bihar through the window.

'Fine.' It was Mehvan who replied.

'I was asking Bihar, but I'm pleased to hear you're doing well too, Mehvan. And you're a good boy to look after your sister like this. How about you, Bihar?'

'I'm okay,' the girl mumbled faintly, staring at the pavement.

Mehvan spat, loud and provocative.

'Bihar's bus is going to be here soon – we'd better go,' he said with a note of insolence.

'Yes. Mustn't be late for school,' said Anna.

Once the investigation had been discontinued and nobody else had wanted to observe the family unofficially, Anna had decided to do this by herself. She showed up outside the Chelkins' house in a patrol car whenever she got the opportunity, and every now and then slowly drove past Bihar and Mehvan's schools at break time. The family had noticed her at once but hadn't dared to say anything. Perhaps they thought they were still on a list of suspects, still under investigation.

Nonetheless, Bihar's situation seemed to have calmed down. Bihar appeared contented and safe; she went to school regularly and in the evenings she sometimes met up with her Kurdish and Somali friends. But the sense of calm could simply have been the result of Anna's presence. And what if the family found out that she was working alone, against direct orders to the contrary? She knew her job could be on the line, but she didn't care. If she turned her back on Bihar and something happened to her, she would never forgive herself.

Anna drove to the police station, parked the car in the exhaust-fumed bay beneath the building and took the lift up to the fourth floor. She had already acquired a sense of familiarity for her office with its bare walls. Perhaps I should buy a plant or something, she mused as she booted up the computer and lifted a folder full of papers on to the table. She opened the venetian blinds; grey clouds still hung heavy in the sky.

Riikka's case had been treading water. Jere's DNA didn't match the sperm found in Riikka's body. His pump-action rifle had been found in a gun cabinet at Riikka's parents' summer cottage, its barrel polished and shining. It was impossible to establish when the rifle had last been fired. According to Jere, this was the previous winter when he had been out hunting hares, though Esko wondered why a lad with a passion for hunting would miss the start of the duck season. He was still convinced that Jere had shot Riikka. But how could he have simultaneously been hundreds of kilometres away in Sevettijärvi? Even Esko couldn't explain away that little detail.

Anna had visited dozens of restaurants in town and discovered many lunch menus offering fish and pine nuts. None of the staff had seen Riikka on the day of the shooting. They had called through the members list of the local hunting association – with no luck. Many people had been out hunting along the shore near the running track, and several of them had been there on the night of the murder.

Two of the hunters had been located, and Anna and Rauno had visited and talked to them. Neither had seen or heard anything out of the ordinary that night, but one of them thought he remembered there being a third person out with the hunt. There had been plenty of birds, so their concentration was elsewhere. Naturally, the .12-calibre rifles belonging to both men had recently been fired. One had seven ducks and one goose hanging in the shed protected by mosquito netting, while the other's catch was already in the freezer, neatly bagged and labelled: mallard breast fillets (20/8); pintail breast fillets (21/8); four teals (1/9).

Both men came across as perfectly normal and sensible; there wasn't the slightest suggestion of mental illness or a guilty conscience and neither seemed to be hiding anything or lying. These men wouldn't even have accidentally shot a shelduck, of that Anna was sure. Still, she didn't want to give up on this line of investigation just yet. They had nothing else to go on.

There was a third person out there somewhere. A third hunter whose prey hadn't flown overhead, its wings rushing in the wind; it had run towards him in a brand-new, scratchy tracksuit.

Had the killer known that it would be impossible to trace a bog-standard hunting rifle? Is that why he'd used this weapon? Or was the killer just as average and nondescript a hunter as the weapon and rounds he had used?

Or she, Anna corrected herself.

For all the manly accoutrements, the killer could just as easily be a woman. Lots of women hunt around here; they also serve as the president and the prime minister. They drink a lot, swear, smoke cigarettes and jump into bed with random acquaintances. They do what they please. They can enlist in the armed forces or go to the police academy. Anna cut her flow of thoughts right there. She had touched the rope that was keeping her in Finland, and that rope burned as though she had slid down it.

And what about Riikka's mysterious new relationship? With the exception of Virve Sarlin, none of Riikka's friends had seen or heard anything, and they had all now been interviewed, their Facebook connections examined, revealing nothing. That being said, apart from a few phone calls and the odd coffee, Riikka hadn't had much to do with them all summer.

On the other hand, everybody seemed to know that Riikka had separated from Jere and was now living with Virve. Every time someone had tried to coax her out to a bar or to the seaside, she had said she just wanted to be alone, but even this hadn't unduly worried anyone. Saara Heikkilä, heavily made-up and with peroxide-blonde hair, had explained to Anna in a nasal voice that Riikka's relationship with her old friends had cooled somewhat once she started dating Jere, the boy that everybody wanted, and when they finally broke up nobody cared to hang out with her any more.

Virve was the only one who had remained a close friend.

Could Virve have made up her story about Riikka's secretive behaviour and her new relationship? She claimed to have stayed at home after Riikka had gone out on her run, but there was nobody to corroborate this. Her neighbours were unable to say whether Riikka, Virve or anyone else had left the apartment that evening.

The police had only Virve's word for what happened on the night of the murder. Was there any way Virve could have done this?

Anna took a deep sigh and replaced the files and case reports in their folders. She had read them all dozens of times, wracking her brains to think how best to move the case forward.

She couldn't think of any new lines of inquiry. Nobody could. They had reached a dead end. Autumn was well on its way and the evenings were drawing in.

More and more often Anna would leave her desk and go outside for a cigarette, though it didn't perk her up at all; more and more often she was missing her evening runs.

After losing enthusiasm for running the marathon, Anna had started running regularly four times a week without any goal other than retaining her sanity. Her weekly programme consisted of two basic runs, one longer run and an interval session. She ran without giving it a second thought. It felt natural; she couldn't live without it.

Now, for two weeks in a row, she had skipped the long run and the intervals. Even on her normal runs she felt increasingly as though her legs were made of lead.

But she didn't want to worry about that now. She would make it up again, when it wasn't raining so much, when she had more time.

Anna glanced at her watch. It was already afternoon. She could use the few hours of overtime that had built up over the last few weeks, go into town for a bite to eat, get home and go to sleep. Tomorrow was her only free weekday all autumn. It made the thought of going home early seem all the more attractive. The investigation had kept her at work until well into the evening several times, and getting to sleep had become a problem. Keeping an eye on Bihar was an added cause for concern. Anna planned to sleep in until late morning; perhaps then she would tidy the flat a little and go clothes-shopping in town. Sari dressed so stylishly, she had noticed, to her embarrassment. Anna always turned up in jeans and a hoodie. How easy life in her patrol uniform had been in that respect.

It wouldn't be until the unit meeting next week that they would decide on any new lines of investigation. Until then, she would have to go over the same old case files, documents whose contents she already knew by heart. Anna hoped that she might be assigned a new case; how nice it would be to investigate bicycle thefts or something similar. New investigations, new cases – it sounded refreshing. But there would be no bicycle thefts for her, not here in the Violent Crimes Unit.

Sari pulled up slowly in front of her house. The garden was cluttered with small plastic buckets and spades, and the yellow swings dangled empty. They hadn't planted anything this summer either; the lawn grew in isolated, tangled clumps and they had become used to the sight of piles of rubble in the garden. Maybe next year, once the children are a bit bigger. We could dig a small vegetable patch, the kids could plant things themselves, watch as they grow. Sari opened the front door and stepped into the hallway. The children's clothes were hanging neatly on their hooks. The sound of laughter came from the kitchen and the scent of food wafted into the hallway. Thank God we can afford a nanny, Sari thought once again. What a luxury to come home after work and have food ready, the laundry done and the kids happily playing. Sari didn't dare imagine what a trial it must be getting them ready for nursery.

'Knock, knock,' she said as she stepped into the kitchen.

Siiri and Tobias jumped from their chairs and came bounding into her arms. Sari hugged them both and felt the endless love flowing within her.

'Right, back to the table. What wonderful food has Sanna made for us today?'

'Macaloni!' said Tobias.

'Oh, macaroni, yummy!' Sari corrected him and smiled at Sanna. 'How's your day been?' she asked the young nanny they had found through an agency and who initially had caused Sari great concern with her dyed blue hair, her heavy make-up, the silver bead in her lower lip and the thin ring through her left eyebrow. Teemu had talked her into it. The girl had seemed smart and confident, and the children had taken to her straight away. Don't judge a book by its cover, her dyed-in-the-wool middle-class engineer husband had convinced her, frowning on Sari's prejudices. Because there had been no one else on offer, Sari had eventually consented – through gritted teeth.

And thank God she had.

Sanna had proved to be worth her weight in gold. As the eldest child in a large family, she was excellent with the kids and knew how to look after the house. She was always in a good mood, had the energy to play with the children, to keep them occupied for hours – and all this without being too lenient with them. Sari felt that her children's behaviour had taken a radical change for the better since she'd gone back to work and Sanna had entered the house. What's more, Sari didn't feel the slightest bit guilty about it. On the contrary, she was enjoying it to the full.

'Siiri was a bit sleepy in the morning, so we didn't go outside for a while,' Sanna explained as she stroked the girl's fair, angelic locks. 'I let them play in their pyjamas until midday. What did we play?'

'Magic forest!' they cried in unison.

This girl's superhuman, Sari thought.

'In the afternoon we went out to the garden. The strap on Tobias's dungarees broke.'

'Don't matter,' he stuttered.

'No, it doesn't matter – we'll mend it,' said Sari.

'All in all, a good day.'

'Great. Thanks so much, Sanna. You're amazing.'

Sanna smiled contentedly.

'What time shall I start tomorrow?'

'Come for nine. Teemu's going to work a bit later tomorrow. You can lie in too.'

'Great. See you in the morning,' said Sanna, waving to the children.

Sari sat down at the ready-laid table, scooped a plate of macaroni

gratin for herself, poured some milk and looked at the clock: 3.30
p.m. Teemu would be back in an hour. She would have a relaxed
evening at home with nothing in particular to do. Because of Teemu's
business trips they had cut back their hobbies to a bare minimum.
They didn't want to let hectic timetables spoil these rare chances to
focus on the children and to spend time together as a family. It was
a good solution; they enjoyed being at home. The children had no
idea that things like stress and time constraints existed.

Her mobile made a gurgling sound. A text message. Teemu had
changed the regular ringtone to a frog's croak, and it took a moment
for Sari to realise the noise was coming from her work phone.

U R so sexy. So sexy there. Yummy yummy.

Sari automatically peered through the window out into the street.
There was no sign of movement. Then she went round the house,
checking all the windows and looking out into the yard.

Were the swings moving? Had the wind picked up?

Have I got some kind of perverted stalker, she thought, and dou-
ble-checked that Sanna had locked the door after her.

Rauno had remained at the station, again. He enjoyed the quiet that
descended on the Violent Crimes Unit after six o'clock once the
majority of the investigators had clocked off. The office doors were
closed, nobody was running along the corridors, the photocopier
wasn't whirring, there were fewer lights on and there was no buzz
of conversation. It was easier to concentrate, to get his thoughts in
order. His work wasn't being constantly interrupted and nobody disturbed him.

Rauno laid the pile of reports on his desk with a sigh and rubbed
his exhausted eyes. Explanations and excuses; at least he could admit
it to himself. He didn't feel so passionately about this job that he
wanted to spend every evening in his office. Far from it.

He didn't want to go home. He knew that his absence was only
making things worse, that when they were having their difficul-
ties they should try and come closer to one another, try and grow

together instead of withdrawing. This was one way of losing his last opportunity to make things right, of making Nina despise him more and more each day. Still, he refused to be the only guilty party.

He didn't know where it had all gone wrong. He had tried and tried, but he'd always felt as though nothing was ever good enough. He was sick of it all.

If it hadn't been for the girls, he would have walked out long ago. Or would he?

Despite everything that had happened, sometimes Rauno felt as though he still loved Nina. Perhaps the feeling was just a habit. They'd been together for seven years. Surely that should be long enough, he thought, and felt a wave of shame and failure. His own parents were still together after 35 years.

Rauno flicked through the reports one last time. There were still plenty of names on the hunting association's member list. This is pointless, he thought, as he decided to call another few names. The killer could be anyone and could live anywhere. He might as well get hold of a list from the neighbouring hunting association and go through them too. What about the Rotary Club? The Women's Institute? Rauno sighed again. Perhaps the bulk of the work was yet to come.

He called five numbers. One didn't answer, and he scored through the other four with a pencil after talking to them. All of them could prove they were somewhere else on the night of the murder – one was even in Thailand. Rauno believed them; what reason did he have not to? It would be impossible to look any more closely into their alibis. He had to trust his own sense of judgement. That's why Rauno had been assigned this task. Apparently he was a good listener. Nina would have disagreed. It was strange how a person could give such a different impression of themselves at work. Which is the real me: the Rauno from home or the Rauno at work? Is it someone else entirely? Someone waiting inside him to develop into the man he really was?

It was too complicated.

It was almost eight o'clock. Rauno filed the reports neatly in their folders and switched off his computer. He would get home just in time to read the girls their bedtime story. At least he still enjoyed that. He didn't want to jeopardise his relationship with his daughters. The fact that it was already beginning to happen was too painful to admit.

When the girls were in their beds and he was reading their story, Nina switched on the television and disappeared into a blue haze of TV entertainment until the early hours. Once the girls were asleep, Rauno went to bed; he was utterly exhausted. Nina spent the night on the sofa, yet again.

When night had given way to morning and the paperboys had finished their morning rounds, Rauno awoke to the sound of his telephone ringing. The call was from the station.

'Do you remember when me and Áron found that body in the Tisza?' asked Ákos out of the blue over dinner.

After a moment's deliberation, Anna hadn't gone into town to eat by herself but had gone to the supermarket, then home to cook Ákos's favourite dish – *bableves*, bean soup – and invited her brother for dinner. She had walked to the other side of the suburb, where blocks of flats identical to her own reached up towards the sky. If I hadn't spent my childhood here, I would never be able to find my way around, she pondered. Everything looks the same, apartment blocks like grotesque skyscrapers as far as the eye can see. The sound of children playing didn't echo from inside the courtyards. The place seemed deserted.

As Ákos opened the door to his messy bedsit, the stench of dejected loneliness had hit her in the face and Anna had found it hard to breathe. My brother, she'd thought. This is my own brother, thrown away and forgotten.

I've done this to him, but this is my chance to fix things. I promise you that. I've been selfish, thinking only about my own success without sparing a thought for you. All she managed to say aloud was: *Gyere enni*. Ákos seemed excited at this surprise invitation and, as Anna had predicted, he was delighted with the *bableves*.

'No, I don't remember. Remind me,' she answered.

They had never talked about Áron, their eldest brother who had died soon after the Croatian war broke out in Osijek and whose memory was beginning to fade. Áron had been only two years older than Ákos, and as children the boys were inseparable. Always together, always getting up to something.

'We'd been drinking down at the *taverna* and started walking home in the early hours, both a bit tipsy. It was a beautiful morning; there was mist hanging above the river and it was warm and quiet. That's why we thought we'd walk back along the shore, though it would take longer. There was a fisherman out on the river in his boat. Do you remember Béla Nagy, the grumpy old man?'

'Yes, vaguely. Réka and I were out there swimming once, and we climbed into the boats along the shore and jumped from their bows back into the water. We hadn't noticed Old Nagy sitting further up on the quayside watching to see when we'd touch his boat. He went crazy when we tried to climb inside his boat, ran all the way down to the shore, shouting until he was red in the face. *Don't you touch my boat!* A short man with a big moustache.'

'That's the one. He was crazy. Anyway, he was already out fishing that morning, and when he saw us he started hollering at us to come and help him, there was something really heavy in his net. Áron was a good swimmer and a bit less drunk, so he swam up to the boat to have a look. *A fene egye meg.*'

'Who was it?'

'Tibor Rekecski. Their family lived quite close, in Kőrös. Do you remember? The guy that drowned after coming down that big slide outside Békavár. He went into the water feet first and hit his head on the rocks on the way down.'

'*A kurva életbe!*'

'His mates tried to dive down and find him; the fire brigade was called and everything, but the river's so muddy and the current is too strong. They couldn't find anything. He'd got caught up in Béla Nagy's fishing net. Áron pulled him ashore. I called the police.'

'I never heard about this.'

'Nobody told you. You were too little.'

'When did all this happen?'

'In '89.'

'So you were 15?'

'Yeah, and you were seven.'

'And out drinking at the Taverna, *Úr Isten!* You were still kids; Áron was only 17.'

'Nobody ever asked for ID,' said Ákos and tried to avoid Anna's eyes by flicking through the newspaper on the table.

When their brother had died and their mother had decided to try and save her other brother from a similar fate, what was left of the family packed a suitcase full of things and fled to Finland. They no longer talked about Áron. Nobody spoke about the conflict, though their mother followed the news carefully. They had stopped talking about their father years ago, so they already knew that it was best to keep quiet about difficult matters.

They had to try and protect their mother. And themselves.

Anna had learned the technique well, and she was perfectly happy not talking about Áron. As far as she was concerned there was no point going over painful things again and again. It was so much easier to let things go and forget about them. That's another reason why the headmaster had been so concerned about her. You have to open up, Anna, let it all out. But Anna didn't know what 'it all' was or how she was supposed to 'let it out'. She had no words for it.

'Have you ever thought of going back?' asked Anna.

'Only about a hundred times a day.'

'Then why don't you?'

'Don't want to.'

'Mum would be pleased.'

'I'd have to move in with her. Jesus, I couldn't deal with that.'

'You could rent your own place.'

'And then what would I do?'

'What do you do here? Live on the dole? You're the worst example of what these swivel-eyed lunatics are always raving on about. They think we're all like that.'

'Someone's got to prove them right.'

'Come on.'

'I don't know. I've been away for so long. And there's no work there either. Most of my friends have moved to Hungary.'

'Then why don't you go to Hungary?'

'*Jebiga*, I'm not going there. Do you want to get rid of me? We've only just—'

'Of course not.'

'That's not what it seems like.'

'*Bocs.*'

'So, are you going to Skype Mum?'

'What about you?' Anna asked, puzzled.

'I thought I'd just listen. I don't want to talk to her.'

'Why not?'

'She'll just start complaining, saying I should come home. Go on, call her. But don't tell her I'm here.'

'She'll want me to tell her how you're doing.'

'Tell her everything's fine.'

'*Hát igen.*'

But their mother wasn't at home. Anna hung up once the answering machine began playing her recorded message. Shame. She was convinced her brother would have wanted to talk to her, after all, if only he'd heard her voice.

'The guys are out in town this evening, said they want to see you again after all these years. They were really excited when I told them you'd moved back to town. They're waiting for you,' said Ákos.

'Where?'

'In Bar Amarillo.'

In addition to his punk friends, Ákos hung out with a gang of young men in their twenties who had escaped the disintegrating former Yugoslavia. For reasons that nobody talked about, they hadn't gone to Sweden, like most people fleeing the conflict. They had found one another here in this suburb; they were wild and handsome, like reincarnations of her missing elder brother Áron, and they had thought of young Anna as an equal member of the gang, considered her something of a mascot, a protector. In this neighbourhood, Anna had never had to worry about anything. Not even the skinheads had dared to harass her. Of course, their mother didn't like these boys any more than she liked the punks; to her mind, everything Ákos did was ruinous. And it was. Anna was the loner, the strange one, the one whose assimilation worried the professionals. Ákos, on the other hand, was always busy; he had friends and plenty to do. Apparently keeping the wrong company is worse than keeping no company at all, Anna thought.

It was through the Yugoslav boys that Anna had preserved a fragile connection to her former homeland. Only rarely did they meet other Hungarians; perhaps they were the only ones in the city. Anna was certain that, despite her protestations to the contrary, their mother had enjoyed the noise that so regularly filled their kitchen, though the language spoken wasn't her own. Their mother had made the boys *burek*. An Albanian, a Serb, a Croatian and a Vojvodina Hungarian – it was like the most ludicrously patriotic propaganda about Yugoslav brotherhood from the Tito era. Anna sensed how they had clung to one another like shipwrecked people holding on to a drifting log, trying to find something familiar amongst all the mindlessness that had brought their childhoods to an end.

Anna's Serbo-Croat was still in working order; it had been preserved just like the men's friendship. Only Ivan, a Croat, had returned home. The infamous gang of immigrants had grown into a club of middle-aged men who smoked and drank a lot, who dwelled on the past too much, who complained about Finland, its football team in particular. All except Ákos now had families, temporary jobs, and their lives were stable after a fashion.

Anna hadn't seen them in years.

A sense of nervous excitement tingled pleasantly in her stomach.

'*Zoran is ott van?*' she asked, trying to sound indifferent.

'Of course, he'll be first in line,' Ákos laughed and gave his sister a teasing look.

'Are you coming too?'

'I'm not in the mood,' said Ákos, but Anna saw how much he wanted to join them.

I spent a year in a preparatory class. At first they thought I should have been there longer – learning to read was really hard – but then they decided to move me to the normal first grade after only a year in preparatory, though I was actually the same age as the kids in second grade. They thought it would be best for me to start at the beginning, while it was still possible given my age – you can't very well put someone who's the age of a sixth-grader back in first grade even if they needed it. In that one year they would have to catch up on the whole of primary school and learn Finnish well enough to be able to survive in middle school, to finish their final exams, go to high school and end up studying medicine. Yeah right. As if it's that simple. Nothing's that simple, especially not the language. Without a language we're nothing. Language is everything, wallahi. *You can get by knowing a language on the surface, you can cope surprisingly well, but study is a different thing altogether, much more demanding than understanding or thinking or pretending you know what's going on.*

Right through primary school I was a year older than everyone in my class, but you don't notice it on the outside, even though some time in the eighth grade I started to feel like a real adult and much older than everyone else. I learned to read in first grade and I picked up this language pretty quick too. I can read Kurdish too, but not as well. I've never read a novel in Kurdish. I read quite a lot in Finnish. There are no books in Kurdish in the library. The teachers kept saying how lucky I was that I was only six when we arrived. Apparently that's the best age to arrive, six or seven, with regard to learning a language, many languages. Mehvan got left behind. He was so little. He lost too much of his own language, and that's why he never learned the new one properly. Or maybe he just can't spell: 'Mehvan's good at skaiting. Mehvan runs in the gardne.'

So there you have it; that was the official part about the system and the language, all neat and businesslike.

Of course, I could always tell what goes on behind the carefully constructed public façade, but I don't want to disturb the hornets' nest. I've decided I'm not going to let bitterness get the better of me. I don't want to end up like Mum and Dad.

But I'll tell you this much: sometimes I found shit in my shoes, quite literally. Wog. My jacket would disappear from the cloakroom. There was a clump of hair caught in a Finnish girl's fist. Name-calling. Whore. Bruises. Nigger. My bag ripped, its contents strewn across the sports field. Cruel fucking laughter. Silent staring. I'd try and blend into the wall, so grey that nobody would notice me, try and do my homework well but keep my mouth shut about it, then people think you're the perfect example of the well-integrated immigrant. And if you've had enough of putting up with all the shit and decide to step out from the wall, you're sent to the special-needs class. Then teachers sit down at meetings and seminars and wonder why there are so damn many immigrant kids in remedial classes. As if they ended up there by themselves, as if nobody put them there in the first place.

And the endless chanting: nigger, nigger, nigger. I've heard it so many times it might as well be my name.

So there are a few examples for you. Thank God I got into high school. That's where my life in Finland really started, my OWN life, that is. And that's where it stopped again almost as quickly.

18

ANNA WOKE to a distant sound. It was pitch dark. The bed was swaying. It took a moment for her heavy head to realise that the sound was coming from her work phone. It was playing an annoying melody somewhere far away.

Anna dragged herself into the hallway. Her leather jacket was lying in a heap on the floor, and the sound of the ringtone in her pocket was growing louder. She pulled out her phone and stared with bleary eyes at the screaming, flashing, trembling screen. It was Esko.

It was 5.30 in the morning. I'm still completely drunk, she thought, even the hall seems to be swaying. Her head was throbbing. She pressed the reject button and put the phone on silent. It was her day off, the first day off she'd had during the week, the day when she was supposed to clean the house and go shopping.

Shit.

'Anna, *vrati se.*'

'*Da, da.*'

'*Ko je bio?*'

'It was from work. Don't talk Serbian to me, I can't speak it any more.'

Zoran burst into laughter.

'There's plenty of work for you here,' he replied in Serbian and lifted the duvet.

Anna eventually got up after one o'clock. Zoran had kept her awake for a while, after which they had both fallen asleep again. Three cups of coffee, two ibuprofens and Zoran's bacon omelette weren't enough to make her nausea go away. Anna's temples ached and she felt sick. She looked at the screen on her work phone and saw that Esko had tried to call her a further three times. Sari, Rauno and Virkkunen had all called her too. Twelve missed calls in total. Virkkunen had sent her an SMS: *Come in ASAP*, it commanded her.

'I have to go to work,' Anna told Zoran as he stepped out of the shower dripping with water and hugged her as she started to get dressed.

'Weren't you supposed to have the day off?'

'Something serious has happened. Everyone's been trying to call me.'

'*Šteta.*'

'*Šta ćeš.*'

Anna had to take the bus into town. She didn't dare take the car, what with her throbbing headache and woozy condition; cycling was also out of the question for the same reason. Zoran wanted to stay in bed with her; he was almost purring around her, trying to stop her getting dressed. Anna wondered what Zoran's wife Nataša would think when her husband finally returned from his night out the day after.

When she arrived at the station, Anna could find neither Esko nor any of the other members of the team. She remembered that her phone was still on silent. She had missed another three calls, and the screen was flashing again.

'Jesus, where the hell have you been?' Esko bellowed down the phone so loudly that she had to pull her mobile away further from her ear.

'I'm in my office.'

She was, in fact, in the toilet. Her stomach had started to churn and her headache had taken a turn for the worse.

'Then get your exotic arse down here. We've got another John Doe.'

'Where are you?'

'On the running track near Häyrysenniemi, near the village of Asemakylä. You'll never guess how he was killed.'

Anna looked in the mirror. She hadn't had time to blow-dry her hair after the shower, and now it was tangled and messy. Large bags hung beneath her reddened eyes. Her stomach was churning and beads of sweat glinted on her upper lip. She felt dizzy.

Why today, of all days, she thought.

'Shot? With a rifle?'

'Dead right. So get a move on. We've been here all morning and Forensics are just finishing up. Virkkunen's furious.'

'There's just one problem.'

'And what's that?'

'I'm not fit to drive.'

After managing to say this, Anna vomited. The phone fell from her hand, pieces of omelette spilled into the toilet bowl, flushed down with coffee and other stomach fluids, in a stream of yellow-brown porridge.

'For Christ's sake,' came a voice from the floor beside the toilet.

Anna asked a patrol car at the station to drive her to the scene of the murder.

It was a bright day. The light seemed to ram the pain further into her skull. She should have brought her sunglasses.

She tried to relax as she sat in the back seat of the patrol car. She closed her eyes and focused on the pain pulsing through her temples and tried to wish it away; she'd read about this method in a women's magazine. It wasn't working. Her head continued to thump as the car turned on to a remote dirt track.

This is déjà vu, thought Anna as birch trees, thicket and every now and then a resilient juniper bush flashed past the window. It was as though she was revisiting the scene of Riikka's murder.

'Are we near the sea?' she asked the boys in uniform in the front seat.

'Yes. This track leads right the way down to the shore, but the running track where the body was found is about half a kilometre before the shore.'

'Quite a coincidence,' she thought out loud. Asemakylä was twenty or so kilometres north of the city, while Saloinen was located the same distance to the south.

Anna was hopelessly late. The forensics officer Linnea Markkula was bent over the body finishing up her work while the forensics team was scouring the surrounding area like a swarm of ants. Esko was standing to one side puffing on a cigarette.

'Look at the sight of you…' he scoffed as Anna appeared on the scene. His voice betrayed a note of satisfaction, of smugness and disgust.

'If I were you, I'd keep my mouth shut about other people's appearance. So, what have I missed?'

'A patrol car came out here at about five this morning after the guy's wife called. She was hysterical, first reported him missing last night.'

Esko pointed to the figure lying on the track. 'The victim is one Ville Pollari. Seems he's been lying there since about the time of the wife's first call.'

'Why does all this seem so familiar?' said Anna and felt a wave of nausea in her stomach.

'Pretty much. Except this time the head's still intact. Killer aimed for the chest, the heart. And this guy was shot at the start of his run. Riikka had almost finished hers.'

'Look at these woods. This is just like at Selkämaa.'

'Yep. The rest of us have been here for hours, so we've noted the similarities.'

'And I'll bet this shoreline is another hunting spot,' she replied, paying no attention to Esko's sarcasm.

'It is.'

Rauno approached them, clearly anxious.

'Guess what they found in this guy's pocket?' he said and nodded

at the figure of a man lying on the running track, his chest ripped
open.

'Well?'

'A pendant on a leather strap.'

A shiver ran down Anna's spine and she felt the hairs on the backs
of her hands stand up.

'What kind of pendant?'

'One with the image of a man in a feathered cap. Exactly the same
as the one we found in Riikka's pocket.'

Anna crouched beneath the yellow tapes and stepped on to the
running track. She took a deep breath as she approached the man
lying dead on the ground. He was relatively young, not yet thirty,
and was wearing a blue tracksuit. He was lying on his back, his
arms and legs outstretched; he looked like a stickman against the
golden yellow covering of sawdust. In the man's chest, right around
the heart, was a large, bloody hole. His strong, masculine chin was
covered in blood spatter.

Linnea was packing up her equipment and stood up with a groan.

'Judging by the body temp and degree of rigor, I'd say between
seven and nine yesterday evening,' she said, stretching her limbs.
'Christ, your muscles get so stiff at this age.'

Anna looked at the dead man and felt the nausea in her stomach
increasing. She had to turn away. She couldn't deal with this. Not
now. Not today.

'I'll let you know before I do the autopsy. You can come and
document it. This case is clearly linked to Riikka's death. Similar
surroundings, similar victim profile, similar MO, and the boys from
ballistics said the rounds from the rifle will probably be a match too.
Almost certainly the same killer. Pretty shocking,' Linnea nattered
on, but Anna couldn't concentrate. She felt faint.

Anna set off anti-clockwise along the track without saying a
word to Linnea. She had to get away; she'd seen too much. The
woods seemed to be swaying around her. How had she managed to

drink herself into this state? She tried to remember what had happened the previous night and tried to count how many drinks she'd had. At home she'd had only one beer, because she hadn't wanted to tempt Ákos unnecessarily. Then she had gone to the bar where Akim, Zoran and a Bosnian guy Anna had never met were waiting for her. There she'd downed at least another four pints. Full pints. At midnight they'd moved on to a nightclub on Hämeentie, which was pretty full for a Thursday evening. Anna stopped counting at the point when Akim had brought ten whiskies to the table. *Pičku mater*, she thought, and she would have laughed if she hadn't felt so horrendous. The situation had got fairly out of hand, but at least Anna's Serbian had started to come back to her. Her old friends were genuinely excited about her return. And so was Anna – last night, at least. Now she wasn't so sure. She was probably still over the limit. Even the fresh air didn't seem to be making her feel any better. Quite the opposite; it was making matters worse.

Then there was Nataša.

Why the hell hadn't Zoran brought his wife along with him? Why was it that Serb men never went anywhere with their wives?

Zoran.

Just when Anna thought she'd finally got over him.

The running track shimmered in front of her like a river. The clear light of autumn made it shine in a myriad shades of yellow. The air betrayed a hint of the winter chill. Anna listened to the fluttering of the birds in the boughs above, chirps here and there, warning calls. The summer chattering had come to an end. The swallows were leaving. She had seen them perching in flocks on the electricity cables.

On any other day she would have enjoyed the beauty of watching nature prepare for the winter. Now a young man lay dead in front of her, her head was thumping and woozy, the inside of her mouth tasted of cat's piss and her legs could barely carry her. She forced herself to do something. First she walked slowly round the length of the track; it was only a few kilometres long, winding but not too hilly. Her heart was racing as if she'd just run a marathon. After this she began investigating the scrubland around the track. She zigzagged in and out of the trees along the edge of the track without knowing what she was looking for.

At the start of the track, the woods were a tangle of thicket bushes that soon gave way to birch trees covered in lichen. The lingonberries were a deep shade of red. Anna knelt down to pluck one. It was bitter, still needed a few frosty nights to bring out the full flavour. I'll have to come out and pick some, she thought, and picked up a sweet wrapper lying among the berries. It's terrible that people litter the woods. When she raised her eyes, she saw a dark figure about a hundred metres away behind the thicket.

It was Esko. He had hidden himself in the bushes like a hare. Anna pressed herself tightly against the nearest birch tree and watched him pull a hipflask out of his jacket pocket, its silver edges glinting in the sunlight. Esko took a long swig, and again Anna felt a wave of nausea rising from her stomach as she tasted the imaginary kick of alcohol in her mouth. Thankfully she didn't vomit this time. She felt better as soon as Esko put the hipflask back in his jacket. Then he fumbled in his trouser pocket and popped something in his mouth. Chewing gum or a mint, she thought, something to mask the smell. What a drunk – boozing at work!

'Esko!' she shouted.

He gave a start and turned round, instinctively touching his jacket pocket as if to make sure the flask was back where it should be and not still in his hand.

'Find anything?' he shouted back, lit a cigarette and began walking towards her.

'A sweet wrapper. Should I give it to Forensics?'

'Why not? You never know.'

'What about you? What are you looking for?' she asked.

'Nothing in particular. Thought I'd come out here for a piss. Wanna watch?'

'I'm going home and back to sleep.'

'Of course. Some dago lover boy there waiting for you, is there?'

Anna pretended not to hear.

'I wasn't really needed here at all. And I don't feel very well either.'

'I heard – and I can see for myself.'

'At least I sort myself out with ibuprofen,' she said and looked at him fixedly. Esko blew smoke in her face.

19

THE FOLLOWING MORNING Anna was at the station before seven. After returning home the day before, her head about to explode and her body feeling like she had been beaten up, she had resolved to quit smoking and get back into active training. In the last few weeks she'd drunk more beer than was good for her, and she decided to swap her daily can of beer for a cup of rooibos tea. Anna had snapped her remaining cigarettes and put them in the bin, taken another painkiller and gone straight to bed. She had slept almost thirteen hours straight.

In all its brutality the second murder was shocking, but it had brought a new sense of energy to the investigation, which had started to stagnate. Perhaps it would be wrong to say that Anna was excited, but she felt a certain agitated tension as she stepped through the door of the Violent Crimes Unit, the same kind of tingling she felt before a running competition.

As always, Chief Inspector Pentti Virkkunen had arrived well before anybody else and asked Anna into his office.

'How do you explain what happened yesterday?' he quipped from behind his desk.

Anna felt a wave of irritation rising within her. If there was one thing she disliked, it was a snooty boss – and she made it clear in her voice.

'It was my day off. It's been marked in the rota since August. Surely I don't need to be ready to come in on my day off? Or do I?'

She remembered that she was supposed to buy herself some new work clothes, which she realised she'd totally forgotten about. She gave her trousers a quick glance: the same pair of jeans she'd worn two days ago. And the same hoodie. Maybe life would be easier if she stopped comparing herself to the endlessly stylish Sari. Maybe she wasn't cut out for power dressing.

'Of course, we can't demand that you make yourself available, but it's still rather disappointing,' said Virkkunen, and for a moment Anna thought he was talking about her work clothes. 'It would have made a great deal of difference if you'd joined us first thing in the morning. To be perfectly honest, I'm counting on you for the success of this investigation. Anyway, I wasn't referring to your obvious hangover. I want to know what you think about the new case.'

'Oh, I'm sorry,' she laughed, embarrassed. 'Well, I haven't really had time to give it much thought yet. But it doesn't look good. The cases are so similar that we must assume it's the same killer. We didn't pay much attention to the necklace we found on Riikka. Of course, anyone could have pieces of jewellery in their pockets. But now that we've found an identical piece on the second victim, it seems important. It's as though it has some special significance. It's like a message.'

'That's what I thought too. It can't be coincidence that two victims, killed in the same manner, are carrying identical necklaces. That pendant means something – but what? We have to find out. Fast.'

'We'll do our best. But there are very few officers on this case, and especially given that our workload has just doubled.'

'What about Esko?'

'What about him?' she started, taken by surprise.

'How are you getting on? Together?'

'Why do you ask?'

'I was thinking of your first day here. The meeting you didn't attend.'

'Esko didn't tell me about that meeting!' Anna could feel herself losing her temper. She didn't understand the point of continually talking about this. Let bygones be bygones.

'So you're accusing Esko?'

'Accusing him? I'm not accusing anyone. But it wasn't a very nice thing to do.'

'I noticed the two of you don't exactly love one another. But are there any problems between you that might hamper this investigation?'

Anna thought about her reply. She looked at Virkkunen's stern face, a face that seemed so ageless. Now was the chance to tell him what Esko was really like when they were alone, let him know about Esko's racist attitudes. She thought of the altercation when they were outside smoking: lack of confidence in her work, spying on her, indirect communication, direct snide insults. Now she had the opportunity to explain why she didn't want to work with Esko a day longer.

'Nothing in particular,' she said.

Virkkunen stared at her, the beginnings of a smile on his face. Anna had the strange feeling that this was some kind of test.

'Do you think Esko has a drinking problem?' he asked suddenly.

Anna was taken aback. What was this all about?

'I don't know. We don't see each other socially. He does his work well enough.'

'Does he drink at work?'

'Not to my knowledge.'

Anna felt uncomfortable. If Virkkunen knew as much as he seemed to, why didn't he confront Esko directly?

She thought of Esko's breath, which always stank of old booze in the mornings. The sip from the hipflask in the bushes. Still, for all she knew, it could have been fruit juice.

'So everything is okay?'

'Nothing to worry about. Except for the bumpy start, things have been going fine.'

Virkkunen gave Anna a sceptical, inquisitive look.

'We're drawing up the new rota this morning. Can we give you the same shifts as before?'

Anna squirmed in her chair. Virkkunen's voice sounded as though this wasn't a question; it was an order. Anna had a hunch – no, she was certain that if she now asked for the rota to be changed, that she was no longer prepared to work with Esko, she would be taken off the investigation altogether. Two days ago she had been frustrated with the case, but this new turn of events had aroused her interest. She was forced to admit that, more than anything else, she was determined to catch the bastard running around with a shotgun. Regardless of Esko.

'I don't see why not,' she replied and was unsure whether she might live to regret those words. She glanced at the smiling face of a fair-haired woman in a tin frame on the desk. The woman appeared to be warning her of something.

'Excellent, that's what I thought, too. Now we can get started on establishing whether there was any connection between Riikka and this Ville Pollari. Did they know one another?'

Relief at the change of subject wiped away Anna's sense of unease.

'There must be a connection somewhere.'

'We need to warn the public, give a statement. Citizens out on a run need to know that a madman with a shotgun might be lurking in the woods.'

'It's not just citizens that might be out running.'

'Excuse me?'

'There could be asylum seekers, Nokia employees transferred from abroad, an international ice-hockey player. They're not all necessarily Finnish citizens…'

'That wasn't exactly my point…'

'I totally agree. We could ask the public for information, anything people might have seen. The killer has to move around somewhere. Someone might have seen a car, a bike or something.'

'This is getting out of hand. We need more people on this case,' sighed the chief inspector.

'…Then she chucked her guts up when I called for the umpteenth time.' Esko's derisive laughter could be heard behind the open door of the staffroom.

'And what did she look like? Jesus Christ, as if she'd had food poisoning and an electric shock all at once. Seems she'd been up boozing until the early hours. We managed to get her out to the scene for less than an hour – the boys from patrol had to drive her.'

So he's an old gossip too, Anna thought as she walked into the room. An awkward silence descended. Sari greeted her with a faint nod of the head, without looking her in the eyes; Rauno seemed to be concentrating on stirring his coffee.

Anna felt a surge of rage rising up inside her.

'Just so you know, I just passed up the opportunity to tell the governor about your racist opinions. And I didn't tell him about the bullying in the workplace, the drinking on duty, though he seemed very keen to know all about it. I didn't breathe a word about all the mornings I've seen you drag yourself in shaking and stinking of not-so-old liquor, and I especially didn't tell him about what I saw yesterday. I just pretended I had no idea what he was talking about.'

The silence deepened. The pipes behind the sink gurgled and footsteps could be heard out in the corridor. The entire police station was waiting, holding its breath.

'Well, at least I'm always on time,' Esko responded with a smirk that didn't quite reach his eyes.

Anna poured herself some coffee without saying anything. She repressed the desire to throw the cup at the wall.

'Come on, Esko, it was her day off,' Sari tried to smooth things over, but fell silent as Anna glared at her. We don't owe that old wanker an explanation, her eyes seemed to say.

The painful silence would not abate. Rauno twiddled a spoon in the sugar bowl; Sari seemed suddenly absorbed in yesterday's headlines on the front page of the newspaper lying on the coffee table. Esko glowered at Anna arrogantly, almost challenging her to a fight. Anna counted to ten, then calmly sipped her coffee.

I refuse to let this jerk provoke me ever again, she resolved. I will not give him the satisfaction.

'Perhaps we should all focus on this case,' she finally said after a moment's pause, eyeing everyone in the room. Sari and Rauno nodded, relieved; Esko looked impassive. Perhaps he was even a bit disappointed, Anna noted to her own satisfaction. He'd been expecting her to lose her temper, to slam the door behind her and disappear into her office in tears.

'As of yesterday, our workload has increased quite substantially,' she continued without waiting for comment. 'And I'm ready to get stuck in. Having a day off can really give you a boost. So – we have two, almost identical murders. What does this tell us?'

The people in the room looked at one another – all except Esko, who had started reading yesterday's paper.

'Somebody with a grudge against joggers,' Rauno suggested.

'A hunter with a grudge against joggers,' said Sari.

'I don't really buy this hunter hypothesis,' said Rauno. 'I've called everyone on the hunting association members list, and none of them seemed remotely suspicious. Of course, you never know…'

'There are plenty of non-hunters with access to hunting rifles,' said Anna. 'Just think how many family members and close friends each of those hunters has. At last in theory, almost everyone in the country probably has contact with firearms, right?'

'As for guns per capita, Finland is pretty near the top of the list,' Rauno admitted. 'But guns are kept behind lock and key, or at least they should be.'

'I'm sure family members know where the keys are,' said Anna.

'Sure. But in my own experience, people involved in hunting teach their kids about gun safety from an early age. These people know what firearms are capable of. They respect guns, they're careful. I think it's unlikely that your average hunter would be running amok with a shotgun. It's more likely to be some computer nerd, someone a bit detached from reality.'

'Well, it's a sick person we're looking for, that much is clear,' said Anna. 'A hunter could suddenly snap and lose his mind.'

'Yes, but I strongly doubt it,' Rauno replied with a smirk.

'It's a wild woodsman,' said Sari. 'But hey, do these victims have anything in common apart from their interest in running?'

'Nothing obvious. This time the victim was a man,' said Esko, and on a whim Anna gave him a friendly smile.

He was taking part in the conversation, despite their altercation. He pretended not to notice her smile.

'And older than Riikka. This Ville is, was, twenty-eight, married with a steady job. Baby on the way, too,' said Rauno.

'Riikka was an occasional jogger trying to lose a few kilos. Ville regularly took part in local orienteering competitions, probably went running every day,' said Esko.

How did he know that, Anna wondered.

'Both were killed near the shore. One to the south of the city, one to the north,' she said.

'It must be the same killer,' said Rauno. 'The same round of ammunition and the same pendant in their pockets. It's the same man.'

'Or woman,' said Sari.

'The pendant is interesting,' said Anna. 'Can anyone tell us more about it?'

'I examined it quite thoroughly yesterday, and it looks like junk, the kind of stuff made in China and sold to tourists halfway across the world. The black disc with the image of the old man is actually plastic and the strap is made of fake leather,' said Rauno.

'Why didn't we take it seriously when we found one in Riikka's pocket?' Anna asked.

'For crying out loud,' Esko snapped. 'It would have been odd if we had reacted to it. There's nothing suspicious about an individual piece of jewellery. Now that there are two of them, things are different – it's clear that they mean something. Either the shooter placed the pendant in their pockets or both victims belong to a … cult or something.'

'We should show it to Riikka's friends and parents,' said Sari.

'I think this is the kind of information we should keep to ourselves,' Esko commented. 'Rauno, try and find out everything you can about it: where it's manufactured, where it's sold and what the image means. Let's think carefully about what information we give to the public. There could be a perfectly reasonable explanation for it, a special offer for anyone buying a tracksuit, something like that.'

'Quite a strange special offer – and coincidentally found on both victims? No way,' said Rauno with a shake of the head. 'But I'll look into it.'

'Do you think we have a serial killer on our hands?' Sari finally put into words what nobody had dared to say.

Again, the staffroom fell silent.

'There hasn't been a third murder yet – to our knowledge, that is,' said Anna. 'According to the FBI, three is the magic number.'

'A serial killer sounds like something from American trash fiction, but you've got to admit there's something pretty sick about these cases. This isn't just drunks beating each other to death,' said Sari.

'Definitely not,' Rauno agreed.

'We've got to find this nutcase,' said Sari. 'Before we *do* find a third body.'

'We have to find a connection between them. There must be something linking these two people,' said Esko firmly.

'I agree,' Anna conferred. 'And when we find the connection, we'll find who did this. We'll have to interview everyone again. Riikka's friends and parents. Jere. Ville's wife, colleagues, neighbours, orienteering friends, hunters and anyone living near the two running tracks. Thankfully Virkkunen is assigning more officers to this case.'

'Really?' Rauno sounded relieved.

'Well, he mentioned it at least. And we're going to ask anyone who might have seen or noticed something to come forward. There's going to be a press conference this afternoon.'

'And who's going to go through all the extra information?' Esko muttered.

'What if Ville was Riikka's new mystery man?' Sari suggested.

'Yes,' Anna cried. 'That's a thought. Of course, Linnea will take DNA samples from the body; we'll be able to cross-reference them with the sperm found on Riikka. If it's a match, that would explain a lot. It might even provide a motive.'

'For Ville's wife, sure,' said Esko.

Virkkunen stepped into the room and poured himself a coffee.

'Anna and Esko: I want you to go to Asemakylä. You'll have to talk to the second victim's wife.'

20

OUTSIDE IT WAS GREY AGAIN. Where had the bright skies of the day before gone? Anna stared at the landscape flashing past, her forehead pressed against the passenger window as Esko drove them north. She noticed that the leaves had turned yellow. When had that happened? Why did time go so quickly?

Taking someone bad news yet again, like an officious vulture, she thought. And again I have to take care of things with that nasty man who isn't going to speak to me throughout the entire journey. At least he deigned to take me in his car this time; I suppose this is progress. Maybe she should tell Virkkunen that things were going well, far better than expected – Esko even allowed her in his car.

Out of the corner of her eye she saw that Esko was looking at her.

She needed a cigarette.

The victim's wife, Maria Jääskö-Pollari, had only been a wife for about a year. She had married a successful man – the man of her dreams, she said. And now she was expecting their first child. A dead man's child, a child that would never know its father.

Anna looked at the woman's face, swollen and expressionless with weeping, and the bulging stomach beneath her black tunic. The two things didn't belong together; they shouldn't be in the same body.

The child would never see its father, yet it would carry a gnawing sense of grief at the back of its mind for the rest of its life, every bit as much as the genes it inherited from its father. We inherit so much, Anna thought, and there's nothing we can do about it.

A familiar sense of melancholy hung around her shoulders, whispering dark prose into her ears. The enthusiasm she'd felt that morning had been erased in a single swipe.

Maria was an economist and had worked as a local councillor in Simonkoski. She had become pregnant just as the transitional period before the merging of two local constituencies was coming to an end, after which Simonkoski would no longer exist as an entity in its own right. Now she was on sick leave with back pain caused by loose joints. She found it all but impossible to sit in the same position for extended periods. She could still walk short journeys as long as she was able to lie down afterwards. She was due to start maternity leave in a month's time, and then she would probably be off work for a year. By the time the child turned three, she would no longer have a job to go back to. It seemed that the only people to survive the cull as the city swallowed up the neighbouring constituencies would be the council bosses.

'But none of that matters any more,' said Maria with a note of bitterness.

Ville Pollari had driven to work at seven in the morning, as he did every day. He was a software engineer at Nokia. Maria had been at home all day, except for a quick trip to the local shop at around ten o'clock. During the day she had done the laundry but hadn't been able to hang it out to dry; bending down to lift the wet laundry from the machine hurt her back too much. She had planned to ask Ville to help her when he came home from work. He helped a lot around the house: emptied the dishwasher, wiped the cupboard doors – all without her having to ask.

That afternoon Maria had cooked some food. She always tried to do this, so that there was food ready when Ville got back from work, though standing in the kitchen was almost as painful as sitting down.

Ville had returned home after five o'clock. They had eaten, Ville had hung out the washing and promised to buy a tumble dryer after pay day. Then he had slumped on the sofa and slept for half an hour. From six till seven he had watched the sports channel and Maria had slouched on the sofa with him, while her husband had massaged the sore areas at the base of her spine. Just before seven o'clock,

Ville's training partner Jussi Järvinen had called him to say that their daughter had a fever and his wife was working that evening.

Ville went running alone.

'Did he often go running with a friend?' asked Anna.

'Ville always did his orienteering training with a friend, usually Jussi, who was a member of the same club. Ville normally went jogging by himself, though Jussi sometimes joined him on his runs, too,' Maria explained.

In her notebook Anna wrote: Jussi Järvinen, daughter with fever.

Ville had left the house at around 7.20 p.m. Maria had lain in bed, signed into her Facebook account with the laptop propped on her stomach. She had spent half an hour chatting with her sister, who lived in Paris. Then her mother had called and they had spoken about all manner of things, including where to find a good deal on a tumble dryer. At around 8.30 p.m. she had switched off the computer and got up to heat the sauna. By 9 p.m. she had already begun glancing at the clock with a note of irritation and called her husband's mobile phone; she heard it ringing in the hallway. At 9.15 p.m. she had telephoned Jussi, who hadn't answered the phone.

Maria had waited another quarter of an hour before calling the police. The duty office had suggested she calm down and wait until morning, saying that there was no point organising a search party at this stage, that things like this happened surprisingly often and that men came home sooner or later with their tail between their legs.

'That officer laughed at me,' she said, devastated. 'Can you imagine? He laughed it off! I shouted at him that Ville wasn't like that, he wasn't that kind of man!'

Maria started to weep. She hid her face in her hands, the sound of stifled sobs emanating from between her fingers. After a moment, she boldly raised her head and glared at Anna and Esko, a look of accusation in her reddened eyes.

'If the police had acted as soon as I called, you might have caught the person who did this. You let that madman get away.'

Anna and Esko held their tongues.

'May I look at your Facebook account?' Anna asked Maria.

'Can I refuse?'

'At this stage, yes, but as the investigation goes on, probably not.'

'Be my guest, read whatever you please,' she snapped and fetched her laptop, catching her breath.

Anna and Esko scrolled through Maria's account. Her small number of friends didn't include anyone from Saloinen. The conversation with her sister had been saved in her chat history at exactly the time she had said. Maria had complained about her back pains and talked of the pain of waiting for things: waiting for dinner to cook, waiting for her husband to come home from work or a run, waiting for there to be something good on TV. And on top of that, waiting to give birth. Her sister had complained about the continual protest marches blocking the streets of Paris.

Nothing suspicious, nothing even remotely violent.

But who would write something like that on Facebook? Lives portrayed on people's walls were more idyllic than those in women's magazines.

What's on your mind, Facebook relentlessly asks. I'm sick of my husband; I think I'll shoot him.

Anna sniffed.

It was clear that Maria didn't know Riikka. She took a long look at Riikka's graduation photograph and shook her head.

'No, I've never seen this girl,' she said, her voice steady and firm.

Neither did she think it was feasible that her husband was having an affair with her or anyone else. Ville wasn't like that, she reiterated. Ville was a good man. He would never have done anything like that. They loved one another, enjoyed each other's company. They were happy.

Maria stroked her stomach and looked through the kitchen window out into the garden where the lawn was still green and healthy, just as it had been all summer.

Anna wanted to believe her. She wanted to believe that there were no infections, no boils lurking in this household and that the child soon to be born would be able to live in an environment that strengthened the beloved memory of its father.

But from experience she knew that people's histories often revealed enormous, all-encompassing lies, all kinds of skeletons. The sense of anxiety tightened its grip on her. It disturbed her concentration, ripped her thoughts from the present moment, from the case at hand, and pulled them towards the ghosts of her own past. Anna gave her head a shake. Focus on the here and now.

'Where was Ville on the evening of 21 August? Do you remember?' Anna asked.

'What day of the week was that?'

'Sunday.'

'Ville always goes for a run on Sunday evenings.'

'Where?'

'Around Häyrysenniemi.'

'What about Selkämaa?'

'Where's that?'

Anna explained that this was where they had found Riikka's body. Maria shook her head. Why would Ville have travelled so far to go running when there was a track much closer? His work forced him to sit behind the wheel of his car quite enough as it was.

'Where were you that evening?' Esko eventually asked.

'Here,' she responded calmly. 'Where else would I be?' She glared at Anna with a look of near contempt in her eyes. It burned. Why is she staring at me? Anna wanted to turn away. She stood up and said she'd like to visit the bathroom. Maria said it was in the hallway. Anna locked the door and stood in front of the mirror. A strange, unfamiliar face stared back at her.

I'm not in control of this, said the mouth in the mirror.

I don't belong here.

As they were driving back into town, Anna asked Esko for a cigarette, trying to test the ice. To her surprise, Esko pulled over at a bus stop and handed her a cigarette. They stepped out of the car and smoked in silence, watching the passing traffic. The tobacco tasted good.

*

That evening Virkkunen was on the news. He appeared on the television in a special bulletin at 7 p.m. He was on the ten o'clock news.
He was on the radio. Tomorrow things would really take off when
the latest developments hit the papers, headlines screaming from the
windows of every shop and kiosk. Anna could almost hear the city
and tranquil countryside around it simmering and drawing breath
in a collective display of fear, as though a bomb had exploded.

She was listening to the radio in a patrol car parked outside
Bihar's house. Virkkunen's matter-of-fact voice went through the
main events relating to the jogging murders as reporters tried to
dig for more details. 'For technical reasons, I can't answer that,' she
heard him reply on more than one occasion.

It was late. The lights were on in the Chelkins' apartment. Every
now and then a shadowy figure appeared at the window. Anna got
the impression that she was being watched, too.

'The police would like to ask members of the public for anything
they might have seen or heard in the area around the Selkämaa
running track on 21 August and the Häyrysenniemi track on 14
September. Any observations could be useful to our investigation,'
Virkkunen continued on the radio.

'How does the killer move from place to place?' a reporter asked.

'That's what we're trying to establish.'

'Should we expect more murders?'

'A ruthless killer is on the loose,' Virkkunen said plainly. 'Until we
establish how he selects his victims, we ask everyone to avoid these
running tracks, especially in the evenings.'

'Is it still safe to go for an afternoon walk?'

There came a rap at the window. Anna gave a start.

'Let me repeat: moving around in the dark, especially near the
shore and along these running tracks, is to be avoided,' said the voice.
Anna switched off the radio and rolled down the window. It was
Payedar Chelkin. He glared at Anna with a menacing glint in his eyes.

'Leave us alone!' he threatened her.

'Remember that you're speaking to a police officer,' she replied and gripped the steering wheel.

'Don't police have better to do?'

'What do you mean?'

'Now you have better to do! You go investigate murders. Go away!'

'The police will do exactly what is required of them.'

'Leave my daughter!'

'You leave her alone, then I can do the same.'

'I not do anything wrong! You go find running killer. You have better to think about.'

'You seem to know a lot about these murders.'

'I see it on news. News full of it.'

'How convenient.'

'What you say?'

'How convenient that we're working on a big murder case; you think we won't have time to investigate you.'

'Police have more important things than my family.'

'There is nothing more important to me than your family,' said Anna; she started the engine and sped away. Bihar's father remained standing on the pavement shaking his fists. In the rear-view mirror, Anna could see him shouting something at her. A chilling thought ran through her mind.

Could Payedar Chelkin be so crazed?

Just then she received another text message.

Anna slowed down and pulled in at a bus stop. The screen on her phone showed an icon the shape of an envelope. Without even looking, she knew where it had come from. Or rather, she didn't know at all.

I wanna fuck u, bitch!

The number from which the message had been sent was different. Of course, this was standard fare for professional criminals: change your number and service provider regularly enough to make tracing the messages impossible. But this message I'm not deleting, Anna resolved.

21

HELENA LAAKSO lived in the village of Saloinen in a small detached house behind the local shop, the bank and a pub, and located about a kilometre from Riikka's house. She was a small, nervous-looking woman, who had read the news in the paper and called the police helpline to explain that she had been out walking her dog on the evening of 21 August and had seen a car driving towards the running track at Selkämaa.

Helena Laakso greeted Anna and Sari, showed them into the living room and gestured for them to sit down in soft, velour-covered armchairs. Pots of tea and coffee had been set on the coffee table along with freshly made scones and small cakes. Mrs Laakso brought in a jug of cream and small spoons, placed them carefully on the tray, agitatedly swiped at a grey hair that had escaped from her loosely tied bun and was hanging across her face. Anna noticed that the woman's hands were trembling with anxiety.

Anna began to wonder whether the sighting of the car was nothing but a lonely old woman's way of getting someone to visit her, of feeling needed and important, if only for a moment, for someone. Sari seemed to be thinking something similar, as she glanced at Anna with a sceptical look in her eyes. Let's see what this is all about, Sari whispered when the lady went into the kitchen to fetch the sugar bowl. Anna looked at the knick-knacks and photographs on the bookshelves: confirmation and graduation photographs, newly married couples and little children, grandchildren presumably. A dog. And where was the dog? Only now did Anna notice that there was no mutt scampering around between their legs, and they hadn't heard a single bark all the time they'd been here.

'So, you were out walking your dog on the evening of 21 August,' Anna began as Mrs Laakso brought the sugar bowl to the table. The lady's restless eyes looked at the tray to make sure that she had brought everything they needed.

'I walk my dog every day,' she replied firmly, dispelling the officers' slightly scatty, uncertain first impression. Her low, powerful voice would have been better suited to another body, one younger and less fragile.

'And where is the dog now?' Sari asked and sipped her coffee.

The woman stopped and looked at Sari with an air of concern.

'Excellent coffee,' Sari added hastily.

It was true. The coffee was strong and black. Caffeine bit urgently into her palette.

Mrs Laakso visibly relaxed and sat down on the sofa.

'Oh good,' she said with satisfaction. 'They told me in the shop that the machine was idiot-proof, but you never know. I've only used it a few times. I bought it yesterday.'

'You have a new coffee maker?' Anna asked.

'Yes, it's one of these new-fangled things that George Clooney advertises on the television. Terribly expensive, but the coffee is simply marvellous. Please, take some milk if it's too strong. I only have strong coffee at the moment. I'll have to order a milder blend and some decaffeinated stuff next time I'm online.'

Helena Laakso smiled at the success of her coffee and no longer seemed remotely unsure of herself. So much for first impressions, thought Anna.

'Ah yes, the dog,' said Mrs Laakso and gave an energetic whistle. There was a scraping of claws against the wooden floor in the kitchen and an enormous bull mastiff came plodding into the living room. It lay down at its owner's feet and didn't pay the guests the slightest attention.

'I've taught him to stay in the kitchen until I call him whenever we have guests. I've always been annoyed at dogs that run into the hallway jumping and yelping. After all, you are my guests.'

The small woman scratched her gigantic dog behind the ears. The dog closed his eyes with an air of calm. With a dog like that nobody would be afraid to live alone or walk alone in the woods.

'You wanted to ask me about the car,' the woman said eventually.

'Yes, that's right. Could you tell us more specifically about that evening? What time did you leave the house and what route did you take?'

'I remember that evening very well indeed, though it was a while ago now. I'd spent three days on a grouse-cooking course with the pensioners' association in the home-economics class at the high school and hadn't had much time to take Mörkö for his walk. Of course, I'd taken him out for a wee and for a short spin round the shops. Once the course is over, I'll take him for a good long walk, I thought. It was a Sunday evening. We left here around seven o'clock. From here it's about five kilometres to the shore. We were there around eight.'

'So you didn't walk along the running track?'

'No. I prefer to walk along the shore, because I can let him off the leash.'

'Was there much traffic along Selkämaantie?'

'No. There never is. The only thing I saw was this red car that passed us outside old Raappana's house. It remember it, because it sped past and threw up a stone that hit me on the thigh.'

'Was it driving fast?'

'I rather think it was.'

'Do you think it was heading towards the running track?'

'It must have gone there, because I didn't see it at the shore.'

'Can you describe the car in any more detail? What make was it?' asked Sari.

'I'm afraid I couldn't tell you. I've never understood cars. My late husband would have known. It was just an average car. Red. Not especially big but not small either.'

'Did you see the driver?'

'No.'

'Not even a glance?'

'I'm afraid not.'

'If we showed you some photographs of mid-size red cars, do you think you would recognise the make?'

'We could try, but I don't think so. They all rather look the same to me.'

'So, the car passed you at around 7.30 p.m. When did you start walking back to the house?'

'We didn't stay there all that long, because there were men out hunting in the reeds. I threw the dog a stick near the end of the path for a while and then we walked back. It was before half past eight. We walked rather more briskly on the way back; we were home in an hour.'

'How did you know that there were hunters by the shore?'

'I saw them.'

'Where exactly?'

'They arrived by car. Two men in camouflage outfits with rifles over their shoulders.'

'What kind of car were they driving?'

'A large black station wagon. The men looked quite young, but they were most pleasant, said hello, and one of them stroked Mörkö, asked what breed he is. Nice young men, but they seemed to be in quite a hurry, said they had to be in position before the birds flew overhead.'

'So, in fact, you saw two cars.'

'Yes, that's right. But those young men were just out hunting,' said Helena Laakso.

'One of those cars belongs to the killer,' said Anna as they drove back towards the city. Sari was behind the wheel.

'The killer drove to the track by car and waited for Riikka. I'll bet it was the red one. The killer knew she'd be jogging out there.'

'And there was no blue Laguna.'

'Right. If it was Virve, she certainly wasn't driving Jere's car.'

'We've already spoken to a couple of guys that were out there hunting. Could they be the same men Mrs Laakso was talking about?'

'I reckon they're probably the same guys, but we should check it out. I'll call Rauno.'

'Good. I'll get Virkkunen to tell one of the assistants to look for images of all potential red, average-sized cars so that Mrs Laakso can try and identify the vehicle.'

'It's probably a waste of time. Most women don't pay attention to cars.'

'I doubt most men pay attention to cars either, but we've got to try. If we could narrow it down to a few possible makes, even that would be something.'

'Riikka receives a call from an unlisted number at 6.30 p.m. Soon afterwards she goes out for a run. Did someone invite her out there?'

Anna's stomach tightened as she thought of the messages she too had received. Should she tell Sari about them? But then she would also have to tell her about the one-night stand with Petri Ketola – and she didn't want to do that.

'It's possible. And if she did, that invitation was almost certainly from the murderer,' said Anna.

'What about the other call earlier in the day? That was from an unlisted number, too.'

'Probably the same person. First asked her out for lunch, then for a run.'

'So Riikka knew her killer.'

'Certainly seems that way.'

'Tracing an unlisted number is very difficult,' Anna said almost to herself.

'I know. People like this change operators and prepaid phones like socks.'

Anna sighed. Perhaps it would make sense to talk to Sari, after all. Instead, she said: 'I've been round nearly all the restaurants in town, and almost all of them serve salmon and pine nuts. And nobody remembers seeing Riikka.'

'They didn't necessarily eat at a restaurant.'

'Right.'

'Why does this all feel so difficult? It's as though we're looking in completely the wrong direction,' Sari sighed.

'I know, orbiting the wrong planet, more like.'

Jussi Järvinen had been invited to the station for an interview. The telephone call had come just as he had arrived home from work and his wife was massaging his shoulders. Thankfully Jussi had a habit of taking work calls behind closed doors in the utility room. His wife didn't wonder why he withdrew there. Though this was no work call.

At the main door, Jussi asked his way to the Violent Crimes Unit. The girl at reception made a call and asked Jussi to wait. Pretty good-looking, he thought, and eyed the girl just a bit too long, making her blush. Soon a large, dishevelled man appeared from the lift, mumbled a hello and took Jussi up to the unit. He had decided not to reveal anything. His private life was irrelevant in this shocking situation. It had nothing to do with Ville's murder. It couldn't. Jussi told himself to calm down.

'Hello,' the man said again once they arrived at the room that must have been his office. 'Esko Niemi.'

The man reached out a rough paw to shake Jussi's hand.

'Hello there,' said Jussi, trying to shake the man's hand firmly and give a good, honest impression of himself.

'Please, take a seat.'

'Thank you.'

'So, Jussi Järvinen. You are Ville Pollari's friend and training partner.'

'Yes, that's right. Please, just call me Jussi.'

'How long have you known Ville?'

'About five years, not all that long. My wife and I moved to Simonkoski near Asemakylä village about five years ago and I joined

the local orienteering club. That's where we met. The Pollari couple
had just moved to the area too, and we started training together.'

'Did you see each other socially?'

'A bit. The four of us would sometimes spend the evening together. Not all that often.'

'When did you last spend an evening like this?'

'I think it was at the beginning of the summer. Yes, a week before
Midsummer, decided to crack open the barbecue season together.
We were at our place.'

'Did anything out of the ordinary happen? Anything you might
remember?'

'No. Everything went just as we'd planned.'

'What does that mean?'

'The food was good and there was plenty of it. The wives chatted
by themselves, and Jussi and I had a few beers. That was it. All in all,
a very nice evening.'

'Did Ville say anything that stuck in your mind? Something that
might be related to our investigation?'

'At the party?'

'There or somewhere else. Did he seem afraid of something? Did
he think anyone was following him or mention anything out of the
ordinary?'

Good, they're only interested in Ville. This is going well. At least I
don't have to lie about anything, thought Jussi, relieved.

'I certainly didn't notice anything. Or then again ... maybe there
was something, now that you mention it.'

'What was that?'

'Later in the summer we went on a long run round Häyrysenniemi and there was a car parked by the track. Ville noticed it, said
he'd seen it there once before, but that he'd never seen anyone else
out running.'

'What kind of car?'

'I didn't look at it all that closely. A fairly old car. Red. I didn't think
there was anything strange about it. At least, at the time I didn't.'

'What time of day was this run? The day Ville mentioned the car?'

'Quite late, nine or ten in the evening. We usually ran quite late. Because of work.'

'The sighting of this car is significant. It could well be linked to these two murders. Try to remember what kind of car it was. Any details you can think of.'

Jussi strained to remember. He tried to think of the last run he and Ville had taken together. It was at the beginning of July, soon after the start of his summer holiday. It was a hot day. That's why they'd set out much later than usual. They had taken Ville's car to Häyrysenniemi; Ville had picked him up on the way. That was their usual arrangement. They pulled up in the parking area, and they had barely switched off the engine when Ville mentioned the car.

'Who else is out here at this hour? That car was parked there the last time I was here, and the time before. I've never seen anyone else out running though,' Ville had said.

Jussi was taken aback at how clearly he remembered Ville's words, words he hadn't paid the least attention to at the time.

But he couldn't remember anything specific about the car.

'Have you seen that red car since?'

Jussi thought hard.

'Not that I can remember.'

'Did Ville visit Häyrysenniemi often?' asked the policeman.

'Three times a week.'

'What day of the week was it when you saw the car?'

'Let me think. My summer holiday started on the fourth of July, which was a Monday, so it was the Friday before that. You know how your holiday always starts on a weekday, but they count the previous weekend too. Yes, it was the first day of July, a Friday evening.'

Esko Niemi made a note of the date.

'Tell me what kind of man Ville was. How did you view him?'

Jussi was so relieved that he could have wept with joy. The policeman was only interested in Ville. It was only natural that they needed to know about him, to build up a profile of the victim. He'd been worried for nothing. What a jerk he was, he thought, only worried about saving his own skin, when his friend had been shot and killed. He would organise a whip-round at the orienteering club and among their circle of friends. His CEO friends were an affluent bunch. They would dig deep to help out Ville's widow and baby.

'Calm. Nice. Quiet, maybe. A real family man. In great shape,' said Jussi. 'Much fitter than me. He was good at motivating people in the team.'

'Did he have another woman on the side?'

'Absolutely not. I mean, I don't think so. I doubt he would have told me if he had, though I just can't imagine Ville doing anything like that. He's so decent. He was.'

'Who would he have told if there had been another woman?'

'I don't know. I don't know any of his close friends. But Ville was head over heels in love with Maria. Baby on the way and everything.'

'Did either you or Ville ever go running around Saloinen?'

'I've never been there, and as far as I know Ville hasn't either. I would probably have known if he had; orienteering was what we talked about the most.'

'Do you own any firearms?'

'Sure, I'm a member of the Asemakylä hunting association.'

'What kind?'

'A couple of shotguns. I've been planning on getting a rifle too so I can go elk-hunting next season.'

'What kind of shotguns?'

'A Mosberg 12/76 and a Sako semi-automatic 16/70. Normal stuff.'

'When did you last fire the Mosberg?'

Jussi stared at the policeman in disbelief. What was he talking about? Surely they didn't think he would have taken out his good friend. He could feel his pulse racing.

'I was out hunting on the first day of the season. I took a few shots but didn't catch anything. I haven't been out since then.'

'What about Ville?'

'He didn't hunt.'

The policeman looked at Jussi from beneath his swollen eyelids. Jussi felt ill at ease. It was as if the copper knew something, could see right through him.

'How often did you and Ville train together?'

'Maybe once a week. Less frequently during the summer. We normally went running through the woods. Sometimes we would go along the running track, but like I said, Ville went there a lot by himself. That's why he was in better shape.'

'When did you fix a time for this run?'

'It's been in my diary for a while now. There's a competition in Sorvala next week, so I thought I'd get in a bit of extra training.'

'Why did you cancel?'

Damn it. They had to ask, of course. What was I thinking?

'Our kid fell ill and my wife was at work. And you can't leave a one-year-old at home by herself,' said Jussi with a chuckle.

'Your wife said she had taken the child with her on a trip.'

The words knocked the air from Jussi's lungs. This can't be happening. Have they called Tiina already? What should I say now? No, I mustn't say a thing.

'Is she getting the days mixed up? They were out of town the day before,' he replied, trying to sound convincing.

'We can check that straight away. Let's give your wife another call, shall we?' the policeman boomed.

'No, there's no need,' Jussi panicked. 'I can explain.'

'Let's hear it.'

'I was at home with another woman. She's my lover. Does Tiina know what I said? About her and the baby? What have you told her?'

'Calm down. We'll need this woman's contact details.'

'I can't give them to you.'

'Why not?'

'I just can't. She has nothing to do with this. Let's not involve her.'

'I'm afraid she has everything to do with it; she can provide you with an alibi for the time of the murder.'

'I didn't shoot Ville!'

'Who can prove that?'

Jussi said nothing. He was in deeper trouble than he'd thought.

He didn't know exactly where the hookers had come from, but there had been two of them at his house, organised for him by a stocky, hairy Russian guy. And they were young too, so this was illegal in more ways than one. What had he got himself messed up with? Did Ville have to get himself killed on that night of all nights?

'You'll just have to believe me,' Jussi cried.

'I'm afraid that's not the way it works. I want that woman's name, or I'll have you taken into custody right away.'

'They called her Ivana. I don't know whether that's her real name.'

'I see, that kind of lover. And where did you meet this Ivana?'

'On an online dating service.'

This was almost true. Jussi had found his first prostitute through an ad in the lonely-hearts' column. That had happened years ago and in a different city altogether. For a long time he had restricted his dalliances to business trips; he didn't want to dirty his own nest, so to speak. But he'd started to get greedy. Tiina was never in the mood. After the baby was born, their sex life had dried up altogether. But he didn't want a divorce; they didn't have any form of prenuptial agreement. The previous winter he had ended up meeting the ringleaders of an organised racket in town. It had been one of those boozy nights out with the company bosses; the evening had started with gushing bottles of champagne and he had ended up in a dodgy bikers' club with his tie askew, his flies open, a can of beer in his hand and a memory blackout. Finding the Russian guy had been easy. He'd promised to make Jussi's dreams of having two at once come true – and relatively cheaply too.

'We need contact details for that woman – or her pimp; it doesn't matter,' said Esko.

Jussi thought about this for a moment. He had two options. Either way he was screwed, that much was certain, but was it better to be charged with buying sex, possibly from a minor, possibly a victim of human trafficking – or with murder?

Ultimately it was a simple choice.

'I don't know the guy's name, but I've got his phone number. He got me the girls.'

'Girls?'

'Yes. There were two.'

'And do they have anything to do with an online dating service?'

'Not really.'

Esko stared at Jussi, who was trying to retain his dignity.

'I see. Wait here for a moment, please.'

Esko picked up the telephone and muttered something. Three painful, endless minutes passed. There came a knock at the door and a plain-clothed officer in his forties stepped inside.

'Hello. My name's DI Kimmo Haahtela. I'm with a different unit; we deal with international crime rackets. You'll be coming with me. Let's continue this conversation in my office.'

Jussi stood up and stared at the floor, humiliated.

'What about Tiina? Will she find out?'

'I'm sure it'll all become clear in the very near future,' said Esko with an air of satisfaction.

Hot bitch! Nice ass. Fuck u hore!

The message had arrived halfway through her shift, and Sari hadn't paid it any attention at the time. Now she was standing in her night-gown in the darkened bedroom looking out of the window, holding her phone. Teemu was away on business again; this time he would be away for three days in a row. What should I do now? There were only two messages, and it had been a while since the first one. He didn't seem very keen for a stalker, and the messages were short. His English wasn't up to much either. But why had she started to receive them after Riikka's murder? Could it really be simply a coincidence?

Sari looked out at the small solar-cell lights lining the garden from the gates to the front door. They were nothing but decoration, like glow worms shining in the dark. They weren't nearly strong enough to light the garden properly. Anyone could be standing out there, lurking, plotting – and I wouldn't see them. The neighbours wouldn't see anything either. What's that car parked over by the street? Is it red? Sari tried to look more carefully, but the darkness blurred the colour and contours of the vehicle. Nobody's going to stalk me, she snapped as she pulled on her shoes and jacket over her nightgown, got her phone ready to call the emergency services, stepped out of the front door and marched up to the car parked on the street.

It was black. Empty. Sari recognised it: the neighbours' eldest son was visiting again. How embarrassing.

Am I really going to let two prank text messages get the better of me? Any teenage idiot could be behind them. What am I thinking?

Sari went back to the house and locked the door carefully behind her. She fetched a spare mattress from the closet and made herself a bed on the floor in the children's room. There she lay and listened to the sound of their calm breathing in the room that smelled of children. If I get one more message, then it's time to act, she decided.

22

THE FORENSIC REPORT from the scene of Ville Pollari's murder was almost as frustrating as the one in the case of Riikka Rautio – but not quite. There was no trace of the killer on Ville's clothes or skin, and they found nothing in the immediate vicinity either. There were no prints or traces of saliva on the sweet wrapper. The pendant in his pocket had been duly wiped clean. But this time the team had been able to isolate three sets of tyre marks in addition to those made by Ville's car. They now had a tyre impression that could belong to the killer's car. At least that was something.

The car is important, thought Anna. So far it was the best lead they had. She called Nils Näkkäläjärvi, who had been assigned to the case from another unit and told to collect images of car models that might fit the description they had been given. The portfolio was now ready, but there were hundreds of pictures and they all looked very similar. Nils wasn't at all optimistic, but said he was ready to show them to witnesses. He planned to start with Jussi Järvinen, whose alibi for the evening of the murder had been confirmed but who had now been arrested for a raft of other charges, and then visit Helena Laakso. After that he planned to visit the houses in the areas around both running tracks.

'I might as well go round both villages and ask about the car,' he said.

'That car is crucial,' said Anna. 'If we can just establish what make it is, we might have a chance of finding it – especially now that we've got the tyre tracks.'

'Let's hope for the best,' replied Nils.

There's nothing in his accent to suggest he's from Lapland, thought Anna. There's nothing in mine either, but our names give us away.

As a rule, minorities weren't oppressed in the former Yugoslavia – except for the Roma, a sin of which the whole world is guilty. At least in theory, all minority groups belonged to the same extended southern Slavic family, though not all of them were Slavs. Anna's hometown of Vojvodina, or Vajdaság in Hungarian, was proudly considered one of the most culturally diverse regions in Europe. The area was home to at least 17 different nationalities; most were Serbs, though there were lots of Hungarians, too.

You could sense something in the air. In all official documentation, names were transcribed to fit the standards of the national language. In passports Sándor became Aleksander, Hungarian surnames Kovács became Kovač, Nagy became Naď, József became Josip and so on and so forth. At the time it had only caused minor inconvenience – some people found it slightly amusing – but afterwards Anna had started thinking about the deeper implications of such a practice. Names really matter. Names tell us where someone is from, sometimes even which village they come from. They tell us what language someone speaks. Our name is part of our identity; it is the clearest external manifestation of who we are. It is a unique, personal expression of who I am.

Is this why the authorities changed people's names? To weaken the influence of the Hungarian identity? To ensure that official records showed the country to be more unified, more Slavic? Anna felt the urge to telephone Réka, to talk things over, to ask what things were like today now that they belonged to Serbia.

Belonged to Serbia, Anna repeated to herself, tasting the meaning of those words. That they belonged to Finland, Sweden, Norway, she thought, and looked up at Nils.

'I'll give you a call when I'm ready,' he said.

'What? Ah yes, thanks,' said Anna as she woke from her reverie.

*

That evening, despite her resolve earlier that day, Anna didn't have the energy to go running. The thought of the shotgun killer lurking in the bushes along the edge of the track was no incentive to pull on her tracksuit and run out of the door.

It had started to rain again, the small drops forming thin rivulets along the kitchen window. She had supper and listened to the news on a local radio station. Joggers were advised to exercise caution. It's actually my duty to stay at home, she thought with a sense of relief and lit a cigarette, this time not even bothering to go out to the balcony.

Anna glanced at the clock; it was almost ten o'clock. Time for bed. She switched off the radio and clambered into bed. Her feet were chilly. She fetched a pair of soft woollen socks, pulled them on, went to the bathroom and snuggled once again beneath the duvet. She tossed and turned trying to find a comfortable position, without success. Her shoulders were tense. After lying in bed for an hour she went back into the living room and put on a CD, a collaborative effort with AGF and Vladislav Delay called *Symptoms*. You can't beat the golden oldies, she thought as she cracked open a can of beer. How do you say 'golden oldies' in Hungarian? She couldn't think of a suitable translation. She thought in Finnish so often these days. It was a shame, but there was little she could do about it.

Electronic music filled the room; Anna lowered the volume. Easy-going music, she thought, almost commercial stuff. The melodic sound combined with just enough experimental noise began to lull Anna to sleep; the sofa turned into a river barge carrying her to the shores of the Tisza, to the summers of her childhood once again. Her father stood on the shore shouting *vigyáz, vigyáz,* as she swam out into the powerful current. *Buta apuka*, she thought, Silly Daddy. After all, their mother was right next to her – and she was a champion swimmer. She would never have swum out to the middle of the river by herself.

Of course, she and Réka used to swim out there in secret. They had been spying on the older boys who had set up tents by the shore and lived there all summer, hidden behind the bushes slightly to one side of the swimming area. She could still smell the bonfire smoke wafting beneath the *bogrács*, inhale the aroma of fish soup, the clay banks along the shore parched by the sun, and the river. Sometimes the boys invited Anna and Réka to join them for some soup. Áron and Ákos were there too. It was the best fish soup she'd ever tasted.

At the weekend there was a disco down by the shore that attracted youngsters from the neighbouring cities and villages, and brawls were a regular occurrence. Ákos had a Mohican haircut, and back then that was enough to start a fight. It was thanks to their father that the policemen from Kanizsa never gave Ákos a beating, but if things at the Strand disco got really out of hand and the police from the neighbouring town were called, Ákos was always their favourite victim. Sometimes he would come home covered from head to toe in dried blood and their mother would weep and cry that the boy would never come to any good. By this time their father was already dead.

Anna woke and realised that the CD had stopped. Silence tingled in her ears. She had dozed off on the sofa. She got up and went out to the balcony for a cigarette. The chilled, moist air bit her bare legs. She leaned against the wet railing. The sleeves of her nightgown were soaked.

She felt a strong urge to call Ákos, to ask if he too remembered, to ask him about their father's death. Anna had been so young at the time, in her last year at nursery school. In the photograph on her bedside table, their father looked just like Ákos.

She couldn't recall his voice. All she could remember was the distant cry of *vigyáz, vigyáz*. She had a vague recollection of her father reading her a bedtime story. Mazsola. It must have been Mazsola.

Ákos didn't answer the telephone. *The number you have dialled is currently unavailable*, the familiar female voice informed her. Anna went to bed. She couldn't get to sleep.

We lived in the reception centre for two years, wallahi. *Imagine, two years. Mum seemed to wake up when we finally got something more permanent, residence permits and an apartment. I don't know what took so long. Not to mention the naturalisation applications. I always imagine that the Department of Immigration as this enormous building, each floor full of cabinets, and when your papers arrive they're filed away in the lowest drawer of the first cabinet on the first floor. Sometimes someone comes along and moves them to the next drawer, then after a while someone else moves them on to the next drawer. So your papers are moving from one drawer to the next, slowly making their way up to the top floor where, in the room at the far end of the floor, there's a huge desk full of more drawers, surprise surprise. All this happens really slowly, because the few members of staff that work there have better things to do than move applications from one drawer to the next – they have to sit at their computers, for instance, and go to loads of meetings all the time – so it's only very rarely that they're assigned to moving paperwork around, once a week at most, and there are millions of drawers. Thankfully the applications never go missing. They don't shout, don't rattle around and they don't get hungry. They never get depressed, frightened or pissed off, and they never complain. It's so much easier to encounter a piece of paper than a real human being. But it takes an age for the papers to make their way to the lowest drawer of the final cabinet, and from there they'll one day make it up on to the desk itself, where, of course, there's another pile of paperwork waiting to be dealt with.*

And one day, the person whose job it is to sign and stamp applications (between 9.30 a.m. and 9.45 a.m.) is on duty and your papers are on the top of the pile and abracadabra you have a residence permit. After that you don't have to worry about little things like being deported, being taken in a police car to a holding cell at the airport and from there herded on to a flight back to where you fucking well came from, because here in Finland we know better than you about whether it's safe to go back there, whether your rights will be upheld or whether you and your children will be able to live a life of dignity like the lives of the Eastern European gypsies, because I'm sure they love living in landfill sites. I'm sure no Finn would ever want to leave a life like that if they happened to be born there. No, no.

Sometimes people even get their hands on the big prize: citizenship. But the desk that deals with citizenship applications is in the President's office and that's why it takes even longer. Just thought I'd mention that.

Once we finally had our residence permits, permanent ones no less, the council agreed to rent us an apartment in Rajapuro. We moved into the ghetto and Mum was thrilled. She never looked out of the windows to see what it was like out there: graffitied concrete walls and half-empty car parks, kids with their heads in bags of glue round the back of the houses. She probably walked to the supermarket with her eyes closed, so as not to break the illusion of the start of our wonderful new life. Still, she must have heard all the drunks. The whole place was a forest built of dirty concrete, a thicket of trees as far as the eye could see, a place with trolls grunting on the pathways and creatures lurking in the corners, a place where the glimmer of a fairy tale shone only in the glazed eyes of the drug addicts.

Mum decorated the bookshelves with junk from Kurdistan, cooked kubba *and* birinc *and listened to old Ciwan Haco cassettes all day long. Dad stapled a green-white-and-red flag to the wall so that the sun would shine even in the middle of winter. He set up a satellite dish on the balcony, and after that the TV was on all the time, belching out news from across the mountains, or at least from Denmark, and our living room had become a vacuum-sealed jar where Mum and Dad were petrified of the slightest leak, because then their new life might start to go off.*

23

'HEY! I'VE GOT IT!' cried Rauno as he rushed into the staffroom where Esko, Anna and Sari were quietly sipping their morning coffee. It was eight o'clock. Sari's youngest had been up all night with a temperature; he'd complained of a sore ear and eventually they'd taken him to hospital. Sari looked pale and exhausted. Esko looked hung-over again. As he raised his cup, black coffee spilled on to the table. His eyes were bloodshot, his hair a mess. Anna didn't look much sprightlier. She had woken up repeatedly, sleeping in fits, without dreaming, without feeling invigorated.

'I've got it! You could at least pretend to be interested,' exclaimed Rauno, dispelling the sullen atmosphere in the room.

'What time do you get to work?' Esko asked sourly.

'Well, tell us what you've found,' said Sari, almost as sourly.

'Guess,' Rauno teased them.

'Just tell us,' Esko thundered.

'The pendant. Look. It didn't even take very long in the age of the internet. I scanned an image of the pendant on to my computer, ran it through a search engine and here you have it!'

Rauno waved a sheet of A4 paper with a small dark square in the corner.

'What the hell is this?' Esko snapped.

'Take a closer look. This is it.'

The fatigued atmosphere of a moment ago was gone. Everyone crowded around the sheet of paper and saw in the dark square the same figure as that in the pendant found in the pockets of both murdered joggers. It was like something drawn by a child. The figure had clumsily jutting limbs and was wearing a feather hat. It looked harmless, almost amusing.

'What on earth is this?' asked Anna.

'Huitzilopochtli.'

'Excuse me?'

'Huitzilopochtli,' Rauno repeated. 'I don't know how you pronounce it. But this is how you spell it.' Rauno wrote out the word
beneath the image. The others looked on, speechless.

'What a ridiculous word,' said Esko.

'And quite a terrible man by all accounts,' Rauno added. 'I've been
reading up on him. Huitzilopochtli was the Aztec god of war and the
sun, the most important of all their gods. A bloodthirsty man, a real
beast. He craved human sacrifices and human blood; the Aztecs were
required to sacrifice lots of people every day to appease him. Imagine,
they used to kill hundreds, even thousands of people every single day.
And it wasn't a tidy affair; it was all blood and guts and religious fervour.
Our killer is an amateur compared to this. And necklaces like this have
never been handed out in any sports shop – I've already checked. So it
certainly looks like the killer put them in the victims' pockets.'

Rauno had printed off a selection of different images of the
ruthless god and the group leafed through them in silence. The
black-and-white image on the pendant was a simplified version.
The colour photographs showed the figure more clearly, complete
with headdress and clothes adorned with numerous feathers, a staff
fashioned like a snake in his hand and something that looked like a
drum. In some of the images, the god's face was black.

The Aztecs were a warfaring people, who enslaved the weaker
Indian tribes and sacrificed people to appease the gods. Huitzilopochtli, in particular, craved bloodshed. In some cases, live sacrifices
had their hearts cut out. Victims were also routinely burned and
drowned. Sometimes the Aztecs even ate their victims.

'Pretty sick, if you ask me,' Esko exclaimed after reading through
Rauno's print-offs.

'And why does he need to have such a difficult name?' Sari wondered. 'It's impossible to say it properly. And there are no instructions
on how to pronounce it.'

'No wonder they had to keep him happy; imagine how pissed off you'd be if you were the greatest of all the gods but nobody could pronounce your name,' said Esko.

'Does the name mean something?' asked Anna.

'Just a minute, it's here somewhere,' said Rauno and began flicking through his papers. 'Here it is. It seems to have several meanings. Here's one: "the one with the hummingbird in his left hand".'

'What the hell does that mean?'

'Should we be looking for a birdwatcher? Someone hunting for hummingbirds?'

'I don't think people hunt hummingbirds,' Rauno mused. 'Not round these parts, that's for sure.'

'Hunting, running and a bloodthirsty Aztec god whose name refers to the hummingbird. Christ! Can they all be linked to one another?' Sari sighed.

'They must be linked somehow,' said Anna. 'What does the hummingbird make you think of?'

'Certainly not human sacrifices.'

'A small, decorative bird whose wings beat so fast that you can't see them move at all.'

'I think of the hummingbird as somehow feminine. It's delicate and graceful.'

'Right, not exactly a grizzly Aztec god.'

'It's colourful. Tropical. Feeds on large flowers.'

'Hummingbirds are endearing, ethereal. They're not cold-blooded killers.'

'Huitzilopochtli,' Rauno repeated.

'The killer hummingbird.'

'Do such things even exist?'

'Seriously, how come you know fancy words like "ethereal"? I'd probably never use a word like that – and it's my native language,' said Rauno.

'Oh, I don't know,' Anna replied. 'It was probably by accident.'

'You're got a natural flair for this. How many languages do you speak?' Rauno asked and looked at Anna in admiration. Anna almost started blushing.

'Come on,' Sari chipped in. 'We all want to know something about you.'

'Well, Hungarian, of course; that's my native language.'

'Oh, so you're not Serbian?' Sari asked, surprised.

'Absolutely not,' Anna laughed. 'But I can speak a bit of Serbian and Croatian and Bosnian, all fairly similar languages. During the Yugoslav years they were all called Serbo-Croat, though they're not exactly identical. Serbian was the national language, and everybody had to learn it from the time they went to nursery school, though the village we were from, Magyarkanizsa, is entirely Hungarian.'

'What language did you speak at school?'

'Hungarians spoke Hungarian and Serbs Serbian. We were always allowed to maintain our own language and culture, to a certain degree, which is more than you can say for the Hungarian minority in Romania. But anyway, my Serbian is fairly rusty these days. Thankfully I've got a couple of friends who help me keep it up,' said Anna and found herself thinking of Zoran.

'Wow, with your help we could infiltrate the Yugoslav mafia,' Rauno suggested.

Anna suddenly felt Zoran's hairy chest against hers, the sound of his gasping breath in her ear.

'No thanks,' she said.

'What other languages do you speak?' Sari asked, fascinated.

'Well, English, of course, like everybody else. And German. And Finnish and Swedish.'

'That's six languages,' said Rauno. 'Impressive.'

'Your Finnish is really flawless,' Sari enthused. 'I don't think I've heard you make a single mistake.'

'Thanks,' said Anna, embarrassed. She never got used to people's compliments, though she knew they were justified. 'It's because I was only a child when we arrived here. I've lived in Finland most of my life, gone to school here. It would be weird if I still had a foreign accent.'

Anna turned her attention to the papers on her desk and started looking through them.

'Let's think for a minute about what this Aztec pendant really means,' she said, trying to divert attention away from her own history and back to the matter at hand. 'What is the killer trying to tell us?'

'That he's bloodthirsty?' Sari suggested.

'Wasn't that obvious without the pendants?' Esko scoffed. 'Could someone who's not bloodthirsty shoot two people to pieces? As a peace offering?'

'Could it mean there's more to come?' asked Anna. 'Aztec gods required tens, even hundreds of sacrifices every day. Does this clue simply mean that the murders aren't going to stop here, that there will be more victims, that the killer isn't satisfied?'

Silence fell across the room.

'It's a chilling thought,' said Rauno eventually.

'Like something straight out of a thriller,' said Sari.

'Perhaps he simply wants to tell us that he is a serial killer,' said Rauno.

'Someone full of hatred, someone who craves human sacrifices,' said Anna.

'Jesus,' Sari whispered.

'What was this what's-his-name angry about?' asked Esko. 'Why did people have to keep him sweet?'

Rauno flicked through his papers.

'It doesn't say anything about that. He was a god, and people were afraid of the gods' wrath. I'll have to check whether there was a specific reason why Huitzilopochtli required so many human sacrifices. And who is our killer trying to appease? Himself? What if he's involved with some kind of Aztec cult?'

'Doesn't seem like an easy-going kind of guy,' Esko commented, and Anna noted how long Esko had been involved in a conversation in which she too was taking part, and how relatively well-behaved he was being.

'This person could be almost anyone – outwardly, at least. It could be someone very decent, very proper. A priest or something.'

'They're the worst of the bunch,' Esko scoffed. 'They make me sick, those Catholic paedoph—'

Sari interrupted him. 'At least we now have something concrete to investigate. Rauno, try and find out where you can get hold of these pendants. I can't imagine these things are very popular; at least, I've never seen them before. And how can we ask the relatives if they know anything about it without giving too much away?'

'Hello there, what do you think about Hutsipochilly? Did your daughter have any connection with the ancient Aztecs? It has come to light that certain Aztec gods might be behind your daughter's murder,' Esko joked.

'It's Huitzilopochtli,' said Rauno.

'No normal person can pronounce a name like that. Except our linguistic genius over there,' he said.

Anna stepped out of the police station into the driving rain. The wind whipped freezing raindrops from the north into her face. Anna decided to walk regardless. She wanted to clear her head, and it was best to do this when she was on the move. She had missed far too many runs. There had been short periods before when she'd gone running much less than usual, but she had always had a good reason, like studying for her final exams. Once she went through an intense period of listening to music. She had lain in bed for three weeks with her headphones on and sucked up the music the way someone dying of thirst might gulp down water. That was back at the time when she had accidentally discovered electronic music. To this day she couldn't explain what it was that fascinated her about it. She had never been a nerd, and she didn't enjoy going to clubs or raves. But there was something so unreal about electronic music; it was so estranged from the world, so full of strange sounds, so marginal and lonely.

Sometimes she hated it.

And now she didn't have the energy to run at all. She smoked every day, drank a beer or two every evening before going to bed, then found she couldn't sleep. She tried to tell herself it was just to do with the murders, but she knew this wasn't the whole truth. She wasn't really afraid, not much at any rate. She was skilled in self-defence – and she was a police officer. She had been trained to react in unexpected, dangerous situations and her route took her through the built-up areas around Koivuharju, far away from the hunting grounds along the shore. These cases had awoken within her something other than fear: they had brought to life a raft of indistinct memories, and fighting them off was beginning to take its toll.

Riikka. Ville. Bihar.

Keeping watch over the girl was too much.

She simply couldn't find the energy to go out running.

Anna was soaked through by the time she arrived at Pizzeria Hazileklek. The restaurant was situated near the centre of town, in a property on the ground floor of a brown, roughcast apartment block from the 1950s, between Pedal&Saddle and TechnoService, a TV repair shop that looked like something from a bygone age.

The aroma of the wood-burner stove and exotic spices struck her as she opened the door. A female voice emanated softly from the speakers attached to the walls, her voice shimmering with distant strangeness. The music bore a faint resemblance to Balkan folk song. The warmth inside felt all the more pleasant after the freezing rain. The candles glowing on the tables and the relaxed buzz of conversation gave the illusion of a late-night evening out, not a quick weekday lunch break. Anna knew the restaurant owners; Maalik and Farzad had fled from Afghanistan. The former university lecturers hadn't wanted to open any old pizzeria or lunch café. They wanted to give people a moment of relaxation for the duration of a meal, an experience that would allow them to forget the stress of work for a moment and take them on a short journey. In addition to the obligatory pizzas, they also served an array of Afghan specialities. It was a popular restaurant.

Water dripped from Anna's dark hair and trickled inside the neck of her jumper as she took off her jacket and scarf and shook off the rain.

'Hello, Anna! Long time no see.' Maalik came out of the kitchen wiping his hands on the white towel dangling from his apron strings.

'Hi, Maalik. How are you?' Anna placed a gentle kiss on both cheeks and they hugged. Farzad appeared and pulled her away.

'My beautiful girl! We're so pleased you moved back home. Where they have kept you? Locked in a closet somewhere?'

'Things at work have been quite busy. But now I'm starving. What delicious food have you got for me today?'

'Help yourself to salad at the buffet and take the *quabili pilau*. A wonderful Afghan dish with vegetables, lamb and raisins. Is very good.'

'Sounds delicious. I'll have one of those, please.'

Anna sat alone for a moment. More customers arrived and the kitchen looked busy.

Maalik and Farzad worked at Pizzeria Hazileklek every day from morning to night and never complained about a thing, though soon after arriving in Finland they realised that here you might as well wipe your arse with a doctoral degree and years of work experience. They were simply grateful that they could be together, that they had food in the fridge and that nobody would try to kill them or put restrictions on their lives. Those were things for which every Finnish citizen should be thankful, Anna thought as Farzad brought her steaming dish to the table. The incredible scent of spices and rice rushed into her nostrils, making her mouth water.

She ate heartily, observing the buzz of people around her, and read the à la carte menu to pass the time. Here, too, you could order salmon and pine nuts.

After finishing her meal, she looked at the freezing weather outside, and the thought of walking back to the station didn't appeal in the least.

'There's a storm brewing,' said Farzad as he brought Anna a tin cup of coffee. 'This one's on the house.'

'Thank you, this is so nice,' Anna said, genuinely touched. 'If ever I can help you guys in any way...'

'There's no need. Come and visit us at home some time. That would be nice.'

'I'll have to come round some evening,' she replied and wondered whether they would ever be able to arrange something.

'You must. How about next weekend?'

'Let's see,' she said as she took out the photographs of Riikka and Ville and handed them to Farzad. He examined them carefully, shook his head and took them into the kitchen to show Maalik. When he came back, he was beaming.

'Maalik see this girl in August. We had an assistant all August. I took holiday. Perhaps I show her the photo. She was serving tables.'

'Excellent!' Anna was thrilled and gave Farzad her card. 'Call me as soon as you've spoken to her.'

Then Anna plucked up the courage to call Rauno and ask him to pick her up. She sipped the black coffee, which was so strong that she had to stir in two spoons of sugar.

It was Esko who came to pick her up. He didn't venture inside but pulled the blue-and-white patrol car up in front of the window and pressed down on the horn. People began looking at one another, and Maalik and Farzad seemed concerned, though they hid this behind their smiles. Anna was ashamed. Furious at his behaviour, she sat in the passenger seat and fastened her seat belt. Neither of them said anything, but Anna felt like shouting something nasty. She reminded herself that she had decided not to rise to his child-ish behaviour and concentrated on staring out of the window. The windscreen wipers opened up a view into the city. The thermometer showed 6°c, but the wind blowing in from the north dragged the temperature down to around zero. The streets were quiet. Only a few people had decided to brave the autumn weather front, and now they were struggling as the wind blew their umbrellas inside out.

'How come you picked me up?' she asked once she felt calmer.

'Don't say you didn't enjoy it. That was an impressive entrance, don't you think?'

I will not shout at him, she thought. I will keep my mouth shut.

'Joke. Virkkunen said that you and I have to interview everyone again in the light of this Hutsilo thing. I thought we'd start with Jere, pay him a surprise visit.'

'Why Jere? He was hundreds of kilometres away when Riikka was shot and there's nothing to link him to Ville.'

'And how do you know that? We haven't asked him anything about the guy. There's something not right about him. We stopped grilling him too early, all because of some half-baked hiking trip. He was still our first suspect.'

'Not officially, he wasn't.'

'You know what I mean. Do you eat there often?'

'Every now and then. Why?'

'The owners are poofs, apparently.'

'So?'

'No matter. I suppose you think everything's perfectly normal.'

Anna bit her lip to stop herself responding.

24

THE FAMILIAR, STUFFY AIR hung heavy in the stairwell. The door
to Jere's apartment was already open and he was standing in the
doorway like a boy scout.

'I saw you from the window; they face out on to the street. That's
why I enjoy sleeping out in the wilderness. It's so quiet your head
almost aches – in a good way.'

Anna glanced around the hallway. She had the strange impression
that something had changed; there was something that hadn't been
there before.

Jere closed the door behind them and handed them a pair of
coat hangers. Anna declined with a wave of the hand and said they
wouldn't be staying long. She wondered why Jere was on such an
obvious charm offensive. Anna heard a noise as the door downstairs
slammed shut and she quickly made her way to living-room window.

'Coffee?' Jere shouted from the kitchen.

'No, thank you,' Anna replied and thought she recognised the
back of the jacket now disappearing into the crowds outside. Just
then she realised what was different about the hallway: it was the
sweet smell of incense. The smell of Virve.

'I'll have a cup,' said Esko, appearing next to Anna in the living
room. Anna gave him a meaningful glance and moved her forefinger
and middle finger in a running motion along the windowsill. Esko
nodded but looked as though he hadn't fully understood what she
was trying to say. Jere soon came through with a tray of coffee.

'What brought you here in such a hurry? Weren't things sorted as
far as I'm concerned?' The boy was trying to sound nonchalant, but
the faint quiver in his voice revealed how nervous he was.

'The only thing that's clear is that you couldn't have shot Riikka, but nothing else is sorted – with regard to you or anyone else,' said Anna. 'You can be sure we'll be visiting you many times in the future.'

'Do you know this man?' Esko asked and pulled a photograph from his jacket pocket.

Jere glanced at the photograph and handed it back straight away. Too quickly, thought Anna.

'No.'

'Are you sure? Take a good look,' said Esko.

'I've already looked and I'm perfectly sure I've never seen this guy. Who is he? Did he kill Riikka?'

'Don't you watch the news? Read the papers?'

'Haven't had time. I'm a bit busy at the moment.'

'What, shagging Virve Sarlin?' Anna quipped.

Jere coughed violently, almost choking on his coffee and sending droplets of liquid flying through the air. Esko looked at Anna and whacked Jere on the back a few times. Eventually he regained his composure, but his cheeks were a dark shade of red. Anna said nothing. Silence was often the best interviewing technique.

'Where were you two days before yesterday between 7 and 11 p.m.?' Esko asked eventually.

Jere was silent.

'Would you like to take another look at that photograph?' he continued.

Still Jere held his tongue.

They waited. Esko stirred more sugar into his coffee, his spoon jangling delicately against the sides of the porcelain cup. He sipped his coffee and calmly replaced his cup on the saucer.

'Listen to me, Sonny Jim. We haven't got time to piss around. I've asked you two questions, and for the first question we are particularly keen to hear your answer. It can't be all that hard for people your age to remember what happened a few nights ago. Now where were you?'

Jere cleared his throat.

'I was here,' he said finally.

'Here? Can anyone prove it?' asked Anna.

'Yes. I was with Virve.' Jere's cheeks reddened again.

Anna and Esko looked at one another. What did I tell you, said Anna's smug expression.

'Can you elaborate?' asked Esko.

Jere thought about this for a moment and eventually decided to give in.

'All right. Virve was here all that day. And yesterday. She came round on Wednesday morning at about ten and we've been here ever since. She left just before you turned up.'

Or at the very moment we turned up, thought Anna.

'So you've been in one another's company for two and a half days?' she asked, slightly amused.

'That's right. Well, we popped out to the shop this morning. Bread and that sort of thing.'

'Have you two been at it long?' asked Esko.

Jere was silent for a moment before continuing. The redness in his cheeks began to fade and he sat up. The arrogant exterior was back.

'What's the point in hiding it any longer? We haven't done anything wrong. We had a bit of a fling before I started dating Riikka, back in high school. Riikka didn't know about it. She thought Virve hated me, but all the time she was gagging for it.'

He gave a smug chuckle. You revolting creature, thought Anna.

'And when Riikka and I broke up, Virve came round straight away to – how should I put it – comfort me. Didn't bother me much. She's a bit weird, not really my type, but in the bedroom none of that really matters. Quite the opposite.'

Bastard, thought Anna.

'Did you know that Virve doesn't have an alibi for the night of Riikka's murder?' Esko asked.

'Yes.'

'And now she has motive too,' Anna added.

'What's that supposed to mean? The thing with Riikka was over, done and dusted. I can have fun with whoever I want. So what if it's her best friend?'

'Did you tell Riikka about it?'

'No.'

'Why not?'

'It's not like we're serious or anything, we just have sex every so often. Virve was worried that Riikka might think we'd been at it while the two of us were still dating, because the break-up was so fresh. And we didn't want to hurt her, Virve least of all.'

'Perhaps Virve is more serious about this than you are,' said Anna. 'Perhaps you were going to get back together with Riikka?'

'No way. You can think what you like. What about the second murder, the man?' he said.

'Oh, so you have heard about it?'

'We bought the paper at the corner shop. Took me a while to put two and two together. Sorry.'

'I see. You realise that two people who give one another alibis aren't generally considered all that reliable?' said Anna.

'You can't prove otherwise,' said Jere.

We'll see about that, thought Anna and asked whether Jere's Remington was still at the police station. Jere took it from his locked gun cabinet. The weapon was clean and gleaming, the smell of gun oil in the barrel.

'So you've got it back?' Anna commented, though she knew that the police were unable to confiscate weapons without good reason.

'Yes, I have. And I'm planning on going home next week to join the hunt.'

'This has just been cleaned,' said Esko.

'All those coppers' fingerprints really started pissing me off.'

'You keep good care of these weapons.'

'They're expensive things. In good hands they can last for centuries.'

'Is this the gun that shot Riikka?'

Jere was visibly shaken and shrunk from a bolshie young man into a cowering little boy.

'Jesus Christ, no, it isn't.'

'What about Ville Pollari?'

'No, it isn't!' he repeated and looked as though he might crack at any moment. The shells around tough lads like this are often surprisingly thin and easily torn, thought Anna. Jere began to sob. He wept like a child.

'I always thought you were taking the death of your ex-girlfriend a bit too calmly,' said Anna.

'I'm not,' Jere whispered. 'It's been hell.'

'So can we start to talk like grown-ups now and tell each other the truth?' Esko asked.

'I'm telling you the truth. I haven't killed anybody.'

'What do you know about the Aztecs?' Anna asked suddenly.

'What?' Jere looked baffled.

'The Aztecs. What do you know about them?' she repeated.

'This is a fucking farce,' said Jere as he dried his eyes on his shirtsleeve.

'It's far from it, believe me.'

'I don't know anything about them. They were Indians in South America or something.'

'Mexico,' Anna corrected him.

At around six o'clock that evening Anna parked her car outside Bihar's house. The wind had picked up considerably and carried the rain in sweeping gusts. Anna thought of the autumn that extended months ahead; it felt oppressive. Dark clouds gathered across the sky earlier than usual, and the street lights around her lit up one after the other, as if to comfort the suburb emptied of people by the approaching storm. Brightly lit windows dappled the sides of the apartment blocks reaching up into the sky. The residents of Rajapuro had fled indoors.

The lights were on in Bihar's apartment too. The kitchen and the smaller bedroom looked out on to the car park. Anna had acquired the floor plan of their apartment from the city housing association.

She had called them up and pretended to be considering renting an apartment in the area. This is how she knew that the living-room and master-bedroom windows were on the other side of the building, in the courtyard surrounded by four tower blocks. Sometimes Anna had watched from the courtyard, sitting by the sandpit, her eyes fixed on the third-floor windows. She also knew that the parents slept in the living room and that Mehvan had a room of his own. The girls shared a room, the smaller of the two bedrooms.

Did Bihar really consider this home? Did she feel at home in this suburb, this city? What about her parents? How can someone from far away in the mountains ever settle down among all this concrete, in a land flattened by the long, dark winter?

In a way, Anna understood Bihar's parents. If her mother had remained here, she would probably have clung on to some grotesque emblem of the past and worshipped it in the small apartment she rented from the city council, weeping for her sons and her daughter. But her mother had had the opportunity to return home, and Anna knew that in this respect she had been exceptionally lucky. The situation at home had calmed down. In fact, the northern areas of Serbia, where to this day there is still a significant Hungarian minority, had been spared the worst of the conflict – like most areas of Serbia, except for Kosovo. Even the NATO bombings in the late 1990s had caused little more than fear and a few broken windows. Most young Hungarian men had fled across the border to Szeged or Budapest to avoid being called up for the Serb army. Some had gone even further. Some had been sent to the front. And some of them had died. Like Áron.

Their mother had returned home as soon as Anna turned eighteen. I've done my duty, she said, and tried to convince the children to come back with her. But it was different if you were young, with a Finnish education to your name, rooted in university studies. Anna wasn't able to go back just like that, once and for all.

Perhaps rooted is too strong a word. For Anna it was a glimmer of the future possibilities that she wouldn't have in her former homeland if she suddenly dropped out of school. One crucial aspect of that glimmer was the fact that she had immersed herself in a new language. Anna had risen to the surface quickly, learned to swim, managed to breathe. And she wasn't the kind of teenager to give up a future like that, no matter how thin the bonds to this country. She had already been uprooted by force once, as a child, when they had no other choice. It was more than just a trifling matter, and something she had no desire to repeat. Anna had decided to stay.

Ákos was another case altogether. He had nothing keeping him here, nothing except the band and now Anna. His studies at the veterinary school in Yugoslavia had been cut short when they fled the country, and his language skills weren't good enough to secure a study position in Finland. Ákos had fallen through the safety net, and there he had remained. There was no horizon, no letter in a bottle, no white doves bringing him olive branches. He had effectively been abandoned. When their mother had returned home, she had pleaded with him to join her; she'd seen that there was no future for him in Finland. But Ákos thought he was far too old to go back to school with a group of teenagers. Things with the band were beginning to pick up around that time; they rehearsed almost every day and were doing gigs in dingy rock clubs across the country. There had been plenty of booze, of course.

Ákos had promised their mother he would start studying as soon as his Finnish was good enough.

Was that another good reason for him not to study this language that people said was a distant relative of their own? Ákos had survived in the band on a smattering of English, and that was the language he still used for official matters at the job centre and social security office. When she had just started at the police academy, Anna had invited Ákos to one of her student parties, and nobody could believe that Anna had a brother who could barely understand what they were saying. Not after meeting Anna.

The whole evening had been a catastrophe. Ákos had drunk far too much and had ended up being rude to Anna's friends, going on about anarchism and his connections to the Yugoslav mafia. Anna was mortified. With hindsight, it was after that altercation that her relationship with her brother had become more distant. And after their mother left, Ákos's drinking took a rapid turn for the worse.

A figure appeared at the kitchen window in Bihar's apartment. It was the figure of a woman, of that Anna was certain. It was probably Bihar's mother, standing there fixedly, a black silhouette against the light. The figure seemed to be looking right into Anna's car. Good, she thought. I want you to know that I'm still watching you, still keeping my eyes open regardless of your husband's threats. I will not let anything bad happen to your daughter; I will protect her from you. Don't you see anything twisted about it, she imagined herself asking Zera Chelkin. Anna felt the urge to sound the horn, to open the car windows and shout her story to the concrete walls around her.

The figure lowered the venetian blinds and twisted them shut. A moment later the same thing happened in the bedroom, the one that Bihar shared with her little sister. That's the end of the show, for now, she thought, and turned on the ignition. As she swerved out of the car park, she saw in the corner of her left eye a white-and-blue police Saab. The patrol car drove into the courtyard via the cycle path, then immediately reversed back. Anna caught only a glimpse of the driver. There was something familiar about him.

The storm hit the city with full force just as Anna arrived at the door of Café au Lait. She struggled against the weather to yank the door open, then a sudden gust of wind almost wrenched it from its hinges. Though the streets were deserted, not everybody had gone home to escape the storm. The café was full of animated conversation and warm light, and the atmosphere sophisticated. Classical piano music could be heard in the background and the scent of coffee tickled her nostrils. Zoran was already waiting at a table in a dusky section towards the back of the café.

Anna ordered a pot of tea and a slice of white-chocolate cheese-cake. Zoran took only an espresso. They exchanged a few words about the howling weather outside, their eyes searching out into the darkening evening more than towards one another.

'*Šta je?* Why did you call?' Zoran asked eventually.

'I don't know. I felt a bit lonely.'

'You know I'm married. There are plenty of things Nataša pretends not to notice, like any good wife, but not for ever. I can't start dating you.'

'*U kurac, Zorane*, that's not what I want.'

'What do you want?'

'Pff, I don't know. Nothing.'

'*Ajde*, Anna. What's the matter? You and me, we've … you know, in the past. You didn't used to be the clingy type, that's why I liked you.'

Anna stirred her tea, watched as the spoon formed a whirlpool in the cup. She had her reasons for contacting Zoran, and there was nothing romantic about them. But suddenly she had felt the urge to say something altogether different to that handsome, dark-eyed man almost ten years her senior, the man she had known since childhood and with whom she had spent a first night of passion after turning sixteen. Even back then, it was clear that they could never be a real couple. You're too young, he had said, and then started dating Nataša, who was only a year older than Anna. You're too independent, is what Anna knew he really meant.

But now she was unable to say anything.

Zoran sipped his coffee. Anna had always been charmed by the Serbs' ability to enjoy the same cup of coffee for hours, to construct an entire social interaction around a single espresso.

And at that moment she realised that this was precisely what she had been missing.

A sense of homesickness tightened her throat.

She wanted to see Réka, to sit on the terrace outside Gong, to have a coffee and chat about things. She wanted to speak Hungarian.

'Have you heard of the jogging murders?' she asked eventually.

'I read about it in the paper. Why?'

'I just wondered if you'd heard anything.'

'*Nista*. Nothing. This isn't a professional job or immigrant gang stuff. Looks like it's some local lunatic.'

'If you hear anything, you'll tell me, right?'

Zoran stared at Anna and sipped his coffee, lost in thought.

'Sure. But trust me, I don't know anything about this. Look, pretty nimble, huh?'

Anna turned and looked towards the counter and watched a man in a wheelchair taking a cup of tea and a slice of cake into his lap and wheeling himself to the nearest table.

'I'd probably shoot myself if I ended up like that,' Zoran continued. 'Still, people can get used to all sorts of things.'

Petri noticed Anna and Zoran and waved. He looked unhappy. Now he'll think I have a boyfriend, Anna thought in horror. And so fucking what? I don't give a damn what he thinks of me.

'You two know each other?' Zoran asked, surprised.

'We must have bumped into each other at work,' Anna replied.

Zoran glanced at his watch.

'I've gotta go. Nati is waiting with the kids. *Zdravo*, honey. See you around.'

Zoran winked and gave her a salacious smile. Anna felt like smirking back at him, but turned instead to gaze out through the streaks of rainwater pouring down the window. Arsehole, she thought.

Half an hour later Anna left the café with a raft of unpleasant thoughts heaving in her head like a sea in a storm. The wind almost blew her over and on the way home gusts of wind gripped the car and shook it violently. Needless to say, Petri had come over to chat with her as soon as Zoran had left. Straight away he asked whether Anna had received any more of those messages. Then he started asking how she was, as if they had once been much closer friends. Anna had forced herself to answer politely, and had even tried to smile a little, asking him about his work, this and that, the things friends talk about. Petri had brought his tea and cake over to her table and sat there for a while chit-chatting. Then he asked her directly why she hadn't wanted to see him again. Anna had been unable to answer. Was she with that man who just left? No. Was it because he was disabled? No. Then why? I don't know. After that Petri didn't say another thing; he wheeled himself outside leaving his half-eaten cake on the table. She had felt like bursting into tears.

Once she got home, Anna was unbearably tired. She smoked a cigarette beneath the kitchen extractor fan and tried to listen to some Pan Sonic, but the twang of guitar feedback left her restless. This isn't even music, she thought and switched to classical. Five minutes of Handel, but even that couldn't relax her. She switched off the CD player and crawled into bed; she huddled beneath the duvet and felt an enormous weight pressing her deeper into the mattress. Her own body felt estranged, distant. It's a good thing there's a storm raging outside, she thought. I don't need to feel guilty for missing my run yet again. I don't have the energy to run another step. All I want to do is sleep and sleep – so why can't I get to sleep?

She closed her eyes and listened to the sound of the wind rattling the balcony railings. She rolled on to her side. She was too warm. She stuck her feet out from beneath the duvet and felt the cool draught from the window against her skin. I'll have to buy some insulation tape tomorrow, she thought, otherwise it'll be too cold in the winter.

At 3 a.m. Anna gave up and got out of bed. The linoleum floor in the bedroom felt like ice against her bare feet. She pulled on a pair of woollen socks and slippers and went out to the balcony for a cigarette. The weather front was already moving towards the northeast, and by now the rain was only spitting. The fatigue was like a dead weight in every muscle in her body. Her shoulders were tense and sore. She didn't dare lean against the railing as she had a strange feeling that it might break, that someone was watching her through the shadows enveloping the apartment blocks, waiting for her to fall.

My family started changing when I was about twelve. Well, I don't know if they changed or whether it was all because I changed. It must have had something to do with me starting my periods, though I didn't get it at the time. That and the fact that I had loads of friends. Suddenly I wasn't allowed to walk to school by myself or walk home afterwards. They got fucking Mehvan to shadow me, the little runt. I wasn't allowed to visit my Finnish friends' places, not even for birthday parties. I tried to ask Mum why, but she wouldn't say anything except that it was all for my own good, for the good of the family, that I'd understand when I was older. I was mad at her and threw a glass bowl at the wall. Naturally, it was a special memento from Kurdistan. She told me to pull my trousers down; I was always allowed to leave my panties on. She thrashed my backside with the belt, not with the buckle like Dad sometimes did to Mehvan. She whipped me and wept, as if it was hurting her more than it was hurting me. I never cried. I gritted my teeth and in my mind I shouted at her in Finnish, saying, you can leather me as much as you damn well please. Mehvan cried, but only much later, secretly, in his own room. Mum always came and apologised after a couple of hours. I always said I forgave her, though I didn't really.

You got used to all the rules quickly enough. I was allowed to spend time with a few other Kurdish girls and Dad's cousin's children – there were loads of them and some of them were really nice and they all lived in Rajapuro. In the eighth grade I spent all summer in Sweden with Mum's relatives. I've got a cousin there who's exactly the same age, and abbou what a summer it was! I had loads of friends and you didn't really think about it when you were playing with them, though all the time, and I really mean all the freaking time, there was an adult relative watching over us. I was just so glad to get away from home for a while. What really irritated me was the way that annoying little shit Mehvan walked at my side to school every morning and how he took the job so damn seriously. He even followed me into the library. Back home I could see in his eyes how he craved Dad's praise and acceptance like a puppy. I never saw him get any praise. Dad thought Mehvan was stupid and that he'd never come to anything, but he still wanted Mehvan to become a doctor. Why do parents always want their children to be doctors? What's so great about spending all day listening to sick people complaining about things, lancing their boils and wiping their arses? You won't see me becoming a doctor, though with my grades it wouldn't be out of the question.

It was only once I got to high school that I realised what a terrible dead-end I was living in: a rotting, amputated dream of Kurdistan preserved in a two-bedroom apartment. By some kind of miracle I'd managed to get Dad to agree to me applying to a high school downtown specialising in science. You needed a really high grade-average to get in. I think Dad thought it was great being able to brag to his friends and relatives about how smart his daughter was, especially as Mehvan gave him so little to brag about. He was lucky he made it from one grade to the next, and believe it or not, most of us are normal people who know the value of a decent education. And because I had a good leaving certificate I got in. Almost the best thing was being able to walk to school by myself; there was no way Mehvan could have taken me into town and picked me up again; he had to get to school himself, and with all the extra bus tickets it would have been too expensive. Of course, they expected me to come home on the first possible bus, and at first they were really strict about it. Dad would even come and wait at the bus stop, but when I only seemed interested in studying they eased off a bit. After a while I started hanging out in town after school, I told them I was going to the library to revise for an exam, and they believed me because even at home I always had my nose in a book and complained that I couldn't concentrate with the TV blaring and Adan whining and asking me to play with her, when all the while I was going to cafés and shops with my new classmates and, later on, with Juse. Gradually I gained my freedom, because at home I was so good at playing the role of the well-behaved Kurdish girl who dreams solely of you know what – a free and idyllic Kurdistan, of course. I even covered our bedroom with maps and pictures to fool them, and they didn't suspect a thing. Maybe they thought the worst was over, puberty had passed without too many problems so now there was nothing to worry about. Their non-existent sense of self-esteem was bolstered by the thought that their offspring, their own flesh and blood was attending an elite Finnish school, albeit that she was the wrong sex. They knew perfectly well that most of the other wog kids in Rajapuro had no hope of doing such a thing, and even if they had selected a husband for me, they probably thought: let her go to school seeing as she's got a head for study and we can get benefits to cover the books and bus tickets. We can have the wedding once she's graduated.

25

ANNA SAT AT HER DESK staring at the flaking surface of the wall. The cold light from the fluorescent lamps stung her eyes, and an infuriating hum filled her ears. She let the sense of numbness spread throughout her body and leaned her head against her hands. Sleep was near. Finally. Small electric shocks rippled through her tense muscles. Each flinch pulled her back to life, keeping her awake, but once she relaxed she sunk into a deeper, soporific state. It felt wonderful. She wanted it to continue for ever.

After Anna had been asleep for a princely twenty minutes, Rauno stepped into her office. Anna didn't have the energy to raise her head.

'Have you been out on the piss again?' Rauno asked after staring for a moment at the woman slumped across the desk.

'No...' came the weak voice from between her arms.

'Should I be worried about you?'

Anna finally raised her head and stared at Rauno, her eyes red and bloodshot. Did he have to walk in just as she'd nodded off? Anna felt like crying. Either that or exploding into hysterical laughter.

'No, you don't,' she replied. 'I'm just tired. Nobody ever asks that racist drunk things like that. Or do they?'

'Don't get upset. I just came into tell you Virve's ready for interview in room number two.'

'Can you help me out here?' she asked, suddenly agitated. 'I'm exhausted. I couldn't get to sleep last night. I can be the bad cop glowering in the background, intimidating and a bit crazy. But please, you do the talking.'

Rauno gave her a quizzical look and nodded his head.

*

'Let's go through this once again from the beginning,' Rauno began. 'Where were you on the evening of 21 August after 8 p.m.?'

Anna pulled up a chair towards the back of the room, sat down and leaned her head against the wall, hoping that she could remain an observer throughout the interview. Her brain felt so stiff from lack of sleep that she feared she would be unable to formulate a single sensible question, let alone react in any way to the girl's responses.

'If I remember right, I've already told you. I was at home all day, all evening and all night.'

'But nobody can testify to that.'

'That's not my fault, is it?' Virve quipped irritably.

'Then where were you on 14 September?'

'I was with Jere at his place. I got there around midday and we were there all day. Jere's already told you all this.'

'Why didn't you tell us that you've been having a relationship with Jere ever since he and Riikka split up?'

Virve looked like she had been preparing for this question and gave a confident smile.

'Oh, it's just sex. Jere and I haven't been shouting about it from the rooftops because we don't want our group of friends – that's Riikka's group of friends, too – to think we had something going on earlier, as if our thing was the reason they split up. It wasn't.'

'You told us that you never liked Jere. Jere, however, has told us a rather different story. According to him...' Rauno leafed through his notes. 'According to him, you two had an encounter with one another in high school and you'd been, er, "gagging for it" ever since.'

Virve scoffed.

'He said that, did he? That's a fantasy all of his own, something he uses to bolster his macho self-esteem. This probably sounds really bad,' Virve said and turned to stare Anna intensely in the eyes. 'But, you see, I'm never "gagging" for anyone, not so that I'd be after them for years. No way, not my style. I'm just looking for a good shag, you know what I mean? And for all his other faults, Jere happens to be just that. Sorry if that really shocks you, but that's just who I am,' she said.

Anna was amused but managed to maintain her poker face. She noticed that Rauno's ears had turned red. Which of them was supposed to be shocked by Virve's revelation?

'So, did you have some sort of encounter during high school?' he asked.

Virve hesitated before admitting to it.

'Yes. One night after a class party. That was it.'

'How soon after that night did Riikka and Jere start dating?'

Again Virve seemed to stall her response, fidgeting with the sleeve of her pullover, her bracelets jangling.

'The following week. But it didn't bother me. I wasn't in love with him or anything.'

'Of course you weren't,' Rauno muttered and continued: 'However, it is profoundly suspicious that after your close friend has just been brutally murdered, you both failed to mention this relationship in interviews with police officers. Withholding information from the police is rather more serious than withholding information from your friend. During police interrogation it is an offence. This casts you both in a very bad light.'

'I'm so sorry,' Virve quipped.

'Did you know that Jere had gone to Lapland at the end of August?'

'Yes. I knew he'd gone off hiking, but I didn't know where exactly.'

'And why didn't you tell us about that either?'

'You asked me whether I knew where Jere was. I didn't know. For all I knew he could have gone south to the Nuuksio national park.'

'By hiding these things and with that attitude, you make your liaison with Jere seem extremely suspicious,' Rauno said with a note of irritation. 'Would you like to hear what I think?'

He continued without waiting for an answer.

'I think you and Jere cooked up this whole plot together. The firearm belonged to Jere and you used it to shoot Riikka. Perhaps Jere committed the second murder. Either that, or you did it. And I'm not the only officer who thinks this is a plausible scenario. In fact, this is one of our key lines of investigation, so I'd advise you to think carefully about lying to us in future.'

Rauno slapped the investigation photographs of Ville Pollari on the table. In the first a smiling man was standing with his arm around his wife in front of their newly built house. In the second he was lying on the running track, his chest blown to pieces. Virve stared at the photographs, expressionless, but Anna saw that behind the mask she was shaking with fear and holding back tears.

'Does this look familiar?' asked Rauno.

'No.'

'Did this man happen to run past when you shot Riikka? Did he see you? Is that why you had to shut him up?'

'No,' Virve shouted. 'No, no, no! I haven't done anything!'

'I think you have, either alone or with Jere. Don't you think it would be better to own up to it now?'

'I've nothing to own up to,' she said.

'Think how relieved you'll be. You won't have to hide or lie about it any longer. It'll all be over,' said Rauno. 'You can finally relax.'

'I didn't dare say anything about Jere or his hiking trip because I was scared that he might have done it,' she shouted and burst into tears. 'You don't have to believe me. I haven't done anything. I was really freaked out. I just kept thinking, what if Jere really loses it and kills me too? I was relieved when I heard he'd been in Sevettijärvi and there was no way he could have done it.'

'Could Jere have done something like this? Could he have lost it and killed someone?' Rauno asked. His voice had changed; now he sounded friendly.

'I really can't imagine … But he got really jealous sometimes. And he was pissed off big time when I let it slip that I thought Riikka might be seeing someone else.'

'Really? He told us that their relationship was over for good.'

'It was, as far as she was concerned. But Jere wanted her back. He never admitted it, but you notice things like that. I'm just a rebound for him. He loved Riikka.'

'How jealous is he, on the whole?'

'Quite a bit.'

'What does that mean?'

'I mean, he starts imagining all sorts of things at the drop of a hat.'

Anna gave a start. She always reacted to words and phrases like this, no matter how exhausted she was. She had made up her mind. Never again would she not ask the questions that needed to be asked.

'Does he ever hit you?' she asked.

Virve was silent for a long moment before speaking.

'Not really. Not, like, really hard.'

'What's that supposed to mean?'

Again the girl seemed hesitant, thinking what to say.

'One time he grabbed hold of me and squeezed my arms and started shaking me. But it was nothing, just a bruise on my arm. Anyway, I'd been irritating him.'

'So you were asking for it?'

'Well, I didn't really say that…'

'Did he ever behave violently towards Riikka?'

'I don't know.'

'You were best friends. You do know.'

'Sometimes he did.'

'Don't you think it's time to forget all about him?'

'But I love him,' she shrieked. 'I always have. Since high school. I haven't done anything bad, not to Riikka and not to anyone else. I haven't. You've got to believe me. Riikka was my best friend, despite everything else.'

Again she started to weep.

'Does the word Huitzilopochtli ring any bells?' Anna asked, still leaning against the back wall.

Virve turned to look at her. She looked aghast and seemed to shrink back as she nervously tugged her sleeves further down her forearms.

'What's that?' she said in almost a whisper.

'Indeed, what is it?' Anna replied and watched Virve. The girl was visibly rattled and was unable to hide it. But there was something else about her. Anna could see that Virve was utterly petrified with fear.

Bihar, standing on the asphalted playground, alone, a dark scarf tightly wrapped round her head, a black trench coat and jeans. She was leaning against the ochre-yellow wall of the school for yuppie kids and didn't notice Anna, who was sitting in a civilian car parked across the street. The car radio belched a babble of chatter into the ether. Anna switched it off.

Bihar's high school was different from the one Anna had once attended. This one was much better. Year upon year, only students with a grade average of around nine would even consider applying. Anna's high school had been in Koivuharju. Her own grade average would have merited a place at a more reputable school, but Anna didn't want to have to get the bus to school, as she already spent so much time doing sports. Koivuharju School had nice teachers and decent results despite the students' diverse backgrounds, and it offered students the opportunity to take extra sports classes. Back then that had been enough, and she hadn't regretted the decision since.

Bihar moved. A tall, lanky boy was walking towards her across the playground. Bihar took out her mobile phone and started fiddling with it.

The boy stood right next to her, but Bihar didn't raise her eyes from her phone. The boy seemed not to notice her either, though he was standing so close. A second, two, three. Then Bihar nodded. The boy walked off.

Got you, thought Anna, her pulse quickening. Then: poor kids, not a chance of making a go of things.

Anna stepped out of the car and walked across the playground. Bihar noticed her and almost ran away, but decided to stay put. Out of the corner of her eye, Anna noticed the boy standing further off, watching the situation unfold, safely surrounded by a group of about a dozen students.

'Don't they want to hang out with you?' Anna asked.

'My friends are all on a double lesson with no break,' the girl responded.

'Who was that boy that was here a minute ago?'

'Don't know. He asked me the time.'

'Does he have bad eyesight? There's an enormous clock over there on the wall.'

'Must have. That's what I thought too.'

'Who was it? Your boyfriend?'

'I can't remember his name. Honest.'

'Of course you can't. How are things at home?'

'Fine.'

'What do you get up to in the evenings? Are you allowed out at all?'

'I don't want to go out. I have to study in the evenings.'

'Is the only reason your parents let you carry on going to school because they know I'm keeping an eye on you?'

Bihar shrugged her shoulders and blew a chewing-gum bubble. The school bell rang abruptly.

'You don't get it, do you?' Bihar hissed and walked off towards the main building.

The boy had disappeared.

Anna would have liked to talk to him too. She should have marched into the school, found a teacher and tried to find out who he was. But she couldn't. Not now.

Now she had to get away.

The anxiety was coming back.

The two-headed eagle was back.

By the time she parked the car in the lock-up beneath the police station, Anna felt as though she couldn't breathe. She undid her seat belt and opened the window, but the cramp in her chest wouldn't relent. Her heart was pounding and sweat tingled on her skin. It's starting again, she thought.

Deep breaths! Calm down!

Anna closed her eyes, tried to think of something different, but the image of a brutalised young girl hung in her mind, lying on the banks of a strange river, with more bodies behind her as far as the eye could see.

For Christ's sake, woman, think of something else!

Bihar was in no danger.

I'm becoming obsessed with this.

It's not normal that I spend my spare time following a girl who, all the evidence would suggest, is completely safe.

I'm losing my mind from lack of sleep. I can't tell what is rational and what isn't any longer, what is true and what false.

Should I just wash my hands of this case altogether, try to spend that time getting some sleep or running?

Anna forced the terrible images from her mind by imaging herself running. Gradually she managed to calm herself down enough that she was able to step out of the car and get on with her work.

Rauno sat at his computer almost night and day. His desk was over-flowing with papers containing any information he could find that had even the most tenuous link to the Aztecs. He had uncovered two small cults in the United States that believed in the Aztec gods. One of them was based on an old farm on the outskirts of San Francisco and had around 15 active members. The other group survived with only a few members somewhere in the Deep South and complained of active discrimination from other people in their community. The two groups appeared to keep some minimal contact. The second group had probably been founded when a few families had left the first and decided to make a start on their own. Both groups were on the US internal intelligence radar, but neither was deemed a significant threat to the general population. Neither group had ever been involved in violent activities of any kind or charged with incitement. A hippie event called the Rainbow Gathering had been held on the San Francisco farm some five years ago. This was the most publicity the group had ever received and the event passed without incident. Rauno got the impression that this was a peaceful group of potheads who got high and posted articles online about their own religion, which incorporated elements of Native American mythology and Aztec gods with communal living, peace, love, vegetarianism and so-called 'soft' drugs.

What had finally aroused Rauno's interest was not the zealous groups themselves but a link to an online retailer selling everything from spelt flour and organic quinoa to Huitzilopochtli posters, plates and necklaces – identical to those found in Riikka and Ville's pockets. The only problem was that the link didn't provide any contact information for the company; all he could find was an online order form. A typical online firm, the kind that people are always being warned about. Rauno placed an order to his home address for a bag of organic beans, which had been harvested in South America for thousands of years, and wrote in the form's ANY QUESTIONS? section that he would like to talk with the company directors about a possible bulk order.

We'll have to get the national police to help us look into these international groups, thought Rauno, my time at work simply won't be enough. He wrote Virkkunen an email asking him to take care of the matter as soon as possible, switched off his computer and rubbed his exhausted eyes in the cool light of the screen as it shut down. He stood up and rolled his tense shoulders. Could he ask Nina to give him a massage, he wondered, though he knew he didn't have the nerve. It was pointless. Nina hadn't so much as accidentally touched him in the last six months, not a hug, a kiss, a touch of the hand. Not to mention sex.

Rauno felt horny. He thought of betraying her. He thought about it every single day. But more than anything he thought of Nina the way she was before, just a short time ago. Laughing, sweet, wonderful, sexy Nina who couldn't get enough of him.

What had gone wrong? What should he do?

And for the first time Rauno felt that it was up to him to do something and not just to wait for the marriage to drift towards divorce. He would have to fight; he mustn't give up. And if things didn't work out after that, so be it. Let them get a divorce – at least he would have tried. He sent his wife a text message in which he apologised for staying at work late and said he would stop in at the sushi bar on his way home.

What else?

That would have to do for tonight. At least it was a start.

Rauno drove to Kyoto Sushi and picked up a large box of assorted maki. Nina loved those. There had been a time when they had thought sushi to be the most erotic food in the world; they had eaten pieces of sushi from one another's bodies and made love afterwards.

He drove home. The house was dark and quiet. In the dimness of the hallway he took off his coat and shoes and carefully peered into the girls' room, where he heard the sound of calm, even breathing.

Nina was sitting in the kitchen by candlelight. She had prepared a pot of green tea, which was infusing as he walked in.

26

ANNA SAT ON THE BALCONY SMOKING. The beautiful late September day was turning to evening and for once she had left work on time. It was perfect weather for running: about 10°C, a gentle breeze, overcast.

But Anna didn't have the energy to go out for a run. She had called Ákos. He had been in a bar somewhere and asked Anna to join him. There's a great buzz, he'd slurred to her on the telephone, come on, my own little sister. Anna had no inclination to check out the buzz, however great. Anyway, Zoran might have been there too. How long had Ákos been back on the drink? She thought back to when she'd last seen her brother. It was less than a week ago. Back then he'd looked good and had been sober. But that was life with a drunk, she knew that all too well. And she also knew that sooner or later her brother would be ringing her doorbell. Sooner, probably. And she would have no option but to answer.

Ákos made her think of their mother; Anna hadn't heard from her in ages. A sense of yearning tightened in her lungs. Or was it all that tobacco? Anna stubbed out her cigarette, went inside and booted up the computer.

'*Szia anyu,*' she said as Skype connected her to her mother's landline. Her mother sounded surprised and happy.

'*Szia drága kislányom, hogy vagy?*'

'I'm fine, thanks. How are things with you?'

'Oh, same old. How's your new job?'

'It's nice.'

'And what about your colleagues?'

'They're nice too,' came Anna's white lie. She didn't need to tell her mother anything about Esko.

'What kind of cases are you working on?'

'Interesting cases. I'll tell you more when I visit.'

'Isn't it awful, my own daughter investigating violent crimes!'

'They're not all as violent as you think,' she lied again.

'When are you coming home?'

'I don't know when I'll have my next holiday. At least I'm racking up plenty of overtime here. I'll have to see if I can combine them into a longer holiday over Christmas.'

'It would be wonderful to have you back for Christmas. What does Koivuharju look like nowadays?'

'Just the same as it always did. Imagine, ten years have passed and absolutely nothing has changed. Well, they've built a few apartment blocks at the end of Takametsä, but that's about it.'

'What about Ákos?'

'He's okay,' she said. Once a liar, always a liar.

'Has he got himself a job yet?'

'No. Where could he work when he doesn't speak Finnish?'

'Still?'

'He'll never learn it. You know him.'

'There was a time I knew a teenage boy full of energy, drive and anger. I always thought he would grow out of it like all the other boys, that the bands and all that terrible music were just a passing phase. But they weren't. I had to bring him to Finland, didn't I.'

Anna couldn't bear listening to her mother playing the martyr. She'd heard it far too often. Her mother seemed to thrive on self-pity and drew her strength from it.

'Mum, you did what you had to back then. There as no way he could have stayed there. He'd been called up for the army. He was already waiting at the police station. Dad's former colleagues were stalling, trying to give us time to escape. At least Ákos is still alive. Isn't that the most important thing?'

'He might as well be as dead as István and Áron. He never calls me, never sends me a letter, a postcard – nothing. When was the last time he visited? He's only visited once, and that was years ago.'

'We haven't seen you much round here either.'

'Oh, don't start that again.'

'You started it. I've already said I'll pay for the flights. There are cheap flights here from Budapest, if you look around online. I can book for you.'

'I think it would be best if you came back here. I haven't the energy to travel these days.'

Anna knew this was nonsense. Her mother was only 62 years old and in perfectly good shape. For some reason, she didn't want to visit them. They had argued about this in the past. Anna suspected that her mother simply didn't want to see Ákos in Finland, marginalised and unemployed.

'Suit yourself, but believe me when I say you shouldn't leave the initiative to Ákos. He's not going to make the first move. Call him. Send him a letter or a card.'

'We'll see. Let's talk about you. Have you found yourself a man yet?'

Couldn't her mother ever talk about something else? She was like a stuck record, raving about Ákos's employment situation and Anna's love life. Should she tell her the truth? That she'd slept with an invalid in August and that it was an interesting experience, or that last winter there had been a skateboarder tearaway ten years her junior, quite a cute guy actually, and a run-of-the-mill Nokia software engineer. That one would doubtless please you no end, but they were only one-night affairs, whereas Zoran seemed to linger in the background all the while. You remember Zoran? Yes, you hated him. But I shagged him again the other week.

'Mum, I'm not looking for a man.'

'Why not? You're not some sort of lesbian, are you?'

'*A fene egye meg, anya!* Why should I spend all my time looking for a man?'

'Surely every decent woman needs a man of her own. Your biological clock will start ticking if you're not careful. You're no spring chicken, you know.'

'I can assure you there are no clocks ticking.'

'Why are you always so difficult?'

'Just leave it, will you?'

'You know how much I've longed for grandchildren. Imagine what it feels like listening to everyone talking about their grand-children … What am I supposed to say? That one of my children is drinking himself into an early grave and the other one spends her entire life working and isn't remotely interested in men?'

'Well, that's the truth. Would it be so terrible to tell people the truth?'

'Anna. You don't understand.'

'You're right. I don't. Goodbye.'

'Don't hang up. Let's talk about something else.'

Only then did they start talking about the goings-on in Kanizsa. Their conversations always followed the same pattern. Anna knew to expect this, and even though every time she resolved not to rise to it, it was no use. She understood only too well why Ákos didn't want to talk to their mother.

The next morning Anna received a call from Farzad. Their assistant had recognised Riikka. She had eaten at Hazileklek on the afternoon of 21 August.

'And she wasn't alone,' Farzad added.

Anna closed her eyes.

'She was with another woman. Older.'

What on earth?

'You want to speak with Jenna? She is here.'

'Thank you,' said Anna. The sound of crackling came through the receiver as the phone changed hands.

'Jenna,' came a young voice.

'Hello, this is Fekete Anna from the police.'

'It's all right, go ahead,' she heard Farzad's voice in the background.

'So, you remember seeing Riikka, the girl in the photograph, eating at the restaurant.'

'Yes. It was 21 August.'

'And how can you be sure?'

'I noticed them because they were obviously arguing. The girl and the woman she was with, that is.'

'Arguing?'

'Yes. They weren't shouting or anything, but you can tell when things are strained between people. And these two were definitely really tense.'

'Did you hear what they were saying to one another?'

'No. They stopped talking whenever I got too close. In fact, I don't think they talked all that much at all.'

'Tell me about the woman.'

'I thought they were mother and daughter, having some kind of argument.'

'So the woman was clearly much older?'

'Yes.'

'What did she look like?'

'Hard to say. She was wearing sunglasses and a headscarf. Average size. Old.'

'How old?'

'I'm a pretty bad judge of age. Everyone over forty looks old to me,' Jenna sniggered.

'Think harder.'

'Sixty. Fifty, maybe.'

'Not exactly an OAP, then.'

'No, definitely not.'

'Are you sure you didn't hear what they were talking about? Anything at all, a single word even.'

'I took their order, asked them if they had enjoyed their meal. They answered fairly abruptly that everything had been fine. I brought the bill. The girl thanked me, the woman didn't. That was it.'

'How did they pay?'

'Separately. In cash.'

A fene, Anna cursed to herself.

'What about when they were leaving?'

'I can't really remember. A big group walked in just then.'

'Do you remember seeing a red car parked nearby?'

'No.'

'Thank you, Jenna. This information could be very useful.'

'No problem, great to be of help. Just get the lunatic quickly. Me and my friends are scared to go out in the evenings.'

As well you should be, thought Anna.

27

RAUNO WALKED INTO ANNA'S OFFICE, clearly agitated.

'I've made contact with the online retailer that sells all the Huitzilopochtli junk. I sent him an offer so tasty he couldn't not get in touch with me. Guess where he's based?'

'Where? Not here, surely?'

'Well, no. It's run by some Russian guy from an office in Moscow. Not the first place I would have thought of. They sell all kinds of mumbo-jumbo stuff, everything from organic produce to new-age trinkets.'

'Organic produce isn't mumbo-jumbo,' Anna objected.

'So why are they selling literature on spiritual development too, healing crystals, feng shui and what have you? Sounds like mumbo-jumbo to me.'

'What did the Russian guy have to say?'

'He said they receive dozens of orders every day from all around the globe, and that they don't keep records of orders by country but by the day they were shipped. But he promised to go through their shipping records and see if there was a shipment of Huitzilopochtli jewellery to Finland. He said it'll take time though. He's the only employee: takes orders, packages them up and posts them, takes care of the warehouse, so he doesn't have all that much spare time. He said those necklaces were a hit in the States – sold a few thousand units.'

'Wow. How much does one necklace cost?'

'Ten euros. Should we order a set for the Christmas party?'

'Hah, that would be hilarious. Let's order some!'

'I don't think Virkkunen would get the joke.'

'Or Niemi.'

They laughed together. It felt good.

'The best of it is, some guy at the National Bureau of Investigation, who specialises in international cases, is going to take over looking into any connections with cults. Which is a good job, because my arse is numb from all that sitting at the computer,' said Rauno.

'Good. I'm sure we can find some other use for your arse.'

Rauno looked at Anna. He was so close. They could have touched one another.

'Joke,' said Anna, taking a step back and trying to smile. 'I mean … there are more important things you could be focusing on.'

Rauno smiled back, perhaps too pleasantly.

Surely he isn't getting any ideas, Anna thought nervously.

'Listen, let's go for a pint this evening,' he said. 'I feel like I really need a decent Finnish beer after all this grim work on the Aztecs. On second thoughts, make that a Czech beer instead. Let's invite Sari and Esko too.'

'Oh, Esko … I don't think I'm really…'

'Yes, yes, it would do you two a world of good to talk outside work.'

'He doesn't talk.'

'Haven't you noticed he's clearly warming to you. He's not nearly as much of an ogre as he was to start with.'

'Maybe.'

'Strike while the iron is hot. Let's go.'

'You could invite your wife too,' Anna suggested.

'She wouldn't come. And who would look after the kids?'

'Shame. It would be nice to meet her.'

'Well. Shall we?'

'All right. But only if Sari comes too.'

'I'll ask her and let you know.'

'Okay.'

Initially Sari wasn't so keen on the idea. Sanna had the day off and her mother was looking after the children. Grandma would be tired and have to go home soon. Anna was exhausted too, to tell the truth.

But still.

She wouldn't be able to sleep anyway. Sari was tired of running straight home from work; a break from her daily routine was tempting. Much to Anna's relief, Esko was the only member of the team who declined straight away. He had other things to do, he said, without expanding further.

Eventually Anna, Sari and Rauno walked along the bustling Sibeliuksenkatu towards Tintti's Bar, a salt-of-the-earth pub that was just waking from its afternoon slumber. It was seven o'clock. The place gave off the stale reek of decades of boozing. A few customers were propping up the bar as though they'd been stuck there for years. Anna and Rauno ordered a pint each; Sari took a pint of cider. They withdrew to a table in the corner.

'Ah, wonderful,' said Sari as she took her first sip of cider. 'I had no idea how much I needed this.'

'What do you think about all the new information that's come to light? The youngsters' interviews and everything?' asked Rauno. 'Wanna bet Virve and Jere hatched this whole thing together?'

'Who was the older woman? The one Riikka was eating with?'

'Exactly. And are Virve and Jere still hiding something?' Anna wondered.

'Do you think somebody could force them to do things like that? Someone posing as Huitzilopochtli?' Sari lowered her voice to a whisper, though the nearest pair of ears was over by the counter.

'The mysterious woman, maybe?'

'She could be some kind of cult leader.'

'Someone who requires human sacrifices.'

'Do you think such a cult could really exist? Here in Finland?'

'Thankfully the bureau will be dealing with that possibility from now on,' said Rauno. 'At least the American nutcases are harmless. I checked with the local police; they have no known connections with Finland, or Europe for that matter.'

'Have there been any new leads from the public?' Anna asked.

'People call us with all kinds of nonsense. We've even had a few confessions. We need to locate that red car,' said Sari.

'Jere drives a blue Laguna,' Rauno reminded them.

'Exactly. How can this be so complicated?' Anna exclaimed.

'What made you want to become a police officer?' Sari asked Anna out of the blue.

Anna was prepared. At least, almost prepared. She had guessed there would be a flood of questions once they got to the bar. It was a wonder she had managed to avoid them for so long. She took a deep breath and began.

'Well, for a start I've always been really into sport.' Until now, she thought, and saw an image of her training schedule, which as autumn had drawn on was as empty as the leafless trees.

'I'd always thought I wanted a job where doing sport wasn't the main thing, but where it really came in useful. I even considered a career in the army for a while.'

'Have you done military service?' asked Rauno.

'Yes.'

'Tell us about that!'

'It's Corporal Fekete to you. At ease, everyone!'

'Christ! Where did you do your service?'

'At the regiment in Sodankylä. I thought of applying for the Reserve Officer School and even the National Defence University, but gave up the idea in the end. I spent one summer working as a temp in our documentation division, dealing with passports applications, driving licences and that sort of thing. It was there that I got a glimpse of police work, and I guess that's where the idea came from.'

Anna had been overwhelmed to get that summer job at the police department. She had read a small item in the newspaper encouraging travellers to apply for their passports well in advance to avoid the summer rush. That had given her idea: she wrote a letter of application and handed it personally to the head of the documentation division. Her application had been received enthusiastically, and the staff at the passport office finally reached their summer breaks slightly less exhausted than they might have, had it not been for the new summer temp. Anna was meticulous with all the paperwork and was a quick learner. Everyone had taken to her immediately. In the staff canteen she chatted once or twice with a nice female officer. She said the job was fascinating but woefully underpaid. Anna had saved her wages for five weeks and put herself through driving school.

'But tell us the real story. Why the police? Why not the army?' Sari asked impatiently.

'I've got family baggage in both professions. I started to get sick of the endless bossing around in the army. I realised it wasn't really my thing.'

The truth was that Anna had joined the army because she wanted to get to the bottom of something. She still didn't know exactly what. She had a strong sense that she needed to examine something, to get an overall picture, to work her way inside the system in order to understand it.

But it hadn't helped. After basic training she felt she understood even less. She had given up trying.

Ultimately, war was always mindless.

'It's the same in the police force,' Rauno commented.

'Not quite. There's a hierarchy, for sure, and everything is carefully regulated, but things aren't as black and white. Here at least people need a brain of their own, you can discuss things. It's not just about obeying orders, so it's far more suited to a pacifist hippie like me.'

'I'll drink to that!' said Sari and raised her pint of cider.

'To hippies!' Rauno shouted.

'And the police force!' Sari added.

'My father was a policeman,' Anna said quietly as she too raised her glass.

They each took a long swig.

'He died when I was little.'

'I'm sorry,' Sari said. 'How old were you?'

'Five. I don't remember him all that well.'

'Can I ask what happened?'

'I'm not entirely sure what happened. All they told me was that he was killed in the line of duty.'

'Terrible,' Sari gasped.

'I'm sorry,' Rauno said awkwardly.

'Thanks, but it all happened so long ago.'

'Shall we have another one? My round,' said Rauno.

'Oh, why not?' Sari answered.

'You guys make me feel like I'm back home – sitting around in bars, raising toasts, buying rounds. Are you sure you're not secretly from the Balkans?' Anna joked.

'Think of us as wannabe Balkans,' Rauno laughed.

Once they had each bought a round, it was late and they were all rather merry. They decided to leave, because one more drink would have meant getting really sloshed. That was the last thing any of them needed, let alone a splitting headache the next morning. Sari jumped into the first taxi, leaving Anna and Rauno to walk back towards the city centre together.

'Should we have one for the road, after all?' Rauno suggested.

'No, I think that's enough for tonight.'

'Pisses me off, the thought of going home,' said Rauno and staggered somewhat. He took hold of Anna's arm, steadied himself and left his hand where it was. Anna felt it burning the skin through her jacket like a glowing hot iron. Damn it, she thought, but she couldn't shake him off; she didn't dare, didn't want to hurt him.

'Why?' she forced herself to ask, though she knew the answer. She'd seen men like this in bars hundreds of times. It was as predictable as age-old TV repeats.

'Things with the wife are going tits up. And now she wants a divorce.'

'Really?'

'Yep. We haven't made any final decisions yet, but we've started talking about it. Fuck it, I was trying to be considerate towards her, brought her dinner and everything – sushi, her favourite – and she decides to use the situation to her advantage, puts the kids to sleep and sits down at the table. That hasn't happened in weeks, you know, we haven't eaten at the same fucking table for God knows how long.'

Rauno squeezed Anna's arm a little tighter. Anna let it happen.

'There she is, pouring tea into cups like nothing's happened, and says perfectly calmly that we should probably get a divorce. Damn it. Says she's been thinking about it for a while and that she can't see any other solution.'

'Do you think there is another solution?'

'I don't know,' Rauno bleated. 'We should try harder.'

'Try what?'

'I don't know. Being together, doing something together.'

'Did you tell her this?'

'No. I threw the fucking sushi in the bin.'

Together they walked north. Anna didn't want to walk all the way home; Koivuharju was quite a distance from the city centre. She decided to get a taxi from the warehouse buildings in the marina, where the town houses gave way to the parkland at Koskipuisto. The park had a bad reputation among residents, but in reality there was hardly any crime there whatsoever. Still, walking through it in the dark wasn't exactly an attractive prospect.

'I'll get a cab over there,' said Anna.

'Can I sleep at your place?' Rauno asked. 'Don't get me wrong, I can sleep on the sofa,' he continued and pressed himself closer to Anna. 'Though, I have to say, you're one hell of an attractive woman.'

'Rauno, you're drunk. Have you had more than just a couple of pints? Go back to your own home.'

'I haven't got a home.'

'Oh, nonsense.'

'Anna, you're magnificent. You're an unbelievably good-looking woman. Let me stay at your place. I promise, I won't touch you,' he pleaded and tried to kiss her.

Anna forcibly shoved him away.

'Stop it!' she shouted. 'This isn't nice any more.'

'So why am I not good enough for you? Do I have to be some kind of cripple to turn you on?'

'Oh piss off, Rauno,' said Anna and ran to the taxi rank, jumped into a car and watched the dark, deserted city rush past her eyes as she tried to hold back the tears. The jetties outside the brand-new apartment blocks on the islands at the mouth of the river floated black against the glinting water, then they reached the slip road on to the motorway and from there the taxi sped up to 120 kilometres an hour past Välikylä and Savela towards the imposing apartment blocks of Koivuharju, towards the apartment in which she would try to get some sleep, the place that she called home.

It struck her that she still hadn't gone to visit the house where she and Ákos and their mother had moved to after leaving the reception centre. It was close by. Childhood. Youth. There it was round the corner.

Anna couldn't get to sleep. She couldn't forget the insinuating text messages from an unlisted number. Now she was thinking about them again.

Could Rauno be behind them?

She tossed and turned in bed until morning, put on her head-phones and listened to Delay's album *Anima*, tried to calm herself down, to forget the text messages, to forget Rauno. She went out to the balcony for a cigarette, stood there shivering in only her pyjamas and dressing gown. She spat on to the asphalt below.

The tower blocks stared at her with hundreds of empty eyes, oozing loneliness.

28

'IMAGINE, THERE ARE ALMOST 600,000 rifles in Finland,' Rauno said to Esko as they drove to Maria Pollari's house.

'So?' Esko replied.

'It's a bloody insane number.'

'Why?'

'That's one rifle for every eight people in this country.'

'So what?'

'Well, it's pretty fucking worrying, don't you think?'

'Not really. What's with all the swearing?' Esko asked. 'Feeling a bit the worse for wear this morning?'

'No.'

'Late night?'

'No.'

The golden boy is lying, Esko thought with an air of self-satisfaction. Rauno's conscientious attitude had always irritated him.

'You've got a rifle yourself – a .12-calibre at that – and I've got two.'

'But I've started wondering whether it's too easy to get a firearm in this country. Even underage kids can get their hands on a gun.'

'For Christ's sake, Rauno, don't talk bollocks. The background checks are ridiculous these days. You have to spend hours proving you're not a self-destructive lunatic with a quick temper. How could they make the protocol any tighter? And as a country lad yourself, you know fine well how bloody important the hunting season is. What else is there for young boys to do? Hunting's a great hobby, keeps kids on the straight and narrow. You don't see country lads hanging around the shopping mall all night; they're in the woods hunting, doing something useful and age-old. They're enjoying being outdoors, getting some fresh air. They're the kind of lads that do their national service without kicking up a fuss.'

'You're right. It's just got me thinking, especially after these shootings. The ecological footprint of game is virtually non-existent. You can't say that for soya.'

'What fucking ecological footprint?'

'Who's swearing now?'

'That's just my irresistible charm. Have you been out hunting this season?'

'Too busy. And there's a bit of a situation about to kick off at home.'

'Jesus, Rauno, all the more reason. Let's go to Jyräväjärvi next weekend, you and me. We'll rent a cottage, have a sauna, get pissed and forget all about your woman problems. Shoot us a few ducks too. What do you say?'

'I'll have to think. Sounds good,' Rauno said, though he knew he wouldn't go.

The Pollaris' house came into view at the end of the path. It was a new, light-blue, detached house with a mansard roof that lent it an air of bygone grandeur. The still of the front garden made the entire house seem deserted. The yellow leaves of the berry bushes fluttered in the breeze. A wind chime jangled on the almost bare branches of a bird-cherry tree. The vegetable patch was empty and untended. Maria Pollari was at home. She invited the officers into the kitchen and asked if they would like some coffee. Both politely refused upon seeing the difficulty Maria had in moving. As she walked she pressed her hands against the base of her spine and groaned in pain as she sat down. They didn't have the heart to cause her any excess trouble.

'What do you want now?' Maria asked, irritated.

'We found an interesting item in your husband's pocket. Here's a photograph. Do you know what it is or why he had it in his pocket?'

Rauno showed her a photograph of the Huitzilopochtli necklace. Maria looked at it carefully.

'I've never seen a necklace like that,' she answered eventually. 'I'm sure Ville didn't own anything like this. Neither do I. How could it have ended up in his pocket?'

'That's what we're trying to establish.'

'What is it?'

Rauno looked at Esko, who gave an affirmative nod.

'It's an image of an Aztec god called Huitzilopochtli,' said Rauno.

'What on earth was it doing in Ville's pocket?' Maria was becoming agitated.

'We don't know.'

'This is sick,' she started to shout. 'My husband is shot while on a perfectly innocent run, then ends up with that thing in his pocket. Which pocket was it in?'

'In his right-hand jacket pocket,' Rauno answered.

'Who put it there? Why?'

'I'm afraid we don't know.'

'It was the killer. It's some sick lunatic. He's going to turn up here and shoot us all,' Maria screamed before falling suddenly silent and stroking her stomach.

'It's perfectly understandable that you're frightened, but there's nothing to indicate that the killer will attack people in their homes. He stalks joggers on the running track.'

'Yes, until now he has, but maybe now he's going to change tactics. Surely he can't repeat the same pattern indefinitely? How many joggers is he going to kill?' Maria was no longer shouting, but her voice was still jittery.

'Could this be something personal?' asked Esko. 'Do you think it's possible the killer deliberately chose Ville?'

'Do you mean, did Ville have any enemies?'

'You could put it like that.'

'Ville had only friends. Not very many, but they were all close friends. Everybody liked him. Nobody could possibly have anything against him.'

'What about people from the past? From before you got married?'

'Ville and I got married a year and four months ago, when he got his job with the city council. Before that we lived in Jyväskylä; that's where we're both originally from. We dated for two years. We were in our early twenties when we met each other at a mass organised by the Lutheran students' association. What past? People that age don't have a past.'

'That depends on the person. Quite a few people that age have a past,' said Esko.

'Ville didn't.'

'What about you?'

'I don't either. I went to confirmation school in Aholansaari and fell in love with one of the older boys. That's my past. Shocking, isn't it?'

'Do you have any connections to Saloinen? Do you know anyone who lives there?'

'You mean the girl killed in August? The one you think was Ville's lover or something equally ridiculous? No. We don't know anyone out that way. Most of our friends are still in Jyväskylä, and by that I mean our true friends. Here we don't have much to do with anyone except for a few work friends and Ville's orienteering friends. They all live in the local area.'

'Did you ever have any arguments?'

'How many times do I have to tell you? No, we didn't. We loved one another. How dare you turn up here and hurt me further?' she screamed.

'I'm sorry,' Rauno apologised. 'All we want to do is find this killer.'

Maria was silent. Only the faint gurgling of the fridge elements broke the silence.

'My back feels like it's on fire; I've got to lie down,' she finally said.

Without waiting for a response she stood up with considerable difficulty, staggered into the living room, her back hunched forwards, and lay on her side on the sofa.

'This has got much worse now that Ville isn't here to help me.'

Maria started to sob.

'Is there anyone who could come out here and help you?' Rauno asked with a note of genuine concern.

Maria wiped her eyes and swallowed her tears, stroked her swollen stomach.

'My mother is here already. She's in town picking up some groceries.' Maria's voice was exhausted. Her eyes momentarily drooped shut.

'Did you notice anything strange about Ville in recent weeks?' Rauno tried again.

'I've already talked about this. I didn't notice anything, because there was nothing to notice. Everything was perfectly normal.'

'Ville had told Jussi Järvinen about a red car he'd seen in the parking area at the start of the running track. Did he ever mention that car to you?'

'No.'

'Do you have any idea who that red car might belong to? According to the sightings, it would seem to be a somewhat older model, an average-sized car.'

'How specific. What make of car?'

'I'm afraid we don't know.'

'Nothing springs to mind, I have to say. My mother has a red car, but it's a brand-new Volvo station wagon. And besides, my mother lives in Jyväskylä and doesn't go jogging.'

'Try and recall the moments when Ville returned from his runs this past summer. What did he tell you? How did he seem? Did he appear worried or concerned about something?'

Maria thought hard, then shook her head once again.

'I categorically did not notice anything out of the ordinary about him. I mean, he wasn't frightened or nervous or anything of the sort. He told me how the run had gone and how he was preparing for his next competition. Though orienteering was only a hobby for Ville, he took it very seriously.'

'What do you know about Jussi Järvinen?' Rauno asked.

'Not all that much. He was a slimy sort of man.'

'In what way?'

'He's a bit too full of himself, the way big bosses generally are. He has a very high opinion of himself. But his wife Tiina seems pleasant enough. They visited us every now and then.'

'When were they last here?'

'June. It was before Midsummer. We had a barbecue in the garden.'

'Did you notice anything odd about the men's behaviour?'

'No,' she replied. 'Ville didn't have a difficult relationship with anyone.'

'Were you in contact with Jussi's wife?'

'No, we weren't friends. They were so different from us. Sometimes I wondered why Ville always wanted to train with that self-obsessed man.'

'Why did he? In your opinion?'

'I've already told you we don't have friends round here. Ville met Jussi through the orienteering club, they live close by, I don't know. Men enjoy doing outdoors things with other men. It doesn't matter who, as long as they get to run around with their dicks out.'

Rauno was amused.

Maria sat up on the sofa, an agonised expression on her face. She clenched her fist and used it to massage the base of her spine.

'Do you have a doctor's certificate for your back problems?' Esko asked.

'Excuse me?' Maria became animated again. 'Of course I have. How else do you think I've managed to be on sick leave for two months? It's over there in the bureau. Take a look for yourself.'

Temperamental woman, Esko thought. I reckon she did more than fall for that older boy.

Esko fetched the paperwork, looked through it and gave Rauno a nod. Loosening of the sacroiliac joints. Intense pain while walking, standing and sitting. Unable to work.

Unable to murder anyone.

The front door opened. A woman's voice could be heard in the hallway.

'Maria! Whose car is that in the drive?'

'There are two police officers here, Mum,' Maria shouted back. 'They want to ask about Ville.'

A chubby woman in her sixties appeared in the living room, like an older clone of Maria Pollari.

'Hello. Sirkka Jääskö, Maria's mother. I came as soon as I heard about this terrible thing. Poor child. They were so happy together.' Maria's mother's voice broke and she stopped talking.

'My condolences,' said Esko. 'It's a good thing you're here to support your daughter.'

'In fact, I'd thought of taking her away, back home for a while, because she's afraid of sleeping here. Is that all right? I live in Jyväskylä.'

Rauno turned to look at Esko, who thought about this for a moment before nodding his consent.

'That's fine. I'm sure it'll be best for her and the baby. Leave us your contact details, because we will probably have to talk to her again,' said Esko.

The sound of weeping came from the living room.

'Maria is in shock. I'm worried about what this will do to the baby. Could you leave us? She needs to get some rest.'

'We were just leaving,' said Rauno.

'When can I have my husband back?' Maria cried. 'I want to bury him! Let me have my husband back!'

'I'm afraid in cases like this it can be some time before we're able to release the body,' Esko said apologetically. 'Given that this wasn't death by natural causes,' he continued quietly.

By now Maria was wailing in rasping, brutal sobs, a mixture of weeping and pain that brought the officers out in goose bumps. Rauno felt awkward, didn't know where to look. He couldn't bear watching her agony.

'Please, leave us,' Sirkka Jääskö implored them in an exhausted voice. 'Go before she loses her mind, before she goes into labour.'

*

'I think the killer chooses his victims at random,' said Rauno as they drove back into town.

'Hangover easing up yet?'

'I haven't got a hangover!'

'Did you try and come on to the wog? Or did she try it on with you?'

'Do you have to be such a wanker all the time?'

'Did you?'

'For your information, that wog served in the Finnish army. And her father was a policeman.'

Esko fell silent. It had started to rain, drizzle at first, then more steadily. The road was wet. The clouds looked like cotton-wool balls after cleaning out the barrel of a gun.

'There's absolutely nothing to connect these two victims. This lunatic probably takes out whoever happens to be running past. He's pretending to be some kind of Aztec warrior. I don't think I'll be going out running any time soon,' said Rauno as stared at the raindrops trickling down the window.

Rajapuro, 9 p.m. Anna was sitting in a patrol car outside Bihar's house, the blue lights on the car roof lazily flashing. Drizzle. Cold. When was someone going to question the fact that she was constantly checking out patrol cars, Anna wondered. Someone will start asking questions, wondering what I'm up to. What am I going to say?

But she didn't care. If she got caught, she would come out here in her own car. They couldn't stop her.

The lights were on in Bihar's apartment. The metallic glow of the television in the living room. What were they watching? Not *Friends* or *Sex and the City*, that was for sure. The occasional glimpse of a figure in the kitchen window, fetching water perhaps. Or going to the fridge. A normal family evening. A normal family.

Right.

Rain glistened on the asphalt like oil; the 10- and 12-storey apartment blocks dwarfed the trees. Kids in baggy jeans were smoking something beneath the roof outside Bihar's doorway, their presence challenging the shadows cast upon them like a life sentence by the surrounding buildings. Ducks caught in the oil, birds that nobody dressed in overalls is going to come and save.

Nobody cares. We are always outsiders.

Strangers.

Others.

Why can't I just stop this? Anna was so tired that she could have fallen asleep in the car. She should have driven straight home from work and gone to bed. Now she would have to take the car back into the city centre, check it in at the depot and only then drive back to Koivuharju – almost an hour's round trip. How would she get any sleep tonight? Fatigue was pressed against her heavy eyelids right now, the heater was blowing a soothing, anaesthetic warmth against her face and she felt languid.

Everything seemed to be in order at Bihar's house. The girl had probably already done her homework, like all hard-working school-girls, and was now watching a Kurdish soap opera on one of the satellite channels and getting ready for bed. Her mother and father would be thanking Allah for such a wonderful daughter and en-couraging her to keep on studying through university. The younger siblings would follow in Bihar's footsteps and one day, not long from now, Finland would see a wealth of highly educated, multilingual, multicultural, second-generation immigrants.

Right.

I'm nothing but a paranoid workaholic, thought Anna as she put her foot on the accelerator, put the car into first gear, released the hand brake and sped off from the Chelkins' front yard.

By the time she arrived home, Anna felt wide awake or, more pre-cisely, the sense of fatigue had momentarily disappeared. She hadn't felt properly awake for weeks: a thick jelly had settled around her brain, her stiff shoulders wouldn't relax even after careful stretch-ing, her heart rate was continually too fast, and her entire body felt constantly as though it was both on overdrive and incapable of functioning properly.

Anna signed in to the police's intranet and started reading Sari's reports on Ville Pollari's phone and bank records. Every call to and from Ville's telephone on the day of the murder had been checked; they were mostly work-related. On his way home he had received a call from Maria, and once he was home another call from Jussi. That was it. Sari had gone through Ville's phone records over the summer and compared them with Riikka's records. What a job Sari has done, Anna thought in awe. Ville hadn't received any calls from any unlisted prepaid numbers and he hadn't called any such numbers himself. Moreover, there was nothing to indicate any connection with Riikka or her circle of friends. Ville didn't even have a Facebook profile. His credit card had been swiped mostly at the large supermarket in Asemakylä. There was nothing to suggest any prior contact with the killer. Nothing whatsoever. Anna racked her brains, trying to think how best to proceed, but her mind was blank. Everything seemed to have reached a dead end, yet again, a dead end with no way out. It was as though the case was stuck in the jelly surrounding her head. And yet she was convinced that there was something she should remember, something she had seen.

Anna eventually managed to doze for a few hours. At least that was something, she tried to console herself, though her head and neck had turned from jelly to burning lava as she clambered out of the tangled sheets at around 5 a.m. She staggered into the kitchen to make some coffee. Her mobile was flashing on the table. She was afraid to look at it; she didn't think she could deal with another message from an unlisted number.

It was Ákos. He'd tried to call her around 4 a.m. So he was on a real bender. Her brother had also sent her a message, which Anna deleted without reading. She knew he would only be asking for money. Then she fetched the newspaper from the mat in the hallway and began leafing through the news items without feeling the slightest interest in them. Someone had sent a brusque text message to the readers' pages: *Why aren't the police doing anything? Decent people are too scared to go out at night.*

Was the writer referring to the jogging murders? Or general law and order? What were they talking about? Come on in and see what we really do, Anna implored the anonymous author, come and watch us lazing around all day long. The police always came in for criticism, no matter what they did.

Whatever. She was already used to it.

What she really needed wasn't what normal people called rest or refreshment.

She wanted oblivion, real oblivion.

Even for a moment.

29

VELI-MATTI HELMERSON raised his eyes from the bright, glowing screen of his computer. What was that clatter in the corridor? As though the door of the neighbouring classroom had rattled. He listened carefully for a moment; sometimes the kids snuck back into school to carry out some kind of prank if the front door was left open. It was strange that schools always attracted pupils in the evenings, especially those that didn't show their faces much during the daytime. Even at this school, the police were called out several times each summer to shoo groups of kids drinking and making a mess in the playground – the school's very own bright young things, who clearly missed the place during the summer break.

He couldn't hear anything. The building again exuded an unbroken silence. The caretaker went round after 4 p.m. locking all the doors in the main building. No pupils were allowed in after that. It was probably Kirsi Koponen leaving her classroom next door. The new fourth-grade teacher was a pretty young woman, who seemed enthusiastic, hard-working and conscientious. They're all like that to begin with, thought Veli-Matti, then they burn themselves out within a few years.

He looked at the clock ticking on the wall. It was almost six o'clock. After his last lesson, he had stayed on to prepare classes for the rest of the week and gone through essays for one of the children's development projects. An extra three hours had sped past unnoticed, time for which he wouldn't be paid. And people still commented on how envious they were of his short working hours.

Veli-Matti decided to call it a day. He switched off his computer, sorted the various papers on his desk, flicked off the lights in the classroom and went into the empty staffroom. The table was cluttered with used coffee mugs. Who's supposed to clear those up, he thought as he recognised a mug belonging to the PE teacher Seppo Vilmusenaho. Spoilt rotten, that guy, always getting other people to do his chores. If I were a woman, would I wash up that mug, he wondered. That's how women behave – taking care of everything and indirectly perpetuating the cycle of underachievement from father to son.

Veli-Matti rinsed his own mug and placed it in the drying cupboard. Then he went to the coat stand, slipped off his work sandals with soft curved soles and put on his walking shoes, pulled on his coat and double locked the staffroom door, as the last person to leave was expected to do. He stepped out into the dark corridor, regularly punctuated with the doors of classrooms, toilets, closets and cleaning cupboards.

Clouds were drifting across the sky, bringing the promise of rain. The wind had whipped up. Veli-Matti felt the chill and pulled a pair of gloves out of his pocket. Two lonely cars stood in the school's asphalted car park: a red Volkswagen Golf and Veli-Matti's own black BMW. Was there still someone at school, he wondered. Who could still be at work? Who owned a car like that? It certainly looked familiar, but there were over a hundred members of staff at the school, if you included the canteen staff and all the cleaners. Veli-Matti couldn't identify everybody's car; it wasn't something that particularly interested him. Though he had felt a wave of irritation when Vilmusenaho had come back from Bosnia with a brand-new Mercedes. A year off work and a ludicrously expensive car. It had felt like an unreasonable amount of good fortune for such an arsehole.

Just as Veli-Matti opened the door to his BMW, which had served him well for the last ten years, and was about to step inside, he looked up at his classroom windows.

The lights were on.

Bloody hell, he cursed out loud. Didn't I just switch them off? He slammed the door shut and turned around, taking a few steps towards the school building before changing his mind. Forget about it, he thought. The council wouldn't go bankrupt if the lights were left on for one night. It had been hours since his light school lunch and he was hungry. He decided to leave the lights on and drive home.

In the fridge were the remains of yesterday's lasagne and a drop of white wine. Veli-Matti reheated the food in the microwave and poured the remaining wine into a glass. It tasted flat and was too cold. A bit like her over there, he thought and looked at his wife who was loading the dishwasher with a sour look on her face. What was the matter with her now?

After finishing his meal, Veli-Matti slumped on the sofa and switched on the television.

'I'm going now,' came his wife's voice from the hallway.

'Okay, I'll probably go for a run,' he replied absent-mindedly and didn't bother getting up to kiss her or give her a hug. She would probably have slapped him if he'd tried.

'Be careful,' she said, though there was no warmth in her voice.

'I will,' he called nonchalantly, though he felt a wave of terror washing through him.

For an hour or so he watched a re-run of a pointless talk show, then he remembered the lights left on in his classroom. The matter started to bug him. What if Vilmusenaho happened to walk his dog past the school and noticed that he'd forgotten to switch off the lights? He would never hear the end of it. It was a niggling thought. Vilmusenaho was just like that, nagged on about people's mistakes, as if in jest, and never forgot things. A thoroughly unpleasant man. It would be best to go on that run straight away, stop off at the school and turn those lights off. Not because of Vilmusenaho; it's the principle, he tried to convince himself. His class had signed up for a project dealing with sustainable development. The students separated their rubbish, tried to use as few paper hand towels as possible and switched off the classroom lights during break time. It was all pointless, he thought, but he had to lead by example. He pulled on his tracksuit, stepped out into the drizzling rain and started jogging at a leisurely pace towards the main middle school in Saloinen. The car park was deserted except for the red Volkswagen.

Still at work, he wondered.

The quiet in the corridors was oppressive.

'Hello?' Veli-Matti hollered from the front door, but not one of the doors in the dark corridor opened up. The school was empty and silent.

Veli-Matti knew the building like the back of his hand and could have made his way around with his eyes closed. He switched the lights on nonetheless. He felt suddenly afraid. He'd been afraid since the end of August, though he was convinced that those terrible events couldn't possibly have anything to do with him, they just couldn't, in all rationality.

He walked past the row of closed doors towards his own classroom. Familiar building, familiar rooms, only familiar colleagues had keys. He would be fine.

After the second murder he had calmed down somewhat. These murders couldn't possibly have anything to do with him, absolutely not.

That being said, he had started restricting his runs to the built-up areas near his house. Everybody had done the same. It was a normal precaution under the circumstances.

When Veli-Matti opened his classroom door, he noticed that the computer was still switched on too. Strange, he thought. How have I become so careless? I'm sure I switched everything off. Irritated at himself, he marched up to his desk and leaned across the computer, switched it off and stood up to leave again straight away.

But the door was blocked.

A dark figure stood in the doorway, aiming a rifle right at him.

'Jesus Christ, what are you…?' Veli-Matti gasped.

'Shut up and sit down,' the figure commanded him and switched off the lights in the room. 'The safety pin is off, this thing's loaded and I know how to use it, as I'm sure you know.'

Veli-Matti sat down in his chair. The lights in the car park shone dimly through the classroom windows, sketching the shadows of the desks across the floor. How could I not have recognised that car, he thought. Is this how it's all going to end?

My work. My life. Everything?

Yes, this is where it's going to end.

I won't see tomorrow.

'There's a present for you on the table. Pick it up and use it. Don't try anything or other people are going to get hurt besides you. They're going to get really hurt. Understand?'

Veli-Matti looked at the syringe lying on the table and nodded.

'What's in it?' he asked, his voice trembling.

'It won't kill you. It'll make things more pleasant. I strongly recommend you use it,' the figure responded.

Veli-Matti stared at syringe. He couldn't do it. He'd never injected himself with anything. Even the idea of a finger-prick blood test scared him.

'Come on, get a fucking move on,' the figure snapped and shook the rifle at him threateningly. 'Do exactly as I say, and nobody else will get hurt. Think of all those sweet little pupils that live round here. What about Eveliina? She's at home right now, all by herself. I've checked. That single mother of hers is on night shift again. If I have to shoot you here, she'll get it too. Maybe a few others as well.'

Insane, thought Veli-Matti. You sick lunatic.

Veli-Matti thought of Eveliina, who was at home doing her homework. A quiet, hard-working girl, every teacher's dream pupil. Her mother felt bad about always being on night shift and leaving her daughter to spend the evenings at home by herself. She'd once burst into tears at the teacher–parent evening; she'd slumped against the desk and opened up to Veli-Matti.

I can't have anything terrible happen to Eveliina, he thought, and with quivering fingers he picked up the syringe and started rolling up the sleeve of his tracksuit.

'That's it. Good boy.'

Veli-Matti hesitated, his heart was racing; he could hear the blood rushing in his head. Then he pressed the syringe into his arm and closed his eyes. The tension drained from his body almost immediately. His heart began to beat calmly again, lazily, and his mind seemed to relax. His limbs drooped towards the floor. Veli-Matti suddenly felt like going to sleep, resting his heavy head on the desk and succumbing to the liberating power of sleep. The classroom rocked like a lullaby. The figure had shrunk to a distant point beside the door, and Veli-Matti no longer had the energy to care.

He slumped against the table and was just able to make out the point by the door approaching him. Like in a film in slow motion, the point gradually assumed a form, propped the indistinct contours of the rifle against the blackboard, disappeared behind him, pulled his limp arms behind his back and slipped a set of handcuffs on his lifeless wrists. Though Veli-Matti was still fully aware of the seriousness of the situation, he felt like laughing out loud. This was his chance to knock the figure for six, to kick the rifle out of reach and run away. And yet he was unable to move even the tip of a finger.

The figure sat down at one of the desks – that was Henrik's place – and waited in silence. After a short while the worst of the numbness seemed to disperse. The objects in the classroom regained their form and Veli-Matti's limbs began to feel like they belonged to him once again. The figure stood up, looked out into the car park for a moment, then nudged Veli-Matti up from his chair with the barrel of the rifle, forced him out of the building and into the car park. He sat him down in the front seat of the red car and drove off somewhere; Veli-Matti didn't know where.

30

EVERY DAY DETECTIVE INSPECTOR RONKAINEN cycled the seven-kilometre journey to the police station where his job was to take calls from members of the public who needed the police's assistance and to pass them on to the correct officers for further investigation. He was expecting a quiet start to his shift, slowly sipping his coffee without any semblance of hurry, because it was a Tuesday morning, and statistically the night between Monday and Tuesday was the calmest of the week.

On this day, however, his telephone rang abruptly before he had even managed to sit down at his desk.

'My husband hasn't come home,' a woman's voice spoke into Ronkainen's ear.

'Can you give me your name, and tell me exactly what has happened?' Ronkainen asked. He glanced at his coffee cup, its contents now cooling on the table.

'My name is Kaarina Helmerson. I live in Saloinen. My husband went for a run yesterday evening and he hasn't come back.'

DI Ronkainen suddenly sat up.

'A run, you say?'

'Yes.'

'Where was he going?'

'I don't know.'

'Let me put you through to one of our investigators,' he said after thinking about the matter for only a fraction of a second.

'Very well,' the woman replied.

'Fekete Anna.'

There were a few Finnish customs that Anna would never get used to, and one of them was to give her Christian name first. Hungarians always gave their surname first.

'Hello, this is Kaarina Helmerson.'

'Good morning.'

'My husband hasn't come home. He went for a run yesterday and hasn't come back. He hasn't left me a message and now he isn't answering his phone. I'm very worried about him. I've read about … things in the paper,' the woman's voice cracked to an agonised sigh.

'Where was your husband heading?' Anna asked immediately.

'I'm not entirely sure. He used to go to the running track at Selkä-maa quite frequently, but after that terrible shooting nobody dares go there any longer. Veli-Matti has taken to running in and around the town, in built-up areas.'

Anna felt her body tense. Riikka was from Saloinen and had died in Selkämaa.

'Sometimes he would go out to Vainikkala and Riitaharju, but to my knowledge he hasn't been there since those … murders.'

'Has anything like this ever happened before? Has he been away from home for a night or two without letting you know?'

The woman began to cry. 'Never,' she said.

'I'm going to end this call and send a patrol car out to check the areas around the running tracks you've mentioned. Is that okay? I'll call you back as soon as I've done that.'

'Fine,' the woman said.

Anna raced out of her office and into the corridor, where she had arrived only a moment ago. For a fraction of a second she hesitated outside Esko's office, thought of continuing to Sari's door instead or going straight to Virkkunen's office, but changed her mind, geared herself up, pounded on the door with her fist and shouted for Esko, who then appeared at the door.

'It's happened again,' she said. 'At least, I think so.'

'Fucking hell,' said Esko and stared at Anna with that familiar

look of disdain. His breath was a fug of garlic and alcohol, which
he had tried to cover up with a throat pastille. Anna felt nauseous.

'Another jogger, a man. He hasn't come home. Wife says he didn't
use the running tracks any more, but before that he'd been a fre-
quent visitor at Selkämaa, Riitaharju and Vainikkala. I'll get patrols
out to all three locations. You should brush your teeth. And wash
your face.'

'Not much use at this age,' he replied.

Anna alerted the patrol units, informed Virkkunen of what was
going on and called Kaarina Helmerson. She put her phone on
speaker; Esko was listening next to her.

'Hello, this is Detective Constable Fekete again. The patrol cars
are now on their way to the scene and they will let me know as soon
as they have any information.'

'Good. Thank you.'

'It could well be that nothing out of the ordinary has happened.
People go missing and reappear all this time. It's actually very com-
monplace, even with people who have never done it before.'

Anna tried to think whether that was actually true or not. It was
just something you said to concerned relatives.

'Veli-Matti would have told me, and besides, he's supposed to be
at work. He never misses work, not unless he's very ill.'

'Have you asked at his place of work?'

'They called me just now. The children started wondering what
had happened when their teacher didn't show up for class.'

'So your husband is a teacher?'

Again the woman's voice cracked. 'Yes. He's a teacher at Saloinen
primary school. 6B should have started their history class at eight
this morning.'

'Why didn't you call us earlier? Yesterday evening, for instance? I
assume your husband isn't in the habit of jogging through the night.
What time did he leave?'

Too many questions at once – again, Anna berated herself. Why did she always have to rush ahead? And the accusatory tone of the questions wouldn't help in the least.

'I wasn't at home last night. I left the house around 6.30 p.m. and that's when Veli-Matti told me he was going for a run.'

'Where did you go?'

'To my elderly mother's apartment in town. I often spend the night there. She won't be able to live in her own home for much longer, but I want to support her as much as I can until the end. I only got home a moment ago.'

'Do you work too?'

'I'm the head of Saloinen high school, but I've been on leave now for about a year, mostly due to the situation with my mother. She's 89 and I don't think she has long left.'

'So you arrived home this morning and noticed that your husband had gone for a run but hadn't come home.'

'That's right. The first thing I noticed was that the car was still in the driveway, so I imagined he was still at home. He almost always drives to work. But when I came in, I noticed that the house was empty. It wasn't long before I realised it had been empty since the previous evening.'

'How can you be sure?'

'The newspaper was still in the letter box; nobody had made any coffee; there were no scraps of supper or breakfast on the table. The bed looked like it hadn't been touched. And his running clothes weren't in a crumpled pile on the bathroom floor; Veli-Matti always leaves them there.'

Kaarina started to cry again. Anna wondered whether she ought to go straight to the woman's house or wait for the patrol units to report back. How long would it take before all three running tracks had been thoroughly checked? If the man had been murdered and everything followed the same pattern as before, they would find him fairly quickly. There had been no attempt to hide the victims; both had been left lying in the middle of the track like a grotesque sign saying *look at me*. Anna guessed they would know within a few hours whether Kaarina Helmerson's husband had been killed on the running track or not.

'Will you be all right or should I send someone over now?' Anna asked.

'I don't really know. I'm sure I'll be fine. I just want to know where my husband is as soon as possible.'

'We all do. I'm sure we'll find him in perfectly good condition. Perhaps he's already on his way home. Maybe he bumped into an old friend while he was out running and they decided to go for a drink somewhere. Something like that. This happens all the time, you know.'

'Yes, you've already said that.'

There was a chill in Kaarina's voice that sent a shiver down Anna's spine. She decided to wait and hear what the patrols found out. Going directly to Kaarina Helmerson's house would be futile. Everything was probably just as she had explained.

Why was murder the first option that occurred to her? Why was it that she believed her own explanations least of all?

Esko went into the staffroom. Anna followed him.

They drank their coffee in silence. Anna's eyes kept trying to press themselves shut and her head was buzzing. Again, she hadn't got to sleep until the early hours. How many times had she dragged herself into work on only a few hours' sleep? How long could she carry on like this? She glanced at Esko; he too looked tired.

'Sleep well?' she asked on the spur of the moment.

'What? Are you taking the piss?'

'No, not at all. Sorry, I didn't mean to—'

'You say sorry a lot.'

'Well, sorry for that too.'

Her phone rang.

Anna pressed the green receiver icon, raised the phone to her ear and listened without saying anything. Then she nodded and ended the call.

'Well, say something, for Christ's sake. Have they found him?' Esko demanded impatiently.

'Yes.'

'Jesus. Where?'

'The same place we found Riikka. Shot to pieces. Huitzilopochtli in his pocket. The third victim.'

'Fuck me.'

There was something different about the area around the Selkämaa running track. It wasn't to do with the autumn, now well on its way, or the bright scattering of dried leaves on the ground, the bare branches or the overcast sky, which the sun would no longer grace with warmth this year.

Anna noticed it immediately.

It was to do with the victim.

Though the previous victims had looked shocking, they both seemed relatively tidy compared to this. At least they had only been shot.

Now something more had happened.

The deceased man was lying on his stomach. Anna cautiously approached the body, trying to keep breathing steadily, though all she wanted to do was run away – fast.

The man had been shot in the head from behind as he lay on the ground. This was clear from the bloody hole in the ground beneath his head, carved out by the force of the shot. The brain and most of the head had dripped into the hole and soaked into the soft sawdust covering the ground. There was virtually no nauseating brain spatter. The scene would have been almost bearable had there not been blood everywhere, as though it had been thrown around with a bucket. The back of the victim's tracksuit top was ripped and slashed and entirely blackened with blood. These marks had not been caused by the blast.

Once the victim had been examined in the position in which he was found, they turned him over. The reason for the large amounts of blood became apparent immediately. The man's chest and stomach had been struck multiple times with a sharp object, most probably

a knife with a long blade. The upper abdomen was riddled with
puncture wounds. It was as though Huitzilopochtli had sought to
tear out his victim's organs. The position of the body and the abun-
dance of blood spatter indicated that the mutilation had taken place
first, then the man had been executed with a single shot to the back
of the head. What's more, the killer had tried to set the man's tracksuit bottoms on fire, but the rain seemed to have stopped the fire
catching.

The killer was not satiated. Quite the opposite.

Anna felt sick.

You damn scrubland, you boring and tedious landscape. Now's
the time to speak up, she whispered, leaving the forensics team and
the coroner to get on with their work and walking off down the
running track to examine the terrain along the edges of the path.
The thicket leaves had dried and fallen to the ground. The willows
jutted upwards like clumps of jagged wicker, the pine forest behind
them was silent. The presence of the sea could be felt, nothing but a
distant sense if you listened carefully. Dark-red lingonberries waited
here and there to be plucked. Anna tasted one. They were good; the
overnight frost had done its job.

When Anna had walked just over a kilometre, the path swung
very close to the shoreline. The rush of iron-grey waves across the autumnal sea could be heard clearly. Anna looked out towards the sea.
The wind whipped water into her eyes. If there had been flocks of
sheep to clear the shrubs, as there had been centuries ago, she would
have been able to see the shore, she thought. A white seagull braved
the chilled air. Anna wondered how long it was planning on staying
so far north. She gathered a handful of lingonberries and tasted the
sweetness brought to them by the hoar frosts. I still haven't managed
to get out berry picking, though I'd planned to, she thought and
turned her back to the sea and the wind. From that angle she saw
in the distance a strange bulge in the terrain at the point where it
formed a small hillock, almost hidden with twigs and thicket. As
Anna clambered closer, she saw that the hillock was formed by two

large boulders, now covered with moss and undergrowth that had sprung up from the build-up of soil and earth on top of them. Anna tensed as she stepped around the boulders. On the northern face of the boulders, the covering of moss had been torn as though someone had climbed up the rock. Anna followed the marks. Above the boulders the willows formed an impenetrable wall. When the trees were in leaf, the shelter from the wall would be perfect. Anna sat down on the damp moss, not caring about the moisture seeping through her trousers. The tangle of twigs in front of her face was thinner at this angle. At this height there was a gap in the willow, from which you looked down diagonally on to the running track a few hundred metres away. Of course, now it was easier to see through the bare branches, but the leaves had only just fallen. Though Anna was no expert, she could see clearly that the branches here hadn't snapped by themselves. The breaks were too clean, too smooth, clearly pruned with a set of cutters. A shiver ran down her back.

She remained sitting there, watching the running track, and ran her hand across the boulder's ancient covering of moss. Its soft, moist surface had a calming effect. After a moment she saw Esko approaching from the left. Anna sat there, motionless, and stared at Esko who was walking briskly, glancing around, seemingly wondering where she was. Absent-mindedly Anna's finger found a small hole in the moss. She stuck her fingertip into the cool of the hole. Something rustled. Anna took a pair of latex gloves from her pocket and carefully tugged a piece of paper out of the hole. A sweet wrapper. And another. Mariannes. Someone had sat here before her, looking through the gap in the willows at people jogging along the track, eating Mariannes. Another shiver, more violent than the first, made Anna's body quiver.

Anna cautiously took out her phone and called Esko. She heard his phone ringing somewhere beneath her.

'Look up,' she said. Esko turned his head but didn't notice Anna until she stood up and started waving her arms.

'Get Forensics up here,' she spoke into the telephone.

*

Kaarina Helmerson lived about a kilometre from Riikka's home. She didn't look surprised as she opened the door of the white-brick detached house to Anna and Esko. Though she was probably approaching fifty, Kaarina was still an impressive sight. A pair of slim-fit jeans accentuated her long legs and the beige wrap-round cardigan revealed her slender waist, a white top showing off her ample breasts. Anna noticed Esko standing up straighter and running his hand through his hair, checking himself in the hall mirror. Anna went to shake the woman's hand. Kaarina's face was now blotchy from tears and worry. Her hand was cold and the handshake weak and limp.

'You don't need to say anything. I don't want pleasantries or condolences. I know. My husband is dead. I can feel it inside; I've felt it ever since I came home this morning. After 27 years of marriage, you just know these sorts of things,' said Kaarina Helmerson, expressionless.

Anna nodded. She took out her camera.

'I have a few photographs here. I must warn you, they are quite shocking, but obviously we have to be sure this is your husband.'

Kaarina Helmerson took the camera. She flicked through the photographs, her face impassive, and handed the camera back to Anna. Tears were running down her cheeks.

'Good God,' was all she could muster.

Anna and Esko waited. Kaarina had closed her eyes and her body had begun to tremble. Her breathing was shallow and agitated. Anna was getting ready to fetch the first-aid kit from the car, in case the woman started hyperventilating, but then Kaarina took a few deep breaths in and out, opened her eyes and spoke calmly.

'It's Veli-Matti. Please, come in. I know you have to interview me, interrogate me. I've made some coffee. Or would you prefer tea?'

Kaarina gestured them into the stylishly fitted white kitchen, where the aroma of freshly brewed coffee lingered in the air. The room was bare and clinical, like something straight out of the pages of an interior-design magazine. An enormous espresso machine stood on the counter.

'Do you have any children?' Anna asked.

Kaarina seemed startled. It took a moment before she answered. She hadn't expected this question.

'No. We wanted some, but that was all a long time ago.'

'How did that affect your marriage?' Anna was surprised by her own line of questioning.

'What's it got to do with anything?' Kaarina snapped.

'I don't know. Our job is to ask … all sorts of things,' Anna explained, trying to find a friendly tone.

'Very well. It brought us to something of a marital crisis, but as I said, this all happened about twenty years ago. We almost divorced over it, actually, but as time passed we came to accept the situation and realised that through our work we were able to share the love that we thought we should have given our own children. It was a very liberating realisation, and it's motivated both of us in our careers. Watching our friends' exhaustion, the stress, the rushing around, we eventually felt a sense of gratitude for having no children. We haven't had to cut back on any hobbies, holidays, anything. Of course, you can't really say these things out loud, at least not to their faces.'

Kaarina gave a dry laugh and sighed deeply. Anna was perplexed at how calm she seemed.

'Did you know Riikka Rautio?' asked Esko.

Kaarina looked at him sternly and answered instantly.

'Terrible, isn't it? We were absolutely shocked when we heard – what a nice girl. Riikka graduated from our school last spring. I know her parents, though not particularly well. Round here everybody knows everybody else, at least by name, and as teachers we obviously know all the families with children.'

'Did your husband ever teach Riikka?'

'I can't remember. I'm sure he would have mentioned it when Riikka died.'

'So he didn't say anything?'

'No, though we talked about it a lot.'

'Did you ever teach her?'

'Yes. I was her Finnish teacher.'

'Throughout high school?'

'Yes.'

'What about Virve Sarlin and Jere Koski?'

'Virve was in the same class. I've never taught Jere, though I know who he is.'

At last, some kind of connection, thought Anna. Two murders have happened in the same location, and two of the victims at least knew one another, lived in the same village, the place where everybody knew everybody else.

'Do you also know a Ville Pollari from the village of Asemakylä near Simonkoski?'

'Who is he?'

'Victim number two.'

'I don't know him.'

'Take a look at this photograph of him. Perhaps you have met one another somewhere?'

Kaarina held the photograph in her hand and stared at it for a long while. Ville, smiling and alive.

'I don't think I've ever seen him. What was his name again?'

'Ville Pollari.'

'What did he do for a living?'

'He was a software engineer at Nokia, worked down town.'

Kaarina thought hard for a moment, then answered unequivocally.

'I haven't heard that name and I've never seen that man before.'

'What about your husband?'

'I don't know. In addition to our common friends, we have friends of our own, though of course we each know most of them by name. I don't recall my husband ever mentioning that name. Was he a jogger too?'

'Yes. He was an orienteering enthusiast.'

'Veli-Matti always went running by himself. It was his way of emptying his thoughts, of forgetting work. I don't think Veli-Matti knew this man, though I can't be sure.'

Kaarina placed the photograph on the kitchen table and her apparent calm began to fracture once again.

'What's going on here? What kind of madman is on the loose? Why aren't the police doing anything?' Kaarina burst into tears and left the kitchen. Anna and Esko sat at the table in silence, their untouched coffee cups in front of them. Anna thought of all the evenings and nights they had spent, without once looking at the clock, trying to catch this killer. All for nothing. They had done everything in their power, and still they had a new victim. Anna felt like throwing herself to the floor and screaming like a child to banish the agony of her frustration and exhaustion. She no longer wanted to do anything at all.

They heard the sound of someone blowing their nose, and Kaarina returned to the kitchen. She stood leaning against the sink and asked whether they would like more coffee. Anna and Esko politely declined.

'I'm afraid there are still many questions we'll have to ask you. I'm sure you understand, this will help us find the killer.'

'Of course. Ask whatever you want. I can cope.'

'You spent last night at your mother's place, but where were you on the evenings of 21 August and 14 September?'

'I can't remember that, can I? Why do you ask?'

'Would you rather we didn't ask a possible suspect that question?' Anna said.

The woman looked at Anna unflinchingly and snorted.

'Of course not. I'm being silly, sorry. But I really don't remember where I was on those evenings. Probably at home or with my mother. Or at Body Pump or the cinema or yoga or at my riding class. I have lots of hobbies. I'll have to check my diary.'

'Could you do that now, please?'

A furrow of irritation appeared between Kaarina's eyes.

'Do I have any choice in the matter?' she said and left the room. A moment later she returned with her diary.

'What days was it again?'

'On 21 August and 14 September,' Anna repeated.

'Let me see. On 21 August, I had Body Pump at seven, followed immediately by relaxation yoga at eight. I use the BodyFitness gym on Suvantokatu, it's right next to my mother's house. I spent that night at my mother's place – that's what this moon here means,' said Kaarina and indicated a small crescent drawn in pencil at the bottom of the entry for that day. Anna noticed that the same symbol appeared very regularly.

'And the other day … Ah yes, I should have remembered that: the school's autumn conference on leadership. It lasted all day: lectures, workshops and a cocktail reception in the evening. I wanted to take part in everything, so I can keep on top of things at work. And there were a few colleagues that I don't see all that often. I spent that night at my mother's place too. I almost always try and combine things in town with looking after my mother. I go to her apartment, we eat something together, I do the dishes and tidy up, go to the gym for a few hours and come back in time to make sure my mother is washed and takes her pills. She sleeps much better when I'm there. And in the morning I can change her diapers straight away and we don't need to wait for the home help to arrive. My mother sometimes has to wait quite a while for them.'

'What time did you leave the cocktail reception?'

'Let me think … around ten, maybe?'

'Who else was there?'

'Do you think I did this? Good God, surely you can't suspect me?' Kaarina was becoming agitated.

'We don't suspect you, and verifiable alibis will help us quite a lot,' said Esko amiably.

'Well, there was Lea Haapala and Kirsti Tuulonen, colleagues and friends from years back. Ask them.'

'Excellent. I'm sure everything's in perfect order,' said Esko so smoothly that Anna wondered whether he had the nerve to start hitting on a widow in shock.

'Do you own any firearms?' asked Anna.

Kaarina looked increasingly uneasy.

'Yes. Veli-Matti sometimes went shooting in the woods. He wasn't a fanatical hunter, but every now and then he would go off and find us something gourmet for dinner – well, he tried, at least,' she said with a forced laugh.

'Could you show us the guns?'

'Of course. They're in Veli-Matti's gun cabinet. Where is it he keeps the key? Bear with me a second.'

She stood up and started rummaging through one of the kitchen drawers. When she found what she was looking for, she led them through the utility room and into the garage, in the far corner of which stood the firearms cabinet. She unlocked the cabinet to reveal a Sako rifle and two shotguns: a slender .20-calibre Merkel and a beautiful .12-calibre Benelli, both engraved. Made to measure. Expensive.

Esko looked down the barrel of the Benelli.

'Has this been fired recently? It hasn't been cleaned.'

'Veli-Matti went down to the shore on the first day of the season, first thing in the morning, spent the whole day there but didn't catch anything.'

'Is that the shore at Selkämaa?' Anna asked.

'I don't know. There's a lot of shoreline around here. He didn't say.'

'We'll have to take this gun for further inspection.'

'Of course.'

Esko packed the firearm into its carry case, propped at the back of the cabinet. He picked up a packet of ammunition too. Anna noticed that the rounds were the Armusa make. Kaarina looked on restlessly, as though she were about to say something.

'Then we'll need a DNA sample. Here's a warrant,' said Anna.

'What on earth for?' Kaarina snapped and opened her mouth.

'Routine stuff,' said Anna and swabbed the inside of the woman's cheek with a Q-tip, which she then packed in a protective plastic container.

'How bad is your mother's condition?' Anna asked.

'Very bad. She can't really get around without assistance. On a good day she can get to the toilet by herself with the Zimmer frame. She can't really see or hear properly any more, and she sometimes has terrible memory lapses. She has Alzheimer's. But she has lucid moments too, and she doesn't want to go into a home. She would prefer to die at home. What else is there to do except help her as much as I can? It's not like I have any brothers or sisters.'

'It's admirable that you look after her so well,' said Esko.

'Yes, well, now it's my turn to look after her,' said Kaarina and gave Esko a faint smile. 'I think people should be allowed to decide for themselves what they do with their lives, even if they don't have very long left. I can't force her into an institution. And thankfully the council provides services, home-helpers and that sort of thing. They visit two or three times a day, depending on how often I can be there.'

'Can your mother confirm the nights that you were with her?' asked Anna.

Kaarina looked doubtful. Then she said: 'I wish I could say, of course she could, but that would be an exaggeration. She might be able to, but then again maybe not. Like I said, she has good days and bad.'

'Does your husband keep old student registers? We'd like to check whether Riikka was ever in his class.'

'We don't keep things like that at home. The school secretary will have them filed away somewhere. Ask her.'

'Fine. And do the Aztecs or the name Huitzilopochtli mean anything to you?' Anna asked.

Kaarina stood staring at Anna and Esko in bewilderment. She wiped the tears from her eyes, which again betrayed a flash of coldness, perhaps hatred or arrogance.

'Excuse me?'

'For technical reasons, we can't go into too much detail, but believe me, the question is highly relevant.'

'Of course I know this and that about the Aztecs – I'm a teacher, after all, and one with a reasonable grasp of general knowledge. But I don't have any personal connection to the subject. Not remotely.'

'What about your husband?'

'Oh for goodness' sake, no! Why are you asking me such nonsense?'

'Does this necklace look familiar?' Anna asked and showed her the image of Huitzilopochtli.

'I've never seen it before. What on earth is it?'

'A necklace like this has been found on all the victims – including your husband.'

'Terrible. What is it?'

'Huitzilopochtli was the highest deity of the Aztecs, a deity to whom the people offered human sacrifices.'

'My God,' Kaarina gasped in shock.

Anna heard her phone beep as a text message arrived. She withdrew into the corridor to read it. Again it had been sent from a newly changed, unlisted number.

A wave of fear and disgust gave Anna goose bumps. The tone of the message had changed; now it was even more threatening. Still, Anna felt a faint sense of relief: at least there was one suspect she could now rule out.

Esko appeared in the hallway.

'Let's go,' he said.

It's not you, that's for sure, Anna said to herself.

Anna's doorbell rang at around 8.45 p.m. On arriving home, Anna has climbed straight into bed and tried to get some sleep, but she felt so cold that she couldn't relax. Perhaps she had caught a chill after sitting on the damp moss. She wished she had an elevated temperature, a fever that would force her to stay in bed and would drain her so much that she would be able to sleep many days in a row.

She had just started to slip into that relaxed state before finally falling asleep when someone began ringing the doorbell. *Picsába*, she shouted and threw her pillow to the ground.

It was Ákos. Her brother was in a bad way. His face was blotchy and gaunt, and his clothes dirty. He stank.

'*Basszd meg, Ákos, aludtam!*'

'*Bocs*, Anna. This is an emergency. Take a look at these papers from the Social. I can't understand a thing. My unemployment benefit hasn't arrived, even though it should have. Now they're asking for more information, *a faszom*.'

'I'm not looking at this now.'

'*Jebiga*, Anna! Help me out here, yeah? Just tell me what they need.'

'*Bocs* yourself. I won't. Take care of your own paperwork.'

'Anna, I need some money. Lend me a hundred, eh? I'll pay you back with next month's benefit.'

'I haven't got any cash. And I wouldn't give you any if I did.'

'Fifty, then. Come on, I'm in the shit here.'

'I can smell that.'

'Give me a break. Just give me the money and I'll go.'

'You won't get a penny from me, that's for sure.'

'Thanks a fucking lot. Bitch.'

'Shut up. Have a shower.'

'Give me a tenner, then.'

'Not a cent. Now go on, piss off!'

'Tight-arsed bitch, no wonder nobody's interested in you. Who would want to look at police scum like that all day? At least give me a smoke, yeah?' Ákos shouted. Anna picked up the packet she'd bought that day and threw it at him; it was already half empty. Without a word of thanks, Ákos left, slamming the door behind him. The stairwell boomed with the sound of banging and stomping.

Anna slumped on to the hallway rug. Her running shoes stared at her accusingly from beneath the coat rack. Anna threw them limply towards the door, but they continued to laugh at her.

She didn't sleep a wink all night. Anna looked out of the kitchen window at the darkened suburb, its tower blocks standing unflinchingly, each on its own plot, without a care for what happened within their walls. Does anyone out there wonder what kind of poor human fate my windows hide, she wondered. That's what I am, a poor human fate, a pathetic soul that will soon go mad. I'll go mad right here in this apartment. I've got to get out.

She decided to pay a visit to Bihar's apartment. Slowly she drove through the northern suburbs towards Rajapuro. The radio was playing classical music. Loneliness condensed like moisture against a nocturnal window.

A red car glided past her on the empty road. The car's headlights blinded her for a moment as it passed; Anna didn't see who was driving. Should she do a U-turn and follow it, stop the car and ask for papers and ID? She hesitated. Even the simplest decisions seemed to get caught in a viscous sludge of fatigue. I'm not turning round, she eventually resolved. The streets are full of red cars, and it would be unprofessional to make a decision like this while my brain is bleary from lack of sleep. In any case, it's gone now.

Bihar's windows were dark.

Of course, Anna thought. What was I expecting? Did I think they would beat Bihar with the lights on and the curtains open, right by the living-room windows, at precisely the moment I pulled up in the yard?

Stupid.

I am stupid. You are stupid. Together we're all stupid, Anna said out loud and laughed.

All decent, sensible people are in bed, asleep.

But I'm still awake. Always fucking awake!

I was bre *the only foreigner in our school. By foreigner I don't mean someone whose parents have come to Finland from Germany or the States or somewhere similar to do some really specialised job for a couple of years and rake in a load of money. There were kids like that at our school. I mean kids like me. And suddenly I was so special and interesting and exotic. In Rajapuro about 35 per cent of pupils have another mother tongue, maybe even 40 per cent. The haggard teachers compare notes and brag about whose class is the most awful.*

But the kids at this new school weren't from out in the sticks. Some of them came in by bus because they were being environmentally friendly. They had hobbies, their parents listened to Mahler and Berlioz and they spent half-term holidays in Barcelona, Christmas holidays in Thailand and skiing holidays in Lapland. Each one of them glowed with the certainty of becoming a lawyer or an economist or an engineer or a doctor or a diplomat. It was a new and strange world to me, and at first I wondered whether I was still in Finland at all, but it wasn't long before I became caught up in it all too. For the first time ever I felt that people actually saw me. I felt like I belonged somewhere.

Once I managed to convince my family that I would wear the hijab, they sometimes let me go to class parties at the weekend. My cool cousin helped out there too – eternally grateful to you, Piya. I'm not angry with you because of what happened. I know you didn't have any choice. We came up with incredible lies to cover for each other. It's amazing that they bought it for so long, but it's just a matter of using the right words and being able to deploy them at precisely the right moment. For almost a year, my family believed I was an active member of a language, culture and politics group for young Kurdish kids, a group that was basically made up of me and my cousin. And my timetable taped to the fridge door featured at least seven different after-school lessons that didn't actually exist. Optional classes, we called them. They didn't know anything about the shorter school days during exam week. If you have to, you can always hatch some new plan. Juse thought my life was really bloody exciting.

Sometimes Mum encouraged me to do something more useful than reading. In her own little mind she must have wondered what I'd do with six As when my rising-star career had already been planned out as the wife of the Kurdish man whose photo she showed me one evening, telling me what an excellent family he was from and that he was a good man. But what they didn't tell me was that everything had already been arranged. I started to suspect the worst when suddenly I was expected to learn to cook all kinds of special Kurdish foods and to clean like I'd never done before. Of course, they'd been preparing me for this since I was a kid, with Mum constantly explaining what a good woman should be able to do and blah blah blah. She tried to force me to cook and bake bread and crochet some ridiculous lace doilies. I was like, for God's sake, I've got a physics exam the day after tomorrow, then maths, and I'm not baking anything. And I didn't bake anything. They put me on house arrest for two weeks, but I told them they might as well put me on arrest for the rest of my life: I'm not cooking all night long and that's that. It was the first time I'd ever openly stood up to them, and immediately I became proof of everything they'd suspected all along: that the Finnish school system was like a rotten, secular dog park and if only we had a nice Kurdish school all of our own, if only we'd had our own wonderful homeland then none of this would have happened. The worst of it was that they started to suspect all my after-school activities.

So I was stuck at home for a few weeks. They lied to our headmaster, saying we were going home for a few weeks and asked to be sent all the homework and exams I'd need to study for. I sat at home and studied like crazy, so I wouldn't fall behind. They took my phone and wouldn't let me use the computer, so I couldn't keep in touch with my friends who all thought I really was in Turkey. Dad said if I did one more thing, said one more word out of place, then he'd take me out of school altogether. That's why I didn't throw a fit or raise my voice when they finally revealed that the creepy guy in the photo was actually my future husband and that we'd been engaged for years.

But it was still a shock.

31

ANNA WENT TO WORK at 6.30. After returning home from Rajapuro she had slept for about an hour, woken up, had some coffee and smoked a cigarette in the kitchen, listened to the buzzing in her head and wondered when she would finally crack. When she didn't crack after all, she decided to have a shower and face the day ahead. But she resolved to sleep the following night. She would have to.

The suburb was every bit as dark and wet as it had been the night before. Anna didn't notice the glimmer of light, the faint augurs of morning rising behind the tower blocks. She didn't even look. And just as she was about to open her car door there in the quiet, almost empty car park, someone grabbed her by the shoulders from behind and squeezed hard. Anna gave a shout; she turned around in a flash, her fist raised and ready to punch the attacker right in the face.

'*Bocs, Anna, bocs, az én vagyok!*' It was Ákos. Anna only just managed to stop her fist striking its target. Her brother seemed spaced out and he was very pale.

'I've lost my fucking keys – can't afford to get the caretaker to come and open the door. It costs 80 euros. I'm skint.'

'I see. So when did you lose your keys?'

'Last night. I need to shower, change my clothes.'

'Where did you spend the night?'

'At a mate's place. Anna, I wanna go clean. Help me.'

Ákos looked terrible. Anna felt sorry for him. She couldn't abandon her brother when he was in trouble. There was nobody here to care for him, nobody at all that he could really talk to. Anna had returned to her former hometown and moved back to the same suburb where her brother still lived. The decision hadn't been motivated solely by her new job and a regular income. It must have had a greater meaning, something to do with her brother, a man whom life had left so crushed. Right there, Anna realised that she had nobody either – nobody but Ákos. And at that moment she knew that if she ever did return home, it would be because of Ákos.

'All right. I'll give you 80 to get the door opened. Not a penny more. I'll come round this afternoon and check that you've cleaned yourself up, then we'll get you into rehab. And I can go through your paperwork from Social Services too. Okay?'

'Great, Anna. I knew I could rely on you.'

A single tear trickled from Ákos's glazed, yellowed eye, as Anna pulled the notes from her wallet and pressed them into his trembling hand. He snatched them greedily and stuffed them into his jacket pocket.

'*Köszönöm, Anna. Nagyon szépen köszönöm.*'

'I'll come round soon. I can't say exactly when – things at work are pretty manic – but probably some time after midday. Okay?'

'Okay. See you later. Hey – you couldn't shout me a couple of beers, could you? I can't go cold turkey straight away; I don't think I'd cope.'

Anna sighed. Reluctantly she went inside and fetched two small cans of beer from the fridge. It was all she had. Ákos stuffed them into his pocket and disappeared.

When she arrived at work, Anna flicked through the papers on her desk without focusing on anything, fighting the urge to have a cigarette. What the hell's wrong with me, she wondered. Why can't I get to sleep? Am I ill? What if I've got cancer or HIV, she thought, horrified.

She tried not to think about all those hazy one-night stands.

Should I go to the doctor?

The thought felt terrifying, as if she were signing her own death warrant. Her eyes were shutting of their own accord; she felt like sleeping but battled against the fatigue. Rauno popped in to bring

her more files, before slipping out just as quickly, muttering something indistinct. Now he hates me too, after that awful night out,
she thought. They all hate me. I'm a failure as a police officer and
a failure as a human being. They blame everything on me being a
foreigner. After this, I doubt a single applicant with an immigrant
background will ever be employed here again – and I was supposed
to be a pioneer, an example to others, fully integrated, fluent in
Finnish, equal to any Finn. Anna felt her pulse quickening and the
hum in her head intensifying.

Anna got up and went out for a cigarette. She took the lift downstairs, opened the back door and walked to the smoking area across
the yard. The empty gherkin jar was full of stinking cigarette ends.
Anna looked at the blackened edges of the jar with a sense of disgust
and imagined that her lungs must look the same. Her cigarette tasted
just as bad as the old butts smelled. She smoked it right down to the
filter all the same.

As she walked back inside, she saw someone watching her from a
window on the fourth floor. It was Sari's window.

Anna went to the toilet and tried to rinse the taste of ashtray from
her mouth with a handful of water, but the taste was ingrained on
the enamel of her teeth. She locked herself in one of the cubicles and
sat staring at the door for a long while. Then she slipped into her
office and began reading the documents Rauno had brought. One
sentence at a time, one line at a time, she forced herself to focus on
them. This is my job and I have to do it to the best of my ability,
she told herself. I can do this. If I don't understand something, I'll
read it again. If I realise I'm not concentrating, I'll read it again. In
this way, she painstakingly went through the details of the killings
once again. But to what end? The files didn't reveal any new information. Would they have to track down all the active joggers in the
city and the neighbouring towns? There must be far more runners
around here than hunting folk. What could they possibly do? Hope-
lessness stared back at her from behind the papers. Compared with
the tempo of American police dramas, real criminal investigations

often moved painfully slowly. But somewhere, somehow, they would break the deadlock and the case would start to unravel. She had to believe it would. As they reached the final strait, things would pick up. How long would that take? And more to the point: would she be able to go the distance?

There came a knock at the door. Sari stepped inside.

'How are you doing?'

'All right. I guess.'

'Is something the matter? I'm really worried about you.'

Anna thought for a moment about what to say, though she would rather have left the room altogether.

'I've been sleeping badly the last few nights, that's all. Actually, I haven't been sleeping much at all. Last night I only got an hour's sleep. But I'll be fine.'

Anna tried to put on a brave smile, though she felt like crying.

'But that sounds really serious,' said Sari. 'You won't cope with this or any other job if you're not getting enough sleep. I've always got a box of Somnor tablets in the cupboard. I never need them, because I know they're there if I can't get to sleep. Just the thought of them calms me down. Have you got any sleeping pills?'

'No ... Pills always freak me out a bit.'

'Listen, call the doctor.'

'What?'

'Call the station's health officer right now; they'll give you an appointment for this afternoon. I've got the number in my phone.' Sari dug her mobile out of her blazer pocket, pulled up the number on the screen and handed it to Anna.

'I'll save this and call them later.'

'Make sure you do,' Sari said sternly. 'We all want things to go well for you. Even Esko mentioned you looked really burned out, and he didn't say it as a put-down.'

Anna felt a wave of irritation washing over her, but to her surprise the feeling shrank and turned into a warmth that stung her eyes.

She took Sari's telephone, went to the window to take down the number and turned her back to Sari, hoping that she hadn't noticed anything. She tapped the number into her own phone and handed the other one back to Sari.

'Make sure to call them. We really care about you,' said Sari as she took the phone, her warm touch lingering on Anna's hand before leaving the room.

Anna remained standing by the window, and didn't bother wiping the tears from her cheeks. She tried to focus on the landscape framed in the window, which at that moment wasn't especially beautiful. A single yellowed bush in the police-station forecourt braved the autumn weather, a solitary dash of colour in the city's otherwise grey canvas. Cars flowed past beneath a cloud of exhaust fumes, four lanes in each direction, and along the edge of the street rose a wall of ugly apartment blocks, built so tightly together they could have grown fast to one another. My own personal protective wall, a wall with no checkpoint, she thought. My wailing wall.

Soon it'll be November. November sucks people dry, drains their energy and gives them only darkness in return.

Huitzilopochtli battled against the darkness too, she'd read in one of Rauno's files. It was specifically this battle that required human sacrifices, so that the sun would once more vanquish the darkness.

And still the days were growing shorter.

Wicked people are full of darkness.

When was the last time someone took care of me?

At the point where her emotions should finally have burst forth, Anna felt only a cold and hollow gap. Finally she packed her camera and notepads into her bag and left for the forensics department to observe the autopsy on Veli-Matti Helmerson.

From the autopsy Anna drove straight to Ákos's apartment in Koivu-harju, though she knew this would make her late for the investigation team's meeting that afternoon. Her brother's unwashed stench greeted her at the door. As agreed, he was at home, but he had no intention of going to the rehab clinic. Again he was blind drunk. Anna was furious and started shouting and raging at her brother, who treated Anna's disappointment the only way a drunken alcoholic knows how – by laughing at her and mocking her. A fat woman stood up from the living-room sofa, lit a cigarette and fetched another can from the fridge. It didn't take much imagination to realise that the events of that morning had been nothing but a bluff.

She felt like killing both of them.

She would never forgive her brother for this.

Beside herself with rage, Anna rushed to the police station and straight into Virkkunen's office. Esko, Sari, Rauno, Nils Näkkäläjärvi and a few other officers brought in as reinforcements had already started the meeting led by Chief Inspector Pertti Virkkunen.

Anna explained that the autopsy had taken longer than expected.

'It's good that you could make it. What do we know about the new victim?' Virkkunen asked her.

Anna heard Esko scoff to himself. Again he hadn't been invited to the autopsy.

I won't let a single old drunk disturb my life, she thought as she plugged her camera into the computer. Concentrate, she commanded herself, forget about those bastards Ákos and Esko, forget about the tiredness, forget everything.

They congregated around the screen.

'It was an interesting autopsy,' she began and was herself taken aback at the frailty and brittleness of her voice.

Anna cleared her throat and poured herself a glass of water from the jug on the table. Sari gave her a worried look. I've got to snap out of this, Anna thought.

'Here we can get an overall picture of the extent of the victim's wounds,' she continued more decisively. Everyone's attention shifted to the computer screen, and she heard the gasps and the muttered expressions of shock. It was no wonder. Mutilated with a knife, the body was a shocking sight, even to the eyes of experienced police officers. Anna continued her account of the autopsy.

'There were 23 knife wounds in total. The blade was long and thin, like one you might use to fillet a fish. The blows were inflicted while the victim lay on the ground, on his back, and before the shooting. We can see this from the direction of the bleeding, though after the initial attack the victim was subsequently turned over and the blood began to flow back.'

'So the guy was lying on the running track with the killer on top of him going mad with a knife, before turning him over and shooting him in the back of the head,' Rauno summed up.

'Sounds strange,' Esko muttered. 'As if the victim just lay down on the track without putting up a fight. Surely there must be signs of a struggle.'

'Perhaps he'd been struck unconscious first,' Nils suggested.

'There were no marks to indicate he'd been hit with anything,' said Anna. 'But his wrists were grazed. Linnea is pretty sure he'd been put in handcuffs. His hands were tied behind his back.'

'How do you put handcuffs on someone running past?' Sari asked.

'We wondered that too, but then Linnea found a small needle mark on his left arm. Here,' Anna enlarged the image and showed them. The mark was only just visible.

'He'd been drugged,' Sari exclaimed.

'So how on earth do you get a syringe into a man running past you?' asked Esko.

'The mark is in precisely the place where a right-handed person would inject themselves,' Anna explained.

'So it is. Jesus, did the killer force Veli-Matti to drug himself?'

'It's highly possible, and at gunpoint it's not even very difficult. It could have happened anywhere, even in the man's own home. The killer would have had to transport the man from one place to another; that would explain the handcuffs.'

'And he had to be drugged in order to get him to the running track in the first place.'

'A place where people are too scared to go running at the moment.'

'Guaranteed peace and quiet.'

'What kind of fixation does this guy have with the running tracks?' Rauno asked.

'He must be a runner himself,' Sari answered quietly. 'Something has happened to him on a running track, something that compels him to carry out the killings there.'

'The knife wounds were inflicted so rapidly that it's hard to establish the order in which they occurred,' said Anna and switched to a close-up of the knife wounds on the victim's chest.

'Christ Almighty,' said Esko.

'What about time of death?' asked Virkkunen.

'Around the same time as the others: after 8 p.m. but definitely before 11 p.m.'

'A former student and a teacher. Strange,' said Sari.

'Have we established whether Riikka was in fact a former student of Veli-Matti's?' asked Anna.

'Yes. The registers from Saloinen primary arrived in my email this morning. Both Riikka and Virve were in Helmerson's class through the fifth and sixth grades.'

'That's an even bigger connection, given that they all live in the same village. And Riikka was a student of Mrs Helmerson in high school.'

'As was Virve.'

'But how does Ville Pollari fit into the equation? He doesn't seem to have any connection to Saloinen whatsoever,' said Virkkunen.

'Maybe we're looking for connections that don't exist or that don't have any significance,' said Sari. 'I think Ville's murder proves that these victims have been selected at random. We found the hideout at Selkämaa. Of course, we can't be a hundred per cent sure that that's where the killer planned the murders – it could be nothing more than a playing area for local kids. But let's assume that the killer used the spot to watch joggers running past. We know that Riikka went there; we know that Veli-Matti went there. The killer simply selected them because they happened to be there at the time. That's it. We need to find a similar hideout at Häyrysenniemi. I think the running track is more significant to the killer than the identity of the victims,' said Sari.

'This is all very good, Sari,' said Virkkunen. 'Sounds plausible. Anna, was there any more news from the morgue?'

'Linnea took DNA samples and ran toxicology tests. That will help us establish exactly what was injected into the victim. She'll be in touch as soon as the results are through. That's all.'

'I've tried to established Veli-Matti's last movements,' said Esko. 'Classes started at nine and finished at three. None of his colleagues noticed anything out of the ordinary. It was a perfectly average day. Veli-Matti had stayed on late to prepare for some school development project. The caretaker locked the front doors at four o'clock; there were still a few teachers in the building at that point. It's a big school, almost a hundred teachers.'

'Wow,' Sari exclaimed. 'In that small village?'

'I know, you wouldn't think it,' said Esko and continued: 'Veli-Matti came home at around 6 p.m., had something to eat and watched TV. Soon after her husband arrived, Mrs Helmerson went into town: first to a gym class, then to her frail mother's place, where she spent the night. As she left, Veli-Matti said he was going out for a run.'

'Did the killer force entry into the Helmersons' house?'

'We'll have to examine the house and ask the neighbours,' said Virkkunen.

'I've been looking into Mrs Helmerson's movements around the times of the previous murders,' said Rauno. 'She claims that she was at a yoga class on 21 August and at a head teachers' social evening on 14 September. Both stories check out. The BodyFitness gym has magnetic cards that regular customers use to swipe themselves in – they get special offers the more they use the gym – and Kaarina Helmerson's card was swiped in for two consecutive classes on the evening Riikka was killed. What's interesting is that the yoga class finished at 9 p.m. Riikka was killed at 10 p.m. An hour is plenty of time to drive from the city centre out to Selkämaa. The head teachers, on the other hand, couldn't remember exactly when they left Kaarina. They had all been having a drink in the hotel foyer and retired to their rooms at around 9 p.m., maybe earlier.'

'Ville was shot between 7.30 p.m. and 9 p.m.'

'Would Kaarina have driven out to Häyrysenniemi under the in-fluence?' asked Sari.

'Head mistresses don't drink and drive,' Esko scoffed. 'When they say they're only having one drink, they mean it.'

'There was nothing of interest on Veli-Matti's telephone,' said Sari. 'On the day of his death he hadn't made any calls and he re-ceived only one call, from his wife.'

'Sari, you talk to the Helmersons' neighbours and get Forensics to go over the house to see if we can find any trace of the killer. Esko and Anna, I want you to talk to Mrs Helmerson's mother,' instructed Virkkunen.

'She's got Alzheimer's,' said Esko, and for a moment it looked as though he gave Anna a conspiratorial smile. Perhaps Anna was so tired she had started to imagine things.

'And we have to talk to all the previous interviewees again: the Rautios, Virve, Jere, the old folk living near the running track. We have to turn every stone once again. What was the name of the old boy who lives at Selkämaa? The one with the sharp memory?' asked Virkkunen.

'Yki Raappana,' Rauno replied.

'You talk to him. He knows you. I've got to get ready for the media storm. We've got a press conference starting soon.'

'Did you call the health officer?' Sari asked as she followed Anna to her office.

'Yes, yes,' Anna lied. 'They prescribed me those sleeping pills you mentioned.'

'Good,' Sari sounded relieved. 'They'll get you sorted.'

Anna remained in her office alone. The clock on the wall was ticking so loudly it made her head hurt. She didn't dare go to the doctor. She was afraid she'd be put on mandatory sick leave. Then she could kiss her job goodbye once the six-month trial period was over. There was no room for wimps in police investigations. You've got to have the psychological stamina.

Nevertheless, at that very moment the thought of being made unemployed didn't seem all that bad after all.

32

AT KERTTU VIITALA'S APARTMENT the autumnal bleakness took on a whole new form: the stuffy, acrid smell of an elderly woman met them at the door. Anna turned up her nose, and she noticed Esko was doing the same. The nurse from the council's home-help service who let them in was a youngish woman with brown hair. With an iron grip, she shook hands firmly with Anna and Esko. You need strength in this job, lifting old people out of bed all day, thought Anna. The work was better suited to men, but with wages even lower than in the police force, the job wasn't all that attractive. Anna felt like opening a window, but perhaps this was forbidden in the homes of octogenarians.

Kerttu Viitala was lying in a bed located right in front of a blaring television set in the living room. The elderly woman was staring at the shopping channel flashing garishly on the screen.

'Is Grandma thinking of ordering herself one of those Turbomuscles?' Anna whispered to Esko beneath the booming aerobics music. Esko chuckled.

He's laughing at one of my jokes, thought Anna, astonished.

The carer heard Anna's joke too, and she didn't find it remotely funny. She rolled her eyes angrily and turned down the volume on the television. Anna felt embarrassed. Kerttu Viitala didn't react at all to the presence of the two strangers standing by her bed.

Anna switched off the TV altogether. The old lady grunted and turned her colourless eyes to look at Anna.

'I was watching that,' she said in a plaintive voice.

'Mrs Viitala, these people are from the police. They'd like to ask you a few questions,' said the nurse, upbeat. Anna sat on the edge of the old lady's bed and shook her hand. Esko greeted the lady too, then stepped back to examine the photographs of relatives staring at him from the bookshelf.

'I'd like to ask about your daughter,' Anna said to Kerttu, raising her voice just as the nurse had done. 'We have a few questions about Kaarina.'

The old lady looked at Anna without saying anything. The nurse began to speak as she counted pills into a glass.

'Kaarina tends to visit in the evenings. She gives her mother her evening pills, a bite of supper, and puts her to bed. She has a night off a couple of times a week, and we come round on those evenings too. Believe me when I say it's rare to have your own child take care of you. Elderly people are left to struggle by themselves, and nobody cares. Home-helpers from the council come round and change their diapers, cook some food, feed them, make sure they take their medication. We haven't got room to house them all. Here we are, Kerttu. Here are your afternoon pills. There's a good girl.'

The nurse stood next to the bed, so close that Anna could smell her breath. And something else, too. Sweat, perhaps. Apparently home-helpers picked up the cumulative staleness of all the elderly folk in the city. Kerttu Viitala groaned as she sat up in bed and raised a quivering hand, blue veins criss-crossing beneath her wafer-thin, wrinkled skin. She took the glass of pills, and with a surprisingly nimble flick of the wrist knocked the entire cocktail into her mouth and swallowed.

'Gosh,' Anna said almost involuntarily.

The nurse was standing by with a glass of water. She raised it to Kerttu's lips and tilted it, a trickle of water running down the front of her threadbare nightgown.

'Good girl,' said the nurse, affected and jaunty, and energetically wiped the old lady's mouth with a sheet of kitchen roll.

Anna watched as the water soaked into the fibres of the cotton nightgown, forming a dark blotch. I want to die suddenly before I turn 70, she thought as she stood up and opened a window. She looked down into the street that bisected the city centre at its busiest point. A constant bustle of people flowed into cafés and shops. Café Penguin, a pleasant and popular place where Anna often stopped for an espresso, could be seen right below. Its terrace had been dismantled and its tethered deckchairs moved to the basement to wait until summer. On the windowsill was a pair of binoculars. When the nurse saw Anna staring at them, she snatched them up and put them in a cupboard in the far corner of the living room.

'Mrs Viitala likes to sit by the window and watch the people walking around outside, whenever she's up to it. That's pretty rare nowadays,' the nurse explained. Her voice was brusque and she stared back at Anna without blinking. The woman's eyes were astonishingly blue. We're disturbing her work, Anna thought. We're disturbing her.

Anna looked down on to the street. The view that opened up from the window was meant for young people, full of energy, people who lived life to the full and had no need whatsoever for Social Services. A view like this wasn't supposed to be looked at from above, through a pair of binoculars, body and soul wasting away, worrying about the missed opportunities of the past. The view invited you to dive in head first and let yourself be carried away by the flow. If you couldn't do that, you belonged elsewhere. In an institution, perhaps, or at the very least further from the city centre.

Anna asked Esko and the nurse into the kitchen. Though Kerttu seemed quite deaf, it didn't feel right talking about her in the same room.

'Have you been looking after Mrs Viitala for long?' Anna asked the nurse.

'Me personally or the nurses in general?'

'Both.'

'Kerttu has been on our books for about a year. At first we only visited every other day to bring her some food. Since last winter the nurses have been coming too. Kerttu's condition went rapidly downhill at around that time, and she couldn't get by with only Kaarina's help. Personally I've been coming here since the winter.'

'Do the same nurses visit every day?'

'No. We have a rotating system, so you might visit the same customer anything from three to five times a week. It depends.'

'Where can we get hold of your rota? We may need to establish which nurses visited on certain dates.'

'Ah yes, of course. You'll have to ask our supervisor at the home-help department. I can give you her contact details.'

'Thank you, that would be great,' said Anna and took the calling card the nurse pulled out of her bag.

'What condition is Mrs Viitala in?' Esko asked.

'Well, you can see for yourself,' the nurse scoffed. 'She's had Alzheimer's for years, and now it's reached the point where Kaarina has to explain who she is. Isn't it terrible? You forget your own child...'

'Kaarina told us that Mrs Viitala has moments of lucidity,' said Anna.

'Did she now? Not that I've ever seen. Of course, Kaarina is here more often than I am. And naturally she knows her mother far better.'

'In your opinion, could Mrs Viitala confirm that her daughter visited her on certain specific dates?'

Again the nurse laughed.

'Absolutely not,' she said. 'Why should she? Has Kaarina done something?'

'We're looking into a case.'

'I have to leave, I'm afraid. We're on a very tight schedule. Please remember to close the window; old people are very sensitive to draughts. And make sure that the door is securely shut when you leave.'

The nurse went back into the living room. Anna and Esko followed her.

'Bye for now, Kerttu. See you the day after tomorrow,' the nurse shouted, holding Mrs Viitala's hand and stroking its wrinkled surface for a moment. The old lady moaned with happiness.

Then she left. The jangle of her extensive collection of keys could be heard from the corridor.

How many lonely old people must there be in this city, Anna wondered, people waiting for the jangle of a set of keys, the sound of the door opening, waiting for someone, anyone, to come and pay a visit? Anna's own grandmother, her father's mother, was 90 years old and still in incredibly good condition. She went to the pensioners' dance evenings, and visited friends and relatives almost every day. The thought flashed across Anna's mind that there weren't any lonely old people back home. Why not?

'She's a good girl, she is, my daughter, to look after me like this,' Kerttu said unexpectedly from the bed.

Anna and Esko took a step closer to the elderly lady.

'Hello, Mrs Viitala,' said Esko, again raising his voice.

'Who is that?' Kerttu asked with a note of concern.

'Esko Niemi and Anna Fekete from the police, ma'am,' he replied.

'The police? Goodness me, has something happened?' Kerttu said in a panic.

'We just have a few questions to ask you.'

'I see. What's the matter?'

Anna again sat down beside her. It felt almost cruel to stand beside the bed, looking down on her, when the person she was talking to was lying there fragile and helpless.

'Could you tell us whether your daughter Kaarina was here the night before last?'

'She's asleep over there in the bedroom.' Kerttu raised a trembling hand and weakly pointed towards the corner of the room.

'Did Kaarina sleep there the night before last?' Esko repeated the question.

'What day was that?'

'The third of October. A Monday.'

'What day is it today?'

'Wednesday.'

'I'm sorry, I would have offered you some coffee.'

'That's fine, we've already had some.'

'Who are you again?'

'We're from the police.'

'Goodness gracious! Has something happened?'

Anna and Esko looked at one another. This was pointless, they both thought. The nurse was right: Mrs Viitala wouldn't make a credible witness.

Esko asked her the same questions once again. And once again the old lady apologised that she couldn't offer them any coffee.

Then Kerttu Viitala felt silent. Her empty eyes fixed on a point somewhere behind Anna and her hand began to fumble for the remote control on the bedside table. The shopping channel flooded back into the room.

Anna tried to clarify a few final points, but Kerttu lay there silently staring at the television. After a moment Anna noticed that the old lady's eyes had pressed shut. Had it not been for the faint sound of snoring emanating from between her furrowed lips, you could have thought she was dead. Anna turned the volume down and closed the window. She and Esko left the apartment. Outside the sun had stopped shining.

At Anna's suggestion they stopped into Café Penguin for a coffee. The warm light shining from the café's windows seemed to invite them to step inside, where numerous gold-framed mirrors reflected and multiplied the light. Anna was reminded of the grand cafés of Budapest. Perhaps she should visit places like this more often, she thought. For a few moments she could imagine she was somewhere else, almost somewhere back home.

Anna couldn't decide whether to have a sandwich or some cake. Tiredness whirled behind her eyes, pressed down on her shoulders and made her feel faint. She really should call the health officer. Otherwise nothing will ever come of this job, she thought, nothing at all.

Esko tapped on her shoulder, and for a moment Anna thought she must have been holding up the queue, but it was because of Virve, who was sitting in the café with another girl. Virve's fair hair was tied in a long plait running down the back of her hemp-green

Indian-cotton tunic towards the floor. Virve gave her an awkward wave, then called over the waiter and asked for the bill.

And at that moment Anna remembered!

She remembered what she knew she had known all along, what she knew she had seen. A shiver ran between her shoulder blades and her pulse quickened.

'When are we scheduled to interview Virve and Jere again?' she asked.

'Tomorrow.'

'Good. I just remembered something. It could be important.'

'Well?'

'Virve visited Mexico back in the spring. I saw a photograph on her Facebook page.'

Esko gave a quiet whistle. Virve glanced up at them and nervously fiddled with the sleeve of her tunic. The familiar jangle of her bracelets carried faintly across the café.

'What did I say all along? There was something fishy about that girl.'

'Don't stare,' Anna whispered. 'What are you having?'

The girls put on their jackets and left the café without looking behind them.

'Coffee.'

'Just a normal coffee? They do really good espresso here, con panna or double, macchiato, cappu—'

'Normal coffee. Burned, bitter, brown liquid poured through a bleached filter, thank you very much, cheap and nasty. I don't touch any of that black muck.'

'This wouldn't have anything to do with your general xenophobia, would it?'

'Say what? You know what you can do with your fancy words. This has nothing to do with anything. I can buy my own coffee, if it's too much to order a normal one. Round here we're not used to treating each other like this.'

Anna paid for Esko's coffee and ordered herself a hot chocolate with whipped cream and a ham sandwich. She seemed instantly more alert. Virve's trip to Mexico couldn't just be a coincidence. Here she was, sitting in Esko's company, in a public café, almost communicating normally with him, though outside the autumn was doing its best to crush those who dared venture into its embrace. She couldn't have imagined doing this a few weeks ago. Esko had certainly undergone something of a change. Anna didn't quite know what had caused it.

But she wanted to find out.

'Why don't you hate me so much any more?'

Esko looked up at her, so taken aback that he seemed almost pleasant. He's not used to people speaking their minds, thought Anna. He's happy to sound off himself without giving his words a second thought, but it catches him off guard when other people do the same. For once I've made him speechless, she thought with a sense of satisfaction when Esko didn't answer straight away but calmly stirred his coffee, considering how to reply.

'Let's say that I still despise everything you stand for, but I don't hate you personally. Not any more,' he said eventually. He looked away; he was blushing.

'You didn't answer the question. Why not?'

'You can be downright bloody infuriating, you know that? I don't know. I suppose I'm starting to get used to you. You're different.'

'Different from who?'

'Different from most immigrants.'

'How many do you know? Personally?'

'Listen, I was a police officer before you lot started turning up here. I've seen the enormous change that's taken place in our society. It started with the Somalis, then a while later came the Yugos and the Kurds and the Afghans and the Africans, and before you know it people are coming in from all directions and we're supposed to pick up the bill for the lot of you. Well, people have had enough. I'll never accept it. Sorry.'

'You still haven't answered the question. How many immigrants do you actually know?'

'I've met plenty in this line of work, and most of them have been suspects charged with serious offences: assault, rape, armed robbery, drugs—'

'That's not what I'm asking. You don't know any immigrants except me.'

'You've got a job, you pay tax and you speak clear Finnish. That's different.'

'I can barely speak my own native language any longer. For the most part I even think in Finnish nowadays,' Anna said quietly.

'I owe you one. You didn't let on to Virkkunen the other week.'

But of course, thought Anna. I should have guessed.

'Virkkunen and I are on pretty good terms, but even he has his limits.'

'A real Balkan doesn't tell tales to the boss – it's as simple as that. I wouldn't know about Finns – decent Finns, that is,' she said.

For a moment Anna wondered whether she'd overstepped the mark, whether Esko was about to slap her across the table or throw his coffee in her face, but instead he burst out laughing so hard that she could hear the tobacco phlegm rattling in his throat. The hearty laughter soon turned to a rasping cough, but there remained a glint in his eyes that made him look younger and less bitter.

'I've cut back since then. I suddenly realised I was fast approaching rock bottom if I needed to have a swig at work too. To be honest, I got a real fright,' said Esko, suddenly serious.

'Good. So you and I can go out Nordic walking one day, okay?'

Esko's coffee went down the wrong way, and he sounded like he was about to suffocate.

'Stop it or I'll choke to death here, and before that I might even start liking you,' he managed to say through a volley of coughing and laughter.

'Well, nobody would worry too much if you were to die, but if you'd started taking a shine to the wog before that, people would never get over it now, would they? Listen, what do you think about Grandma back there?'

'I think it looks like our good-looking widow's alibi is pretty flimsy after all,' he replied.

33

RAUNO WAS IN A PATROL CAR driving towards the city. He was returning from a meeting with his old acquaintances Aune Toivola and Yki Raappana. And he had something interesting to tell the team. As she did every day, Aune had gone to sleep early on Monday evening – without her hearing aid – and hadn't heard a thing. Yki Raappana, on the other hand, had heard a car driving towards the shore at around 9 p.m. on Monday evening. After Riikka's death he had begun paying particular attention to people moving around on the path. The old man wouldn't admit to being afraid, but Rauno could smell his fear. It was no wonder, he had thought, being a decrepit old man living in a remote place where someone had been brutally murdered. He would certainly have been afraid, or would at least have been on his guard. Poor Yki had been on his guard since August – and his alertness was of great use to the investigation. After hearing the car, Yki had gone out into his front garden. It was already dark at that time of night. Soon afterwards he had heard a shot. There was still the occasional duck shooter wandering around late in the season, so the sound of gunshot was nothing out of the ordinary. Except that now the sun set at around 7 p.m., so any birds flying over in the evening would have passed hours earlier and no hunter would have been able to make out prey in the dark – unless that prey was the size of a grown man.

Yki had put on some extra clothes and decided to wait outside until the car came back along the path. And it came back soon enough. Yki had crouched down in the bushes near the edge of the path and had seen a red car hurtling past. And the best of it was, Yki knew one make of car from another: it was a Volkswagen Golf, an old model, precisely the kind that had been sighted in the vicinity of the previous murders. He hadn't been able to make out the registration number; his sight wasn't as sharp as it had been when he was younger and it was too dark. It had looked as though the plates were covered in mud. He said he might have seen the same car drive past once before. The previous time Yki had only managed to get a fleeting glimpse of it, so he couldn't be entirely sure. The old man proudly showed Rauno a blue jotter where he had noted down details of every car he'd spotted on the path since 22 August. There weren't very many of them, perhaps an average of seven a day. He had guessed that the killer would return to the scene of the crime. Rauno had praised the man, and Yki could have burst with glee. Apparently as a younger man he had considered taking a job in the police force. Rauno commented that Yki's career as a forester had been a loss for the police service; a man this sharp could have been a lot of use. Yki was thrilled and offered to make some coffee. Though Rauno was eager to get back to the station with the news, he didn't have the heart to refuse. The old man had already taken up plenty of his time.

Now Rauno felt like putting his foot on the accelerator and getting back to the station as soon as possible. This was a breakthrough. With this information they would quickly identify the old red Volkswagen, and there was no doubt it would belong to the killer.

He exceeded the speed limit without even noticing it. There was little traffic and he hadn't yet reached the city limits. Just then he saw something black in the corner of his right eye. In a split second, he realised that the black spot was moving – and that it was coming towards him. Rauno slammed on the brakes. The car began to swerve across the road, still slippery from the rain. The huge male elk stopped in the middle of the road as if demanding to be hit. This is the end, was all Rauno had time to think before the impact.

Sari was finding it hard to concentrate. She was sitting in her car near the Helmersons' house looking alternately at her telephone and at the houses along the street. She had received another text message. The tone was the same as before, sexist and intimidating. Frightening. It was time to get to work on finding out who was sending them. And she would have to interview all of Helmerson's neighbours. Where should she start?

Sari shifted her phone from one hand to the next. They had to catch the killer. This prank caller was a much smaller threat, if indeed a threat at all.

Unless they were one and the same person.

Sari didn't want to give the possibility any more thought. She contacted a friend at the National Criminal Police who specialised in mobile phones, computers, data surveillance and everything in between. He promised to do all he could. Sari got out of the car and began walking towards the first house on the street, the neighbours opposite the Helmersons. The front garden was large and well taken care of; the house had a handsome brick façade. It was the same as all the houses and gardens in the area. There was no answer when Sari rang the doorbell. She tried again but there was no one at home. She made a note of the name on the letter box and went to the next house. An elderly, grey-haired man was outside raking the garden.

'Good afternoon,' said Sari and showed her identification.

'Afternoon,' the man replied, propped his rake by the shed wall and asked her inside.

'I'm sure you've already heard the news,' she said.

'Yes. Terrible stuff. We all keep the doors locked these days. People don't dare go about their business now. Feels like there's someone aiming a gun at me when I'm out here raking the garden.'

'Did you see anything suspicious going on at the Helmersons' house two evenings ago?'

'Not that I noticed.'

'Did you ever see a red car?'

'Veli-Matti drives a black BMW. And Kaarina has a silver Nissan. I haven't seen any red cars round here, no.'

'What about people? Anyone other than the Helmersons?'

'They have visitors every now and then, but I haven't seen anything out of the ordinary.'

'If you think of anything, please call me. Even something that might seem insignificant could be very important,' she explained and handed the man her card.

'Very well. I'll be in touch if something comes to mind.'

The man escorted Sari to the gate, returned to his rake and continued gathering piles of leaves on the grass.

Sari went to the next house.

This time the door was opened by a woman in her fifties. The coffee was already brewing. Good, she thought. This woman clearly keeps her eyes open.

Sari introduced herself and explained why she was there.

'Oh yes, I've seen a red car – quite frequently, in fact,' said the woman. Sari couldn't contain her excitement.

'When? Was it here two evenings ago?'

'No, I haven't seen it for a while now.'

'During the summer?'

The woman thought for a moment.

'No, it wasn't there in the summer either. But in the spring it was parked out there quite a bit. Whenever Kaarina went to her mother's place, that red car would turn up soon afterwards. Well, not every time but quite often. It wasn't parked in the Helmersons' driveway or even outside the house, but over there, a bit further away.'

'Think carefully. Precisely when in the spring was it here?'

'Well … from March until May, perhaps?'

'How often did you see the car?'

'Hard to say. A dozen times in total?'

'Did you see who was driving it?'

'It was a woman.'

'What did she look like?'

'You know, *that* kind of woman.'

'Er, what kind of woman?'

'The kind of woman that sleeps with married men. A whore,' the neighbour hissed.

'What did she look like?'

'I never got a good look at her. I don't really know.'

'Short, tall, thin, fat, blonde, brunette?'

'Average size. I don't know about her hair.'

'What about age?'

'I've no idea. But they're generally younger, aren't they?'

Sari approached the window from where you could see on to the street. From this window the Helmersons' front door was completely hidden and the front garden was at too sharp an angle to get a good view. It would be impossible to get a proper look at anyone visiting the Helmersons' house.

A red car had been sighted in the area last spring, almost six months ago. What on earth could this mean?

'Still, sometimes I thought it looked like Kaarina.'

'Excuse me?'

'Yes, sometimes it looked as though it was Kaarina Helmerson driving that car.'

Sari's telephone rang. It was Virkkunen.

'I've told Forensics to leave the Helmersons' place for now.'

'Why? I was going there next,' Sari exclaimed.

'We've just received a call from Seppo Vilmusenaho. He's a PE teacher at Saloinen primary – Veli-Matti's colleague. He said he saw the lights on in Veli-Matti's classroom at around 6.30 p.m. on Monday evening.'

'And?'

'And there was a red car in the school car park. At the time, he didn't pay the car much attention, because he'd been so interested in the classroom lights. Seppo told us he'd been annoyed that Veli-Matti could be so careless, given that he was leading the school's Green Energy Project. He had decided to mention the matter to Veli-Matti, but as soon as news of the murder came out he remembered our call for any sightings of a red car. Seppo believes that the killer was there in Veli-Matti's classroom.'

'Could Veli-Matti have jogged back to work?'

'I've sent Forensics out to the school. Get down there. The Helmersons' house can wait.'

'Okay. And by the way, the red car has been spotted around this neighbourhood. Last spring.'

Virkkunen whistled quietly.

'We're on to something,' he said. 'We're finally on to something.'

The running tracks around Häyrysenniemi were deserted. Nobody dared go out there any longer. Now the track was lined only by the evenly positioned street lights. Anna had driven from Café Penguin directly to Asemakylä. Throughout the journey happiness flickered inside her.

Esko had accepted her, out of the blue, without forewarning, just like that. Anna hadn't dared hope for such a thing. She had prepared herself to put up with Esko's snide comments and verbal attacks till the end of time.

Still, the deserted running track succeeded in quashing her happiness. Would anybody ever dare run here again? This time Anna didn't wander off along the track. She decided to start her investigation from the spot where you could see both the parking area and the start of the track: the scene of Ville Pollari's murder. Anna turned her back to the street lamps and the running track and scanned in the opposite direction.

The terrain was mostly covered with thick scrub, but running south from the start of the track there was a strip of older pine forest. That's one place there wouldn't be thicket to block someone's view. Anna walked along the strip of land, covered in lichen and moss. The ground was even, no hills or bumps where anyone could have been hiding. Anna was about to turn back when she noticed something behind a large pine tree. From a distance it looked like nothing but a tangle of metal. She ran up to the tree and found a folding deckchair knocked to the ground, perhaps blown over by the wind. Its metallic parts were rusty, the fabric frayed at the edges. It could have been lying there for years.

Anna righted the chair and sat down on it, facing the running track. She could just make out the parking area; Anna could see the faint contour of her car. With a pair of binoculars, it would have been easy to watch people running round the track, she thought. Was the deckchair here by accident? Could this have been the killer's vantage point?

Anna carefully examined the area around the chair but couldn't see any sweet wrappers or anything else of interest. She took the chair with her to give it to the forensics team. Perhaps they would be able to find some fingerprints on it.

On her way back Anna stopped at the Pollaris' house, but it was as deserted as the running track. Maria had gone to her mother's house in Jyväskylä. I hope everything's okay with the baby, she thought as she sat at the end of the Pollaris' driveway for a moment and let her eyes press shut, almost falling asleep.

Again she was woken by the sound of her telephone.

It was Rauno's wife, whom Anna hadn't yet met. Nina Forsman was calling from the hospital. She was so hysterical that Anna could barely make out a word. She understood that something serious had happened to Rauno. Anna shook the sleep from her body with a cigarette, and as soon as she had smoked it, she set off for the hospital.

Inside the hospital, everything was white and so bright that it hurt Anna's head. Floral-print curtains in the emergency room attempted to soften the feel of being in an institution. Rauno was lying on a metal-framed bed, linked up to numerous tubes and monitors. His face was hidden behind a large oxygen mask. A petite woman sat next to the bed. She jumped up as Anna stepped into the room and offered a delicate hand. She's like a bird, the thought flashed through Anna's mind, not like a mouse at all.

'Hello, I'm Rauno's wife – Nina. I don't think we've met.'

'Fekete Anna. Sorry we had to meet like this. Where are the girls?'

'I took them to my mother's. I haven't told them anything yet. I don't know what to say. They're still so little,' Nina agonised.

'The doctors here can give you advice on what to do,' Anna tried to comfort her. 'There's no rush. They don't need to hear it straight away.'

'Yes,' Nina whimpered. 'You're right.'

'What happened?'

'He hit an elk. It's a miracle that he's still alive.'

'What's his condition?'

'I don't know exactly. The doctors don't know. He's got some fractures in his right thigh and he's broken several ribs.'

'What about his head?'

Nina began to weep.

'He might not…' she stammered. 'He might never wake up. Or if he does, he won't be the same Rauno that we all know.'

Anna began to tremble. The room felt cold. Was there a window open somewhere? Anna examined the windows, but there was no way of opening them. What a ridiculous thought – an open window in an emergency room where people are fighting for their lives. Rauno's struggle seemed peaceful. He was calm, as though he was sleeping off his exhaustion. Anna realised that she wished she was lying there instead of him. She felt like removing the tubes and waking him up, ordering him to go home and sort out whatever had gone on between him and his wife. Anna would lie down there herself, there beneath the warm blankets; she'd pull on the faded hospital gown, place the oxygen mask over her mouth, connect the sensors to her chest, head and fingers, insert the drip into her own arm and drift into a liberating slumber. What a wonderful state. Only death could be better than this.

Thankfully Rauno didn't look like he was dying. The steady beeping on the monitor showed that his heart was beating evenly and kept alive the glimmer of hope that he might just pull through this. His face had been spared the worst of the damage. That was something.

'And I'd just decided to get a divorce,' Nina said all of a sudden.

Anna snapped back to the real world, yanked herself into that state of consciousness needed to communicate with people, to listen to them and comfort them, the state she no longer had the strength to deal with. She didn't know what to say, and decided not to say anything.

'I doubt it'll be possible now,' Nina continued.

'Take things one step at a time,' said Anna.

'For the children's sake. After this, dealing with a divorce would be too much for them.'

'For them, yes, but for you too.'

'What can I tell them?' Nina continued sobbing. 'How can I bring them here to see their father like this?'

Anna took Nina's hand and pressed it gently. She didn't have any answers, in any language.

'Why did you call me?' she asked eventually. 'I mean, we don't know one another…'

'I don't know,' Nina replied. 'Was there … Is there anything going on between you two?' she asked abruptly.

'What? Not at all. Don't even think that,' said Anna.

Nina gave a cautious smile as tears trickled down her cheeks.

34

ANNA DROVE TO RAJAPURO and parked outside Bihar's apartment block. All her fatigue had gone; she felt like a machine that worked simply by pushing a button. Though it was getting late, she decided to go in and have a few words with the family, just to remind them that she was still keeping an eye on them. Perhaps she needed the reminder more than the Chelkin family. Her motivation had begun to dwindle as the days grew shorter, and on more than a few occasions Anna had resolved to give up checking on Bihar. Yet she always came back. It was like an irritating disease that wouldn't go away. Christmas would be the absolute deadline for this farce. If nothing had happened before that, she would call it a day. And still she had the niggling worry that she might never be able to let go.

The windows at the Chelkin household were as dark as the residents' eyes. It seemed that there was no one at home, but Anna decided to give it a try nonetheless. She stepped inside. The walls in the stairwell were covered in graffiti tags. She rang the Chelkins' doorbell, but nobody answered. Where were they? There was generally always somebody at home. As she returned to her car, Anna saw a patrol car gliding from the car park back on to the street. This time she was certain who was driving.

What the hell was he doing here?

The same thing she was doing?

She called Esko.

They agreed to meet back at the station. 'I thought you weren't going to get involved in checking on the darkies unless you had to,' she snapped at him.

'Maybe I did have to.'

'Tell me what's going on!'

'I'm not telling you anything.'

'Oh, here we go,' she shouted. 'Listen, don't pretend to be all matey with me if you don't mean it. You don't need to suck up to me, whatever Virkkunen says. I can't deal with this!'

A rage whipped up inside her bringing tears to her eyes. She felt like a child whose trust had been betrayed.

'Calm down! I want to *show* you something, not tell you.'

Esko took Anna down to the archives where video recordings of police interviews were stored. He took a laptop from one of the cupboards and set it up on the table.

'I watched this yesterday. It's the interview with Bihar.'

'Why? Why did you watch it?' Anna was puzzled.

'I saw you in the car park outside their house back in September while I was out on another case. I realised you were traipsing out there all the time checking on the family, but I decided to let it go. To be honest, you were pissing me off so much back then, I planned on saving the information until I found an opportunity to use it.'

'Damn it, Esko.'

'Once an old bastard, always an old bastard, right? Now shut up and listen. A while ago I started wondering why you refused to drop the case, like we agreed. You'll burn yourself out with all that extra work. I guessed there had to be something suspicious about the Chelkins after all. So, for my own peace of mind, I came down here and watched that interview again and ... Well, see for yourself.'

Anna watched Bihar on the screen as she waited. She looked lonely.

The girl was glancing around nervously and biting her nails. Those nails had been varnished many times, the multi-coloured layers of varnish now flaked and worn. They looked terrible. Then Anna walked into the room.

Gosh, I look stern, she thought. I should have tried a milder approach, more motherly and protective. Would Bihar have opened up more if I'd done that?

The interview began, and Anna remembered every word, as though they had been spoken only a moment ago; that same sense of desperate anger as the girl recanted her story and protected her father filled Anna all over again. She didn't want to watch this, to relive that frustration, her own failure over and over.

'Just take it easy and watch,' said Esko as he noticed Anna squirming. 'Watch very closely, right to the end.'

Anna saw herself bringing the interview to an end and standing up to leave the room.

Bihar lagged behind.

Oh yes, I remember that, she thought. I wondered what she was doing. Was there still something she wanted to say? She didn't seem to want to leave the room.

And suddenly, perhaps on the screen for no more than a second, Anna saw it.

She is standing at the open door; the corridor looks like an illuminated cave behind her. Bihar is standing by the interview table, pulling up the long trench coat covering her body. She looks up, directly at the camera. Her eyes look so empty, so dead, and yet they seem to be imploring anyone watching. She opens her coat, and it's as though the camera catches a sound and cries for help.

It was written on her T-shirt. White painted letters in rough brushstrokes against the black fabric of the T-shirt. A simple word.

HELP.

Anna's eyes blurred and her head started buzzing so much that she could feel the veins in her temples bulging. When was the last time I saw Bihar? I was there today, but I didn't see her; there was nobody at home. Why didn't I notice her cry for help earlier on? Why haven't I watched these tapes again? That's why we record them of course, so that we can analyse them, investigate them, watch them over and over. I haven't done that. How long is it since we conducted that interview? That was over two months ago. When was the last time I saw Bihar?

I can't remember.

Panic consumed her. She gripped the armrests on her chair and closed her eyes tightly. It was coming now, the emotional collapse that had been knocking at her door for a long time on all those sleepless nights. She couldn't cope with this. This was the final straw.

'Take it easy,' said Esko. 'Calm, now.'

'I've really screwed this up,' she said.

'Then it's a good job you've got a partner who's alert enough to notice these things and sort them out,' he said and took Anna by the hand. He rubbed Anna's hand in his fingers, yellowed by nicotine, until she gradually began to calm down.

The game wasn't over yet. She had feared the worst from the outset and had regularly shown the family her continued presence. Two months had passed and nothing had happened, so in all probability everything was fine now too. They wouldn't dare do anything, not under the constant scrutiny of the police. And now Esko was here to support her, the racist, drunken old bastard. Anna started to laugh as relief shimmered within her. Nothing bad could possibly have happened.

'*Pease pudding, hot and cold*,' whispered Esko, tickling the back of Anna's hand.

'What?'

'Haha! Finally something our language genius has never heard of!'

'You can't make pudding from peas.'

'It's a kind of porridge.'

'Ugh. I've never understood Finns' obsession with porridge. Disgusting stuff, if you ask me.'

'Porridge is tasty and healthy,' said Esko, almost offended. 'I have a bowl of oat porridge every morning; can't start the day without it.'

'Right. Don't you mean barley porridge? The liquid kind?'

'Shut it!'

'We have to get out to Bihar's place. I'm not sure when I last saw her. It might be as long as a week.'

'You're right, we have to go there, but first we have to plan things carefully,' said Esko. 'Have you heard the saying "less haste, more speed"?'

'Of course I have. But enough of the pea porridge, okay?'

It was already 8.30 p.m. by the time Anna, Esko, Sari and a squadron from Patrol, as well as the interpreter who had been at the initial interviews, whose private number Anna had kept just in case, had assembled outside Bihar Chelkin's apartment. Everything had been carefully planned, the Child Protection Agency had been informed and a team of social workers were on standby.

They had decided to go later in the evening, so that the girl would definitely be at home. Anna and Esko went to the door, while the others kept watch in the yard to make sure nobody tried to run away. Anna and the interpreter ran up to the third floor. As a precaution Esko took the lift.

Anna rang the doorbell. The younger sister Adan opened the door and burst into tears upon seeing the police officers. Anna and Esko had decided to turn up in uniform, as this often commanded greater authority. Now nobody would try to pull the wool over their eyes. Now they would get him. Adan ran back into the apartment shouting something, and Payedar Chelkin appeared in the hallway. The man let out a stream of Kurdish words that sounded like curses. The interpreter remained silent.

'Where is Bihar?' Anna shouted. 'Bring her out here! It's time we took her somewhere safe. And as for you,' she turned to the interpreter. 'You will translate every word, every grunt, exactly the way it's said. Everything.' The interpreter tried to say something, but by now Bihar's mother had come into the hallway. Everyone was shouting and screaming at once. Zera Chelkin was weeping and shrieking. Bihar's father was bellowing angrily; Adan's sobs could be heard from one of the bedrooms and Mehvan was peering through one of the open doors, a look of shock on his face. The situation was chaotic, to say the least.

Anna shouted above the noise. 'Everybody quiet, for Christ's sake! This is the police!'

The interpreter shouted the same in Kurdish, but it was meaningless. The family had fallen silent.

It must be my Balkan roots, but I certainly know how to use my voice, Anna thought with satisfaction.

Zera lowered her head. Mehvan disappeared into his sister's bedroom. Once the situation had calmed down, Payedar quietly explained what had happened.

Bihar had disappeared.

Anna and Esko looked at one another in the dimness of the hallway. Anna pulled the front door shut behind her; another door had opened on the floor above, the lights in the stairwell had been switched on and a nosy neighbour was creeping around in the corridor.

Bihar hadn't come home from school.

This had never happened before.

Her parents seemed genuinely concerned.

They had planned to inform the police tomorrow at the latest.

Because this had happened before, after all. Several times apparently.

When Bihar had been with that Finnish boy.

'Where have you taken her?' Anna shouted. 'Answer me. Where is Bihar?' The parents looked distressed. They were unable to say anything. In the girls' bedroom Adan started crying again.

Anna reported Bihar missing right there in the Chelkins' hallway. They would have to alert the border agency and customs officials in case she tried to leave the country. How far away could she possibly be? The school confirmed that Bihar had been there all day, until four o'clock. Her last lesson was German. Now it was nine o'clock, so that was five hours ago. If she'd been taken somewhere by plane, she could be very far away. Either that, or she could be in Sweden.

Crossing the border into Sweden was easy; you could take anything across, at any time – even people. She would have to inform Interpol.

Then they would simply have to wait.

'In cases like this, girls are often sent back to their home countries, where they are instantly married off to men considerably older than them,' Anna later explained in the staff room at the Violent Crimes Unit. Night had fallen on the police station too; in addition to them, there were only a few officers on night shift.

'Either that or she's already dead. That's how these things go. Girls just disappear, and nobody ever finds out what happened.'

Anna drummed her fingers on the table and drank her coffee.

'How are you bearing up?' Sari asked suddenly.

Pretty bloody terribly, Anna felt like responding. To be honest, I'm at the end of my tether.

'It's just that you seem to take this case so personally,' Sari continued.

Yes, Sari, I do take it personally. Far too personally.

'Sure, this is pretty difficult,' she finally said out loud. 'That girl really touched me. But I'll be fine.'

Anna slumped against the table. Sari watched her, concerned, then gently stroked her back.

'Any news on Rauno?' Anna asked.

'No change. All of his organs are functioning, but he's still unconscious,' said Sari.

'Damn it. As if we needed that too. Damn it, damn it, damn it,' Anna cursed.

'I think we all need some sleep,' said Esko. 'There's no point staying here worrying about things we can't change. We need to be ready tomorrow. It's been a long and draining day, and tomorrow will be no different.'

Not exactly music for going to sleep, thought Anna as she sipped beer straight from the half-litre can and tapped her left foot to the mystical beat as though she were walking through the alleyways of a large city. The Sistol album she'd ordered had finally arrived. It had been lying on the hallway rug in a flat cardboard package beneath a pile of flyers and free newspapers.

Now rats were scavenging through the stinking rubbish bins. Homeless junkies lay by the walls watching her pass, their eyes gleaming. A blue wave of light washed across the graffiti-covered surface of the concrete walls as a police car sped along the adjacent avenue in hot pursuit of a criminal.

It was well past midnight. She had only just come home and hadn't bothered to have a shower. Tomorrow she would have to go for a run, she thought and wondered who she was trying to fool. She hadn't run a step all autumn. She was so tired that every part of her body ached. She tried to make sense of all the indistinct things that had burst from her past to her present, things that had suddenly jumped into focus and were now shouting at her so loudly that everything else was drowned out.

Vigyáz!

Fatigue pulsed in her body like a tumour. I have emotional cancer, she thought and fetched another can of beer. And I don't think I'm going to overcome it. She smoked a cigarette on the sofa and fetched the ashtray from the balcony. Sistol's strange techno sounds emptied her head one beat at a time.

She smoked another cigarette. Smoke rings rose up to the ceiling, shrouding the room in a grey mist.

Heavenly Father, anyone who's listening, let me sleep just one night, was her final, desperate thought before the gates opened to a deep, peaceful sleep.

Juse is different from all the other boys I know. To be honest, I've always thought boys were a bit stupid. Mehvan is an idiot and all my boy cousins are idiots and all the snotty-nosed kids at Rajapuro primary are super idiots. Juse has light-blue eyes and his hair is cute the way it sticks up in every direction and he's quite skinny. We were in the same group for a history project, then one day he came and chatted to me during break time and asked me out for a coffee. That's where it all started. I fancied him straight away. He's so funny, utterly crazy and always makes me laugh. He said he'd noticed me on the first day of school and wondered who that beautiful, quiet, smart girl was. I was embarrassed, but it's really nice to hear someone saying things like that, especially if you're not used to it. At first we were just good friends; we'd talk and talk, and all that free time I managed to swindle for myself we spent together, but it wasn't long before the relationship got more serious. The attraction was really strong right from the start, and it was mutual. I told him all about my family and my background, everything. Juse had plans on how to soften up my parents, but with that he showed how naïve he was. No Finn can truly understand what honour, namus, really means to our people.

One of my aunts, or a second cousin of our second cousin's neighbours or whatever she was, had seen me and Juse around the town holding hands when, according to my timetable, I was supposed to be at school reading up for my extended chemistry exam. That's when all hell finally broke loose. After that, everything happened quite fast. They found out that there was no Kurdish club, and when she was threatened back home Piya told her parents about a couple of class parties I'd been too. So, in other words, it turned out that for the best part of a year I'd had plenty of opportunities to spend time alone with boys – Finnish boys – and that there was a special boy in the picture too. Which, of course, to them meant that I'd already lost my virginity and that I was essentially a slut. They would have to call off the engagement, because who wants to marry a fallen woman? They could wave goodbye to the family's honour; Bihar had destroyed that.

Dad was furious. Still, he managed to behave with surprising calm – he didn't beat me or anything. That's when I knew they meant business. It felt as though they'd been planning this day for a long time. Perhaps they had.

Juse received a death threat at the same time as they took me to my aunt and uncle's place in Vantaa. Dad and my uncle were smart enough to send it from a prepaid phone and they didn't mention any names. Juse decided to delete the message, he was so pissed off. I was really mad at him afterwards, because that would have been evidence.

35

THE MORNING MEETING about Rauno's accident was over. The corridor and offices at the Violent Crimes Unit were quiet, as though any noise might have disturbed Rauno as he lay in the hospital. There was a shocked and despondent atmosphere in the unit. Any motivation to catch the killer was gone, now replaced by concern for their colleague. What's more, Bihar's disappearance was distressing. Even Virkkunen could sense it. Now he had to lead his team, give them emotional stamina. With Rauno out of the picture, they would have to work harder than ever. The killer must not be allowed to benefit from the crisis enveloping the investigation. We mustn't allow him that pleasure, that advantage, Virkkunen had said as he rounded off the meeting. The officers nodded woefully, but Anna felt as though she was on the verge of giving up. She had slept well all night and woken up feeling surprisingly alert, something she barely recognised any more. For once her head hadn't been throbbing, and she'd almost felt like going for a run. Now the fatigue was creeping back. It wasn't going to give up just like that.

A pale Virve was waiting in the corridor of the Violent Crimes Unit. She stepped into Anna's office, sullen and nervous. She was wearing a retro-style dress with a large printed pattern and thick dark-brown socks. A Palestine scarf was tightly wrapped round her neck, and this time her long hair had been sloppily tied up in a bun. She took off her red duffel coat and held it in her arms.

'How are you?' Anna asked.

Virve scoffed but didn't say anything.

'Several matters have come to light as part of our investigation, and I'd like to ask you a few questions about them. Then I'm going to take you down to the holding cells where we'll register your details.'

'What does that mean?' Virve gasped.

'It's just a routine procedure. We'll take your photograph, finger-prints, a DNA sample and note down any distinguishing features. I have a warrant for it here. The information will all be destroyed if you're proven innocent.'

'Am I being charged?' Virve's panic was rapidly beginning to escalate.

'No, not at the moment. So it's important that you tell the truth and don't try to hide anything from me.'

Virve's breathing was shallow and her eyes were shifting restlessly. She nodded to indicate that she had understood.

'Where were you on Monday evening?'

'At the cinema,' she replied instantly. 'With Emmi. You saw us together at Café Penguin.'

'Which cinema were you at and what were you watching?'

'We were at Aurora. Brad Pitt's latest film. It was rubbish.'

'What time was this?'

'The showing started at nine and ended at eleven.'

'And before that?'

'I was with Emmi all day.'

'And have you been to Mexico?'

'Yes,' she whispered.

'When?'

'Last spring, straight after our exams.'

'Who were you travelling with?'

'I was alone.'

'Alone? Why?'

'I wanted to go by myself.'

'Why?'

'I don't know. I suppose I just wanted to get away from every-thing, friends, school, Mum, everything.'

'Was it because you wanted to learn about the history of the Aztecs?'

'It's really interesting, but that's not why I went.'

'So why did you go?'

'I managed to get a really cheap flight.'

Virve was extremely nervous. She fidgeted with her dress, kept touching her hair and bracelets, crossing and uncrossing her legs.

'Why do you keep asking about the Aztecs?'

'Because they're linked to all three murders. That's why. And you happen to have visited Mexico.'

'I haven't done anything!' Virve raised her voice.

'Don't worry, we'll be the judge of that,' said Anna, keeping her composure.

'But I haven't. You've got to believe me.'

'Let's go down and get you registered, shall we?' said Anna and gestured to Virve to follow her.

Anna and Virve walked through the police station and up to the top floor, where the holding cells were located. The whole floor stank of cigarette smoke. Anna realised that she hadn't smoked a single cigarette since arriving at work that morning and felt the desire for nicotine like a sumptuous tingling in the tissues along the inside of her mouth. Why isn't the yearning for nicotine enough? So often the mere thought feels better than the act itself.

The registration department was situated right in the middle of the floor, surrounded by the holding cells. It was grey and lit in pale fluorescent light, like all the other rooms in this building, though this one had no windows. The bleak room had a computer, photographic equipment and a fingerprinting machine that looked like a scanner. On a table in the corner stood an older, manual version of the same machine. Anna wondered whether it had been left there on purpose, in case of a power cut or some significant infrastructure catastrophe.

'Let's take your fingerprints first, then the DNA sample and the photos to finish off with,' said Heikki, a young guy who had graduated as a media assistant and who doubtless had a very different idea of his future career when he began his studies, but who had since realised he was lucky to have a job at all. In a twisted way he found working with criminals fascinating. Working here, he had plenty of juicy stories to tell his mates, far better than anyone in a regular, boring job. He had even registered the couple that had dismembered a woman and stuffed her in a suitcase last summer; he'd processed motorbike gangs, members of the Yugoslav mafia and other professional criminals whose scars and tattoos he had documented in detail.

Once they had taken her fingerprints, Heikki glanced over the warrant for the DNA sample and asked Virve to open her mouth. With a practised hand, he swiped the inside of her cheek with a cotton-wool bud and pushed it into a plastic tube.

'There we go, that's ready for analysis,' he said.

'This is horrible,' Virve whispered. 'It makes me feel like a real criminal.'

'Really?' Anna commented. 'Guilty conscience?'

'Will you listen to me for once? No. This room is terrifying. All these fingerprints and samples ... it's as if I'd really done something bad. This is awful. Why are you taking these?' Virve started to cry and looked at the door as though she wanted to rush out. Anna could see that the girl was beside herself.

'Take it easy, now,' said Heikki as he gently took Virve by the shoulders and sat her down. 'You sit there for a moment. Right, now listen to me. These procedures are routine parts of a police investigation and it's perfectly normal that the subject of the procedures – that's you – finds them stressful and intrusive. You're not the first person to start panicking up here. If you're found to be completely innocent, all of this information will be destroyed and there won't be any trace of you in the police system. So let's all take a deep breath, get these photographs done, then that's us for today.' Heikki chatted away to Virve and the girl visibly calmed down. He's slick, thought Anna. I must remember to commend him later.

'That's the way. Good. There's nothing to worry about. First we'll photograph your face, then if you've got any distinguishing features or tattoos, we'll need to photograph them too. Do you have anything like that?'

Virve wiped her tears on her sleeve and didn't say anything.

'Do you have any tattoos or scars or large birthmarks or...'

Virve stared at the old manual fingerprinting machine, as though she was suddenly unable to understand what they were saying. Her eyes bore a look of resignation. Anna and Heikki waited. Eventually Virve rolled up the sleeve on her left arm.

On her forearm, just above the wrist, was a colourful, resplendent orchid and from inside the flower, with its long curved beak, a beautiful hummingbird was supping nectar.

'Should we take her in?' Esko asked Virkkunen, to whose office the whole team had been summoned. Virve had been left to wait with Heikki in the registration room.

'She can prove that she was at the cinema when Veli-Matti was shot,' said Anna. 'I just called the cinema and the girl she claims to have been with. The film played until 11 p.m. Nobody left during the screening.'

'What about before the screening?' asked Sari. 'Veli-Matti wasn't shot very late in the evening. She could have done it before the film started.'

'She was with this Emmi from 5 p.m. onwards. They went swimming before the film. It's just not possible. Virve can't have killed Veli-Matti.'

'This whole thing was cooked up by Virve and Jere, I've said so all along. Christ, now we've finally got the one with the hummingbird in her left hand! All autumn we've been wondering what on earth this Hutsilo thing means. We can't let her go now. It's time to put a stop to these killings!' Esko bellowed.

'What did you get out of Jere?' Virkkunen asked Esko.

'Nothing much. Apparently he's stopped shagging the hippie girl. He's ready to confront the grief of losing Riikka and doesn't want to hide any more, nonsense like that – and from a grown man too. On Monday he was at a lecture, then he spent the evening and night with the university's hiking society in Varpaneva. The story checks out; the hiking society confirmed it. They're crazy folk, going off camping by a bog in the middle of the week at this time of year. But I'll be damned, there they were. All evening and all night.'

'So they can't really be in it together if they were both somewhere else at the time. There would need to be a third person involved, and that sounds pretty far-fetched,' said Anna.

'Didn't we speculate that they could belong to some kind of cult?' asked Sari. 'Rauno found a few on the internet. Then there are the online retailers. We need to get into Rauno's email account; the Russian guy should have written back to him by now with information on whether there were any shipments of those necklaces to Finland.'

'I'll sort you out with the passwords,' said Virkkunen.

'Good. But what if this really is some sick cult where everybody takes turns at killing someone?'

'It's possible,' said Anna. 'But do you really think some of them could go crazy and start sacrificing people together? I mean, in real life?'

'There are examples of mass suicides. People do all kinds of crazy things in the name of religion.'

'Suicide is a bit different, though.'

'I don't know. But if that's the case, who is their leader? Jere doesn't have any hummingbird tattoos.'

'It's Virve, obviously,' Esko spluttered. 'She's the one with the tattoo. She's Hutsilo. The boss, the highest bloody deity.'

'I don't buy that,' said Anna. 'I've interviewed her three times.'

'We need to grill these two about the Aztec connection. But we certainly can't arrest Virve, not on evidence this flimsy,' said Virkkunen.

'But it can't just be coincidence that the killer leaves images of a bloodthirsty Aztec god on each victim, then we find a tattoo directly linked to the necklaces on the wrist of a girl who was one of our first suspects. It cannot be coincidence!' Esko shouted.

'No, it can't,' Virkkunen conceded. 'And I'm sure it isn't. But that aside, one tattoo doesn't prove that Virve is the killer or some kind of cult leader, especially as she has a watertight alibi. It's circumstantial evidence. Continue with the interviews. If these kids have some connection to that god or any cult, find it. Now!'

'Seems like you're in the habit of roughing up your girlfriends, doesn't it?' Esko commented to Jere Koski, who was still sitting staring at his hands in Interview Room 2. 'Virve Sarlin has described you as jealous and violent. Is that true?'

Jere looked up.

'I don't wanna be like that,' he said in despair.

'What do you mean?'

'Sometimes it just bursts out. It's like I can't control it.'

'What bursts out?' asked Sari.

'The aggression. It's like my head goes blank. I totally lose it.'

'Does this happen often?'

Jere looked at them, puzzled, as though suddenly he had no idea where he was or who he was with. Then he gave a cautious smile.

'No, thank God. I've tried to train myself out of it. I don't want to be like…'

He stopped all of a sudden.

'Like who?' Sari prompted him.

'Like my dad,' Jere all but whispered.

'But you are, after all. Yes?' Sari asked.

'Yes, I suppose so. Fuck it.' Jere clenched his fists so hard that his knuckles turned white.

'We found old bruises on Riikka's body. They were quite large and in strange places, so they couldn't have been caused by bumping into the table. The forensics officer suggested she might have fallen from her bike, a few weeks before her death. Were you somehow involved?' Sari asked.

Jere seemed to swallow the word *yes*, so quietly that it was barely audible.

'Speak up,' Esko commanded.

'Riikka came round to my place to pick up the last of her things. There was a dress and a pair of trousers, and she needed them. I asked her if we could give it another shot. That's how it started.'

'Tell us more. Tell us everything.'

'She was wearing some sort of summer dress. She looked so nice. It was a really hot day. I must have tried to hug her or something, but she shoved me away and said it was too late. I told her I'd found a group online called MANagement, that they had a branch in town and that I'd start attending their sessions. If only she'd take me back. I even showed her their brochure. I'd printed it off.'

Jere took a breath, plucking up the courage to continue.

'I had such a wonderful girlfriend, and yet I was such an idiot I managed to ruin everything. I turned into just the kind of man I swore I never would. But I never laid into her the way my dad used to beat Mum.'

'So how did you lay into her?' asked Esko.

'I've only done it once before, and even then it was more like squeezing and shaking than anything; I never hit her. Then I hurled her to the floor and ran outside. I was shit scared of myself. It was after that that Riikka started thinking about splitting up. And that's why she eventually left, though I didn't behave like that any more. I walked away if I could feel myself losing control. Except that one time last summer.'

'We'll talk about that in a minute,' said Esko. 'So, you'd printed off the brochure for this MANagement support group? Then what?'

'She just kept saying it was too late, what was done was done. Then I asked if there was someone else. She didn't answer, but I could see it in her face. That's when I really lost it. I hit her and shoved her against the wall but she fell backwards and hit the coffee table. I'm surprised it didn't break. That's where the bruises came from. It was then that I realised I'd never get her back. There went my last chance. I was at rock bottom. That's why I took off to Lapland, to calm down and think things through.'

'But in the meantime, you'd started fooling around with Virve,' said Sari.

Jere looked embarrassed.

'Yeah. She turned up, started throwing herself at me and I thought, what the hell.'

'And you hit her.'

'I lost my temper, once, when she said Riikka was seeing someone else. I didn't hit her; I shook her. I managed to control it. And unlike Riikka, Virve forgave me. She believes that I want to change.'

'You realise that a tendency for jealousy and violence doesn't look very good in the eyes of the police,' said Esko.

'I know. I'm not exactly thrilled with it myself. But you know I was in Lapland when Riikka died. And anyway, I wouldn't have killed her. I loved her. And I've never had anything against Veli-Matti; he was a cool teacher. And I didn't even know that other guy!'

'What about Virve?'

'What about her?'

'She doesn't have a decent alibi for the first two murders.'

'She was at my place on one of those evenings.'

'I said a decent alibi. You could be protecting her and lying to us,' said Esko.

'Why would I do that?'

'I don't know. Fear?' Esko suggested.

Jere began moving restlessly.

'This whole thing is really frightening. I mean it. Listen, Virve, me and loads of our friends – we've all been shit scared since this all kicked off. Nobody so much as goes out for an evening walk any more. But Virve was with me in my flat when that guy was killed. I guarantee you.'

'Yes, and you were in Lapland when Riikka was killed,' said Sari.

Jere sniffed, then burst into tears. Esko looked away.

'It's all my fault,' Jere stammered. 'If I'd been able to control myself, Riikka would have come back to me. She would never have left me. Then none of this would have happened. She would have been at my place, safe. Fucking hell, this is all my fault!' he cried.

'Still, make sure to get in touch with MANagement,' said Sari. 'Call them today. I've heard lots of good things about them.'

Jere wiped his face on his sleeve and nodded.

'I want to get better,' he said. 'I can't deal with the thought of being like my dad. I'd rather kill myself.'

Sari handed him a tissue.

'And what about the Aztecs?'

'What about them?'

'Does anything come to mind? Does the word Huitzilopochtli ring any bells?'

Jere stared at them, his eyes frozen.

'What is it then?' he asked.

'I think you already know,' said Sari.

'It sounds familiar, as if I've heard it somewhere.'

'Think back.'

There was a long silence.

'Virve's tattoo,' he said eventually.

'So you do know,' said Esko.

'I'm fucking scared that it might be Virve,' he said.

Anna returned to Virve and took her back to her office.

'Do you remember last time, we asked you what you know about Huitzilopochtli?' Anna asked. She tried to sound as calm and friendly as possible. Interviewing someone who is afraid can be useful, because it often coaxes the truth out, but if the interviewee is too scared, they can shut down completely. You had to be able to treat a frightened interviewee with cotton gloves, but Anna was horrified at her own lack of experience. Back in Patrol, she'd never had to interview anyone, except if her patrol was the first responder on scene. The longer this case dragged out, the weaker she felt herself to be.

Anna tried to hide her yawn. What impression would that give an interviewee?

'I remember,' said Virve and finally plucked up the courage to look Anna in the eye – a show of honesty. Sometimes, at least.

'I remember it too. You seemed startled. Why was that?'

'You saw my tattoo, didn't you?'

'Tell me about the tattoo. When did you get it, where and why?'

'I got it done in May when I came back from Mexico, at a place downtown called Pink Ink. Why? Well, why do people usually get tattoos? It's fashion, isn't it? I think of it as a graduation present to myself.'

'Why that picture in particular? The hummingbird.'

'I've always really liked them; it's nothing deeper than that. Then I designed the image – I'm pretty good at drawing, by the way – and I took it into the shop. They gave me a quote, and two weeks later it was there on my arm. That's it. Honestly.'

'Did you know that Huitzilopochtli means "the one with the hummingbird in his left hand"?'

'Yes, I learned that when I was in Mexico.'

'And you still wanted to get a tattoo like that?'

'Well, it's a fairly gruesome double meaning. Back then, I just thought it was really cool. Why do you keep asking about this? What's my tattoo got to do with all this? I'm really frightened; I keep thinking there must be a skeleton in the closet somewhere, something that's going to get me banged up for killing Riikka, Veli-Matti and that other guy.'

'Do you own any Aztec jewellery?'

'No. None whatsoever.'

'You have quite a lot of jewellery.'

'Yes, but no Aztec jewellery to my knowledge.'

'Did you buy any jewellery in Mexico?'

'Yes, this bracelet,' said Virve and raised her jangling hand. 'That's the only one.'

'Do you belong to any religious groups?'

'The Finnish Lutheran Church. I've been thinking of rescinding my membership.'

'What about Jere?'

'He's not thinking of rescinding anything.'

'Does he have any interest in the Aztecs?'

'I doubt it. Who would be interested in a bunch of crazy serial killers?' Virve fell silent, as she realised the full implication of her words.

'The victims all had some kind of Aztec symbols on them, didn't they?' she asked Anna.

Anna nodded.

'I knew it. I guessed this must have been it the first time you asked about them. What is it? Are you allowed to tell me?'

'A necklace with the image of Huitzilopochtli.'

'Somebody's trying to set me up.'

'Who would do that?'

'No idea.'

'And why?'

'I really don't know.'

'Think. How many people know about your tattoo?'

'Everyone's seen it. Everyone who has anything to do with me, that is. During the summer it's on display all the time. People are always noticing it; complete strangers come up and ask me about it. I'm sure the whole city knows about the weird girl who spends all summer on the terrace outside Café Penguin, the one with the hummingbird on her left arm.'

'Huitzilopochtli,' said Anna.

'Exactly.'

'Jere knew the story about Virve's tattoo. And he was afraid that Virve might be the killer, because we'd started asking about the Aztecs,' said Esko when the team met for lunch at the station cafeteria. Grey cream-of-vegetable soup and liver steaks. I wasn't supposed to eat here ever again, Anna thought. She noticed that nobody else seemed enthusiastic about the food either.

'What the hell's the matter with kids these days, when they won't even tell the police the truth? If I suspected my bedfellow might be a crazed murderer, I'd go to the police and tell them everything,' said Sari.

'The first victim was their good friend, and they were worried they would be suspects because they had started fooling around with one another. So they already had a guilty conscience. Then they both started worrying that the other one was guilty. People have freaked out and started hiding things for far less. But their attempts to withhold evidence don't seem particularly premeditated. I think it was more a panicked attempt at self-preservation,' said Anna.

'Still, we can't rule them out just yet. They've got it all: the hummingbird, a weapon, a motive, everything. There must be a third accomplice,' said Esko.

'So what's the motive for Ville Pollari's murder?' asked Sari.

'He must have been a witness.'

'And what about their former teacher Veli-Matti?' asked Anna.

'They needed another kill. Hutsilo commanded them,' Esko muttered.

'And whose is the red car, the one that's been seen outside the Helmersons' house all last spring and in the vicinity of all three murders?' asked Virkkunen. 'Neither Virve nor Jere owns such a car.'

Nobody was able to answer.

'Let's keep these two here as long as the law allows. You two go and examine the Helmersons' house. Talk to the widow again,' Virkkunen instructed them. 'We've got to move on this.'

36

'HERE AGAIN?' said Kaarina Helmerson as Anna and Esko stood at her front door. She looked haggard: dark shadows beneath her eyes, her hair tied in a messy ponytail.

'Hello,' said Anna and showed her the search warrant. 'We'll need to have a look around, examine Veli-Matti's things. You know.'

'Of course. Knock yourselves out.'

'If you could sit on the sofa for the moment, please. Technically you shouldn't be here at all,' Esko said to Kaarina, taking her by the hand, walking her into the living room and gently pressing her shoulders until she was sitting on the sofa. She didn't resist. Her movements were robotic, devoid of any personal volition. Esko looked worried. He remained sitting next to Kaarina as Anna began examining Veli-Matti's office.

The desk and sofa bed, together with the shelving unit recessed into the wall, left just enough floor space to open out the sofa bed. Anna opened the cabinets. Three shelves filled with folders and piles of papers, student support, IT funding applications, forms, lesson plans, teachers' curricula, history essays, English exam papers.

Anna quickly flicked through each of the folders, but couldn't find anything out of place in the teacher's cabinet. Underwear, shirts, socks. What am I really looking for, Anna wondered. How can I find anything, if I don't know what I'm looking for?

Her phone rang.

It was Linnea Markkula.

'Hahaa!' the coroner chuckled without any greater introduction.

'Well?' Anna replied impatiently.

'I've just got the lab results.'

'And?'

'The substance found in Veli-Matti's blood was haloperidol, good old Vitamin H. In Finland it's sold under the product name Serenase. It's used for the treatment of schizophrenia and delirium. In the States it's been used to help sedate people being deported, to make the operation as peaceful and pleasant as possible for all parties. It's quite interesting: the substance takes effect quickly, and effectively paralyses the subject, but it's hard to get your hands on it and you have to be bloody careful when administering it. Professional stuff, I'd say. You can't get stuff like this over the counter at your average chemist.'

'So what does all this mean?'

'Hard to say. Is the wife a doctor or something?'

'No. She's a head teacher.'

'Well, somebody stuck that stuff into Helmerson's arm. You should look for a phial of it. Small, brown, made of glass. Hey, fancy going out on the town on Friday night? You could bring that brother of yours along…'

'Come on. I've got to find that phial.'

'Hey, don't hang up! There's more. I've had my lab team working flat out.'

Sari was sitting at the computer in her office, trying to concentrate. She had found a telephone number for the Helmersons' neighbour who hadn't been at home, but there had been no answer. Now she was writing up the accounts of the neighbours she had interviewed. She couldn't focus. Her husband was away on business again. The children hadn't been sleeping well, and in the mornings they'd been tired and sniffly. She was so worried about Rauno that she felt a tightness in her chest. Bihar's disappearance gnawed at her insides; it was a huge failure on her part. Sari couldn't help but blame herself. After all, she'd been initially convinced that something suspicious was going on. She should have believed Anna and demanded that they keep an eye on the girl. Now it was too late. What on earth had happened to her?

Sari gripped the computer mouse, her knuckles white, and clicked open a new email. It was from her friend who had been looking into the mysterious messages. Not that again, she thought and felt a strong desire to destroy the message without reading it. She turned towards the window, where a light rain had started to patter. Then she forced herself to read the message.

Her friend had established that one of the messages was sent from the Välikylä area of town and two others via the base station situated right next to the police station. He said finding out any further details would be impossible. The phone from which they had been sent was untraceable. But he told Sari to get in touch again if she received any new messages. Then they could try something else. Sari felt herself breaking out in a sweat. What did all this mean? The police station was situated on a busy street right in the city centre; thousands of people walked past it every day. That being said, Sari couldn't help thinking that the person sending the messages was somehow following her, that these messages weren't a teenage prank after all, that they were linked to the murder investigation – and she still hadn't told anyone about them. Had she made yet another irrevocable mistake?

Sari looked at the clock; it was almost four o'clock. Soon she would be able to leave. Was everything okay at home? Sanna would surely have got in touch if the kids had developed a fever. She called Sanna. The mobile rang, but nobody answered. They'll be outside now, of course, she thought and looked at the driving rain behind the windowpane. She tried to write her report, but it was futile.

She tried calling again. Still no answer. Sanna was usually very conscientious and kept her phone with her at all times. She could easily have left it at home; either that or it was ringing quietly at the bottom of her bag, somewhere at the other end of the house. She would never hear it above the kids' racket. Sari sent her an SMS: *Call me immediately*. Again she tried to concentrate on the files on her desk.

This is pointless. Best get home right away, she thought as her telephone rang. For a fraction of a second she felt relief, but it wasn't Sanna. It was Kirsti from Forensics.

They had isolated a trace of haloperidol on Veli-Matti's desk in his classroom. So Veli-Matti had been drugged at the school. Quite brazen, she thought – and risky. The killer had the audacity to break into the school, a building with over a hundred employees, and from there to take Veli-Matti to Selkämaa in handcuffs. Didn't this guy worry the least about getting caught? And how had he gained entry? You'd have to go through several locked doors to get to Veli-Matti's classroom, and yet there were no signs of forced entry. Sari shivered. If the killer was this sick, what was he capable of? She thought of her children. The feeling of worry pricked her skin like a sharp needle and its deceptive fingers closed around her throat. She saved her unfinished report, switched off the computer, took her coat from the hanger and pulled on her boots.

She called home again.

No answer.

Anna sat down at Veli-Matti's desk, took a deep breath. She wondered what to do next and decided to follow her original plan. She moved into the bathroom. The large mirrored cupboard was full of cosmetics. Designer brands flashed in Anna's eyes as she lifted the various bottles and placed them on the edge of the sink.

And there it was, behind everything else. A small glass phial, just as Linnea had said. The label bore the name SERENASE.

Anna returned to the living room. Esko was sitting on the sofa holding Kaarina's hand. Her hair was unkempt and there were smudges of make-up beneath her eyes. What had initially given the impression of a well-presented, stylish head teacher who took good care of herself had, in a few days, faded to reveal an ageing, suffering woman. I wonder if I look that wretched, thought Anna and glanced at herself in the mirror. Yes, I do, she had to admit.

'We've checked your story for the nights of each murder, and I'm afraid you don't have a verifiable alibi for any of the three evenings.

Your mother's memory isn't good enough to confirm that you were with her on the evenings in question,' said Anna and suddenly felt a wave of pity for the woman.

'I was there,' Kaarina replied, her voice clipped.

'Of course, the fact that we can't verify your story doesn't automatically mean that you're a suspect,' said Esko.

Anna gave him a cautionary glower, but he pretended not to notice.

'Good,' said Kaarina and gave him a tired smile.

Anna showed Kaarina a photograph of Virve's tattoo.

'Does this look familiar?'

'It's the Sarlin girl's tattoo, isn't it?'

'Yes. What do you know about it?'

'Well, it was hard not to pay attention to all that bragging at the school graduation party. There she was, parading around in a sleeveless dress and shoving her arm in everyone's face. Trying to be so individual, of course, though nowadays almost all the kids have covered themselves in all manner of squiggles.'

'Do you know what this tattoo means?'

'It's a hummingbird. And a flower.'

'But what does it mean?'

'I haven't the foggiest.'

'It's Huitzilopochtli.'

'Good God. You don't think Virve...?' Kaarina couldn't bring herself to complete the sentence.

'Do you think Virve could have done this?'

'I don't know. Surely not. She was never a very pleasant student, but a murderer...?'

'The only problem with this theory is that Virve has an alibi for the evening of your husband's murder.'

'Really?'

'If Virve is embroiled in this, she must have some kind of accomplice. Either that or someone who knew about her tattoo is trying to make it look as though she is guilty. Who could that be?'

'I have no idea,' Kaarina replied coldly.

'Were there any problems in your marriage?' asked Anna.

'No. Of course, in a long marriage there are always ups and downs. I've already told you about the infertility, but other than that there was nothing.'

'Infidelity?'

'No.'

'You're quite certain?'

Kaarina was silent. She let go of Esko's hand, touched her cheek and stroked the surface of the sofa with her fingers.

'Can one ever be a hundred per cent certain?' she asked.

'So what's this?' asked Anna and showed her the phial. Esko stood up.

'I really don't know.'

'It was in your bathroom. In the cupboard above the sink.'

'It's not mine. I don't know what it is.'

'It's the substance that was used to drug your husband before he was shot.'

'I've never seen that before! I don't know how it got there!' Kaarina screamed.

Esko glanced at the phial with a look of disbelief.

Anna waited. She would soon have to break the other news too. She mustered all the courage she could. Why was this so difficult?

'Your DNA was found on sweet wrappers we discovered at Selkä-maa. And the sperm found in Riikka's vagina belonged to your husband,' Anna finally blurted out.

Kaarina turned to look at the window, behind which the final leaves on the hedgerow were defiantly holding on to the balding branches and the lawn was covered with a yellow-and-brown quilt, the kind that primary-school pupils draw every autumn.

'Did you really not know about the relationship between Veli-Matti and Riikka?' Anna asked.

'Now would be the time to speak up,' Esko gently encouraged her.

Kaarina cleared her throat. Then she stood up and fetched a glass of water.

'Very well,' she said eventually. 'I found out about the affair the day Riikka died. I accidentally found a telephone in the pocket of Veli-Matti's tracksuit as I was putting it in the washing machine. My first reaction was to ask him what on earth this was – I didn't know he had a phone like this. Then curiosity got the better of me and I looked through the list of calls and messages. He'd only ever called one number. And the messages ... He'd never sent me messages like that.'

Kaarina's face contorted in a pained grimace. She took a deep breath before continuing.

'I sent the number to directory enquiries. It belonged to Riikka Rautio, Veli-Matti's former student. My former student. She was all but a child!'

Anna and Esko waited in silence as Kaarina wiped her eyes and blew her nose.

'I sent that little slut a message from Veli-Matti's phone inviting her for lunch at Hazileklek. You should have seen her face when she realised who was waiting for her.' Kaarina gave a hollow laugh. 'I told her to put an end to it. This ... relationship was ridiculous. But I wasn't behaving normally; I was beside myself.'

'How did Riikka react? What did she say?'

'I'm sure she was every bit as flustered as I was. She promised to leave him, apologised over and over. We left it on a note of mutual understanding, if such a thing was possible under the circumstances. I can't believe the little bitch hopped straight back into bed with him. She's quite the actress.'

'What happened next?'

'From the restaurant I went straight to my mother's place. I spent the whole night there, because I wanted to calm down before confronting Veli-Matti. I wanted to think carefully about what to say to him. That's why I went to my gym class. Exercise helps to clear my head. I've never been the type to lie down in the face of problems.'

Or you were simply trying to provide yourself with an alibi, thought Anna.

'When I heard the next day that Riikka had been murdered out on the running track – word gets round this village like wildfire, you know – I decided not to tell Veli-Matti that I knew about the affair.'

'Why not?' asked Esko.

'I was afraid that he might have done it.'

'What about the phone?'

'I left it in his tracksuit pocket and I haven't seen it since. And as for those sweet wrappers, I have no idea. I never eat sweets. Except very occasionally. At my mother's place.'

As she dashed out of her office, Sari knocked into Nils Näkkäläjärvi, who had stopped right outside her door. Nils chuckled. Sari cursed angrily.

'I'm in a hurry. There's some sort of emergency back home.'

'Hey, listen. I've got something,' said Nils.

Sari's phone beeped as a message arrived. The restlessness inside her was slowly turning to outright panic.

'Out with it then.'

'I've been looking into that red car for weeks. You can't imagine how much I've…'

'Spit it out!'

'Kaarina Helmerson's mother Kerttu owns a red Volkswagen Golf, exactly the kind of car we're looking for. Quite a coincidence, don't you think?'

'It's not a coincidence. Call Anna.'

'Surely a demented old woman doesn't drive around any more?'

'Of course she doesn't. Nils, listen. Stay there. I've got to read this message, and I'm frightened to death.'

Nils looked at Sari somewhat bewildered and nodded. Sari took out her telephone. Her hand was surprisingly steady, though her guts were churning with terror. She took a deep breath and clicked it open.

Hi there! All fine. Phone was on silent :) Made salmon soup for tea. S.

37

'I DON'T THINK KAARINA DID IT,' said Esko as he and Anna stepped out of the holding cells and walked across to the smoking area in the yard.

Towards the end of their visit, they had received orders from Virkkunen to arrest Kaarina Helmerson. Kaarina hadn't resisted and hadn't tried to protest her innocence.

'I knew it would end like this,' she had said. 'But I didn't do it,' she continued, calm and collected.

She had asked permission to wash up the few dishes and take out the rubbish before they left, so that it didn't start to smell. Then she had telephoned the council's home-help department and told them that she would be unavailable to look after her mother and agreed that the carer would visit three times a day. She had watered the flowers, pulled on an expensive-looking wax coat and a stylish pair of outdoor shoes and followed Anna and Esko out to the car without resisting in the least. Her poise was almost noble. Anna had sat beside her on the back seat. The drive back into the city had been as quiet as a funeral cortege.

'I mean, Ville Pollari doesn't fit into this pattern at all, unless he was a witness to Riikka's murder. But why the hell would he have been out running around Selkämaa in August, so far away from home? He never visited the place.'

Of course you don't think she did it, because you're besotted with her, thought Anna but held her tongue.

'You shouldn't trust your intuition,' she commented instead. 'We should let the facts speak for themselves.'

Esko looked almost offended.

'Kaarina had free access to that gun cabinet,' Anna reminded him. 'And the tyre tracks found at Häyrysenniemi are a match for Kerttu Viitala's red Volkswagen. You're the one that said her alibi wasn't up to much. And it certainly isn't; she hasn't got one. This is a classic tale of the woman scorned. After years of disappointments and infidelity, something finally snapped.'

'What about the necklaces? Why did she put the Hutsilo pendants in the victims' pockets?' Esko tried to defend her.

'Kaarina was Virve's teacher. Though she claims otherwise, she must have known about the various meanings of the tattoo. So Jere and Virve were innocent after all,' said Anna.

'Pretty cruel to try and frame your former students for murder. If you ask me, something doesn't add up here.'

'Come on, everything adds up,' said Anna. 'You should be glad we've finally wrapped this case up.'

Esko muttered something and lit another cigarette; Anna stubbed out her own. It tasted good, a bit too good, she thought and wondered how she could start weaning herself off them again.

When she went back inside, Anna walked up to Sari's office. Sari was just checking Rauno's email account.

'Any news on Bihar?' she asked.

'Nothing. She hasn't been seen at the airports or harbours, and there's been no news from the Swedish border either. The family is being charged with "hiding" the girl,' said Anna, drawing inverted commas in the air with her fingers. 'The investigation has been transferred to another team. They're trying to establish whether she's still alive or whether she's been sent abroad somewhere. And how the family is involved in all this.'

'At least Bihar didn't mysteriously fall off the balcony,' said Sari.

'Not yet, at least,' Anna replied.

'I'm so worried about her.'

Anna sighed, avoiding Sari's eyes.

'Me too, but there's nothing we can do about it.'

'Isn't it shocking that Veli-Matti Helmerson was attacked at school? That Kaarina…'

'I know, it's terrible. Did they find anything else at the school?'

'The classroom was full of fingerprints, hairs, fibres, everything you can think of, so to save resources Forensics decided not to examine it any further. There's plenty of evidence as it is.'

'Look at this,' said Sari and pointed to Rauno's emails. 'This came from Moscow this morning,' she said, her voice victorious.

'A shipment of ten Huitzilopochtli necklaces was sent to the city's central post office at the beginning of July. The name on the order was Veli-Matti Helmerson.'

'That's that then,' said Anna.

A strange sense of emptiness consumed her.

Was that it? Was this what they had been investigating, going over detail by detail, throughout the long autumn? Was the case so simple, so quickly resolved after all?

At the same time she felt a cautious excitement.

This really was the end of the case, once and for all, and soon it would be over altogether. Soon the rush would be over. Soon she would be able to redeem all those hours of overtime.

She could sleep. Finally.

'By the way, have you received any weird text messages this autumn?' Sari asked all of a sudden.

'Yes. How did you…?' but Anna was cut short as Sari waved an old Nokia mobile phone in front of her face.

'So have I,' she said. 'And they're from this phone.'

'What?'

'Every now and then I've received nasty text messages from an unlisted number. I looked into it, and it turns out the messages were sent from the city centre, right next to the station. Of course, that's not much to go on – this area must have the busiest mobile-phone traffic in the city – but the other day I happened to bump into that patrol officer Sami. You remember, the guy from the gym? What a

prick. I was on my way home, and I was already a bit freaked out –
I'll tell you about that later. Anyway, there he was, standing in the
foyer, typing away at this phone. I don't know what came over me; I
just had a really strong hunch. I ran up to him, grabbed the phone
and ran off. Take a look!'

Anna picked up the phone and opened the messages in the
phone's outbox.

I fuck u till u die.

That's the one she had received while she was at the Helmersons'
house with Esko.

That and all the other disgusting messages were there in a neat
folder, their recipients listed only as A and S.

'So he realised he had to change the SIM card, but he wasn't smart
enough to delete the messages from the phone's memory. Maybe he
read them at night and fantasised.'

'What are we going to do about this?' Anna asked Sari.

'We'll come up with something. He'll get what's coming to him.'

They both smiled.

38

DARKNESS HADN'T COME RUSHING into the city, brash as a troubadour, but still it had taken everyone by surprise. Suddenly people noticed that it was dark all the time. It was dark when you went to work, to school, and it was dark when you trudged through the driving rain and sleet to the local shop and back home. In the November darkness, the desperate plight of the homeless didn't bear thinking about; not having a place to leave, a place to return to. In the darkness. Despite of the darkness.

Of course, the darkness had announced its arrival through the gradually encroaching evenings, rudely edging the summer out of its way, as it does every year. People knew to expect it, yet it had succeeded in creeping up behind them and startling them with a whisper. *It's me again. Are you ready?*

On a good day, an orange glow might hang behind the apartment blocks for a moment, but for the most part the days passed unchanging through the colourless landscape.

Somewhere else it might have been possible to relax, to let yourself be carried along by the quiet, the stillness, to descend into the darkness as it appeared, to find the beauty in the myriad shades of grey that defined the restrained winter landscape, to let your mind rest with the rhythm of nature. In the city, nobody would even think of such a thing.

Puddles of sleet seeped up through the soles of your shoes, into your socks, chilling your feet. If only it would snow, people said, begging for mercy; it would be so much lighter. Then when the snow did come, everything went crazy: trains and aeroplanes were late; there were fatal car pile-ups on the motorway; the price of electricity went through the roof. Shops ran out of spades and snow shovels. Flu spread through the city. Alcohol sales reached record levels.

And in the mornings you had to go to work, though it was the last thing anyone wanted to do. Beneath the glare of LEDs and fluorescent lamps, people were expected to unflaggingly present a play directed by market forces, a performance called Western civilisation.

It was the eve of Kaarina's trial. Anna was on her way to meet Ákos. She had taken her brother to the rehab clinic in Kivelä when, repentant and in very bad shape, he had turned up at her door to apologise.

Anna had forgiven him – almost. And though she knew that by helping him she was actually helping to prolong his illness, she couldn't turn her own brother away.

Now Ákos was doing much better. The tremors and the voices were kept at bay with sedatives, liberally dished out at the clinic. On principle, Anna thought it was wrong to treat addiction with other substances that caused addiction, but now she didn't have to strength to care. The priority was to get Ákos back on his feet. At least for a while.

As she wandered along the street, she noticed the Pink Ink tattoo studio and remembered that Virve had said this was the place where she'd had the hummingbird etched into her left arm. On the spur of the moment, Anna stepped inside. A young girl with multiple face piercings was sitting at the counter leafing through a magazine.

'Hi there.' The girl raised her eyes from the magazine and greeted her.

'Hello,' said Anna and showed her police ID. The girl looked frightened.

'I'd like to ask about a tattoo. Do you remember a girl who came in here back in May and got a tattoo of a hummingbird sucking nectar from an orchid?'

'Yeah, I remember her,' the girl said. 'It turned out great! But I don't do the tattoos here. I only do piercings. Timo!' she shouted. 'The police are asking about the hummingbird sleeve you did back in the spring.'

From a room at the back emerged an enormous man, his face, neck and arms covered in tattoos. The sight was imposing. And quite sexy, Anna realised and smiled at the man.

'Fekete Anna from the police. Hello. Do you remember this tattoo?'

'Sure. I remember all the pieces I do.'

'Do you remember the customer?'

'Which one?' Timo answered.

Anna's heart skipped a beat.

'Excuse me?'

'There were two of them.'

Two hummingbirds. *Jézus Mária.*

'First there was a blonde hippie chick, then a few weeks later another woman, a bit older maybe, a brunette. She had really muscular arms.'

'Do you have a name for this other woman? The brunette?' Anna asked, barely able to contain her sense of agitation.

'We should have. People normally give a name when they book in. Give me a minute, I'll have a look.'

The man walked over to a computer and started typing. Even his fingers were tattooed. They were beautiful in their own brutal way.

'Here it is. *Jaana.* No surname; I tend not to ask.'

'I'll take your card,' said Anna pointing to a little box of business cards next to the computer. 'In case I have any more questions.'

'No problem,' the man replied and looked at Anna just a little too long.

Jaana, Anna thought feverishly as she walked back out into the street. Who is Jaana? Have I heard that name somewhere before? Was it in the list of students we got from the school in Saloinen? Anna called Esko and asked him to look into it. Then she telephoned Riikka's parents, Virve and Maria Pollari to ask if they knew anyone by the name of Jaana.

No, was the abrupt answer.

'Just a minute,' Anna said out loud and stopped in her tracks in the middle of the pavement.

Now she had to think carefully.

It was apparent that Kerttu Viitala's car had been sighted both at Selkämaa and Häyrysenniemi. At both running tracks they had found hideouts where the killer was able to observe the victims. And at the hideout at Selkämaa they had found sweet wrappers with Kaarina Helmerson's DNA. And Veli-Matti had been screwing Riikka. And Virve had a hummingbird on her left arm. And so did another woman too.

And it wasn't Kaarina Helmerson.

Who could have had access to Kerttu Viitala's car? Just then, Anna remembered the binoculars on Mrs Viitala's windowsill, the ones the old lady had allegedly used to watch the crowds of people down below whenever she was up to it.

Anna telephoned the holding cells and asked to speak to Kaarina. Afterwards, even more agitated, she called Esko once again.

'You were right. It looks like we've charged an innocent person after all.'

39

ANNA FORCED HERSELF to eat a couple of sandwiches and drink a cup of tea, though she wasn't hungry in the least. Tonight she would have to have all her wits about her. She went into the living room and switched on the television, which she hadn't given to Ákos after all. She drew the line at financing her brother's drinking debts, either with cash or by giving him things to sell off. Again there was nothing interesting on the television. She channel-hopped absent-mindedly, jumping up occasionally as though she had just remembered to do something. She put the laundry in the machine, washed her teacup, dusted the coffee table and the bookshelf, watered the heathers in the box on the balcony, though she knew they didn't need it. She glanced at the thermometer installed on the balcony door and was surprised to see the temperature reading was two below zero. She remembered her new daylight lamp, still unopened in the kitchen cupboard. Was it too late to start using it, she wondered as she went into the kitchen and opened the box. The lamp was rather beautiful; its oval glass looked frosted. She placed the lamp on the table and switched it on, just to test it, and was taken aback that the bright light didn't dazzle her. This must be effective, she thought. I'm going to use this in the mornings while I read the paper.

She glanced at the clock. A few hours to go yet.

Restlessness sent small electric impulses through her muscles. She couldn't sit still.

She would spoil the plan if she didn't calm down.

All of a sudden Anna felt a strong urge to go running. The feeling of quite how much she had missed exercise all autumn was like the pain of losing a close friend. It was the most effective way of keeping her wits about her, better than any sleeping pills or antidepressants: the running she loved so much. And at the drop of a hat, she'd traded it in for beer and cigarettes. What an idiot she'd been. She would have time to go for a short run. Just to see what if felt like after such a long break.

It would calm her down and relax her tensed muscles.

The theatre to play out later that evening would go more smoothly.

Anna picked out a warm anorak made of smooth material and pulled on her trainers. They felt snug and familiar, like the embrace of an old lover.

Very quietly Anna walked down the stairs and opened the front door. The sharp, frigid air met her outside; it felt fresh and crisp. With brisk steps she walked to the beginning of the track running around behind the suburb, and as the asphalt gave way to the soft sawdust path, she dived into the darkness of the forest and picked up her speed to a gentle jog.

It didn't feel too bad.

At least, not to start with.

But it didn't feel easy either. This run must be on my tired body's own terms, she decided and continued slowly on her way, moving steadily further away from the street lights. She was concentrating so hard on listening to her body that she didn't notice how dark the forest had become. And she didn't hear the approaching footsteps.

Her heart could have stopped when all of a sudden a bright light flashed behind her and a woman's voice said: 'Well, well. Little Miss Policewoman. Haven't seen you around here for a while.'

The voice was taut, without a shred of happiness at seeing her again. Anna glanced over her shoulder and saw the figure dressed in black running a couple of metres behind her. The jogger was wearing a headlamp, its beam of light bouncing along the track like an amorphous ball, its edges occasionally illuminating Anna. The glare of the lamp prevented Anna from seeing the jogger's face, but she knew who it was, knew exactly how piercing were the blue eyes lurking in the light's shadow.

'Hello,' Anna replied. 'I haven't been running for a few months now.'

The jogger gave a hollow laugh.

'No wonder you're so slow. I caught up with you rather more quickly than I thought.'

The woman was now running alongside her. Though she had appeared very suddenly, she didn't look at all out of breath. To her relief, Anna noted that the woman wasn't carrying anything in her hands and had no rucksack.

She wouldn't dare, Anna thought. Not a police officer.

'It's quite late for a run,' the woman said. 'We've met out here before. Do you remember? Back in the autumn.'

'I remember,' Anna responded. She was so out of breath that she couldn't speak properly.

'I was sure you must have recognised me when we last met. But you didn't. Some police officer you are,' she laughed scornfully.

All of a sudden the woman switched off the lamp on her forehead. The darkness swallowed them whole. In a short time, her eyes had adjusted so well to the light of the lamp that now Anna couldn't see a thing. She stumbled and almost tripped over. Again the jogger gave a menacing laugh and pushed right up against her. 'Careful,' she said. A ripple of disgust ran the length of Anna's arm.

They ran next to one another through the darkness. Anna tried to calculate how much of the track remained. If she sped up a little, they would reach the corner with the fallen tree in just over five minutes, and after that the track would wind its way back round towards civilisation. From there it would be another fifteen minutes of brisk running before they reached the main road. But the risk that she might not be able to go on was increasing all the while. All the cigarettes she'd smoked that autumn were kicking in. Her entire body felt like lead, and there was a stinging sensation in her lungs.

Another twenty minutes. It seemed like an eternity.

'Aren't you afraid, running out here in the dark?' the woman asked her.

She was still so close that Anna could just smell her breath. And there was something else too. Blood? Hatred? Perhaps it was the suffering of all the people she had killed; the smell of death was ingrained in the fibres of her tracksuit.

'Not usually,' Anna replied.

She increased her pace a little. She could do it. She would have to.

'Are you frightened now?'

'Should I be?'

'I don't know; depends who's out here with you.'

Anna felt the adrenalin pumping renewed energy into her legs. So something good came of this fear after all. Again she sped up a little. The woman still didn't seem the least out of breath.

'What is there to be afraid of now that the hummingbird is finally in its cage?' the woman snapped and ran on ahead at such a speed that she immediately disappeared into the darkness.

Anna stopped where she was and breathed heavily, her hands resting on her knees. Her heart was pounding in her chest. The forest around her was silent, waiting expectantly for the arrival of winter. She could no longer hear the sound of footsteps running away. Anna listened carefully for a moment, then slowly unzipped her anorak and slipped her hand into the inside pocket. The black metal had warmed beneath her jacket. She removed the gun from its holster. Its weight felt soothing, calming. She walked onwards, the pistol in her hand. In the darkness the woman couldn't possibly make out the silhouette of the gun at the end of her arm.

She walked briskly, scanning the surrounding woods, her senses on high alert. She wanted to get away from the track as soon as possible. She wanted it all to be over. She wanted to get home and enjoy all that overtime, to sleep. Heavenly Father, or whoever you are, please let Rauno wake up and let me get home safely, her mind cried out.

The familiar fallen tree lay at the side of the path like an ominous boulder. From here it wasn't far back to the road and the lights. Soon she would be safe.

At that moment there came a faint rustling sound in the bushes. Anna stopped still and gripped the pistol's handle with both hands. She thought she could make out movement in front of her, somewhere to her left. She raised her weapon and waited, waited and listened. Nothing happened, only the boom of her racing heart thumping in her ears. It was nothing. The woman was long gone.

Just then a black figure charged out from behind the roots of the fallen tree, coming right towards her at a terrific pace. Anna caught a glimpse of the long barrel of the rifle and the horrific grimace on the woman's face just as the shot thundered out, deafening her and knocking the air from her lungs. Anna could feel the pellets tearing burning holes in her skin. Now it was finally over, she thought as she fell to the ground in agony, just before her consciousness was swallowed by a deep silence.

40

LIGHT. A rushing sound.

Noises.

Someone speaking, somewhere.

Anna stroked the surface where she lay. It wasn't sawdust. It felt like slippery cotton. She sat up with a groan. She was in a bed. The bed was surrounded with bright mist. Figures were moving around her. They approached the bed. They spoke.

'Jesus, Anna, you scared us!' Esko's rough voice boomed from the nearest of the figures.

'Thank God you were wearing your vest. Otherwise you would have died.'

It was Sari.

'Am I in hospital?' Anna asked. Her eyes were gradually beginning to focus. She could make out the faces of Esko and Sari. They were beaming with smiles.

'Yes – and you're in one piece too. Only a couple of pellets caught your left shoulder. It's just a scratch,' said Esko. 'But you lost consciousness when the shot hit you in the chest. It must have packed quite a punch.'

'I remember,' she said quietly. 'It felt wonderful, as if I was falling asleep.'

'Anna! Don't say things like that. Look who's here!' said Sari pointing across the room.

A third grey figure approached the bed. A moment later Rauno's head came peering through the misty light.

'Hello there,' he greeted her jovially from beside the bed.

'Rauno!' Anna cried.

'That's me. I woke up last night, and now I'm racing around the hospital in a wheelchair. The docs said it's a miracle. I suppose it is, now that they've told me what happened.'

'What about the killer?' Anna asked cautiously.

'She's in a secure room at the end of the corridor. She didn't have quite as much luck as you did, but she'll live.'

'What really happened out there on the track?' asked Anna.

'Esko shot the lunatic just as she discharged the rifle at you. You shot at her too,' said Sari. 'Esko hit the target; your bullet flew off into the woods.'

Esko looked pleased with himself. Anna braced herself for some kind of barbed comment, but none was forthcoming.

'The rifle she'd been using was the Helmersons' beautiful Benelli. She'd made copies of the keys to the Helmersons' house, probably from Kaarina's set of keys while Kaarina was staying with her mother. We don't have all the details yet. We'll have to wait until the killer is up to being interviewed.'

'But we confiscated the Benelli and put it into evidence.' Anna was puzzled.

'That's right. But there was another rifle in Veli-Matti's gun cabinet. Remember the Merkel? We hadn't confiscated that one. She picked it up, and that's the one she used to shoot you.'

'That was another stroke of luck,' said Sari. 'It's not nearly as powerful as the Benelli.'

Anna listened in silence.

She could have died.

But she was alive.

What would have become of Ákos if she had died?

'And what could be easier than having another set of keys cut to Grandma's old car that no one ever uses?' Sari continued. 'Home helpers have unfettered access to their elderly customers' homes. They have all the keys, and nobody ever sees what they get up to. The nurse planned and prepared everything in the course of her normal work, and made it look as though Kaarina was the culprit. And Virve.'

'Just think what kind of lunatics are out there, going in and out of helpless old people's houses,' Anna whispered.

'It doesn't bear thinking about,' Sari said.

And though none of them wanted to, they all saw themselves as old people: demented, defenceless, lying in bed, waiting for the rattle of a set of keys, a brief visit from the nurse. How many years did they have before that happened?

'The binoculars suddenly flashed in my mind,' said Anna. 'They seemed so out of place there on the windowsill. It was like one of those Spot the Oddity tests. When I called Kaarina to ask about them, she didn't know what I was talking about. So I called the council's home-help supervisor and discovered that one of the nurses assigned to Mrs Viitala was called Jaana Tervola. And what do you know, this same Jaana Tervola was on duty when Esko and I paid Mrs Viitala a visit.'

'But why?' Sari wondered, bewildered. 'Why on earth did she do all this?'

'That's precisely what we'll be asking her once she's recovered,' said Esko.

'But why were you out on the track with that psychopath?' Rauno exclaimed. Esko replied on Anna's behalf.

'When Anna realised what was going on with the tattoos and everything else, she called me straight away. We had a team meeting and planned a little ambush. We telephoned this Jaana and said that she might be able to help Anna clarify a few details regarding the case. An informal meeting was arranged for 10 p.m. in a nice little pub downtown, so that Jaana wouldn't start to suspect something was going on. We were going to try and make her slip up, because we didn't have any physical evidence against her. We wanted to startle her into spilling the beans. It all worked a bit too well.'

'Esko and Sari were supposed to sit at the back of the bar, pretending to be customers – a natural role for Esko,' said Anna.

'Shut it,' Esko scoffed.

'We needed to cover our backs. And Anna was going to be wearing a wire,' said Sari.

'Is that above board?' asked Rauno.

'We okayed all the details with Virkkunen,' Esko explained. 'But I had a bad feeling about it. I thought I'd keep an eye on things before the agreed meeting, just to be sure. After all, we were setting a trap for someone who was potentially pretty volatile.'

'Thank God you did,' said Sari.

'I saw Anna going out for that bloody run. Christ, she hasn't done any exercise all autumn, if you don't count chain-smoking out in the yard with me. She's been depressed and bloody stressed out, and tonight of all nights she decides to get her life back in order. I followed her to the start of the track. I parked the car by the side of the road and waited, and before long I saw a woman sprinting into the woods after her. I couldn't see who it was, but I feared the worst, so there was nothing for it: I had to go in after them. I called for back-up and started going round the track in the opposite direction. Christ, I was shit-scared I would be too late.'

'But you weren't,' said Anna.

Esko grabbed Anna and held her in his bear-like arms. Anna could smell the mint pastilles, barely covering the scent of booze.

'Thank you,' she whispered into his ear.

'What are we going to do with you?'

Anna had to go. She wanted to see for herself, to look, even for a moment, at the woman who had murdered three people in cold blood and whom she had been hunting all autumn. She wanted to see the woman now, weak and wounded, before the interviews, before the trial, before Huitzilopochtli could regain his strength. Just to glance at her, thought Anna. That's enough.

The hospital had quietened. Visiting hours were over, dinner had been served and cleared away; only a handful of nurses were still wandering the corridors. Anna found Jaana Tervola's room easily.

The police officer sitting in front of the door lowered his book, stood up and greeted Anna like a soldier. Then he opened the locks on the door, briefly examined the room and let Anna inside.

'She's asleep,' he whispered.

Anna stepped inside the room. At first glance it looked like any other hospital room: a bed, a drip, dimmed lights that hadn't been switched off though the patient was asleep, a glass of water on the bedside table.

On closer inspection, the glass was made of plastic. Instead of a window, there was a rough, grey concrete wall. The bed was made up with the same light-blue sheets and thin blanket as were on Anna's bed.

Anna shuddered. Beneath the blanket she could see the arm on to which the drip and needle were taped. Some form of healing substance dripped in a steady stream from a bag hanging next to the bed and straight into the patient's vein. The hand moved. The blanket was drawn further up. The orange orchid glowed in the dim light of the room. A green-and-black hummingbird, shiny and metallic, was sucking nectar from inside the flower with its long tongue.

'It's beautiful, isn't it?'

Anna was startled. The voice came from beneath the blanket. It didn't sound weak at all.

Anna didn't answer.

'It's not the same as the other one, in case you're wondering. Come closer and take a look. Do you see? The colours are different. And my hummingbird has a much greedier expression; it's digging its beak deeper into the flower.'

Anna stood stock still. The woman sat up from beneath the blanket. Her eyes fixed themselves on Anna.

'Frightened again? I told you, there's nothing to be afraid of now that the hummingbird is in its cage. You're quite the coward, aren't you? But no matter, be like that. Do you want to know why I got this tattoo?'

Still Anna said nothing. Something warned her against speaking, though the woman seemed to be feeding her little questions like pieces of bait.

'I'd been watching that whore, Riikka. I followed her when she went out running, trying to slim that fat arse of hers. I saw the little thief move in with the hippie girl. And that's when they started plotting to take everything away from me.'

The woman heaved herself up, her posture now much straighter, and pushed her forearm out from beneath the blanket.

'I first saw the tattoo when I was looking out of Kerttu's window with the binoculars. The tattoo struck me, started whispering to me. It was the binoculars that gave me away, wasn't it? It was the only mistake I made, leaving them out on the windowsill. Pretty good though, don't you think? Only one tiny little mistake in an otherwise perfect plan.'

But that was enough for us, thought Anna.

'I saw the way those little sluts sat around giggling, knocking back sparkling wine and flirting with passers-by as though life were nothing but a breeze. It was maddening. For a while I followed one of them, the hippie girl with the tattoo. I approached her and talked to her, as if in passing; she was at a nightclub showing off her arm and offering her backside to anyone who'd look. She was so damn arrogant. And drunk. Telling people every detail – the trip to Mexico, her final exams, the story of her tattoo, how painful it had been, how much it had cost. People are so unbelievably stupid.'

The woman was staring at Anna with ice-cold eyes. Her face was hard and expressionless, but Anna was sure she could discern behind them a sense of concealed pain. Esko must have hit her hard. Good, thought Anna.

'The stupid hippie brat didn't even realise that she was giving me everything I needed. Take it, take it, there's your revenge! The deity Huitzilopochtli, right here on my arm. Be my guest, take his power, use it, become him, exact your revenge. The hummingbird spoke to me in that nightclub, its voice was clear and bright, but I'll never tell anyone what it said to me. Its voice echoed in my ears; it grew and grew until it was shouting. And so I became the one with the hummingbird in her left hand. I became the Hummingbird! And no one takes anything from the Hummingbird without permission. Nobody. And still, everything was taken away from me. *He* was taken away from me. He abandoned me, but the Hummingbird will not be abandoned without exacting punishment!'

'But you are Jaana,' whispered Anna.

The woman's face contorted with rage. She tried to struggle up into a sitting position, but couldn't, and her tattooed arm was thrashing so much that she knocked over the stand with the drip. She was kicking her legs so wildly that the bed began to rattle and shake from side to side. Anna noticed that one of Jaana's arms was handcuffed to the bed frame. The woman started shrieking, curses raining down on Anna. The policeman on guard at the door and three nurses rushed into the room, and together they held the flailing woman down on the bed. Once they had secured her, one of the nurses injected some form of sedative into her arm. Jaana Tervola's body went limp and she fell silent.

Anna crept back to her own room in shock. She wrapped herself in the hospital blanket, which couldn't quite keep out the cold, and stared for a long time at the flaking, cracked surface of the ceiling. The night nurse came and asked if she wanted to talk. Anna shook her head. Everything's fine, she said. Then she shook one of the tablets from the bottle of pills into her hand, placed it on her tongue, took a sip of water and waited for sleep to consume her.

41

ANNA SWITCHED ON her computer. She had only just been discharged from hospital. The doctor had given her an initial two weeks of sick leave, with the option of extending it if necessary. Not because Anna had been seriously injured or was deemed otherwise physically incapable of working, but to give her time to recover from her traumatic encounter with the Hummingbird. Anna had also finally mentioned the insomnia she'd been experiencing all autumn. The doctor's brow had furrowed with Hippocratic concern.

Life can be so strange, she thought as she booked plane tickets for Ákos and herself. A flight to Budapest, then two hundred kilometres along the motorway in a rented car. Then across the EU border and they would all be there together once again.

Home.

From their front door in Koivuharju to the front door in Magyarkanizsa, complete with connecting flights, the journey would take less than seven hours.

It was so close.

And yet so far away.

Outside it was dark. Grey slivers of sleet slapped against the window. The first pathetic attempt at snow so far. Would they have a decent winter at all this year?

Jaana Tervola had recovered sufficiently and had already been interviewed. The home-helper had had a brief affair with Veli-Matti Helmerson back in the spring. They had met one another at Kerttu Viitala's house. Veli-Matti had been standing in for his wife, who had come down with a particularly vicious bout of flu, and he had taken care of his mother-in-law for a few weeks. For Jaana it had been love at first sight, but it was unclear quite how serious Veli-Matti had been about their fling. Anna suspected that the relationship might have been largely the product of Jaana's disturbed mind. In any case, he had met his former student, who in the intervening years had grown into a young woman, on the running track at Selkämaa – the same place where, according to Jaana, she and Veli-Matti had often met up with one another. Eventually Veli-Matti had abruptly ended the relationship with Jaana by text message.

She had planned her revenge at her vantage point in Selkämaa and at Häyrysenniemi, sitting on the old garden chair with her binoculars. During a search of her apartment, they had found sets of keys to the Helmersons' house and for Mrs Viitala's house and car. Jaana had revealed that she went in and out of the Helmersons' house as and when she pleased and had driven the old woman's car hundreds of kilometres – without anyone noticing a thing. People can be so gullible and stupid, she had laughed.

Ville Pollari had had nothing whatsoever to do with Jaana, Riikka or Veli-Matti. The killings had to be made to seem like the work of a crazed serial killer, Jaana had explained. What does that make you then, Anna had wondered. Many things were still unclear. Jaana Tervola refused to answer certain questions and sometimes spoke such gibberish that it was hard to get an overall picture of events. But there was no doubt that they would establish the remaining details in time – as much as was necessary, that is. The initial case report would be long and difficult to compile – her first report as a criminal investigator.

Anna's private email account flashed as a new message arrived.

Finally, she thought and began reading the dreamlike story of a real-life nightmare that appeared on her computer screen.

If I hadn't made the call that night they would've killed me for sure. There was death in the air, wallahi; it wasn't far off. Or they might've sent me to Turkey or somewhere and married me off to the first guy who'd take me. And believe me, there would've been plenty of takers! Some lucky old git would have bagged himself a young sex slave that it would've been his duty to treat badly for ever. That would've been death too – a life sentence.

When the cops turned up at our place (I gave the home address because I wasn't even sure where I was), Dad said straight off he was gonna kill Adan. I could hear my sister screaming with terror in the background. Dad's voice was so cold. He said if I didn't take back what I'd said to the Emergency Services and come up with some kind of explanation, like it was a dream or something, then nobody would ever see Adan again.

The idea of taking revenge only came later, before the interviews. Dad was really nervous that the cops wouldn't swallow any far-fetched stories about it all being a bad dream once they started interviewing us all. That's when he decided to say the call was just an angry young girl's attempt to get back at her strict parents. It must have sounded pretty convincing, I'm sure. And, in a way, it was true.

I couldn't put Adan in danger. I had to lie.

I made the T-shirt during an art lesson the day before the interviews. My teacher said it was great, that sometimes she'd wanted to shout for help when she was younger. In any other situation it would have felt encouraging or something. I've always been irritated by teachers banging on, 'I so understand you', and all that. In that situation it just felt absurd. They understand fuck all. They're just molly-coddled big kids that think a detention is an effective punishment, because they would've died of shame if they'd ever been given one.

Juse thought my T-shirt was great, but he didn't think it would work. He was shitting himself that my folks would find out and kill me – and Adan. He wasn't worried for himself, said they wouldn't dare touch a Finnish kid. I wouldn't be so sure about that.

Not all Kurdish girls live like this. I know a Kurdish fitness model. She's always working out and showing off her body, parading around Europe in a tiny bikini, and her family is really proud of her. Not all Muslims live like this either. Believe it or not, most of us are a totally normal bunch. And don't forget that some Christians are brought up just as strictly as we are; think of the South Sudanese. And Finland has a huge problem with domestic violence, which of course Finns don't think is comparable to our situation. Finnish people's behaviour is 'only' because of the booze, and anything that's caused by the booze is almost wholly acceptable or at least justifiable. That's what people will tell you.

I don't know what causes these things. I know loads of Muslim girls in Rajapuro that wear make-up and go out shopping and openly hang out with their Finnish friends – even with boys. Their families might not particularly like it, but at least they give them the freedom to do as they wish. It's well cool. If I ever have children, I want them to be free. And now I'm going to be free too.

Just like that Nasima Razmyar, Immigrant of the Year. OMG, you should have seen her doing the rumba on Strictly! *Dad yanked the plug out of the wall and started shouting so much that his chest was bulging, saying that's the last time we'll ever watch that whore in his house. He didn't get it, didn't understand that that's exactly why she took part in the show in the first place: to show people stuck in their ways (like my stupid family) and their children that anything is possible.*

They threw a right party once the investigation was called off, and started setting me up with Plan B, a guy somewhere in Germany, older and even more revolting than the first. That would make sure I didn't get any ideas and would put an end to my sinful life, and, more importantly, the family's tattered honour would be saved. They thought they could carry on just as before.

It was great when you started following me and keeping an eye on us in the yard. Dad was livid. Literally, so angry that you wouldn't believe it. They couldn't take me out of school after all. They couldn't lock me at home. They couldn't send me to Germany, let alone kill me. That's where Plan C came in, and they had no control over that plan. It was so cool.

I feel sick with worry every time I think about you creeping around the documentation division at the police station in the middle of the night. It's terrifying. Imagine if someone had walked in and seen you putting together that passport. They'd have banged you up or something. And you'd have been kicked out of the police, for sure.

Still, it makes me laugh. It's incredible, just like in the movies. You're so cool – I can hardly believe it. I hope you don't get into trouble because of me. Or Esko. Give the old drunk a nudge from me and tickle him every time he comes out with any of his racist crap. I still can't believe he hid me at his place until everything was sorted. Amazing. And that's the other miracle – that things actually did get sorted. You made me the Angel of Rajapuro, who wasn't stoned to death in the end, but who flew away on wings of her own.

The new name is going to take some getting used to. I keep starting to say Bih… But I'll learn.

High school is great; they enrolled me as soon as I arrived. I've already made a couple of friends; we eat together and sometimes go to the movies in the evenings. The hostel is okay too. At the moment there are eight girls here from all over the world. I share a room with a girl from Syria, whose older brother was the only one in the family to defend her; he arranged for her to be sent here when the situation at home started to resemble mine. Imagine, her older brother! The most important member of the family after the father. How come he wasn't involved in it all? It makes me think that all this will change one day. There is hope. It's crazy that you even knew an international safe house like this existed!

So everything's finally going well, but I'm still really worried about Adan. The thought of her being taken into foster care feels awful, but at least now I know she's safe. It's hard for me that we can't keep in touch. I hope she's been placed with a nice family. Thanks for forwarding her my message. Otherwise she'd be frightened all the time; she'd think I was really dead. But I'll see her again. At the very latest when she turns 18 and can travel out here by herself.

As for my fucking arsehole of a family. It serves them right that they think they're still being investigated for my disappearance. Now it's their turn to sit at home shitting themselves, wondering what's going to happen next — just like yours truly did for years. It's not like they can be convicted of anything, because there's nothing to link them to my disappearance. I know it sounds cruel, but I don't pity them in the least.

Maybe Mehvan. But just a bit.

Love B.

P.S. Juse is applying for school exchange next year. Guess where?

After reading everything carefully, Anna deleted the message and removed it from her email trash folder. Then she destroyed the email account altogether; it had been created for one reason only. Now nothing could link her to Bihar or her disappearance. Finally Anna switched off her computer. She expected to feel a sense of relief, but there was none.

From her wallet she took out the business card that she had been turning in her fingers every now and then for some time now.

Pink Ink. Professional Tattooing and Piercing. Because You're Unique.

She thought of that striking face, covered in tattoos, the arms and fingers decorated with ink patterns.

Then she dialled the number on the card.

THANK YOU

Thank you to Aino, Ilona and Robert for the love, the creativity, the light that shines from each and every one of you.

Thank you to everyone at Otava, particularly Aleksi. Thank you to Jaakko, Maija and Jani for advice regarding police procedure, to Satu for tips on forensic science and to Sari for correcting a few medical details. As you can see, details aside, imagination still won the day.

Thank you to my mother for reading to me indefatigably when I was a child. Without you this would never have happened.